FIVE BY FIVE 2

NO SURRENDER

D1603245

FIVE BY FIVE 2

NO SURRENDER

William C. Dietz
Kevin J. Anderson
Brad R. Torgersen
R.M. Meluch
Aaron M. Allston

Edited by Kevin J. Anderson

WordFire Press
Colorado Springs, Colorado

ISBN: 978-1-61475-071-0

Published by
WordFire Press, an imprint of
WordFire Inc
PO Box 1840
Monument CO 80132

WordFire Press Trade Paperback Edition – August 2013
Printed in the USA
www.wordfire.com

CONTENTS

LEGIO PATRIA NOSTRA
THE LEGION IS OUR COUNTRY

A Legion of the Damned® story

WILLIAM C. DIETZ

CHAPTER ONE

War makes thieves and peace hangs them.

George Herbert
Standard year circa 1620

The moon HE24-6743

If the moon had a name, it was a Hudathan name, since the satellite was orbiting a world that the Hudathans laid claim to. But, like everything else in the sector of space sandwiched between the Hudathan Empire and the Confederacy of Sentient Beings, the moon was open to attack.

Legion Captain Damien Chozick was strapped into a chair located aft of the control well in which the ship's captain, pilot, and navigator were seated. And, as the thirty-year-old destroyer escort *Mohawk* crept even closer to the moon, all eyes were on the wrap-around screen in front of them. One side of the Hudathan base was obscured by dark shadows, while the other was brightly lit. Craters pitted the surface of the moon and some were filled with what Chozick assumed to be junk. Crawler tracks ran between them.

The purpose of the mission was to pound the moon base into submission, land, and gather intelligence. Then Chozick and his legionnaires were supposed to destroy key components of the facility on their way out. A hit-and-run operation of the sort that they had carried out many times in the past. Except that something was wrong. The ridgeheads weren't shooting at the *Mohawk*, but they should have been. Why not? Were the Hudathans incompetent? Never. What did that leave then? A trap? That made sense. The aliens were waiting for the *Mohawk* to get closer, and, once she did, the bastards would open fire.

The DE was only a couple of hundred feet off the surface and creeping along. A docking tower loomed up ahead. It was at least three hundred feet tall and, in spite of its flimsy appearance, capable of servicing two ships at a time. That was because each vessel would weigh only a fraction of what it would on an Earth normal planet. One landing cradle was empty but a Hudathan transport was cradled in the other. It was surrounded by a complicated tracery of robotic machinery, some of which was connected to the ship.

That was strange. The freighter should be making a run for it. And the trap, if there was one, should have been sprung by then. As the DE coasted toward the base, the ship's sensors probed the surrounding area for any signs of life. The technician's voice was tight but calm. "Scanning... Scanning... Scanning... There are patches of heat but all of them are static so far. The only sign of electromechanical activity is an automated docking system that is broadcasting in Hudathan."

Lieutenant Commander Angie Dickerson was the *Mohawk's* commanding officer. And like the ship herself, had been called out of retirement to fill a slot that should belong to someone twenty years younger. Her white hair was worn in a crew cut, her eyes were like chips of turquoise, and she had the no-nonsense manner of an officer who had seen most everything. "Alright Captain Chozick... This would be a good time to join your company. I suggest that you secure the Hudathan ship before going down to inspect the rest of the base. If the freighter blows, and takes the *Mohawk* with it, you'll have a long walk home."

The odds that the ridgeheads would blow up a ship *and* toast a docking tower to destroy the *Mohawk* were pretty slim, but it paid to be cautious. Chozick said, "Roger that," as he freed himself from the six-point harness and stood. The DE's argrav generator was on, so it was a simple matter to make his way down the main corridor to a sealed hatch. Once it cycled open he entered a second passageway. It led to another hatch and the sign that read, "UNPRESSURIZED COMPARTMENT". Racks of equipment were located on both sides of the entryway.

While at battle stations, all of the ship's crew members were required to wear skintight counter-pressure suits and keep their helmets close at hand. Chozick was no exception. So all he had to do to get ready was secure his brain bucket to the suit's neck ring and put on a combat rig with integral air supply. After running a series of tests to make sure that everything was operating properly, he entered the lock.

Once the air had been removed, hatch two opened into a cargo compartment that could be used for a wide variety of missions, including the transportation of ground troops. In this case, Bravo Company, 2nd Battalion of the 4th Regiment. Bravo Company was an infantry outfit to which a platoon of cavalry had been attached to give it some extra heft. And that was potentially important when battling aliens who stood eight-feet-tall and weighed three to four hundred pounds.

Had Chozick been a different sort of officer, and had his company been comprised of the usual mix of ex-criminals, misfits and adventurers for which the Legion was known, someone might have shouted, "Atten-hut!" But Chozick had gone to considerable lengths to recruit only the most venal soldiers into his outfit. So his arrival was greeted with remarks like, "There he is", "Here we go", and "Listen up".

Most of the legionnaires were bio bods, but some ten-foot-tall cyborgs were present as well, and could be seen toward the back of the hold. "Okay, we're about to dock, so grab something solid," Chozick advised them. "And keep your eyes peeled once we're clear of the ship. The Hudathans should be shooting at us by now, but they aren't, so something strange is going on.

"The 1st platoon will remain here and guard the *Mohawk*. Once we get outside you'll see that a Hudathan ship is berthed side-by-side with this one. The 2nd platoon will enter and secure it. As that's taking place, the 3rd will make its way down to the surface and await further

5

orders. Remember, there isn't much gravity out there, so if you jump up off the ground it will be a long time before you come down. *If you come down.* So follow the low grav protocols they taught you in basic."

Chozick's comments were interrupted as Dickerson's voice was heard in their helmets. "Standby for docking in five, four, three, two, one." The last digit was followed by a heavy impact as the *Mohawk* settled onto the cradle formed by four skeletal arms. One bio bod landed on his ass. That provoked gales of laughter from the others along with lots of snide remarks.

"Last, but not least," Chozick said, "it is our patriotic duty to liberate any valuables that the ridgeheads left laying around. But remember, all for one, and one for all. Anyone who tries to short the team will wind up on the KIA list. Do you copy?"

There had been three such deaths during the last ten missions, and all of the legionnaires were aware of it. So there was no response other than silence. Chozick nodded. "Good... Put your helmets on, seal 'em, and stand by."

A light flashed two minutes later and the legionnaires heard a warning tone as Chozick led them into a huge lock. Once the door closed behind them an antibacterial mist fogged the lock. The moment the decontamination sequence was complete, Chozick led them across a ramp to the walkway that paralleled the ship. He went first because that was his inclination and because the men, women, and cyborgs under his command expected him to take the same chances they did. That was part of the unwritten contract that bound them together. The planet Krang hung over them. Most of the visible surface was tan, but the poles were white, and patches of blue could be seen through holes in the cloud cover.

The ramp bounced slightly as Chozick slip-slid forward, weapon at the ready. *Now*, he thought to himself. *Now they'll spring the trap.* But nothing happened as he led the 1st platoon across a connecting causeway to the alien ship. It was small and capable of landing on a planetary surface. The hull was aerodynamically smooth, but somewhat bulky, not unlike the whales in Earth's oceans.

After arriving on the cradle that supported the freighter, Chozick turned left and made his way to the point where an open hatch gave access to a large Hudathan-sized lock. Chozick waved a demolitions team forward. Then he turned to discover that the company's new Field Intelligence Robot was standing a couple of feet away. The name

"Orson" was stenciled across the android's chest, but everybody referred to it as "Shithead."

Was the robot what it purported to be? An intelligence gathering device conceived by some fat-assed staff officer? Or was it somebody's effort to spy on him? Chozick didn't know or care because Shithead's life expectancy was less than two hours long.

There was a verbal warning followed by a soundless explosion, a flash of light, and a sudden trash storm as air rushed out of the compartment just beyond the lock. That should piss the ridgeheads off, but there was no response as Chozick checked the heads-up display (HUD) projected on the inside surface of his visor.

A variety of information was available to him; including a line diagram of where he was in relation to the *Mohawk*, POV shots for every person in the company, and more. At the moment, he wanted to ensure that his helmet cam was functioning properly so he would have footage for the battalion's Intel officer to look at. Not because he cared, but because it was necessary to *look* like he cared, and Shithead wasn't going to make it back. Fortunately the helmet cam was in good working order so that, plus footage from the rest of the legionnaires, it would give the chair warriors something to do.

The lighting was dim inside the ship—but not so dim that Chozick couldn't recognize the dead body for what it was. Or *had* been. Because the sudden loss of pressure within the ship had done horrible things to what had been a Hudathan. "He died of natural causes," Shithead observed, as it knelt next to the pile of raw meat. The robot's hands were steady as they took a tissue sample.

"How do you know that?" Chozick demanded.

"He wasn't wearing a pressure suit," the robot replied. "And, based on that, I think it's safe to assume that the rest of the crew died of natural causes as well. A highly communicable disease would explain it."

That was a breathtaking leap in Chozick's opinion, but one that seemed to be born-out as the legionnaires pushed deeper into the ship, and came across more bodies. Plus the robot's theory explained why none of the aliens were clad in pressure suits and didn't try to defend their ship. As for the base, well, time would tell.

Form follows function, or so the saying goes, so, even though Hudathan minds had been responsible for designing the, ship it bore similarities to Human vessels. Two main corridors ran parallel to each other. Passageways connected the corridors together and provided

William C. Dietz

access to various compartments. The legionnaires didn't have enough time to investigate each nook and cranny. But when they saw something that might have some value they were quick to grab it. So it wasn't long before Chozick spotted bio bods carrying enormous back swords, bulky sidearms, and all manner of alien knickknacks. Would the loot slow them down in an emergency? Of course it would—but that was one of the tradeoffs Chozick had to accept in order to have the type of company he wanted. The kind that was going to put some serious money in his pockets one day. Chozick's thoughts were interrupted by the sound of Dickerson's voice in his helmet. "This the Captain... Give me a sitrep. Over."

Chozick told her about the bodies and passed Shithead's analysis off as his own. "Okay," Dickerson said. "An epidemic would explain it. But remember that some survivors could be holed up somewhere—and a Hudathan ship could arrive at any moment. Should that occur the *Mohawk* would be easy meat for them. So finish the job as quickly as you can. Over."

Chozick wanted to say, "Get over yourself, bitch," but didn't. He acknowledged the order by chinning his mike two times, instead.

The next transmission was from First Sergeant Kobo. An especially brutal noncom who liked to punctuate his orders with a swift kick in the ass. "Got something, boss. I think you should take a look."

A straight up company commander would have insisted that Kobo use proper radio protocol but that was the sort of thing that Chozick's people resented. The officer was in the control room at that point. Two Hudathans were present but both were dead. "Yeah? Where are you?"

"In the hold."

"On my way." Chozick turned and saw that Shithead was seated in front of a terminal. Downloading data? That's the way it looked. Not that it mattered. "Take me to the hold," Chozick ordered.

Shithead had never been to the hold, but didn't hesitate. "Yes, sir." Chozick followed the android down a corridor and into a side passageway. It led to a lift. Once inside, Shithead chose one of five oversized buttons. That was when Chozick realized something he should have noticed before. The robot could read Hudathan! And, given its function, that made sense.

The elevator came to a stop, the door slid open, and Shithead stepped out. Chozick followed it down a corridor, past what might

8

have been an engineering space, and through a lock. Kobo and a couple of bio bods were waiting in the compartment beyond. The noncom was big and looked bigger with the helmet on his head and the life support package on his back. Chozick nodded to him. "Whatcha got?"

"There's a bunch of boxes in the hold," Kobo answered, "but only one of them has a transparent lid. And it's located in the middle of the compartment, all special like."

Special treatment could be an indication of something valuable. Chozick nodded. "Show me."

Kobo led the officer back to the point where a large box sat resting on a couple of stands. Two lights were focused on the container which might be a further sign of its importance. Chozick stepped up to the container and looked down through the transparent duraplast. The first thing he saw was a skeleton, a *Hudathan* skeleton, with a long staff lying next to it. Chozick frowned. "You brought me down here to look at a dead Hudathan?"

Kobo was about to speak when Shithead answered for him. The robot had produced a thin cable which connected it to the jack panel at the head of the casket. "The body is that of Ho-La," it said solemnly. "He was a monk, a famous monk, who left Hudatha to live on a planet called Rain. His remains are one hundred and twenty-three years old and were on their way to Hudatha for safekeeping."

"*Why?*" Chozick demanded.

"Ho-La has a status similar to that of a Human saint," Shithead replied. "Though largely ignored, his teachings are greatly respected by all six Hudathan clans. It may be that the Hudathans were afraid that the Ramanthians would conqueror Rain, find the remains and desecrate them."

Chozick took the information in. A saint. A highly respected saint. How much would the ridgeheads pay to get the remains back? A million? *Five* million? It was a strange opportunity but one with considerable potential. "Sergeant Kobo, please accept my apologies. You are a fucking genius. Seal this container and move it to the *Mohawk* right away."

Kobo nodded. "Got it boss." Then, having turned to the bio bods, he growled at them. "Well, don't just stand there... Find something to protect the coffin with. I'll call for some T-2s. They can carry it."

Chozick looked at Shithead just in time to see the wire disappear into the robot's olive-drab colored body. "Lead me down to the surface."

Shithead departed with Chozick and some bio bods following along behind. They left the ship, followed a causeway to the tower, and were on their way to the ground when Dickerson pinged him again. "The Captain here... Why can't we see your video feeds? Or hear any radio traffic? Over."

"It must be some sort of technical glitch," Chozick lied. "But I'll keep you informed. We cleared the ship and we're on our way to the base. Over."

"All right," Dickerson said irritably. "But pick up the pace. "We're sitting ducks. Over."

"Copy that," Chozick replied. Then, after breaking the connection, "Bitch."

A platoon of bio bods and some T-2s stood waiting as Chozick and his party arrived on the surface. The bipedal cyborgs stood ten-feet tall, could run at speeds up to fifty-miles per hour, and operate in a complete vacuum when necessary. For the purposes of the current mission each borg was equipped with grasper hands and carrying an energy cannon.

In terms of firepower each T-2 was the rough equivalent of eight fully armed bio bods. Two of them led the way as the legionnaires crossed a large expanse of open ground to reach the base. Tracks ran every-which-way across the surface of the moon, but most of them converged on a single spot. And that was the entrance to what Chozick imagined to be the headquarters building.

Unlike the hatch on the ship, the outer door was closed. "Blow it," Chozick ordered. "We'll split into teams once we get inside. I'll take the 1st squad, Lieutenant Ember will lead the 2nd, and Sergeant Howers will be in charge of the 3rd. Remember, we could run into survivors, so be careful."

Chozick's words were punctuated by a silent flash and a sudden dust storm. The interior had been pressurized, just as the ship had been, and any Hudathan not wearing a suit was dead meat. And ugly meat, at that.

They entered a huge lock. Tracked ground vehicles were parked next to a stack of cargo modules. Incoming supplies? Outgoing garbage? Intel would want to know. Chozick pointed to the pile. "Check those modules Sergeant Howes... and take Shithead with you. It can read Hudathan."

As Howes and his party split off Chozick and the rest of them passed through an open hatch and entered the building beyond. Chozick turned left at the first intersection while Lieutenant Ember and his legionnaires went right. The deck was littered with trash that had been sucked towards the lock when it blew. Some of it crunched under Chozick's boots as he passed the first of what would eventually be eleven dead bodies. Hudathans who, with only a few exceptions, were stretched out on bunks. A fact that suggested that they too had been terribly ill.

But *how*? Had the ship brought the disease to the station? Or had the personnel inside the base been sick when the freighter arrived? That was the sort of thing the spooks would try to figure out. Personally, so long as he and his people were safe, Chozick didn't care. And, by his reasoning, there was very little reason for concern. First, because it was very unlikely that a Human would be susceptible to a Hudathan disease. But, even if he was wrong, the entire company would have to pass through the antibiotic mist before they could reboard the ship.

After a quick tour of the hydroponics section Chozick and his team were headed back toward the lock when Howes spoke. "Hey, boss... Do you read me? Over."

"Roger that, over."

"We got something here. A container of what Shithead says is hafnium. Personally I ain't never heard of the stuff but Shithead says that the brass would want us to bring it back."

Chozick knew the android was correct because the officer made it his business to understand which substances were valuable and why. Hafnium was used to make high-temperature ceramics and the nickel based super alloys that were critical to manufacturing nozzles for plasma arc torches and nuclear control rods. That meant hafnium was *always* valuable. But now, in the middle of a war, the stuff would be priceless! *If* Howes was correct. "You're sure?"

"Hell no, I'm not sure," the noncom replied. "Shithead is sure. It wants us to load the container onto the ship."

"Shithead is correct," Chozick said, as his heart began to beat a little faster. "Round up as many cyborgs as you need and take that container up to the *Mohawk*. Over."

"I'm on it," Howes assured him. "Over."

Chozick could hardly believe his good fortune as he and his team exited the building. He could see Howes and four T-2s up ahead. They were carrying a cargo module between them, and puffs of moon dust shot up with each step. This was what Chozick had been hoping for. A BIG score. More than that, his personal freedom. If he had the balls to take the opportunity and make something of it. But *did* he?

*   *   *

Dickerson was feeling antsy and struggling to conceal it from the bridge crew. The *Mohawk* had been docked for one hour, twenty-six minutes, and seventeen seconds by that time. An eternity from her point of view, because the DE was stationary and, therefore, vulnerable to any vessel that happened along, which was bad enough.

But the fact that she didn't trust Captain Chozick made the situation even worse. The legionnaire hadn't done anything wrong. Not that she knew about anyway. But Dickerson was sixty-two years old, had dealt with a lot of people, and had learned to trust her instincts. And there was something about Chozick's coal chip eyes, his bladelike nose, and his thin lipped mouth that left her cold. So the incoming radio call came as a relief. "We're about to re-board," Chozick said. "I'll come forward and give you a report as soon as all of my people have cleared decontamination and are strapped in. Over."

"How long will that take? Over."

"Fifteen, max. We'll hurry. Over."

Thus reassured, Dickerson gave orders for all personnel to begin their preflight checks. That was more of a formality than anything else, since the crew had been ready to lift from the moment the ship put down. Still, it gave them something to do as Dickerson watched Chozick and his ruffians enter the lock. She wondered what was contained in the cargo module that the T-2s were hauling aboard. The fact that it was the *second* container the legionnaires had brought back might be an indicator of success. Dickerson turned away from the screen as the external hatch closed and antibacterial mist filled the lock.

There were plenty of things to think about as the *Mohawk's* crew prepared to get underway—so Dickerson didn't notice when Chozick entered the control room fifteen minutes later. She heard his voice and turned to see that he wasn't alone. Three heavily armed legionnaires stood flanking him. Dickerson frowned. "This is a restricted area, Captain... Please order your subordinates to return to the hold."

"*I'll* be making the rules from now on," Chozick said, and aimed a gun at her. Dickerson raised her hands to block the bullets. *I was right*, she thought to herself, and then it was over.

*   *   *

The gunshots were unnaturally loud in the close confines of the control room and Chozick saw Dickerson jerk as the slugs struck her chest. Her head flopped forward but a six-point harness held her upright.

Chozick lowered the pistol as he looked around. The pilot, navigator, and three techs all wore expressions of shocked disbelief. "We have the XO," he said calmly. "And the chief engineer. Both have agreed to cooperate. The plan is to take the *Mohawk* out to a planet on the rim. Those who wish to join us, and share in the take, can. The rest of the ship's personnel will be dropped at a point where they can find transportation. That means you have every reason to cooperate. Are there any questions? No? Fine. Let's get underway."

*   *   *

Shithead should have been dead. *Would* have been dead had it been Human. That's because the robot had been standing in line, waiting to enter the *Mohawk's* lock, when Chozick shot it in the face.

But unlike Human beings, Shithead's CPU was located in its torso rather than its head. So although the bullet destroyed a sub-processor responsible for speech the rest of the android's capabilities were unaffected. That meant Shithead was "alive" to the extent than any robot was alive, but had the good sense to fake its death, and was lying on its back as the *Mohawk* took off.

As repellors flared and the ship grew steadily smaller Shithead didn't feel any sense of anger or hopelessness. What was, was.

Finally, once the DE was lost among the unblinking stars, Shithead knew it was safe to stand up. Chozick was supposed to destroy key components of the base as he withdrew but hadn't. *Why?* The answer was obvious. The Human had experienced a malfunction of some sort. It made no difference. Shithead's duty was clear: Find a way off the moon, convey what it knew to the proper authorities, and request a new speech synthesizer. . In that order.

So Shithead followed the causeway to the tower and stepped onto the elevator. Once the robot reached the ground it began to walk. Each step produced a puff of bone dry dust which took a long time to fall.

As Shithead approached the crater it could see a tangle of what might have been old hydroponics tanks, the remains of a crawler, and a pile of scrap metal. None of which were of any interest. No, the android's attention was focused on the Human-made space ship it had seen from the top of the tower. It looked like a navy tug and lay in two pieces. Shithead didn't know how the tug had been acquired, or why the Hudathans cut it in two, nor did it care.

What Shithead wanted to know was whether the vessel was equipped with one of the new FTL comsets. If it was, and if the robot could get the piece of equipment up and running, it could call for help.

With that in mind, Shithead made a beeline for the bow section, entered through a large hole, and made its way to the control room. But, after scanning the interior with its headlamp, Shithead was forced to conclude that the lowly tug wasn't equipped with an FTL comset.

What about message torpedoes? Every ship carried them, and as it turned out, the tug was no exception. Unfortunately the nacelle from which the missiles were launched was located *under* the hull. And even with the moon's light gravity that section of the tug was too heavy for Shithead to lift.

So the robot was about to start for the headquarters building when it noticed something interesting. The tug was equipped with *two* lifeboats! One on each side of the hull. However, due to the way the ship was positioned, the boat on the port side was inaccessible. Still, that meant the boat on the starboard side was exposed. Or would be if Shithead found a way to open the bay where the boat was kept.

First, however, the robot needed to enter the escape craft and verify that it was still operable. An easy task, and one that went well. Thus encouraged, the machine went looking for an accumulator that still had some juice in it. After locating a power source, it was necessary to run a jumper cable from it to the servos that controlled the bay doors. They opened smoothly.

Having exposed the lifeboat to space, the next task was to charge the launching system which, under emergency conditions, would blow the emergency vehicle out into space. Unfortunately, part of the launch mechanism was damaged beyond repair. That meant the robot had to remove the broken parts and replace them with components salvaged from the port bay. A process that took three additional hours.

Finally, having restored the launching system to full functionality, it was time for Shithead to enter the tiny cockpit and strap itself in. Lifeboats were intentionally easy to launch, so all the android had to do was flip a red cover out of the way, and push a green button. The response was instantaneous. The control board lit up, a five-second count down began, and a signal was sent to the newly rejuvenated air compressor. It blew the lifeboat out and up. And, thanks to the moon's microgravity, there was plenty of time for the little in-system drive to fire. Shithead was jacked into the vessel's NAVCOMP by then, and ordered it get clear of Krang's gravity well as quickly as possible.

Then, once the lifeboat was well underway, it was time for the android to issue additional orders. The ship wasn't large enough to rate a hyperdrive, so Shithead couldn't jump to its destination. But it could head into Human space, find a nav beacon, and use its emergency com capability to send a message. Would the plan work? Shithead didn't know and didn't care. In the absence of something productive to do, it went to standby. There were no dreams, just a state of readiness, and that was all any robot could ask for.

CHAPTER TWO

Coincidence is God's way of remaining anonymous.

Albert Einstein
The World As I See It
Standard year, 1949

The planet Algeron

Even though the planet Algeron had a breathable atmosphere and something close to Earth normal gravity, there was one way in which it was very different. And that was the fact that mountains divided the northern hemisphere from the southern. They were called The Towers of Algeron, and their highest peaks dwarfed Everest on Earth, and Olympic Mons on Mars. They were so massive that, if placed on Earth, the Towers would have sunk down through the planet's crust. But that wasn't going to happen because the mountains weighed half what they would on Earth due to the gravity differential between Algeron's relatively small poles and its equator.

All of which was fine with Legion Captain Dean "Deacon" Smith. It was the two-hour-and-forty-minute days that he disliked. But what was, was. And the short days, the bad weather, and hostile natives were a large part of why the first emperor had given the planet to the Legion more than a hundred years earlier. The unspoken reason being his heartfelt desire to keep most of the Legion off Earth where, if led by the wrong people, it could have been a threat to him and his family. Because the emperor knew what the Legion's motto meant: *Legio patria nostra*. "The legion is our country." Meaning that the men, women, and cyborgs who served in the Legion were ultimately loyal to each other rather than whatever government happened to be in power.

Smith knew all of that, of course—but was focused on his job. Which was to find the bandits responsible for Private Coster's death and take them prisoner, or, failing that, to kill them. Because the Naa bandits viewed the Legion the same way they would look at a tribe. A strong tribe could take revenge. A weak tribe couldn't. So the last thing the Legion's brass wanted was to be perceived as weak.

Most of Smith's company was back at Fort Cameron. But he, along with Lieutenant Mary Josy, and her twenty-four-person platoon were following a mishmash of dooth tracks up a narrow trail. The legionnaires had been following the tracks for two local days by then and, as the sun began to set, Smith knew the temperature would fall. Once that happened it might start to snow. If so, the tracks would disappear within thirty minutes.

That would be bad, but far from disastrous, since one of the bandits had stolen Private Laraby's brain bucket, and it was "on." As a result, Smith could "see" the helmet's location on his HUD. So, unless the Naa threw their prize away, or turned the power off, the platoon could track them down.

There was another possibility however... What if the bandits *knew* how the helmet worked—and were using it to suck the platoon into a carefully planned ambush? A lot of legionnaires had been killed by underestimating the Naa.

Lieutenant Josy and her cyborg were up in the point position. The T-2 could detect heat and electromechanical activity, but couldn't see over the ridge above. Knowing that Smith sent the platoon's drone up to take a look. The can-shaped robot could fly at altitudes up to three hundred feet, send pictures back, and even serve as an interpreter if necessary. The machine made a soft whirring sound as it vanished into the gloom.

The bio bods activated the night vision technology built into their helmets as another two-hour-and-forty-minute night got underway. It was helpful, but wouldn't provide a decisive advantage. The Naa could smell what some of them called "the stinks" from a hundred yards away. Their retinas were equipped with twice the number of rods that Humans had, and they were very attuned to the environment. So much so that the Naa had been known to sense the presence of alien troops even when there were no physical cues to go on. They were also excellent shots and increasingly armed with weapons stolen from legionnaires like Private Laraby.

By leaning back in the harness and bending his knees, Smith could absorb the up and down motion as Chang carried him uphill. Like all of the T-2s Chang had been a bio bod originally and now, having lost most of his body, was living life as a cyborg. It was, he said, "A lot better than the alternative."

Each cyborg had a story. Some had been legionnaires to begin with. Chang was an example of that. But others, those who had committed capital crimes, were often given a choice between life as a cyborg or a dive into the big abyss. Did that suck? Yes, it did. But most people thought that some life was better than none at all. Smith's thoughts were interrupted by an incoming transmission. "This is unit Zero-Two," the drone said flatly. "I am streaming video on channel three."

Smith brought channel three up on his HUD. It looked like Zero-Two was just over the ridge looking down on what the map overlay said was the village of Crooked Creek. And, judging from appearances the settlement, was under attack. It consisted of about twenty huts surrounded by a palisade.

The north side of the defensive wall was on fire, and Legion issue tracers were slicing the night into an assortment of geometric shapes. From what Smith could see, it appeared that the bandits were so intent on looting the village they were unaware of the Humans who were following them. The choice was his. According to the orders Smith had been given he could "...take any actions necessary to apprehend or kill the bandits responsible for Private Laraby's death."

So, if Smith wanted to, he could go down and kick some ass. He wasn't required to do so, however, since the Legion had a long tradition of allowing the indigs to kill each other. But in his mind,

Smith reported to an authority higher than the Legion. Psalm 82:3 read: "Defend the weak and the fatherless; uphold the cause of the poor and the oppressed." And it didn't take a genius to see that the village of Crooked Creek was oppressed. Smith chinned his mike. "Alpha-Nine to Alpha-One. You saw the video. If we hurry, we can attack the bandits while they're focused on the village. Over."

*   *   *

Lieutenant Josy was anything but surprised. In addition to leading the 1st platoon, she was the Deacon's XO and accustomed to his ways. No one knew why he had given up civilian life for an organization staffed by adventurers, misfits, and criminals. A self imposed punishment perhaps? A fall from grace? That was *her* theory. As for the name, well, it seemed as though half the people in the Legion were named "Smith," and running from something. "Roger that, Nine." Then, over the company push, "This is One. Put it in gear, people. The fur -alls are shooting at each other on the far side of the ridge and Nine wants to party. Over."

*   *   *

Smith heard a flurry of affirmative clicks as Josy and her T-2 began to pick up speed. Then it was time to hang on as Chang followed suit. It took ten minutes to reach the top of the ridge and start down the other side. Half of the log palisade was on fire by then. And that meant things weren't going well for the villagers. "Nine to Zero-Two... Enter the village, let the villagers know that we're going to attack the bandits from the west, and tell them not to fire on us. Over." Having received an acknowledgement, Smith switched to the company push. "This is Nine. Do not, I repeat do *not* fire on the village without an order from me. One will take us in. Over."

The last order made it clear that Josy would lead the attack. That would not only signal his faith in her, but give him an opportunity to see how the officer handled herself.

There was a mad scramble to get down the hillside quickly, and Smith was forced to hang onto the grab bar in front of him as Chang took the slope in a series of gigantic leaps. Once they were on level ground, Josy ordered the 1st squad to circle around to the east where it could stop the bandits if they attempted to run. She led the rest of the platoon in with guns blazing.

There was a lot of confusion so it was difficult to tell how many bandits there were—but two dozen seemed like a pretty good estimate. They were mounted on the enormous six-legged animals the Naa called dooths and, as was their habit, the warriors were circling the beleaguered village while they fired into it. A strategy that made them hard to hit but opened them to friendly fire.

Every now and then one of the bandits would ride his dooth in through one of the fiery gaps. But, as far as Smith could tell, none of them ever came out. A sure indication that the villagers had been able to hold the inner compound.

Had the legionnaires been part of an infantry regiment, a different approach would have been in order. But, thanks to their mobility, the two person cavalry units could run their opponents down. Smith felt Chang surge forward firing both arm-mounted weapons at once. The energy cannon was lethal but lacked the punch that a .50 caliber machine gun round could deliver.

A dooth-mounted rider appeared up ahead and both went down in a welter of blood as Chang's fire converged on them. Then they were past the bodies and Smith heard himself utter a whoop of joy. That was followed by a surge of guilt; for to enjoy war, to enjoy killing, was a sin.

Thus chastened, Smith monitored the company push as Josy's platoon made short work of the bandits who were circling the village. Three of the brigands tried to escape, ran into the 1st squad, and were cut to pieces.

For their part, the legionnaires suffered only three casualties, none of which were serious enough to require a dust off. It had been a successful action and Smith told Josy that over the platoon push so everyone could hear.

Then he freed himself from the harness and dropped to the ground. It had begun to snow, and flakes whirled around the officer as he made his way over to a still-smoldering gap in the palisade. Most of the fires had been extinguished by then, and a cloud of steam billowed into the air as one of the villagers threw a bucket of water onto a glowing timber. Smith kept his weapon pointed at the sky as he stepped through the opening and into the open area beyond.

That was when the drone appeared. It was keeping company with a Naa warrior. Like all of his kind, the indig was humanoid, had a slender frame, and was covered by a coat of short fur. Though similar to a Human's the Naa's face had a slightly feline cast to it. Smith noticed that the local was armed with a Naa made rifle and wore a cross belt to which three sheaths were attached. Two were empty. "I am called Strongarm Knifethrow," the Naa said. A slight overlap could be heard as the drone made the necessary translation.

Smith reached up to remove his helmet which he tucked under his left arm. "My name is Captain Smith. Your people fought bravely."

What Smith saw in the Naa's eyes required no translation. The sadness was clear to see. "What you say is true—and I thank you for it. But we are a small village and many lives were lost."

"The gods have them," Smith said. "They shall feast tonight."

Knifethrow looked at the Human. "You know of the gods?"

"I read about them," Smith replied.

"And you believe?"

"I believe in one god but he has reason to deny me."

"The gods are fickle," Knifethrow observed. "Your god will change his mind."

"I hope so," Smith replied. There was a pause. Then, after a moment of silence, he spoke again. "Except for those items which belong to us, the rest of the bandits' belongings will be left with you. That includes the surviving animals."

The items in question wouldn't make up for lives lost. But the loot would help the village to rebuild. Knifethrow offered Smith the forearm-to-forearm grip that was reserved for adult warriors. "Thank you."

"You're welcome," Smith replied. And the conversation was over.

The newly fallen snow made a crunching sound as the legionnaire worked his way back to the point where Chang was waiting. Josy was present, as well. Her visor was open to reveal straight cut black bangs, even features, and a nose stud. "I have a present for you," she said, and gave Smith the helmet. The name LARABY was stenciled across the front of it. Smith felt for the power button and pushed. Then he turned to look at the village. The sun had broken company with the eastern horizon, and a cold gray light suffused the scene. A female was crying and a shot rang out as someone put a wounded dooth out of its misery. "Vengeance is mine saith the Lord," Smith said. "But where the hell *was* he?"

Josy looked up into Smith's tortured face. "If there is a god," she said, "maybe he was here. Maybe that's why most of the villagers are alive."

But Smith's eyes were on something far away, and she knew he wasn't listening. Her gaze shifted to Chang. He shook his enormous head. There was no way to reach the Deacon. Not when he was in one of his moods.

Once the legionnaires were ready, they turned west and began the long trip back to Fort Camerone. The snow was falling faster now, and it laid a white shroud over the land. Another two-hour-and-forty-minute day had begun.

*   *   *

It took eleven local days to complete the journey to Fort Camerone. It had been rebuilt after being destroyed years earlier. And now that it was home to the government in exile, work was underway to expand the complex. The area, formerly referred to as Naa Town, had been razed to make room for what was commonly called "the new fort" . To support the larger structure, a spaceport was being built off to the west, and a training complex was under construction, as well.

So, as Smith and his legionnaires neared the fort, they passed between multiple check points, were tracked by eyes in the sky, and repeatedly asked to identify themselves. A process that made Smith increasingly grumpy. Finally, having answered the same question a dozen times, he lost his temper. "Who the hell do you *think* we are? How many T-2s do the Naa have?"

That earned him some sharp words from a faceless major who took the opportunity to remind Smith that assumptions can get people killed. So Smith was already in a bad mood as the platoon entered the fort. A ramp led down into the subbasement where the cyborgs were quartered. The corridors were large enough to let two twenty-five ton quads pass each other. Side passageways led to the bays assigned to individual units.

The rest of the company was there, which meant that the 1st platoon had to endure a barrage of friendly insults as they entered the area. Then it was time to unload weapons, hose the cyborgs down, and run tech checks on each one. Once the work was done the bio bods were allowed to get some chow, take showers, and log some rack time. All except for Smith and Josy, who were slated to appear in front of Battalion Commander Colonel Leo Price at 1400 hours. And, since it was already 1330 when the message arrived, they had thirty minutes in which to make the hike. Not enough time to eat or take a shower.

"It was a mistake to get into that major's face," Josy said, as they got off a lift. "I'll bet he was on the horn to Price a minute later."

Smith scowled. "Fuck him."

Josy gave him sideways glance. "You told me that the use of profanity is a sin."

"The major is an asshole," Smith responded darkly. "God knows that. So he'll forgive me."

Josy laughed as a door slid open allowing them to enter battalion headquarters. A large desk blocked the way—and a no nonsense sergeant was seated behind it. "Good afternoon, Captain... What can I do for you?"

"My name's Smith, and this is Lieutenant Josy. We're here to see the Colonel."

The sergeant's eyes flicked to a screen and back again. "Yes, sir. Unfortunately, the Colonel is running late. Please take a seat. I'll let you know as soon as he's available."

So, in spite of the fact that they were tired, hungry, and dirty, the officers had no choice but to sit and wait. It was 1433 by the time a general left the colonel's office and the sergeant looked their way. "The Colonel is free now... You can go in."

Josy followed Smith as he circled the reception desk and made his way back to an open door. A knock block was mounted on the wall, and Smith was about to make use of it, when Price looked up from his terminal. The colonel's head was shaved, his skin was brown, and his eyes were a brilliant green. "No need for that, Captain... Come in and take a load off."

*   *   *

Once they were seated Price inquired about the mission. While Smith spoke Josy took a look around. There were pictures on the walls. Price on a T-2, Price in front of a quad, and Price with General Booly. And there were knickknacks too. Josy was taking inventory when she heard her name. "Congratulations Lieutenant Josy," Price said. "It sounds like you led a very successful patrol."

That was when Josy realized that Smith had given her credit for defeating the bandits. She was about to object when Price cut her off. "That's why I sent for the two of you... The Naa aren't the only ones who have to deal with bandits. We have some of our own. But, before I get into the specifics, some background information will be helpful.

"As you know, the bugs have control of Earth and we're getting our asses kicked on planets like Gamma-014. So we need help. First from the Clone Hegemony, which owns 014, and then from the Hudathans if we can get it. They believe that *all* races represent an existential threat to them. But, if we can convince them that the Ramanthians are the greatest threat, then we would have some very effective allies. With that in mind we have cut back on the number of missions into Hudathan held space—and some very high level government officials are trying to bring them around."

*   *   *

"That would be wonderful," Smith said sincerely.

"Yes, it would," Price agreed as he stood. "So keep that in mind during the meeting."

Smith was about to say, "What meeting," when the colonel turned to a side door. Having sensed his presence it opened onto a conference room. Price led the way. As Smith entered he was surprised to see that a robot was standing on one side of the room—and a Hudathan was perched on a corner of the table. The reason for that was obvious. The alien was so large that he couldn't sit in one of the chairs. "War Commander Tola-Sa, please allow me to introduce Captain Smith, and Lieutenant Josy. They're the officers I told you about."

Smith had seen pictures of Hudathans, and knew they were large, but didn't realize how large until coming face to face with one. Tola-Sa was about seven feet tall with broad shoulders and thick arms. A bony ridge ran front to back along the top of a hairless head, dark eyes stared out from under craggy brows, and his frog-like mouth looked hard and uncompromising. A translator was clipped to the cross belts that the Hudathan wore and, when he spoke, some overlap could be heard. "It's a pleasure to meet you Captain... And you as well Lieutenant. The colonel tells me that you specialize in killing criminals."

It was true that Smith's company had successfully tracked down a number of bandits. But he hadn't considered it to be a specialty. Nor had he set out to kill them. Far from it. According to James 2:13, "Judgment without mercy will be shown to anyone who has not been merciful."

But it was also true that, in spite of his best intentions, most of the bandits that Smith went after wound up dead. So he wasn't sure what to say. "We do our best, sir."

Price nodded indulgently. "By now you understand where this is going. The War Commander and I want you to find a criminal, a *Human* criminal who, until very recently, wore the same uniform that you do. A captain named Damien Chozick."

Smith frowned. "A captain? What did he do?"

"That's why Orson is here," Price replied. "It was attached to Chozick's command when the crimes were committed, and can provide you with a firsthand account of everything that took place."

Price turned to the robot. "Start your report just prior to landing on moon HE24-6743."

As Smith looked at the android, he noticed that a section of its face was bright with new metal. A repair, perhaps? Smith thought so as Price ordered the lights to dim and Orson launched into its report. Though tied together with some flat, unemotional comments, most of the narrative consisted of holographic POV video shots with accompanying audio. The images were suspended over the middle of the conference room table. And, as Smith watched, he saw the landing, the Hudathan skeleton, and Chozick ordering a subordinate to place the hafnium on the *Mohawk*. The final shot showed the renegade drawing his pistol and pointing it at the camera, which ,was to say, Orson. That was followed by a spark and sudden darkness.

"That's right," Price said. "Chozick assumed that a bullet in the head would destroy Orson's CPU. But he was wrong. Orson's CPU is located in its chest! So it played dead, waited for the ship to lift, and went looking for another way home. The journey took the better part of three months. And, if Orson were Human, we'd be hanging medals on him."

Smith looked from Price to Tola-Sa and back again. "So, given the War Commander's presence here, it's my guess that you want us to find the remains."

"Yes," Price said emphatically. "And the hafnium if you can. Both belong to our Hudathan friends. But recovering the reliquary is the most important of the two. The theft of Ho-La's remains by a human military unit would end any chance of an alliance. And once you catch up with the renegades I want you to kill them. *All* of them. They are currently missing in action. Let's keep it that way."

Smith frowned. "We'll do our best, sir. But I won't promise to kill Chozick and his legionnaires. Not if they surrender. It wouldn't be right."

*　　*　　*

Price opened his mouth as if to speak and closed it again. Judging from the expression on his face, he was angry. Very angry. Seconds passed as he stared at Smith. Josy figured that a lightning bolt was about to fall—never mind the fact that the order was illegal. But maybe Price considered that, because, when he spoke, the tone was surprisingly conciliatory. "Alright, Captain... If Chozick or any of his legionnaires surrender you can bring them here."

Smith nodded. "Yes, sir. So, where are they?"

Price looked at Tola-Sa and back again. "We have no idea."

CHAPTER THREE

All warfare is based on deception.

Sun Tzu
The Art Of War
Standard year circa 500 B.C.

The space station Orb 1, in orbit around the planet Long Jump

As Chozick began to circle "B" deck, the holographic image of a woman appeared in front of him. "Hi, honey," the simulacrum said. "I'm horny, how about you?"

The image shattered as Chozick stepped through it. This was what? His twentieth visit to the hab? Something like that. But the almost overwhelming assault on his senses still came as a shock. Disembodied voices whispered marketing slogans into his ears, zip ads roamed the surrounding bulkheads, and a whiff of exotic perfume found his nostrils. "It's called *Galaxy*," a floating pitch ball told him. "And it will change your life."

All of that and more was part of the daily routine on Orb 1, the last stop before ships set out for the rim worlds beyond, and a hub for every sort of business deal imaginable. And every sort of pleasure as well. The latter being of major importance to Chozick's renegades who, if they became restive, might rebel. But things had gone well so far.

After departing moon HE24-6743 Chozick and his legionnaires forced the swabbies to enter hyperspace and set a course for Long Jump. And it *was* a long jump. The better part of three weeks had elapsed as a series of leaps carried them ever closer to their destination.

The ex-legionnaires gambled, got into fights, and had to be pacified from time to time. But Chozick knew he was riding the proverbial tiger—and was careful to rule with a light hand. Because he had plans, *big* plans, and would need some cannon fodder to make them work.

Eventually the jump came to an end. And when it did, Chozick ordered the ship's XO to land the DE in an unpopulated part of Long Jump's surface, which was easy to do, because there were only a few million sentients on the planet.

Once on the ground Chozick made good on his previous offer. Those members of the crew who wanted to leave were given ten days worth of rations and a map. Two officers and four enlisted people elected to stay.

Then, before the newly freed swabbies were allowed to leave, Chozick had them shot. The bodies went into unmarked graves—and Chozick ordered his "associates" to paint new numbers on the ship's hull and give her a new name. The *Star Queen* had a nice ring to it. Chozick figured that the *Mohawk* and everybody aboard her was listed as MIA by then, and, so long as the ship's name didn't pop up somewhere, it would stay that way.

Though overworked, the remaining sailors managed to get the ship off the ground and successfully docked with the space station above. That was when Chozick went about recruiting the kind of crew members he could rely on. Cutthroats, to be sure, but noncoms like Kobo would keep them in line.

Chozick sidestepped a robo vendor and took a left. Both sides of the busy corridor were lined with tiny hole-in-the-wall businesses. Chozick passed a travel agency and a nail salon before arriving in front of the nondescript hatch. The sign on the door read, NOOL HANDRA, SHIPPING BROKER.

Chozick knew the title was accurate, even if Handra made most of his living from activities other than shipping. He palmed the hatch and it hissed open. That allowed Chozick to enter a small reception area. There was a desk and there, seated behind it, was Handra's daughter.

Chozick knew Kella to be short, as all Thrakies were, which meant the chair was boosting her up. She had large light-gathering eyes, pointed ears, and horizontal slits where Human nostrils would have been. Kella was dressed in what passed for high fashion on Orb 1. That included spray-on face glitter and lots of internally-lit jewelry. "Good morning, citizen Vemy," she said brightly. "Go on back. My father is expecting you."

Chozick said, "Thanks," and made his way back to a featureless door. Then he heard a click and knew that a lock had been released. By Kella? Yes, that made sense. The barrier slid out of the way, then closed behind him. The inner office was very different from the sterile reception area. Fine art graced the walls. And, where the far wall met the deck, a row of pillows gave Handra something to lean on. He was of indeterminate age, affected a red pillbox hat, and was swathed in a matching robe. A generously proportioned robe that could conceal just about anything weapons included. "How nice to see you," Handra said in flawless standard. "Please have a seat."

There were no seats. Just the plush rug located opposite Handra. So Chozick sat on the floor. A low table separated them. The top was inscribed with alien hieroglyphics and home to a hand comp, air stylus, and Handra's "form". Chozick knew that almost every Thrakie had a form, or miniature robot, all of which were handmade. Some were programmed to perform simple tasks—but most served as electromechanical pets. Judging from appearances, Handra's form fell into the latter category. Like its owner, the robot was bipedal and equipped with two arms. It did a handstand and proceeded to walk about the surface of the table as the conversation began.

"I received your message," Chozick said. "You have news for me?"

"I do," Handra said solemnly. "I received a response from a Hudathan official named Oro Bo-Ka. He wants you to know that your request was received—and the ruling triad is scheduled to consider the matter in two standard weeks."

"*Two weeks?* I sent the message, the video, and the finger bone a month ago."

Handra shrugged. "One must be patient. And remember... It took the message more than two weeks to get here. So chances are that the meeting Tola-Sa referred to has already taken place."

Chozick felt a sense of rising desperation. Because of the war, there was no way to contact the Hudathan government, other than through the Thrakies. A race of aliens which had been chased into Human space by a fleet of robotic warships years before and had eventually been granted asylum. They claimed to be neutral where the current conflict was concerned—but had a well-known tendency to play both sides against the middle.

But the Hudathans were the only ones who would pay for the reliquary—and the Thrakies were the only ones who had the means to contact them. Besides, were it possible to conduct face-to-face negotiations with the ridgeheads, only a crazy person would choose to do so. If there was a faster way to wind up dead, Chozick couldn't imagine what it would be. "Please send a confirmation," he said. "And let me know when the next message arrives."

"I will," the Thrakie promised.

"I guess that's it then," Chozick said, as he prepared to stand.

"There is one more issue," Handra said, as the form climbed up onto his shoulder. "And that's the matter of payment."

"You'll get paid when I do."

"That is not the way the contract reads," the Thrakie replied. "Line 2 of paragraph 157 specifies that an interim payment of twenty thousand credits is due upon receipt of the first message from the Hudathan government."

Chozick scowled. "How do I know the message is real? You could have made it up."

Handra sighed in much the same manner as a parent might while dealing with an especially difficult child. "Here," he said, as he flipped a disk into the air. Chozick caught it. "That," Handra said, "is the device the message arrived on. Drop it into a reader. Assuming you speak Hudathan, you'll be able to verify what I told you."

Chozick slipped the disk into a pocket as the form wrestled with Handra's ear. "I can't pay you yet. But I will soon."

Handra nodded. "I'm glad to hear it. But I'm afraid it will be necessary to withhold any future messages until I have the money in hand."

Chozick wanted to shoot the Thrakie, but figured the alien was armed. And how would he communicate with Hudathans if Handra was dead? The Human forced a smile as he stood. "No problem... I plan to pay you before then."

There was a click as the lock was released. "Excellent," Handra replied. "Have a nice day." The form waved as Chozick left.

*   *   *

The town of Sunrise on the planet Long Jump

It was raining. Not a driving rain, but a persistent mist that settled over the mourners like a shroud and, eventually, found their skin. The procession started in front of Kim's funeral parlor, and followed main street to a hill made out of mine tailings, where row upon row of grave markers stood. Some of the graves belonged to people who died of old age, but not many, the town was too young for that. Most of the dead were miners killed in accidents. And there, at the front of the procession, walking arm in arm with Reverend Goolsby, was Boss Ryker.

The mine owner had always been big, but he was even larger now. He'd been a laborer once, and muscular, but years of good living had put thirty extra pounds on him. And that had something to do with a bad hip. Every step caused him pain.

It was important to lead the procession however. To show the mine workers and their families that he cared. Because running the mine, the town, and most of the surrounding countryside required more than the simple application of force. A certain level of support was necessary. And, in order to get it, Ryker had to convince the locals that he cared about them. That was why the families of the five dead miners would receive a month's pay and whatever amount of money they owed the company store would be forgiven.

But business was business, and if there was no one who could step forward to take the dead man or woman's place, the family would have to leave its company owned house to make way for a new employee. It was sad, but what could he do? He was only one man after all—and couldn't support a town full of moochers.

So Ryker limped up the spiral path as the mist fell around him. The prime real estate at the top of the hill had already been claimed, so the miners were going to be buried two thirds of the way up the slope. Their graves had already been dug and were starting to go soft after hours of rain.

Ryker didn't like to think about dying, so, rather than listen to Goolsby's drivel, he took the opportunity to look out over his kingdom. Copper Mountain was off to his left only half visible in the mist. And there, on the flat land below, was the town of Sunrise. It was a tidy community with arrow straight streets all of which were laid out grid style. The spaceport? He'd built that... As well as the school, medical clinic, and park.

"Mr. Ryker?" Goolsby inquired. "Would you like to say a few words?"

That was when Ryker realized Goolsby had finished and it was his turn to speak. It was something he'd done many times before and didn't have to prepare for. His eyes swept the downcast faces around him. "This is a sad day... Five of our friends and loved ones are gone but they remain here in our hearts. I can see their faces now, happy to start a shift, and to provide for their families. Let's hold those images in our minds so that these fine men and women will always be with us. Thank you."

It was bullshit of course... Every word of it. But the people around Ryker nodded and some even managed to smile. That was the part that amazed him. How some empty platitudes could make them feel better. He was grateful, though, because what would he do without them?

Once the bodies were in the ground, the townsfolk followed the trail down to the foot of main street and, from there, many went to spend the rest of the day in the town's saloon. It was always a profitable enterprise, but never more so than on the day of a funeral. Ryker wasn't going to spend any of his time drinking, however. He had a business to run.

Ryker's office was located in the Sunrise bank, *his* bank, on the second floor. It was surrounded by a wall, and built like a fort. Armed guards nodded respectfully as he passed through the gate and climbed the steps that led to the front door. A mercenary dressed in body armor was there to open it for him. "Good morning, boss."

"It's raining," Ryker pointed out, "and I just attended a funeral. But I appreciate the sentiment."

The bank was closed for the day, so the lobby was empty. Ryker took a hard right, opened a door, and climbed a flight of stairs to the second floor. That made his hip hurt, so he was cranky by the time he entered his office. And the sight of "Stick" Matthews sitting in his chair, smoking one of his cigars did nothing to improve his humor.

"Oops! Sorry, boss," Stick said as he jumped up out of the chair. "I was killing time, that's all."

"Yeah, sure," Ryker said as he rounded the cluttered desk to claim his seat. "*And* stealing my cigars."

Stick was seated on one of two guest chairs by then and completely unapologetic. He was tall, thin, and too well dressed for the town of Sunrise. "You'll forgive me," he predicted confidently. "I brought you a deal. A *good* deal."

That was the reason why Stick got away with so much. He spent most of his time on the space station where he was always on the lookout for business opportunities. Some legit and some less so. "Okay," Ryker said indulgently. "What have you got?"

"There's a new player on the space station," Stick answered. "A guy named George Vemy. He owns a DE that must be forty years old. I figure he bought it surplus and fixed it up. Anyway, he claims to have a ton of hafnium sitting in the ship's hold and he's looking for a buyer."

Ryker frowned. "Have you seen it?"

Stick shook his head. "No. Vemy won't let visitors on his ship. But the sample he gave me tested out. This is the good stuff, Boss—so I figured you would be interested."

And Ryker *was* interested. Trading valuable metals was a profitable sideline. "And you were correct, Stick... Well done." Ryker pointed to a well stocked bar. "Pour yourself a drink. Let's talk this through."

*　　　*　　　*

Aboard the Star Queen

For the first time in a long time Chozick felt happy. His efforts to find a buyer for the hafnium had been successful—and he would soon have three million credits to tide him over until the Hudathans bought the skeleton. That would bring in *fifty* million. Enough to start the mercenary outfit he'd been thinking about. Not just any outfit, but one equipped with cyborgs. Just like the Legion. It would make his group so special that clients would be willing to pay premium prices.

Such were Chozick's thoughts as the *Star Queen* completed a full orbit of Long Jump and began to slow. His buyer, a man named Ryker, had agreed to pay cash on delivery. And in this case that meant a deposit at one of Orb 1's three banks. A deposit which Ember would verify before the hafnium was unloaded.

Would Ryker try to hijack the hafnium? He might. Chozick had done some research and, according to Handra, Mr. Ryker had a bad reputation. But Chozick figured that a destroyer escort plus a company of ex-legionnaires should provide more than enough protection.

So, as the ship circled the town of Sunrise, Chozick felt happy. And when he saw that the area around the small spaceport was nearly deserted, he felt even happier. There was a truck, and a small group of men, but that was to be expected. Chozick, who was seated at the rear of the control room said, "Put her down."

The man who had been XO under Dickerson was the captain now—but everyone still referred to him as XO. A nom de guerre that was fine with him. He issued a series of orders that brought the DE to a hover. Then, with the dignity befitting a vessel of her age, the *Star Queen* lowered herself onto the large patch of heat fused soil that functioned as the town's spaceport. There was a solid thump followed by the usual creaks and groans as the DE's frame was forced to support all of the ship's weight.

Chozick was dressed in one of the new uniforms he had supplied his bio bods. They were similar to those issued by the Legion, but with what he considered to be improvements. Small things, mostly, but the first step towards creating his mercenary army. The Legion helmet had been repainted, but was otherwise the same. Chozick chinned his mike as he made his way back to the hold. "Remember everything I told you," he said, "and things will go smoothly. Drop the ramp."

A rectangle of light appeared as the ramp went down. Chozick thumbed his visor up and out of the way as he clumped down onto the ground. Kobo and a bio bod named Farley followed him. Both were heavily armed.

As Chozick stepped off the ramp, Stick Matthews came forward to shake hands. "We meet again," he said cheerfully.

Chozick nodded. "Where's Mr. Ryker?"

"He asked me to handle the transaction for him," Stick answered smoothly.

Chozick shrugged. "Okay... It makes no difference to me. Make the transfer. My man will verify the deposit and radio the ship. Once he does, we'll bring the hafnium out."

"Of course," Stick said, as he produced a hand com. "Three million, minus five hundred thousand for the landing tax, leaves two-point-five mil. I'll authorize the transfer now."

"Whoa," Chozick said. "*What* landing tax? That's bullshit."

"You're welcome to your opinion," Stick said politely, "but the spaceport has a legal right to impose a landing tax as set by the port commissioner."

Chozick scowled. "And who is the port commissioner?"

Stick smiled. "That would be Mr. Ryker."

"Okay," Chozick said. "The deal is off. Tell Ryker to take his landing tax and shove it up his ass."

Stick murmured something into the com and Chozick heard a crackling sound from behind him. All three renegades whirled in time to see the front end of a monstrous machine break through the surface of the tarmac! Seconds later a huge claw reached out to secure a grip on one of the *Queen's* landing skids. How much did the subterranean beast weigh? Ten tons? Twenty? More than enough to prevent the ship from lifting off. But the DE was far from defenseless. Chozick chinned his mike. "Blast that thing. Do it *now*."

The *Queen's* belly turret swiveled toward the mining machine, but stopped as some sort of drill shot up out of the ground to skewer it. "Sorry," Stick said. "But once a ship lands on our spaceport the fee must be paid. So I suggest that you unload the hafnium. Two and a half mil is a lot of money. Take what you can get and be happy."

Chozick caught movement out of the corner of his eye and turned in time to see a couple of men pull a cover off the truck. The pedestal mounted energy cannon made a whining sound as it traversed around to point at the spaceship. Chozick chinned his mike. "Destroy the truck."

One of the ship's guns burped coherent energy and the truck vanished in a flash of light and a clap of thunder. Pieces of fiery debris were still falling as Chozick turned back to Stick. "You took it too far," the renegade said grimly, "and now you're going to pay. Kobo, we're switching to plan B."

Stick watched in horror as a column of T-2s marched down the ramp. Except for the first three, the rest of the cyborgs were carrying bio bods, and all of them were armed. The movement was so fast that the pistol seemed to materialize in Chozick's hand. "Ryker... Where is he?"

Stick was frightened but not enough to turn on Ryker. "I don't know. He ..."

Chozick pulled the trigger and a third eye appeared between the two Stick already had. The body fell with arms out-flung. The hand com skittered away. There was a crunching sound as Kobo stepped on it.

"Okay," Chozick said into his mike. "Don't kill anyone you don't have to—but secure this town. I'm looking for a man named Ryker. Speak up if you find him."

There was some resistance as they entered the town, snipers mostly, but none of it made any difference. Chozick and his T-2 led the way, and it wasn't long before his renegades were in control of the town hall, the police station, and the power plant.

Then, acting on a tip from a citizen, Chozick went looking for the bank. It wasn't hard to find. And when he got there, Chozick could tell that Ryker was inside. Nothing else would explain why it was so well protected.

Having seen the nine-foot tall duracrete wall that surrounded the building, Chozick wanted to know what was waiting behind it before he and his company attacked. He was a businessman now, and his people were assets. Especially the cyborgs.

So Chozick told his troops to take cover in and next to the surrounding buildings while he sent a drone in to check things out. It wasn't long before the flying robot drew fire and had to pull out. But not before the device got a good look at some mortar pits, well placed machine guns, and mercs armed with rocket launchers. The latter being weapons that could have been used to bring them down. So, why hadn't they? Because they *wanted* him to see what he was up against. That suggested a leader, a *good* leader, who wanted to conserve his or her resources. After all, why fight if you didn't have to? This was about money rather than politics.

Chozick gave orders for his people to remain where they were and rode his T-2 forward. Once he was about three hundred feet away from the wall, the durasteel gate opened and a merc appeared. She was clad in black body armor and wore two pistols. As the woman came closer. Chozick saw that she had red hair, freckles on her face, and was a bit husky. Not fat, but sturdy, as if raised on a heavy gravity world. She stopped and looked them up and down. "That's a Trooper II... But it's wearing a non reg paint job—so that makes you deserters."

"Since you're familiar with cyborgs you know what they can do," Chozick countered. "If this comes to a fight we'll win."

"Not necessarily," the woman replied. "But even if you do, the causalities will be high."

"I have a DE," Chozick said. "You know that... You saw it circle the town. We can grease you from above."

The woman made a face. "There is that."

"Yes, there is. But it doesn't have to end that way. You could pull out. I'll let you go. Or, if you're interested in a merger, I'm looking to expand. What's your name?"

"They call me Red."

"Okay, Red. My name is Damien. You have three choices: Fight a losing battle, take a walk, or enter into a merger. Which is it going to be?"

Red was silent for what might have been a minute. Finally, with obvious reluctance, she spoke. "I'll take option three."

"Good," Chozick replied. "Here's the deal ... Ryker agreed to buy a ton of hafnium from me for three mil. But, when I arrived, he tried to charge me a five-hundred thousand credit landing fee. That pissed me off so now I'm going to confiscate everything he has. I'll take ten-percent off the top, you'll get five, and equal shares will go to *all* the troops. Yours and mine. What do you say?"

"I like it," Red replied. "But my people have a say in what we do—and they will insist on that if we merge."

"You can't run a military unit like a democracy," Chozick said. "Both of us know that. But my troops can cancel my ticket anytime they want to. I know it and they know it."

Red nodded. "That makes sense. I'll be back shortly."

A full twenty minutes passed. And Chozick was beginning to wonder if Red was up to something when the gate swung open and the merc reappeared. She wasn't alone. As Red came forward Chozick saw that she was holding a leash. It was attached to a portly man who was walking with his head down. When Red was twenty feet away she stopped. "Damien, this is Mr. Ryker. Mr. Ryker, this is Damien. I think he has a present for you."

Ryker looked up, and was just about to speak, when a bullet passed through his mouth and exited through his neck. It didn't kill him, but the next one did. The mine, the town, all of it belonged to Chozick now ... And it was just a matter of time before the Hudathans would pay for the skeleton. Life was very, very good.

CHAPTER FOUR

Military strategy is shaped by the availability of supplies.

Tral Heba
Ramanthian Book of Guidance
Standard year 1721

The planet Algeron

When Smith awoke, it was to the feeling that there was something he was supposed to do. But *what?* Then it came to him. He was supposed to find Chozick and bring him to justice. And that was God's work. "Blessed are they who maintain justice, who constantly do what is right." Psalm 106:3.

God's universe was a huge place, however, and full of places where evil could not only hide, but flourish. In spite of their best efforts, the Confederacy's intelligence operatives had been unable to find the renegade. And, try as he might, Smith couldn't imagine himself in Chozick's place. That made it practically impossible to guess where the son of Satan was.

Fortunately, he had a sinner close at hand. A person who made no secret of the fact that she was a blasphemer, an occasional drunkard, and a serial fornicator. And that was his executive officer Mary Josy. Perhaps she would be able to help.

So Smith showered, shaved, and went to breakfast. Or was it lunch? It was difficult to keep track of time on Algeron. Then he went looking for Josy. The company was enjoying a two-day stand down, so she was off duty. And on Algeron there was only one place where a mostly godless person could go for fun, and that was the officers' club.

The O club was about fifteen-minutes away from where Smith's company was quartered. The light was dim, the music was too loud for Smith's taste, and he could smell the alcohol. The sweet, sweet liquid that had given him so much peace before taking his life away. He steeled himself against the pull of it and went looking for Josy. He wasn't familiar with the layout, and the club was huge, so that involved a good deal of walking around.

It didn't take long to discover that the officers were self-segregating. Infantry sat with infantry, engineers sat with engineers, and cavalry sat with cavalry. And that was where he found Josy. She was seated at a table in cavalry country. Three equally junior officers were at the table all playing some sort of drinking game. That bothered him. *Why?* Because he was jealous? No, yes, maybe. "There you are," he said. "Mind if I join you?"

Josy didn't want Smith to join the table, nor did the others, especially the two cavalry officers. They knew Smith by reputation and didn't want to suffer though a lecture. But they couldn't say "no" to a company commander and didn't. "This *is* a surprise," Josy said truthfully. "Have you been here before?"

"Once," Smith answered. "During my orientation tour."

The cavalry officers exchanged looks and stood. The taller of the two spoke. "I hope you'll excuse us, sir ... We have a field exercise coming up—so it's time to grab some shuteye."

"No problem," Smith said. As the officers left he turned to the other person at the table. A navy pilot who should have been with the zoomies on the far side of the room but had chosen to hang out with cavalry instead. *Why?* The answer was Josy. Smith smiled. He was old for a captain, at least thirty-five, and came across as even older. "So, son ... Shouldn't you be checking your parachute or something?"

Josy started to object but the flier shook his head. "That's okay ... The captain is right. Duty calls." And with that he downed the rest of his drink and left.

Smith turned to find that Josy was staring at him. "What the hell was *that?*" she demanded.

"There's no need to swear."

"Bullshit. *You* swear."

"Only under great stress," Smith replied. "Besides, he was navy."

"I *like* the navy ... And I was going let him land on my pad."

Smith made a face. "You're disgusting."

"Right ... So, why are you here?"

"I, that is to say *we*, are supposed to find Chozick."

"And?"

"And I wondered if you had given the matter any thought."

"Not really," Josy replied. "I've been busy."

"Okay ... Well, there's no time like the present. You heard Colonel Price. The brass doesn't know where Chozick is. Maybe we can come up with something."

Josy shook a stim stick out of a half empty pack and set fire to it. She sucked the smoke deep into her lungs before allowing it to dribble out through her nostrils. Smith caught a whiff of the smoke and felt the old hunger. It wasn't about stim sticks. It was the combination of stim sticks and alcohol that he craved. A stimulant *and* a depressant. Stupid, stupid, stupid. "Those are bad for you."

Josy took another deep drag. "So is getting shot at ... But you never object to *that*. So let's think about the Choz ... He went over the hill. *Why?*"

"Because he's a thief and the chance to steal both the skeleton and the hafnium was too good to pass up."

"Okay," Josy agreed. "But did he go his own way? Or did he keep the company together?"

Smith considered that. "Based on what we know so far it looks like Chozick went out of his way to bring scum bags into his company. People who shared his values and would follow illegal orders. So would he ditch them? I don't think so. And remember ... That sort of arrangement cuts both ways. It's quite possible that Chozick's people wouldn't let him split. Not without paying them first."

"Good point," Josy said. "So, where would they go?"

"The rim."

"Yeah, but *where* on the rim? He could be on any one of a thousand planets."

Smith knew that was true. Chozick and his borgs could be anywhere. Then it hit him. Cyborgs! Chozick's company included a detachment of twelve T-2s. And every one of them would require spare parts. Lots of them. Far more than any company would take on a mission.

So where would he get them? Not on the open market because war form parts were highly regulated and traditionally manufactured on Earth. But the Ramanthians were in control there. Yes, new factories were under construction elsewhere, but just starting to come on line. That was why Smith and his peers had to battle each other for parts. So there was only one place where Chozick could get what he needed and that was Algeron! But how? And from whom? "Come on," Smith said. "We're going to the personnel department. Then we'll go visiting."

"Visiting? What the hell for?"

Smith plucked the stim stick out of her hand and stubbed it out. "What's the old saying? You're known by the company you keep?

Well, let's see who Chozick liked to hang out with. I'd be willing to bet that one of them works in supply."

Josy made a face. "You don't gamble."

Smith smiled. "No, not anymore. Come on. We have work to do."

*   *   *

The warehouse was large, dimly lit, and primarily staffed by robots. That meant Staff Sergeant Lester Orko had plenty of time in which to sit in his office, throw his boots up onto his desk, and watch porno. And that's what he was doing when a T-2 named Tanaka kicked the door in. Orko was taken by surprise and nearly fell over backwards as two officers entered the room. One of them was holding a laser equipped pistol. The red dot floated up off his chest as she came over to press cold metal against his forehead. "Hi," she said sweetly. "My name is Lieutenant Josy—and this is Captain Smith. We're here to talk to you about a turd named Chozick."

"You can't do this," Orko objected. "I have rights!"

"Yes, you do," Josy agreed. "You have the right to tell me what I want to know or I will blow your balls off. Then I'll file a report stating that my pistol discharged accidentally. Captain Smith will back me up, then he'll have to go to church, and God will forgive him. Meanwhile you'll be living in the stockade and singing soprano. So what'll it be? The low down on Chozick? Or a ballectomy?"

Orko's eyes shifted to Smith. "She's kidding, right?"

Smith shrugged. "She's a sinner, son. And you never know with sinners. I can't say that I approve of her approach—but God moves in mysterious ways. Who am I to intervene?"

Josy smiled evilly and tilted the weapon down so that the red dot was centered on the supply sergeant's crotch. "Okay!" Orko exclaimed. "I'll tell you ... Get the bitch off me."

"The bitch is an officer," Smith said primly. "As such, you will address her in the proper manner."

"Please, ma'am," Orko said contritely. "Please aim your pistol somewhere else."

"That's better," Josy allowed, as she pulled Orko and his rolling chair away from the desk. "Now you can have a nice chat with the captain while I take tour your terminal. Uh, oh, look at this ... Porno! You *are* a bad boy."

Smith dragged a stool over to where Orko was sitting and spent the next twenty minutes talking to the noncom while Josy reviewed his records. The people in personnel had been slow to cooperate at first—but quickly changed their minds after a brief com call with Colonel Price.

Based on the data they gave him, Smith had been able to compile a list of people who had served with Chozick. With that information in hand he had conducted a series of interviews. Most of the people he spoke to had been interviewed by military intelligence. But Smith didn't stop there. He went to see their acquaintances, and *their* acquaintances, until someone tipped him off to a supply sergeant named Orko. A well-known "fixer" who could seemingly summon hard to find spare parts out of thin air.

Eventually, based on computer records, plus Orko's admissions, the full story came to light. About a month after Chozick and his people went on the MIA list Orko received a package from a civilian pilot. One of hundreds who came and went all the time.

Inside the wrapping, Orko found a box containing six gold wafers plus a request for certain T-2 parts. The document wasn't signed, but Orko had done business with Chozick in the past, and had a pretty good idea of who he was dealing with. There had been two packages since, both delivered by the same pilot, a woman named Peebo. "But how did you pull it off?" Smith wanted to know. "T-2 parts are very hard to find."

Orko was reluctant to say—but agreed to do so when Smith threatened to let Josy interrogate him. "I took the parts of T-2s in the morgue," he confessed. "And why not? They were waiting to be recycled."

Smith knew that was partially true. Worn out war forms were stored in a facility commonly referred to as "the morgue". But given the situation on Earth, *all* parts were valuable. Even those with sixty or seventy percent wear. "So you sent worn out parts to Chozick?"

"Not worn out ... *Used*. And I told him that. He knows the score. There's no way that I could send new parts."

That made sense and Smith had what he needed. Which was to say Orko, who was going to be incommunicado for the next month, and recordings of everything the supply sergeant had said. They didn't know where Chozick was—but they would soon.

*   *   *

Angelica Peedo had just broken orbit, and was headed for the nearest jump point, when two aerospace fighters swooped in to take up positions to either side of her courier ship. The orders to turn back came as a surprise to both her and the vessel's only passenger—a wealthy Human who had business interests on the rim.

But Peedo wasn't worried until she landed at Fort Cameron and a pair of military policemen came aboard the ship. Then, with cuffs on her wrists, she was led to an office located deep within the fort. A number of people were waiting there. "I'm Colonel Price," one of them said, "and this is War Commander Tora-Sa."

Peedo turned to see a Hudathan step out of the shadows and wondered what the hell was going on. A ridgehead? In Fort Camerone? That was unheard of. The introductions continued. "The young lady is Lieutenant Josy—and the man standing next to her is Captain Smith. We want to speak with you."

The ensuing conversation lasted an hour. By the time it was over a number of things were clear. Peedo knew Chozick as a man named George Vemy and he, like other clients she had, paid her to carry small shipments of freight for him. Did she know what she had been transporting for Orko? No, that was none of her business. And where had she and Vemy met? The answer was aboard a space station in orbit around a planet called Long Jump.

Smith felt a tremendous sense of satisfaction as the final piece fell into place. Now they knew where the treacherous bastard was. "So," Price said, "we're making progress. But speed is important. Chozick made use of an intermediary to communicate with the Hudathan government. He wants fifty-million for the reliquary and they're stalling him. But how long before he moves to another location? Or sells the remains to someone else at a deeply discounted price? You and the lieutenant did an exemplary job of figuring out where he is. Now is the time to go get him."

"I'll need a week to get ready," Smith replied.

Price frowned. "A *week?* What for?"

"To train my people," Smith explained. "We know Chozick still has his cyborgs. That's why he's buying parts for them. So, if it comes to a fight, it will be a brawl in which T-2s will have to battle T-2's. And my people aren't trained for that."

Judging from the expression on Price's face, that hadn't occurred to him. And seeing the possibility of an advantage, Smith was quick to follow up. "Plus I need a freighter. A ship that won't attract attention but can duke it out with a DE if necessary."

William C. Dietz

War Commander Tola-Sa spoke for the first time. "Why not send a battle group? Then you could take control of the space station and the planet if you needed to."

Price made a face. "I wish we could ... The truth is that we don't have one to spare. Plus, even if we did, I fear that Chozick and his renegades might slip through our fingers. A stealthy approach is best, and Captain Smith is correct, it will take some time to find the right vessel."

He turned to Smith. "I can see that you have given this matter some thought."

"The lord takes care of those who take care of themselves, sir."

Price looked at Josy who smiled beatifically. "That's right, sir ... *and* the lord takes care of those who carry a big stick."

"Now that's funny," Tola-Sa said, without cracking a smile. "The lieutenant could be a Hudathan." The meeting was over.

*   *   *

In order to make the necessary preparations in a short amount of time, Smith and Josy had to split up. His responsibility was to get the company ready to fight—and hers was to make sure they had all the materials required to do so. That included food, ammo, and yes— spare parts. No small job, and one she tackled with her usual energy.

That left Smith free to make plans. Unlike Chozick, who was an infantry officer with T-2s attached to his unit, Smith was a cavalry officer. So it was tempting to show up off Long Jump with a full company of thirty six cyborgs and an equal number of bio bods. Tempting, but risky. That was because he couldn't predict what would happen next. T-2s were great on open ground. But what if he had to go after the renegades on Orb 1? Bio bods would be more useful in that kind of situation.

So, after giving the matter some thought, Smith decided to allot himself fourteen T-2s. That was two more than Chozick had. Plus he was going to take what he thought of as "the equalizer", Meaning one of the Legion's quads. In addition to the fourteen bio bods who would team up with the T-2s, Smith was going to need some foot soldiers. About seventy of them if he was to achieve parity with what Chozick had. The obvious solution was to take two platoons of regular infantry.

But Smith had what he thought was a better idea. Rather than a detachment of legs, he'd take seventy of the bio bods presently serving

42

in Colonel Price's cavalry battalion. They knew what T-2s could and couldn't do. Plus they could help with maintenance. Then, as an insurance policy, he would give every squad a rocket launcher. That would give them a chance if they had to confront a T-2.

Finally there was the matter of zappers. Meaning the pistol shaped devices issued to cavalry officers in case one of their borgs went bonkers. That didn't happen very often. But, when it did, a zapper could bring even the largest cyborg to its knees by disrupting its electrical systems.

Of course, anything that can be activated can be deactivated, given the right knowhow. Which raised an interesting question. Would Chozick want to keep the zapper option in place? Maybe, although, if he did, a single zapper armed bio bod could disable *all* of his cyborgs in a matter of seconds.

And what about the cyborgs themselves? Would they allow Chozick to retain that kind of power over them? No, Smith didn't think so. They were renegades after all—and would want their freedom. So it was safe to assume that the deserters would be invulnerable to zappers.

Then there was the opposite possibility to think about. What if Chozick or one of his bio bods was to fire a zapper at Smith's T-2s? That would be disastrous. So Smith had no choice but to deactivate the submission systems in the borgs that were slated to accompany them. A risk? Yes, half of them were murderers, after all. It was a chance he'd have to take.

The possibility of T-2 versus T-2 combat wasn't covered in any of the training manuals so there was nothing to go on. All Smith could do was divide his newly reconfigured company into halves, provide all personnel with training weapons, and turn them over to lieutenants Tran and Noll. A satellite and a computer would be used to score the battle.

The setting was the euphemistically named "Happy Valley" located just east of the fort and west of the famed High Hump Hill. A spot often used for training exercises and littered with weather worn trenches, icy mortar pits, and crumbling earth-walls. And, as was often the case on Algeron, it was snowing. Each platoon had a flag and orders to: A. defend it, and B. capture the other teams' ensign. All while Smith watched them from a point halfway up High Hump Hill.

The differences between the two officers quickly became apparent in the way they dealt with the situation. Noll fortified an area at the south end of the "field" and assigned one T-2 and a third of his bio bods to protect it. Then he sent a T-2 and sixteen legionnaires up the left side of the battlefield as a feint. The idea was to draw some of Tran's forces away from his flag and open it to an attack from Noll and the rest of his platoon. A force that included the remaining cyborgs.

It was a reasonable plan in Smith's opinion, one that would probably be successful against most opponents, but not Tran. She was a free thinker and Smith watched admiringly as the junior officer sent a token force to deal with what she had correctly identified as a feint. Then she ran the rest of her platoon straight at Noll's base bringing her flag with her! An unusual strategy that took Noll's platoon by surprise. And, spread out as they were, left them unable to stop the invaders. Their flag fell soon thereafter.

Once the exercise was over Smith knew a lot more about two of his three platoon leaders. But what about the T-2s? While watching them Smith had been reminded of a football game in which Tran's cyborgs functioned as guards. That was instructive. And as night fell, they went at it again. And again. Until all of them were exhausted.

Then it was time to eat, sleep, shower and start again. And with each passing day the legionnaires got better. But after forty eight hours of additional training it was time to stop and prepare for the lift off. That involved repairing gear, performing maintenance on the cyborgs, and dealing with minor medical issues.

Finally the day of departure arrived, and Smith was looking forward to a hassle free lift. But when he arrived at the spaceport, it was to find that War Commander Tola-Sa and twelve Hudathan marines were waiting for him. All wore full kit, including armor and back swords. Packs were stacked; ready for loading. Price came forward at that point, and Smith turned to confront him. "What's going on here?"

There was no, "Good morning, sir," but if Price noticed, he chose to ignore it. "Sorry, Smith ... but War Commander Tola-Sa received a last minute directive from his superiors. They insist that Hudathan troops take part in the mission. It's a matter of honor."

Smith wanted to tell Price and Tola-Sa why the last minute decision was a bad idea ... Including the fact that the Humans and Hudathans would need translators in order to communicate, hadn't trained together, and had no reason to trust each other. But he could see the look in Price's eyes and knew what the officer would say if he objected: The Confederacy was losing the war—and new allies could make an important difference. So he swallowed his concerns and gave Price the answer he wanted to hear. "Sir, yes, sir. And the chain of command?"

Price looked relieved. "You'll be in command."

Smith looked at Tola-Sa who nodded.

"There's one more thing," Price interjected. "I'm sending Orson along. It will document the mission and, who knows: Orson has a number of different capabilities and one or more of them might come in handy."

The truth was that Smith didn't care if Orson came along or not. He had other things on his mind. "Yes, sir."

"Good. Lieutenant Josy and the *Chicago* are waiting for you in orbit. The *Chicago* belongs to a commercial shipping line and looks the part. Nobody will connect her with the military. That's the good news."

Smith frowned. "And the bad news?"

"The *Chicago* is lightly armed. If you try to go toe to toe with the *Mohawk* , you'll lose."

Smith wanted to swear. "I see ... Is there anything else I should be aware of?"

"Nope," Price said comfortably. "Have a nice trip."

CHAPTER FIVE

The troops should be exercised frequently, cavalry as well as infantry, and the general should often be present to praise some, to criticize others, and to see with his own eyes that orders ... are observed exactly.

Frederick the Great
Instructions for His Generals
Standard year 1747

Aboard the freighter Chicago

The *Chicago* was a freighter, so the ship had very few cabins. Not that it mattered, because Smith insisted that everyone, officers included, live together in the hold. The purpose being to force integration between the legionnaires and the Hudathans. Translators helped solve the language problem—but creating a sense of mutual respect was a more difficult task.

So once the *Chicago* entered hyperspace, Smith sought out Tola-Sa in order to explain his concerns. And the other officer was quite supportive. "I agree," Tola-Sa said. "A great deal is riding on this. A lack of cooperation could be disastrous."

Given how fiercely independent the Hudathans were Smith was both surprised and gratified by Tola-Sa's response. But, when he took a moment to think about it, Smith came to an important realization. Tola-Sa was in a difficult situation. Tola-Sa was in the position of reporting to someone two levels lower than he was. And, worse yet, he and his troops were on a ship packed with aliens. A situation almost certain to trigger the xenophobia that the Hudathans were famous for. Not to mention the fact that, if things went poorly, it was quite possible that Tola-Sa's superiors would hold *him* responsible for the mission's failure.

So Smith worked with Tola-Sa to devise a variety of exercises designed to create some unity within the short period of time available. The first step was to integrate the company to the extent possible by seeding Hudathans in at the squad level. Next, he designated two of them as noncoms, with authority over Humans.

Then Smith and Tola-Sa devised a series of exercises that put squad against squad. And it wasn't long before Humans discovered that it was impossible to beat the Hudathans at arm wrestling, unless you were a T-2, in which case the situation was reversed.

"You've got them working together," Josy commented, as she appeared at his side. "That's no small accomplishment." Tug of war was a favorite among the troops and they were about to begin another contest.

Smith looked at her then back to the impending battle. The cable was taut, and it was interesting to note how both sides were using Hudathans and T-2s to anchor their ends of the rope. "All of us are God's creatures," he said. "So we have similar needs. And we're inherently good."

Josy looked up at him. "Even the Ramanthians?"

"Even them," Smith said soberly.

Josy thought about that for a moment. "I'm sorry, sir," she said. "But that's bullshit." Then she walked away.

*   *   *

The space station Orb 1, in orbit around the planet Long Jump

Chozick hadn't visited the space station since landing in the town of Sunrise weeks earlier. There was too much to do. There was a town to take control of, a copper mine to learn about, and fifty-seven mercenaries to get acquainted with. All of which required a great deal of time and effort. That meant his plan to sell the skeleton back to the Hudathans had been relegated to a back burner. So the message from Handra came as a welcome surprise. After months of waiting the Hudathans were going to send an emissary to Orb 1.

The *Mohawk* had been repaired, but rather than employ the ship for such a short trip, Chozick made use of the DE's shuttle instead. And he made a point out of arriving on the space station a day early for some R and R. Ember was there to meet him. The ex-lieutenant was Chozick's business representative on the space station. An occupation he was well suited for, so long as he received a sufficient amount of direction.

The two men left the docking ring for B deck, where Chozick hoped to get a good meal. Ember was something of an expert on the station's eateries by then, and suggested a place called the Taj. Once the two men had been shown to a booth and ordered drinks, it was time to catch up. Chozick provided a summary of everything that had been accomplished on the ground, and Ember talked about his adventures on the station, most of which involved women.

There was a pause while the second round of drinks arrived. After the waiter left, the narrative continued. "And speaking of women ... Did you know Lieutenant Josy?"

Chozick shook his head. "Nope. I never met her."

"Well," Ember said, "I spent a night with her once—and it was *very* enjoyable. Anyway, imagine my surprise when I passed her in the main corridor earlier today."

Chozick felt a mild sense of alarm. "The Legion has troops on Orb 1?"

Ember shook his head. "Not that I know of ... She was in civvies. On vacation, most likely—or maybe she went over the hill. There was a man with her. A tall guy with black hair, a gaunt face, and stooped shoulders."

"Did she recognize you?"

"Nah, she was too busy schmoozing the tall guy."

Chozick's mind was racing by then. Ember was an idiot ... But no news there. Was Josy's presence on the station a coincidence? It was a big galaxy, after all. But the timing could only be described as strange. First, the message from the Hudathans, now this. It shouldn't matter though... The Confederacy was at war with the Hudathans. Yet there was something about the situation that didn't feel right. Chozick forced himself to remain calm. He sipped his drink. "Tell me something, Rex ... How are we doing where parts are concerned? When was the last time you received a shipment from Orko?"

"It's overdue," Ember admitted. "But don't worry—I'm on it."

But Chozick *was* worried. The fact that Orko hadn't sent any parts could mean nothing or everything. What if the idiot had been caught somehow? And spilled his guts? Worse yet what if the brass knew about his attempts to ransom the skeleton? The meeting scheduled for the next day could be a trick. A way to get him alone where he'd be vulnerable.

Chozick stood, his leg struck the table, and a drink spilled. "Pay the bill. We're leaving."

*   *   *

Smith felt nervous as he, Josy, and Tola-Sa made their way through crowded corridors. And for good reason. A lot was riding on the upcoming meeting. *If* Chozick showed up, and *if* they could grab him, it might be possible to avoid a battle. Or, if they *had* to fight, it would be easier to win.

Smith was in civilian clothes as was Josy. Tola-Sa was dressed in a hood, voluminous cloak, and boots. His size caused him to stand out, but not as much as one might expect, since all manner of exotic beings walked the halls of Orb 1.

A short trip down a side corridor took them to a plain door and a sign that read, NOOL HANDRA, SHIPPING BROKER. Once inside they were greeted by a diminutive Thrakie who was wearing too much makeup. She sent them back to a door which slid out of the way. They entered a dimly lit room and Smith was about to speak, when six men attacked. They were dressed in black and had been waiting in the shadows.

It was a small space, so there was very little room in which to maneuver. Smith felt a burning sensation as an energy bolt slicked across his cheek, heard a thud as Tola-Sa punched a man in the face, and realized that Chozick wasn't going to show up.

But there was no time to pursue that line of thought as one of the hired thugs wrapped his fingers around Josy's throat and she head butted him. Blood was pouring out of his nose as the man reeled backwards and Smith kicked him in the groin. The spacer fell, clutching his privates and suffered even more when Tola-Sa accidentally stepped on his head.

The Hudathan was having a good time until a Human stabbed him in the right arm. Tola-Sa uttered a grunt of rage, took hold of the handle, and jerked the blade free. Then having secured a grip on his opponent's throat, Tola-Sa drove the knife down through the top of the Human's skull. The body joined others on the floor.

Meanwhile Smith had an arm around another man's throat. Josy kicked the thug in the knee and kicked it again as Smith let go. "That's enough," Smith said as the man began to whimper. "Mercy is a virtue."

"Mercy is stupid," Josy said, while allowing herself one last kick. She looked for another opponent but the battle was over. Bodies, most of which were dead, littered the floor. Smith was still in the process of learning to interpret Hudathan facial expressions but was pretty sure that Tola-Sa looked happy.

"The door is locked," Josy said, as she tried it for a second time.

William C. Dietz

"I have the key," Tola-Sa assured her, as a gigantic boot hit the door.

It crumpled and gave way when Smith pushed on it. He was ready to grab the Thraki who had been sitting at the front desk but she was gone. "Come on," he said. "Let's find citizen Handra. There's an excellent chance that he knows where Chozick is."

Smith turned to Josy. "Contact the ship. Tell Lieutenant Noll to place the entire company on high alert—and send two cyborgs out to join us. We might need some additional muscle. Once they show up on the security monitors the cops will freak out, so we might as well contact them now."

To their credit, the station's security beings responded quickly. They took one look at the room full of bodies and were about to arrest everyone in sight when the T-2s arrived. That, plus Smith's threat to declare martial law, left the police officers with no choice but to cooperate. And with their assistance, Smith found Handra and his daughter in a short period of time. There weren't that many places to hide so they had taken refuge in the suite of rooms which Handra maintained on C deck.

Having cornered the Thraki, Smith suggested that Tola-Sa handle the interrogation. That prospect was enough to scare the hell out of Handra who hurried to spill his guts. Chozick was on Long Jump in a town called Sunrise. Plan A had ended in failure. It was time to try Plan B.

*　　　*　　　*

Aboard the freighter Chicago

The *Chicago* shook violently as the ship continued its descent through Long Jump's atmosphere. Only eight hours had passed since the battle on the space station and Smith was worried. Based on information supplied by Citizen Handra they had been able to locate Lieutenant Ember. Like Handra, he broke after spending a few minutes with Tola-Sa and told them all about Sunrise, the mine, and the additional troops Chozick had.

Smith's thoughts were interrupted as the Captain's voice came over the intercom. "Okay, everybody ... Hang onto your panties. It looks like they spotted us. Evasive maneuvers will begin *now*."

The bottom of Smith's stomach seemed to disappear as the *Chicago* fell like a stone. Then the freighter was underway again and seemingly

50

headed straight up. Gee forces pushed the legionnaire down into his seat and someone threw up as loose items hit the deck. That was followed by what felt like an extreme roller coaster ride.

But the evasive maneuvers didn't work. Something hit the *Chicago* and hit it hard. Alarms began to hoot and howl. Smith uttered a silent prayer. *Yea, though I walk through the valley of the shadow of death, I will fear no evil, for thou art with me ..."*

The prayer wasn't enough. "We're going in!" the Captain shouted over the intercom. "Hang on!"

Suddenly the ship rolled and Smith found himself hanging upside down in his harness. Then the freighter flipped right side up again and hit hard. Intermittent screeching sounds were heard as the *Chicago* hit the ground and skipped like a stone on a pond. It landed one more time and coasted to a stop.

Every second would count, and Smith knew it as he hit the harness release. "This is Nine," he said, chinning the mike. "They will attack from the air ... Every cyborg who can will exit the ship and form an AA network. Fire when ready.

"Able bodied bio bods will follow the borgs and seek cover. Leave the wounded on the ship. That's an order. Over."

It was cold and Smith knew there was a very real chance that people would die as a result of his order. But the *Chicago* was a sitting duck. And if it were destroyed *everyone* would die. The wounded and the medics alike. And if Smith lost the medics, then other causalities would die later on. He was playing God and hated it. Daylight flooded the hold as both the port and starboard hatches opened. Having positioned herself next to the starboard hatch, Josy yelled, "Go! Go! Go!"

In keeping with Smith's orders the cyborgs went first with those bio bods who could scuttling along behind. But there wasn't much they could do as the DE came in for the kill. The ship filled half the sky as it hung there supported by flaring repellors. As the DE started to pivot, an artificial dust storm made it hard to see. "They're going to fire a broadside at us!" someone yelled. Smith realized that was true. The turn would allow the renegades to bring more weapons to bear on the *Chicago*.

But the cyborgs had linked their onboard computers into a single network by then and half of them were armed with so-called "cans". Meaning that each carried a pair of shoulder mounted rocket launchers. So each T-2 could deliver twelve independently targeted missiles. They fired in unison, and as rockets sleeted into the air, the cyborgs who weren't armed with cans let loose with their arm mounted energy cannons, and their fire converged on the enemy vessel as well.

The DE's shields were down so that it could fire its weapons, so the hull took the full force of the well-coordinated barrage. Smith saw the bright flash produced by a secondary explosion and heard a loud BOOM.

The *Queen* staggered, began to tilt, and righted herself. Then, with only two thirds of her repellors firing, she turned away and began to retreat. But one of the borgs hadn't fired yet. And that was the four-legged beast that Smith thought of as "the equalizer".

The quad stood twenty-five feet tall and weighed fifty tons, so he had taken longer to exit the ship. But having cleared the wreck, Corporal Ray "Pinky" Jackson was ready to fight. And when he fired his missiles they followed each other like bullets shot from a gun. Each struck within feet of the previous projectile and that created a flash point that seemed to pulse like a strobe. Together the missiles blew a hole in the DE's stern and one of them found the engine room. When it did, there was a massive explosion followed by a circular shock wave. The blast knocked Smith onto his ass and burning rubbish fell from the sky as he stood up. Smith chinned his mike. "Nice shooting *Sergeant* Jackson—you're going to get a pay raise."

A reedy cheer went up as Josy appeared at Smith's side. "So, what do you think? Was Chozick aboard?"

"I doubt it," Smith answered. "But it doesn't make any difference. There are the rest of them to deal with as well."

"What if the reliquary was aboard the DE?"

"Then we're in big trouble," Smith answered. "Come on ... There are wounded to tend to."

*   *   *

It took the better part of four hours to provide the wounded with first aid, salvage what they could from the wreck, and dig shallow graves. One cyborg, one Hudathan, and nine bio bods had been killed. Eventually Smith planned to come back and give all of them proper burials. But that would have to wait. Chozick knew that an attack was coming and every passing hour gave him more time to prepare for it.

So as bio bods loaded supplies into Sergeant Jackson's cargo compartment, and the platoon leaders checked their troops, Smith met with Tora-Sa and Josy. "Here's how I figure it," Smith said. "Chozick will assume that we're after him, which is true, but we're after the reliquary as well. And that's the more important of the two objectives."

Tora-Sa nodded. "You are correct ... Although I look forward to taking Chozick's head. His skull will make a nice addition to my collection."

Smith made a face. "Yes, well, be that as it may ... I think we can take advantage of the situation. I will lead the 2nd and 3rd platoons against the town while the two of you take the 1st and circle around. It's my hope that you can find a way into the mine. And that, according to Ember, is where the reliquary is stored."

"Access can be gained via a vertical ventilation shaft," a fourth voice said. "I will lead you there."

All three turned to find that Orson was standing two feet away. Smith had paid scant attention to the robot during the trip out but here it was. "There are a number of satellites in orbit around Long Jump," the android said matter-of -factly. "I hacked one of them and made use of it to take aerial photos. The ventilation stack is clear to see."

"Well done," Smith said, as he turned to Josy. "Hand your borgs off to the other platoon leaders, enter the mine via the shaft, and secure the reliquary. No heroics. Once the remains are safe we will have accomplished the most important aspect of our mission. Then we can go after Chozick, starve him out, or wait for the navy to bomb the place. It hardly matters. Contact me right away once you have the reliquary."

"Okay, but I reserve the right to shoot Chozick if I run into him," Josy said.

"But not in the head," Tola-Sa countered. "That would ruin my trophy."

Smith shook his head sadly. "Both of you are going to hell. You have your orders. Execute them."

There was no reason to hurry. Not in Smith's opinion. Josy and Tola-Sa would need plenty of time to circle around and approach from the south. But the other platoons would have to advance or Chozick would become suspicious.

So Smith sent drones forward to act as scouts, followed by the bio bods, and T-2s. Sergeant Jackson brought up the rear.

The light had begun to fade by the time they reached the outskirts of town. The legionnaires could fight at night but so could their opponents. So Smith decided to harass the enemy during the hours of darkness and attack Sunrise shortly after dawn. The symbology of that

William C. Dietz

appealed to him. "He will bring forth your righteousness as the light, and your justice as the noonday." Psalm 37:6.

That was the plan, or would have been, except that Chozick wasn't about to sit around and wait for the enemy to attack on their terms. And, thanks to his drones, he knew where the enemy units were. The first indication of that was a distant thump followed by screech and a loud explosion as a mortar round landed within three feet of a cyborg and her bio bod. Both were killed instantly.

Then shells began to rain down all around, killing Smith's legionnaires, and forcing the survivors to seek cover. But the incoming mortar bombs could be tracked. And it took Jackson's onboard computer less than a minute to calculate all of the necessary firing solutions, load them into missiles, and fire. Bright explosions marked the enemy mortar pits. *A tooth for a tooth*, Smith thought grimly as his binoculars swept the area ahead, *and a missile for a missile*.

But no sooner had some sort of equilibrium been restored when something monstrous burst out of the ground next to Jackson. The construct was even larger than the quad was. Two skeletal arms slid under the war form's belly. Then, with the ease of a little boy turning a beetle over onto its back, the mining machine flipped the cyborg. The equalizer had been put out of action—and a monster was on the loose.

*   *   *

Josy could hear the muted sound of explosions off in the distance as Orson led her platoon around Copper Mountain's southern flank. Her team had been stripped of cyborgs because it was unlikely that a T-2 would be able to climb a super steep slope or drop through what could be a tight ventilation shaft. So her team consisted of a drone, Orson, Tora-Sa, two of his Hudathan troopers, and forty legionnaires.

They weren't encumbered by heavy packs, so the soldiers were able to jog cross country as the android led the way. The ground was generally open but broken by occasional ravines and outcroppings of ancient rock. The landscape had a greenish tint—but that was a small price to pay for the ability to see at night.

Even though the Deacon was pulling most of the enemy troops his way Josy expected to encounter some opposition. Surely the renegade wouldn't leave his southern flank unprotected. But after more than thirty minutes of running, that appeared to be the case. Josy knew how dangerous assumptions could be, however, and decided to give her troops a five minute break while her drone went forward.

54

Minutes passed, the drone gave the all clear, and the platoon took off. The mountain was to their left and the sides looked steep. That could be a big problem and might explain why they hadn't run into any bad guys. Maybe Chozick thought the mountain could take care of itself.

Another forty minutes passed and Josy was starting to get tired as Orson slowed and held a hand up. Then, as the column came to a stop, it pointed upwards. "The ventilation shaft is directly above us," the robot declared.

Josy looked up and didn't like the view. The slope was so steep that it would be necessary to use ropes. *If* someone could free climb the mountainside first.

But before they tackled that problem there was something else to consider. Were guards posted up above? If so, they would certainly take notice when a platoon of troops started up the mountain.

So Josy took control of the drone. She could fly it using a wireless remote and could see what it "saw" using the HUD projected on the inside of her visor. Unfortunately the drone had a heat signature that any sentry worth his or her salt could detect. So Josy kept the robot in against the mountain, flying only inches away from the largest rocks in hopes of escaping detection.

The drone was about two hundred and twenty feet up when Josy spotted what she'd been looking for. A Human-shaped blob of light could be seen standing next to a ghostly looking heat stack. It was holding something up to its eyes. Binoculars? Yes.

Carefully, lest she move the robot too much and draw attention to it, Josy delegated control of the machine's single weapon to herself. What happened next would be critical. If she missed the sentry, or merely winged him, an alarm would be given. And if that occurred, reinforcements would be sent. Worse yet, the renegades would retain control of the reliquary.

Josy held her breath as she eased the luminous crosshairs onto the target. There was an intermittent breeze from the west so tiny movements of the joystick were required to keep the glowing X on target.

Then, as her thumb came down on the firing button, the sentry turned out of the sight picture. Josy swore and made the necessary adjustment. Her thumb mashed the button and the energy bolt punched a hole through the lookout a fraction of a second later. There was no report. The sentry went limp and the weight of the weapon dangling across his or her chest was enough to pull the dead body forward. Josy was about to shout a warning when the corpse landed next to a startled legionnaire. There was a thump followed by an emphatic, "What the hell?"

"Sorry about that," Josy said as she put the remote away. "I'll holler next time. Bring some cord. Let's see if the drone can carry it up and around the ventilation stack. Maybe we can use it to hoist a rope up. That would save a lot of time. Let's get going."

*   *   *

Having accomplished its mission, the orange monster was trying to retreat underground when Smith went after it. "Come on!" he shouted. "Let's kill that thing!"

Two bio bods were close enough to respond as Smith ran straight for the hole the machine was backing into. He jumped, landed on the front end of the monster, and shouted into the mike. "Find the driver! Kill him."

The order made sense, but was easier said than done. Smith staggered as the soil strewn deck tilted and he was forced to grab a support to prevent himself from falling off. There were lights, all protected by wire mesh, but the dirt raining down from above made it hard to see.

Smith heard a scream and knew one of his legionnaires was dead. "God damn you!" the officer yelled as the engine roared and he battled his way toward a dimly seen light. The cab? Smith hoped so as the monster tried to buck him off and a fist-sized rock hit his shoulder. He saw a safety rail and grabbed onto it as the machine backed down the tunnel it had created earlier. That was the threat ... The damned thing could surface and attack again. But not if the operator was dead.

Smith was closer, by then, and could see the cab. But that meant the operator could see him as well—and soon emerged long enough to fire a pistol at the legionnaire. Smith heard clanging sounds as bullets struck all around him but was unhurt. *Thank you, Lord*, he thought to himself.

But then the ceiling caved in and drove him to the deck. He struggled against the weight of the soil, fought his way free, and realized that his assault rifle was gone. It made no difference. Smith stooped to collect a rock before staggering toward the cab.

Then he was there, peering at the operator through an armored window, as he followed a grab rail to the left. The machine jerked to a halt as the operator came out to shoot the apparition that was clinging to his machine. He pulled the trigger and the weapon clicked empty. Smith laughed wildly. "Vengeance is mine, saith the Lord!" the legionnaire shouted, as he brought the rock down with both hands.

The operator was wearing a helmet and a protective suit. He staggered under the force of the attack, tried to retreat into the cab, but couldn't escape. The second blow destroyed his visor and the third smashed into his face. He brought both hands up to protect the bloody mess and collapsed as Smith struck again. "He's dead, sir," the little private said. "You can stop now."

Smith let go of the rock and heard a clang as it landed next to the body. He swayed like a drunk as the private tried to support him. "You're sure?"

"Yes, sir," she said.

"Good. See if you can turn this thing off ... And lead me out of here."

"I'll try, sir," the private said. And she did.

*   *   *

It took what seemed like an eternity for Josy's platoon to climb the steep slope and enter the ventilation stack via an access door. It wasn't necessary to rappel down the shaft because it was equipped with rungs. The same rungs the lookouts relied on. There was a tunnel at the bottom of the stack which didn't seem to be in use at the moment. And that made sense, given the battle that was raging in town.

Finally, once all of Josy's people were in the tunnel, it was time to seek out Chozick's operations center and the reliquary that was stored there. Fortunately, there were signs to point the way—along with occasional safety placards.

The tunnel was dimly lit, large enough for two ore carriers to pass each other, and ran consistently downhill. The platoon hadn't traveled far when Orson spoke to Josy over the platoon freq. "Look up and to the right."

Josy looked, saw the camera, and realized that it was pointed at her. So much for the element of surprise. She offered the lens a one-fingered salute and delivered a warning to the platoon. "They know we're here so it's just a matter of time before we make contact. Keep it tight, eyeball those side tunnels, and watch our six. Who knows? They might attack from behind. Over."

But when the attack came it was from the front. The first sign of trouble was a distant rumble and four white dots that quickly morphed into huge ore carriers traveling up-tunnel side-by-side. "This is One," Josy said. "Take cover. I want rockets on those trucks... Fire when ready. Over."

The tube jockeys went to one knee, took aim, and pulled their triggers. The heat seeking missiles couldn't miss. They hit massive grills and exploded. Both trucks ground to a halt and one of them erupted into flames. But as troops surged around the vehicles they'd been riding in, it was apparent that they'd been shielded from the force of the explosions. They opened fire and fountains of dirt jumped into the air as what sounded like a wasp buzzed past Josy's left ear. Two legionnaires fell. The rest returned fire.

The renegades had gone to ground by then and the firefight had the makings of a standoff until the burning truck exploded. The blast threw shrapnel up-tunnel and killed half a dozen of Chozick's troops. It was a real, as well as psychological blow—and Josy hurried to take full advantage of it. "Follow me!" she shouted, and ran down tunnel. Those who could followed.

That was too much for the remaining renegades. They turned and ran. Or tried to. But a wall of flame blocked the way. That forced them to turn back in order to defend themselves. The move came too late. Tola-Sa and his Hudathans were there with swords swinging. Heads came off, blood flew, and bodies collapsed as the huge aliens did their work.

"Stop!" Josy shouted, as the remaining dropped their weapons. "They're surrendering."

Tola-Sa managed to take one more head before heeding the order. "Sorry," he said, wiping his sword on a body. "My blade was thirsty."

Josy placed the prisoners under guard and assigned a squad to stay with the wounded and protect them. Then she led the rest of the legionnaires toward the still smoldering trucks. They had lots of ground clearance. Enough to crawl under. And that was what she planned to do.

*   *   *

Even though he didn't want to send his troops into the town of Sunrise during the night, Smith was forced to do so, or risk losing what little bit of offensive momentum he had. So after emerging from the tunnel, he sent his T-2s into the town. The idea was to use the cyborgs as shock troops while squads of bio bods sought to hold whatever ground was taken.

What ensued was a bloody block-by-block battle fought against Chozick's troops and some of the townspeople who took pot shots at the invaders from doors and windows. It was a foolish thing to do, but understandable since most of them didn't know about the reliquary, or its importance. So Smith spared them to the extent that he could without putting his legionnaires at additional risk.

It was nasty work. But inch by inch, and foot by foot, Smith's legionnaires pushed Chozick's people back. And by the time the sun rose, Smith's company had control of the town. What they *didn't* have was the reliquary, and repeated attempts to make contact with Josy had been unsuccessful. Had her platoon been wiped out? Or were they inside the mine where radio signals couldn't reach?

There was no way to know, as Smith led two squads of bio bods into the no man's land of sheds, trucks, and piles of rusting equipment that lay between Sunrise and the copper mine. He was rounding the front end of an old crawler when the renegade made contact. "This is Chozick. Let's talk."

The transmission came in via the command freq. And why not? Chozick was using Legion standard com gear. "Okay," Smith said. "What would you like to talk about?"

"First, tell your people to stay where they are, and stop firing. I'll do the same."

Smith scanned the area in front him through a pair of binoculars. Everything looked normal enough. "Roger that. Hold one."

Then, cognizant of the fact that Chozick could hear, Smith spoke to his people. "This is Nine ... I'm in contact with the renegades. Maintain your present positions and hold your fire. Over."

Having kept his word Smith switched to command frequency again. "All right ... The cease fire is on. Place your weapons on the ground and come out with your hands over your heads. Over."

Chozick laughed. "Very funny, Nine ... I thought you were after me. After *us*. But then my scouts saw the Hudathans. They want the skeleton and you're here to help them get it. And that makes sense in a twisted kind of way. The Confederacy is about to go under and the ridgeheads can save it. Well, that's fine with me ... Give us a ship plus five million credits, and we'll leave the box of bones behind. Or keep coming and we'll destroy them. The choice is up to you."

Suddenly a *third* voice came over the command channel. And it belonged to Josy! "Not so fast asshole. It turns out that *we* have the reliquary ... *And* the hole you were going to hide in. So it's like Captain Smith said. Put your weapons down and your hands in the air."

There was a moment of silence. Smith figured Chozick was on the horn checking to see if Josy's claim was true. Then, having received no reply, he was forced to confront the truth. With Josy behind him barring any chance of retreat, he had nowhere left to go.

The silence was broken by a *fourth* voice. "This is Orson. I'm here with Lieutenant Josy. I suggest that you allow me to speak with Captain Chozick."

Smith was sick of all the killing and, if there was a way to take the surviving renegades alive, then he was for it. More than that, he had a duty to do so ... "Thou shalt not kill." It wasn't a suggestion. It was a commandment. Yet he had violated it over and over. Maybe, just maybe, he could meet God with a little less blood on his hands. "Okay," Smith said. "Go ahead. You heard it Chozick ... Orson is coming out to talk to you."

There was no reply. But, as with the drones, Smith could see what the robot saw on his HUD. And that gave him an Orson-eye-view of a rectangle of light with legionnaires crouched to either side of it. Then he was walking out into bright daylight with the sheds, trucks, and rusty gear piled beyond. He could see the renegades now, most of whom were kneeling, weapons at the ready. A man stood and turned. Smith could see the look of surprise on his face and hear his voice. "Shithead! Is that *you*? Well I'll be damned."

"Yes," a new voice said. A voice that Smith recognized as belonging to Colonel Price! "You should have aimed lower."

Chozick frowned. "Who *are* you? What's going on?"

Smith was wondering the same thing. Had Orson been programmed to channel Price? That's the way it appeared. But *why*? Then he remembered the order Price had given him. The one he refused to obey.

"Say goodbye," Price said.

Chozick frowned. "Goodbye? Wait a minute ... Let's talk, let's ..."

When Orson exploded, a horizontal blast wave erased Chozick and the rest of the renegades. Smith's visor went dark to protect his eyes and the helmet acted to dampen the sound. But he could feel the heat as the wind blew past him and was sucked back in. The second clap of thunder was weaker than the first, and left Smith feeling angry.

The Legion had been planning to kill Chozick all along. And, being unable to count on him to do it, they sent Orson. Had the robot been programmed to knife the renegade if it got close enough? Or to shoot him? Probably. But he was carrying explosives just in case.

"Well," Josy said, as she strolled out into the sunshine. "That takes care of that. Mission accomplished. Let's round up our people, call for some transportation, and go home."

ABOUT THE AUTHOR

New York Times bestselling author **William C. Dietz** has published more than forty novels some of which have been translated into German, French, Russian, Korean and Japanese. Dietz also wrote the script for the *Legion of the Damned* game based on his book of the same name and co-wrote SONY's *Resistance: Burning Skies* game for the PS Vita. He grew up in the Seattle area, spent time with the Navy and Marine Corps as a medic, graduated from the University of Washington, lived in Africa for half a year, and has traveled to six continents. He has been employed as a surgical technician, college instructor, news writer, television producer and Director of Public Relations and Marketing for an international telephone company.

Dietz is a member of the Writer's Guild and the International Association of Media Tie-In Writers. He and his wife live near Gig Harbor in Washington State where they enjoy traveling, kayaking, and reading books. williamcdietz.com

William C. Dietz

PRISONER OF WAR

KEVIN J. ANDERSON

AUTHOR'S NOTE

According to unofficial military policy, the U.S. Air Force knows exactly what it takes to make the best fighter pilot: balls the size of grapefruits, and brains the size of a pea.

Some might say that it requires all the good qualities of a fighter pilot to walk in Harlan Ellison's footsteps. Harlan is always a hard act to follow, and it's daunting even to try.

When I first talked with Harlan about doing a sequel to his classic Outer Limits *teleplay, "Soldier," he was very skeptical. Given the sheer number of abysmal sequels and bad spinoffs that have graced bookstore racks and theater screens, I suppose he had good reason. "I've never done a sequel to a single one of my stories," he told me. "I never felt the need. If I got it right the first time, I've said all I needed to say."*

In the course of my writing career I have gathered a rather impressive (if that's the word) collection of rejection slips—something like 750 at last count—and I never learned to give up when common sense dictated that I should. So, I went back to Harlan. "Look, you've developed a sprawling scenario of a devastating future war, where soldiers are bred and trained to do nothing but fight from birth to death. Are you telling me that there's only one story to be told in that whole world?"

So, I got to play with Harlan Ellison's toys.

Kevin J. Anderson

"Prisoner of War" is my tapdance on Harlan's stage, set in the devastating world of "Soldier". It is a story about another set of warriors in a never-ending war, men bred for nothing but the battleground—and how they cope with the horrors of…peace.

As a final note, this story was published in an Outer Limits *volume that never got distributed. I love the story, and I hope that here in* Five by Five *it finds a wider audience.*

—KJA

The first Enemy laser-lances blazed across the battlefield at an unknown time of day. No one paid attention to the hour during a firefight anyway. Neither Barto nor any of his squad-mates could see the sun or moon overhead: too much smoke and haze and blast debris filled the air, along with the smell of blood and burning.

A soldier had to be ready at any time or place. A soldier would fight until the fight was over. An endless Now filled their existence, a razor-edged flow of life-for-the-moment, and the slightest distraction or daydream could end the Now ... forever.

With a clatter of dusty armor and a hum of returned weapons-fire, the defenders charged forward, Barto among them. They had no terrain maps or battle plans, only unseen commanders bellowing instructions into their helmet earpieces.

Greasy fires guttered and smoked from explosions, but as long as a soldier could draw breath, the air always smelled sweet enough. Somehow the flames still found organic material to burn, though only a few skeletal trees remained standing. The horizon was like broken, jagged teeth. No discernible structures remained, only blistered destruction and the endless bedlam of combat.

To a man who had known no other life, Barto found the landscape familiar and comforting.

"Down!" his point man, Arviq, screamed loudly enough so that Barto could hear it through the armored helmet. A bolt of white-hot energy seared the ground in front of them, turning the blasted soil into glass. The ricochet stitched a broken-windshield pattern of lethal cuts across the armored chest of one comrade five meters away.

The victim was in a different part of the squad; Barto knew him only by serial number instead of a more personal, chosen name. Now the man was a casualty of war; his serial number would be displayed in fine print on the memorial lists back at the crèche—for two days. And then it would be erased forever.

Barto and Arviq both dove to the bottom of the trench as more well-aimed laser-lances embroidered the ground and the slumping walls of the ditch. As he hunched over to shield himself, the helmet's speakers continued to pound commands: "KILL ... KILL ... KILL ..."

The Enemy assault ended with a brief hesitation, like an indrawn breath. The soldiers around Barto paused, regrouped, then scrambled to their feet, leaving the fallen comrade behind. Later, regardless of the battle's outcome, trained bloodhounds would retrieve the body parts and drag them back to HQ in their jaws. After the proper casualty statistics had been recorded, the KIA corpses would be efficiently incinerated.

In the middle of a firefight, Barto and Arviq could not be bothered by such things. They had been trained never to think of fallen comrades; it was beyond the purview of their mission. The voice in the helmet speakers changed, took on a different note: "RETALIATE ... RETALIATE ... RETALIATE ..."

With a howl and a roar enhanced by adrenaline injections from inside the armor suits, Barto and his squad moved as a unit. Programmed endorphins poured into their bloodstreams at the moment of battle frenzy, and they surged out of the trench. The Enemy encampment could not be far, and they silently swore to unleash a slaughter that would outmatch anything their opponents had ever done ... though this most recent attack was assuredly a response to their own previous day's offensive.

Moving as a unit, the squad clambered over debris, around craters, and out into the open. They ran beyond monofilament barricades that would slice the limb off an unwary soldier, then into a sonic minefield whose layout shone on the eye-visor screen inside each helmet.

With a self-assured gait across the no-man's land, the soldiers moved like a pack of killer rats, laser-lances slung in their arms. They bellowed and snarled, pumping each other up. As he ran, Barto studied the sonic minefield grid in his visor, sidestepping instinctively.

From their embankment, the Enemy began to fire again. The smoky air became a lattice of deadly lines in all directions. Barto continued running. Beside him, Arviq pressed the stock of his weapon against his armored breastplate, pumping blast after blast toward the unseen Enemy.

Then a laser-lance seared close to Barto's helmet, blistering the top layer of semi-reflective silver. Static blasted across his eye visor, and he couldn't see. He made one false sidestep and yelled. He could

Kevin J. Anderson

no longer find the grid display, could no longer even see the actual ground.

Just as his foot came down in the wrong place, Arviq grabbed his arm and yanked him aside, using their combined momentum. The sonic mine exploded, vomiting debris and shrapnel with pounding soundwaves that fractured the plates of Barto's armor, pulverizing the bones in his leg. But he fell out of the mine's focused kill radius and lay biting back the pain.

He propped himself up and ripped off his slagged helmet, blinking with naked eyes at the real sky. Arviq had saved his life—just as Barto would have done for his squad-mate had their situations been reversed.

Always trust your comrades. Your life is theirs. That was how it had always been.

And even if he did fall to Enemy attack, the bloodhounds would haul his body to HQ, and he would receive an appropriate military farewell before he returned to the earth—mission accomplished. A soldier's duty was to fight, and Barto had been performing that duty for all of his conscious life.

As he activated his rescue transmitter and fumbled for the medpak, the rest of the soldiers charged forward, leaving him behind. Arviq didn't even spare him a backward glance.

*   *   *

Some said the war had gone on forever—and since no one kept track of history anymore, the statement could not be proved false.

Barto knew only the military life. He had emerged from a tank in the soldiers' crèche with the programming wired into his brain, fully aware, fully grown, and knowing his assignment. If ever he had any questions or doubts, the command voices in his helmet would answer them.

Barto knew primarily that he had to kill the Enemy. He knew that he had to protect his comrades, that the squad was the sum of his existence. No good soldier could rest until every last Enemy had been eradicated, down to their feline spies, down to the bloodhounds that dragged away Enemy KIAs.

Winning this war might well take an eternity, but Barto was willing to fight for that long. Every moment of his life had encompassed either fighting, or learning new techniques to kill and to survive, or resting so that he could fight again the next day.

There was no time for anything else. There was no need for anything else.

Barto remembered when he'd been younger, not long out of the tank. His muscles were wiry, his body flexible without the stiffness of constant abuse. His skin had been smooth, free of the intaglio of scars from a thousand close dances with death. Barto and his squad-mates—apprentices all—had fought hand-to-hand in the crèche gymnasium, occasionally breaking each other's bones or knocking each other unconscious. None of them had yet earned their armor, their protection, or their weapons. They couldn't even call themselves soldiers. ...

Now consigned to the HQ infirmary and repair shop, as he drifted in a soup of pain and unconsciousness, Barto revisited the long-ago moment he had first grasped a specialized piece of equipment designed to maim and kill. The soldier trainees had learned early on in their drill that any object was a potential weapon—but this was a spear, a long rough bar of old steel with a sharpened point that gleamed white and silver in the unforgiving lights. A weapon: his own weapon.

He spun it around in his hand, feeling its weight—a deadly impaling device that could be used against the oncoming Enemy.

Later, his advanced training would, of course, include hand-to-hand combat against other soldiers, human opponents ... but not at first. All trainees were expendable, but if the young men could be salvaged, then the military programming services would turn them into killers.

For months, Barto received somatic instruction and physical drilling by one of the rare old veterans who had survived years of combat. The veteran had a wealth of experience and survival instincts that could not be matched even by the most sophisticated computers. He made sure that Barto fought to the limit of his abilities.

Swinging the spear against nothing, feeling his body move, Barto reacted to the barked commands of the veteran instructor. Response without thought. He learned how to make the weapon into a part of him, an extension of his reflexes. He was the weapon; the spear was just an augmentation.

Then they gave him a taste of blood, real blood. They wanted him to get in the habit of killing.

The small metal-walled arena was like an echo chamber, a large underground room with simulated rock outcroppings, a fallen tree, and other sharp obstacles. Barto didn't question of reality of the scenario. The environment itself was a tool to be used.

During that exercise, the veteran instructor let him wear his helmet ... but nothing else. Stripped naked, he gripped the spear in his hand and glared through the visor. The helmet earphones gave him reassuring commands in his ears, directions, suggestions. Otherwise, Barto felt helpless—but no soldier was ever helpless, because a helpless man could not become a soldier.

Underground, the arena door groaned open, and barricade bars moved away. Barto tensed. He gripped the metal shaft of the spear despite the sweat on his palms.

Suddenly, a whirlwind of bristles and scales, sharp hooves and long tusks launched itself like a projectile. An enhanced boar with scarlet eyes snarled and plowed forward, searching for a target, something against which to vent its anger.

And Barto was the only other creature in the room.

On high pedestals in the gallery above, three enhanced cats watched, blinking their gold-green eyes. The feline spy commanders observed for the invisible overlords who wanted to see how the freshly detanked soldiers reacted in their first real life-or-death test.

The boar charged. Barto jabbed with the spear, but he was too tentative. Before, he had only thrust at imaginary opponents and an occasional hologram projected inside his visor. Now, though, the boar came on like a locomotive. The spear glanced off, opening a mere stinging scratch in the creature's skin. Barto had not imagined its hide could be so tough, its bones so hard. He had made the first, terrible mistake in this duel.

The trivial wound enraged the beast.

Barto dove to one side over a synthetic rock, and the boar rammed into the artificial tree trunk. It spun around, shaking its head, tusks gleaming. The ivory spears in its mouth looked much more deadly than Barto's primitive weapon. The boar attacked again.

A moment of panic rose up like an illusion, but he pounded it back, and the fear evaporated, bringing a rush of adrenaline. The chemical and electronic components in his body released the substance, making Barto see red rage of his own.

The enhanced boar recovered itself and snorted. Barto knew he had a better chance of striking the target in motion if he didn't use a tiny pinpoint thrust; instead, he swung the heavy metal bar sideways like a cudgel. The sturdy steel bashed the creature's thick skull. The sound of the impact rang out in the hollow room.

The cats watched from their pedestals.

The boar squealed and thrashed. Barto saw that its eyes held an increased intelligence, like that found in the feline spies and in the daredevil bloodhounds that retrieved bodies from the battlefield. The boar responded with a calculated counterattack, trying to outthink this naked human opponent, this would-be soldier. Barto smiled: the boar was the Enemy.

In the frenzy of battle, Barto no longer thought like an intelligent human being. Instead, he relied only on instinct and unbearable bloodlust. He rushed in without forethought, without care, without any sense of self-preservation. After all ... he had a spear.

The boar tried to feint, to react, but Barto gave the Enemy no chance. He swung again with the staff, drawing a bright red line of blood and putting out one of the beast's eyes. Crimson and yellow body fluids oozed through smashed skin on the boar's snout. It leapt forward, driven by insanity and pain.

Now Barto used the spear with finesse.

A great calm flowed through him, as if the rest of the world had slowed down, and he saw exactly what to do, exactly where to hold the spear. The sharpened point neatly plunged through the ribcage of the beast and skewered its lungs and heart. Showering a wet-iron smell in the air, the creature lay quivering, trembling ... dying.

When Barto came back to his senses, he saw that his legs had been slashed open by the boar's tusks. The deep gouges left him bleeding, but oddly without any sense of pain or injury. He looked down and studied the corpse of his opponent, the Enemy. Now he had killed. Barto had fresh blood on his hands, real blood from a vanquished opponent.

He liked the sensation.

He knew that this had been no simple exercise. He knew the boar could well have killed him, and that other trainees who had vanished from the barracks must have failed this part of their instruction.

But Barto had succeeded. He was a killer now, and he was one step closer to becoming a soldier.

*   *   *

Time didn't matter. For a soldier, time never mattered. He awoke hours, or days, later back in the HQ infirmary and repair shop—

patched up, drugged, but fully aware. A hairless chimpanzee tended him, leaning over in a cloud of disinfectant scents and bad breath. The chimp medical techs knew how to bandage and fix battlefield wounds. They could do no surgery that required finesse, but the soldiers required nothing that needed delicacy for cosmetic effect.

Once injured, if a soldier could be fixed, he would be sent back to the battlefield. If his wounds caused the chimp med-techs too much trouble, he would be eliminated. Every surviving member of the squad bore his share of scars, burns, scabs, and callouses. No one paid attention to these trophies of war; they were part of a soldier's life, not a badge of honor or bravery.

Since Barto hadn't been eliminated, he assumed he must have been fixed.

He sat up on the infirmary cot, and the hairless chimpanzees hurried over, uttering quiet reassurances, a few English words, a few soothing grunts. Triggered by his awakening, a signal was automatically sent back to his squad commander.

Barto listened to an assessment of his repaired leg, his stitched muscles and skin, and his bruises and contusions. Not too bad, he thought. He'd suffered worse, sometimes even in training with other soldiers (especially during the initial few months, when they'd first been given their own sets of armor).

He remembered that back then his comrade Arviq, in particular, had thought himself invincible. ...

During downtime before the soldiers crawled into their assigned sleeping bins, the other squad members were required to file through the infirmary to see their injured comrades. Some came only because of orders to do so; most of them would rather have been sleeping.

But the invisible commanders planted instructions to go to the infirmary simply so that other soldiers could see the wounded, could see what could happen to them if they weren't careful ... but also so they could see that they just might survive.

Recovering, Barto sat up in the uncomfortable infirmary bed and watched the other soldiers come in. His pain went away with another automatic rush of endorphins to deaden his unpleasant sensations ... or perhaps his own determination was enough to quell the nerve-fire of agony.

The fighters filed by. He recognized few of them, all strangers without armor and helmets, though he could have identified each one by the serial numbers displayed on their fatigues. These were soldiers, cogs in a fighting machine. They didn't have time to be individuals.

When Arviq came up at the end of the line, he stood brusque, nodding gruffly. "You'll mend," he said.

"Thank you for saving me," Barto answered. It was the closest thing they'd had to a conversation in a long time.

"It's my duty. I await the day when you can fight with us again." He marched out, and the others followed him. Barto lay back and attempted to sleep, to regain his strength. Through sheer force of will, he growled at his cells and tissues to work harder, to knit the injuries and restore him to full health. ...

Day after day, lying in the infirmary and waiting proved far more difficult than any combat situation Barto had ever encountered. Finally, after a maddening week of intensive recuperation, directed therapy aided by medical technology and powerful drugs, he was released from his hospital prison and sent back to the front.

Where he belonged.

*   *   *

The battlefield screamed with pain and destruction, explosions, fire, and death—but to Barto, after being so long in the sheltered quiet of the infirmary, the tumult was a shout of exuberance. He was glad to be here.

The soldiers raced across the ground, each in his own squad position, weapons drawn. They had already driven back the Enemy, and now the fire of laser-lances grew even thicker around them as the others became desperate. They pressed ahead, deeper into Enemy territory than they had ever gone before.

Their helmet locators for sonic mines and shrapnel grenades buzzed constantly, but the reptilian part of Barto's brain reacted without volition, hardwired into fighting and killing. He dodged and weaved, keeping himself alive.

His point man, Arviq, jogged close beside him, and Barto extended his peripheral vision behind the dark visor to enfold his comrade into an invisible protective sphere. He would assist his partner if he got into trouble—not out of any sense of payback or obligation, but because it was an automatic response, his own assignment. He would have done the same for any other soldier, any member of his squad—anyone but the Enemy.

Precision-guided mortars scribed parabolas through the air and exploded close to any concentration of soldiers who did not display the proper transponders. Amidst screams and thunder, a massive triple detonation wiped out over half of Barto's squad, but the others did not fall back, did not even pause. They drove onward, continued the push. The fallen comrades would be taken care of somehow, though no one knew how the bloodhounds would ever make it this deep into Enemy-held territory.

This far behind the main battle lines, the Enemy numbers themselves were dwindling, and Barto fired and fired again. The laser-lance thrummed in his gauntleted hands, skewering a distant man's chestplate and leaving a smoking hole.

But it wasn't really a man, after all. It was the Enemy.

The chase continued, and the survivors of Barto's squad ran in the direction of what must have been Enemy HQ. In his dry, dusty mouth he could taste the sweet honey of victory.

But suddenly, unexpectedly, they triggered a row of booby-traps that did not appear on their helmet sensors. Camouflaged catapults popped up, spraying near-invisible clouds of netting, monofilament webs as insubstantial as smoke but sharper than the most deadly razor.

The flying webwork engulfed four soldiers near him, and they fell into neatly butchered pieces. But oddly enough, so did three of the Enemy men rushing in retreat, as if they themselves hadn't known of these defenses. But their own visor sensors must have been keyed to boobytraps they themselves had planted. ...

Though the questions astonished him, Barto did not pause. His job was not to analyze. Paraplegic computer tactitions and the invisible battlefield commanders did all that work. The voices in his helmet told him to push forward, and so he pushed forward.

Arviq ran beside him, still firing his laser-lance—and numbly Barto realized that most of the other soldiers were dead. His squad had been decimated ... but the Enemy was nearly eradicated as well.

War often required sacrifices, and many soldiers died. But a victory would pay the bloody cost ten times over. They had never gone so far.

The thrill of seeing the Enemy nearly exterminated gave Barto all the enthusiasm he needed, even without an adrenaline rush augmented by injectors in his armor. With a shared glance behind opaque visors, he and Arviq both had the same thought, and ran forward with their four remaining companions. They couldn't stop now.

Then large gun emplacements popped out of the ground, more massive than anything he had ever seen before. Barto reeled in unaccustomed confusion—the Enemy had never exhibited technology like this! Automated fire rained down on them, super powerful laser-lances far more devastating than any of the hand-held rifles.

Soldiers screamed. The blasts were like belts of incinerating flame, vaporizing armor and leaving not even bones for the bloodhounds to retrieve. The firepower pummeled anyone who came close, whether friend or Enemy. They had no chance, no chance at all.

An explosion ripped out a deep crater ten meters from them. Someone screamed, but Barto had no voice. The automated superlasers continued to track across the ground, pinpointing armor, crushing any movement. Barto watched the beams sweep closer, vaporizing everything in the vicinity. His four remaining squad members died in a puff of blood-smoke and molten armor plate.

On impulse he grabbed Arviq and shoved him hard toward the fresh crater. Together, the two dove into the raw trench just as the splash of disintegration passed over them. The voices in his helmet turned to a rainstorm of incomprehensible static.

Within moments the battle stopped. Everyone else was dead.

All of the laser fire and explosions ceased. All the Enemy, all of the squad, every living thing had been annihilated.

Without saying a word, Arviq hauled himself to his hands and knees and reached over to shake Barto, who also recovered his balance. The two of them sat panting for a moment, stunned but still determined. Neither of them—in fact, no one they knew—had ever been so far behind Enemy lines.

They rose up slowly and carefully into the crackling silence, afraid of other targeted automated systems. Clods of dry dirt fell from their armor. Dust and crackling ash roiled through the air ... but nothing else moved.

"We won?" Barto asked. "Is the war over?"

"I hope not." Arviq turned to him, his mouth a grim line beneath the opaque visor of the helmet. "The war will never be over. But we may have won this battle."

Barto raised his helmet over the rim of the blasted crater. No weapons responded to the motion. The battlefield remained eerily quiet with only the faint sound of coughing fires and settling dust.

"Must be the Enemy encampment," Arviq said with a grunt. "Increased defenses— maybe even HQ." He grinned. "Success!"

But Barto wasn't so sure. Moving with tense caution, he climbed away from the crater. "No, not HQ. The defenses killed as many of them as us. ID transponders useless."

Arviq joined him, sole survivors on the sprawling battlefield. Barto could see where the huge gun emplacements had raised up. Adjusting his visor filters, he spotted different infrared signatures, metallic traces, solid structures and hollow passages beneath the scarred ground.

Amazed, Barto crept forward. "We've discovered something. We're required to investigate."

"No, back to HQ," Arviq said. "We must report. Our squad was wiped out."

But Barto shook him off. He stood determined, looking ahead across the scabbed landscape. "Not until we have hard reconnaissance. This could be important."

Arviq hesitated only a moment. Neither outranked the other, and they had no time for argument, but the other soldier quickly came to his own decision. "Yes. Reconnaissance is part of our mission."

Most of the time, sly intelligence cats would creep through the darkness, observing Enemy strongholds and reporting back to HQ. But the squad had gone farther into Enemy territory than any known advance, and they might have new information. That was the most important thing. They weren't doing it for the glory or for a possible promotion, or for any sort of reward. Barto and Arviq would take the risk because it was their duty.

"My head, my thoughts ... are empty," Arviq said, tapping his helmet.

Barto adjusted his earphones, but still received no transmission and no commands. An uneasy silence echoed in his head. The speakers growled no more repetitive commands to attack and kill.

"How can you stand it?" Arviq looked at him.

Barto took a deep breath. "No choice. Tolerate it."

Crouched low, they trudged toward the automated gun emplacements, but the motion sensors did not reactivate. The weapons had gone through their program and wiped out the threat. Somehow, the two comrades had slipped through the cracks. They could move forward.

Barto and Arviq found a metal hatchplate in the half-hidden superstructure of the enormous laser-lances. Barto sat down and pressed his helmet against the hatch, carefully listening for any vibration, fully tense. Any moment now he expected the destructive fire to rain out again.

He tugged on the hatch, looking for access controls. "We can infiltrate," he said. "It's an underground bunker. Maybe weapons storage. We can bring supplies or power packs back to HQ."

Together they wiped off dust and blasted dirt from the plate, used tools from their armor belts to crack open the seals, and, finally, they lifted the heavy hatch.

Still no voices came to their heads, no instructions. The two soldiers were on their own. Barto didn't like it one bit.

They dropped down into the opening, where a steel ladder led into a maw of shadows. They descended, gripping rung after rung with gauntleted hands. If this was Enemy HQ, Barto thought, it was a much larger complex than anything he and his squad had ever lived in.

Finally the ladder ended in an underground tunnel with the hatch cover high above them. Barto paused for a moment to scan the surroundings, then they walked forward into dim silence. The tunnels seemed empty, barely used, abandoned for a long time. Barto realized the Enemy soldiers could not have emerged from this place. No one had walked down these access tunnels in a long, long time.

As point man, Arviq led the way. He strode forward, hands on his weapons, ready for anything. A soldier had to be flexible and determined. The small tunnel lights gave little illumination, but their helmet visors augmented the ambient photons.

Cameras in their helmets recorded everything as reconnaissance files to be downloaded back in HQ. They continued for what seemed like miles, trudging deeper and deeper into the Earth. This place was an important facility, possibly a central complex ... but Barto couldn't begin to understand it.

From up ahead came a faint throbbing from generators and heavy machinery. Finally, they saw brighter light, thick windows, rectangular plates that shone through to another world, a subterranean complex that seemed like a mythical land. Inside huge grottoes, pale ethereal people moved about wearing bright colors. Plants of a shockingly lush green, garish hues that Barto had never seen before drew the two of them forward like magnets.

"What is this?" Arviq asked. "Some kind of trick?"

"Paradise."

As the soldiers approached, unable to believe what they were seeing, they crossed an unseen threshold, a booby-trap. They heard a

Kevin J. Anderson

brief hum, a crackle of power-surge. Barto reacted just in time to feel a sinking despair—but not fast enough to get out of the way.

A pressing white light engulfed both of them, swallowing them up. In an instant, Barto's visor turned black, then so did his eyes.

*   *   *

When he awoke, the assault on his senses nearly knocked him back into protective unconsciousness. Sounds, smells, colors bombarded him like weapons fire. His armor and helmet had been stripped away, leaving him vulnerable; without it, he felt helpless, soft-skinned, like a worm.

The bed beneath him was warm and soft, disorienting. A gentle and cozy light surrounded him instead of the familiar garish white to which he was accustomed back in his own barracks. Each breath of the humid air was perfumed with a sweet, flowery scent that nauseated him.

Was this an infirmary? Barto turned his head gently, and a raging pain clamored inside his skull. The place reminded him, oddly, of the time he had been helpless and healing from his previous injury ... but he saw no hairless chimpanzees, no robotic medical attendants. The sheets were soft and slick, vastly different from the other rough, sterile coverings.

Grogginess smothered his mind and body. Barto tried to return to full awareness ... but something was wrong. His body remained sluggish and unresponsive, as if the accustomed chemical stimulants were not being released according to program. He needed adrenalin; he needed endorphins.

Arviq lay on another bed beside him, similarly prone, similarly stripped of his armor. When Barto turned his head and directed his gaze in the opposite direction, he was astonished to find another person by his shoulder. Not one of the enhanced animals bred to attend the regiment ... but a woman, a lovely creature with short, honey-brown hair and a shimmering purple garment so brilliant and dazzling that it made his eyes ache.

Responding with combat readiness, he sat up with a lurch—but the woman rushed over and shushed him with a gentle touch. "Quiet now. Everything's all right. You are safe here." Her voice sounded like sweet syrup. Alien.

Arviq stirred beside him, groaning in confusion and growing rage.

76

Then Barto remembered a legend, a story told on the field during the quiet times between battles when some soldiers were more frightened than others. It was a hopeful myth of what happened to brave and dedicated fighters after a death in battle. Was this ... Valhalla?

He glanced over at Arviq, his face contorted with confusion. His eyes glimmered with dark fires. "Are we dead?"

The woman laughed like tinkling crystal. "No, soldier. We are people like yourselves: human beings."

She didn't look like him, though, or any other person he had ever seen. Barto shook his head, refusing to acknowledge the pain left over inside. He'd had enough experience with pain. "You're not ... soldiers."

The woman smiled and leaned closer to him. A warmth radiated from her scrubbed and lotioned skin. He had never noticed a person's physical features before, never paid attention ... and he'd never seen anything so beautiful in his life.

"Everyone is a soldier," he said, "either for our side, or the Enemy."

The woman continued to give him a slightly superior smile. "You are soldiers, my friends ... but we are not. Not here." She gave a gesture to indicate her entire underground world. "After all, it's a war. You're fighting and dying." Her thin, dark eyebrows rose up in graceful arches on her forehead. "Did it never occur to you to ask exactly what you're fighting ... for?"

With a sudden burst of energy and an outcry of rage, Arviq lunged up from his bed, reaching out with clawlike hands, his face full of fury. Even without armor or weapons, any soldier knew how to kill with his bare hands. Somehow he found the energy to lash out, to propel himself into a combat frame of mind.

The woman staggered back from the infirmary beds, startled. Barto saw shadows, more people moving behind observation windows, automatic devices activating. There was another flash of white light, and again he lost consciousness.

*　　　*　　　*

When Barto awoke once more, he was alone in a room, clad in soft pajamas with more slick sheets wrapped around him. He found his bed too pliant, too yielding, as if it meant to be comfortable with a vengeance.

Kevin J. Anderson

The gentle sound of running water trickled from speakers embedded in the wall. The white-noise had a soothing effect, the opposite of the perpetual, pressuring commands that had droned into his ears from helmet speakers. Now, the image of a soporific, bubbling brook made him want to lie motionless in a stupor.

He no longer even seemed alive.

This room was smaller, the walls painted pastel colors instead of clean white. The illumination was muted and warm, like sunlight through amber. It made his head fuzzy.

Stiffly, Barto rolled over and found that Arviq wasn't with him this time. His comrade had been taken elsewhere. Was this some sort of insidious Enemy plan? Divide and conquer, separate the squad members.

Had he fallen into some new kind of warfare that went beyond violence and destruction to this personality-destroying brainwashing technique? Barto snarled and tried to find a way to escape—a captured soldier's duty was to escape at all costs.

He didn't hear a door open, felt no movement of the air—but suddenly the beautiful woman stood there with him, setting a platter down on a ledge formed out of the substance of the wall. She leaned over his bed, her entire body smelling of gentle flowers and perfumes. She smiled down at him, parting soft lips to reveal even, white teeth. Barto started, ready to fight with hand-to-hand techniques even without his armor or his weapons—but she made no threatening move.

"My name is Juliette," she said, then waited as if he was supposed to recognize some significance to the name.

He answered as he had been drilled. "Barto. Corporal. E21TFDN." He rolled off the serial number in a singsong chant, "Eetoowun teeyeff deeyenn." He had spoken it more than any other word in his lifetime. Then he formed his mouth into a grim line. That was all he had been trained to say. The Enemy rarely, if ever, took prisoners. Everyone died on the battlefield.

"I brought food for you ... Barto." Juliette picked up a steaming, spicy-smelling bowl from the tray on the ledge. It contained some kind of broth laced with vegetables, even a little meat.

Though he could withstand long periods of fasting, Barto realized how hungry he was. He'd been trained to shut off the hunger pangs and nerve twinges in his digestive system. But he also knew to take nourishment whenever possible, to maintain his strength.

78

She extended a spoon, and Barto raised his head to accept a mouthful. The spoon was metal with rounded edges. Even such a crude and innocuous weapon could be used in many different ways as a killing instrument. He could have snatched it from her—but he did not, taking the mouthful instead.

The flavors exploded around his tongue, and Barto nearly choked. It was too intense, too spiced, too fresh—experiences his mouth had never had. Back in the barracks, all soldiers ate a common meal, a protein-rich gruel that served as sustenance and nothing else. He'd never before dined on a preparation in which someone had cared about its flavors. He didn't find it at all pleasant.

Juliette gave him another mouthful, and he forced himself to eat it. But he did not let down his guard for an instant.

"The stun-field should have no residual effect on you, Barto," she said. "You'll regain your strength in no time." Her voice sounded odd in his ears, pitched with a higher timbre, musical rather than the implacable instructions that had poured into his ears from the helmet's speakers.

"I'm strong enough," Barto said. "Where is my comrade?"

"He's safe and being tended—but we thought it best to separate you." She took the bowl away, then stood back to appraise him. "I'm curious about you, Barto, Corporal, E21TFDN. I want to be your friend—so let's just use our first names, all right?" She brushed her hand along his arm, and he recoiled at her touch; it felt like warm feathers tickling across the skin. "Can you stand up? I'd like to take you for a walk to show you where you are."

Barto did not argue with her. Regardless of her intentions, Juliette's offer would allow him to continue his reconnaissance. She could show him whatever she wished, and he would gather information. Without the helmet visor and its implanted cameras, he would have to observe with his own eyes, and remember details. But it could be done.

As he swung off the bed, the loose-fitting pajamas felt strange on him, not hard enough, not safe. He walked on the balls of his bare feet, every muscle tense, searching for mysterious threats as Juliette led him out of the room. She took him down underground corridors into even richer light. They passed beautiful images of scenery, forgotten forests and lost mountains ... waterfalls and lakes unlike anything he had ever seen on the battle-scarred combat fields.

"Who are you people?" Barto said. "What is this place?"

Kevin J. Anderson

"We're civilians. We went underground centuries ago to escape the fighting, while our armies defended us against the invasion."

Barto tried to assess the information, to fit it like puzzle pieces into the sparse information in his mind. "My squad is ... part of the defenders? We fight against the invaders?"

She looked at him with a curious, placid expression. Her pale skin, delicate bone structure, and pointed chin gave her an ethereal, elfin appearance. "No one knows which side is which anymore."

Other people, similarly pale-skinned and soft-looking, observed the pair as they walked by. Some smiled, some drew back in fear. Many regarded him with cold, fish-like interest. Juliette seemed to enjoy the attention she received just by being with him.

Barto scanned his surroundings for a way to escape and return to his squad. But then he remembered that, except for Arviq, all of his comrades were dead, annihilated by the immense gun emplacements that protected this underground shelter. Back at his own HQ, the databases must have already recorded him and his point man as casualties of war.

Juliette talked as they continued, her voice a pleasant melange of words. She told him of their days of peace and shelter down below, how the survivors had made an entire world down here by excavating tunnel after tunnel. There, the civilians did what she called "the great work of humanity"—composing music, dabbling in art, writing poetry and literature ... though, if they remained isolated down here without experiencing the hard edge of life, Barto didn't know how they found any material to incorporate into their creations.

Though she turned at intersections, descended to different levels, walked in circles, Barto never lost his bearings. He imprinted a map of everything they encountered, knowing he might need to use it later. On his own.

Juliette took him to a greenhouse where the smells nearly stifled him: humid air, the odors of vegetation and mulch, flowers bursting forth like explosions from mortar-fire. Pollinating insects flitted from blossom to blossom, and brilliantly ripe vegetables and fruits made his eyes hurt.

He heard the drip of irrigation systems, saw colorful birds hopping from plant to plant, and a shiver went up his spine. Everything was so quiet here, so gentle. It made him feel too full of energy, too restless.

Barto remembered when he'd been forced to recuperate in the HQ infirmary as the hairless chimpanzees tended to him. He had been bored and frustrated ... but with a goal—to heal, so he could go back and fight. He had managed to wait until his body returned to its optimal condition, when he could go out and serve his purpose in life.

Here, though, these people had a quiet calmness about them, an air or superiority ... with nothing else to do. Juliette seemed to enjoy it, seemed proud of being a civilian.

Barto had never experienced such vibrant beauty, the smells, the music ... the sense of peace. His body rebelled at the thought, but as the hours went by in the beautiful woman's company, he began to feel his resistance crumbling. This was all new to him.

As she showed him their underground "paradise", Barto followed her and listened. Finally, in exasperation, he turned to Juliette and asked, "So there's no war here?" He couldn't believe it. Such a concept had never occurred to him. "No battles?"

"Oh, we have a little." Juliette smiled, then gestured him forward. "Here, let me show you. Maybe you'll find it comforting."

She led him down smooth passages where the temperature grew cooler, the smell more metallic. They walked down glass-walled hallways until they reached a control center.

Battle-plans. Tactical maps. Troop movement displays.

"This is how we maintain our edge, Barto, and our window on the outside world." Juliette's people sat at stations in front of the shifting screens, their fingers raised across control panels. Terrain grids spread out in front of them in bristling colors.

High-resolution panels showed other soldiers, people in familiar armor and helmets, jittery point-of-view images transmitted from visor cameras. Civilian men and women leaned over, punching in commands and speaking into microphones.

"Move left. Open fire."

Another man with a deep voice droned, "Kill the Enemy. Kill the Enemy. Kill the Enemy." He sounded bored. The others looked very relaxed in their positions.

Barto stared with shock as he realized that these were the voices he'd heard in his helmet all his life: directing him, helping him plan his attack. These were his ultimate commanders in the war.

Astonished, Barto looked over to see Arviq also standing inside the control room, chaperoned by a civilian man, also dressed in a loose jumpsuit. His point man's chaperone demonstrated the workings of the controls. Arviq's eyes were wide as he watched the battle.

Kevin J. Anderson

Sensing the new arrivals, Arviq looked up to see Barto. Their eyes met, and hot understanding flashed between them. This was the ultimate headquarters of their army. Arviq reeled from the revelation, but Barto felt a nagging question in the back of his mind. He wondered if other civilians in this control room might be directing the Enemy troops in a similar fashion.

Safe in their protected bunkers, these isolated civilians played the deadly war like a game, an exercise. They'd lived here for so long, so comfortably, they seemed uninterested in winning the conflict or ending the crisis ... merely in maintaining what they already had.

"So you see, Barto," Juliette said, touching his arm again; this time he did not withdraw so quickly, "we understand what you go through. We're familiar with the war, we're there with you inside your head during even the most terrible missions. We know how difficult it is for the soldiers." She smiled. "That's why I'm very glad to offer you asylum here. Stay with us." Now she sounded coy. "I'd be ... very interested in getting to know you better."

Arviq glowered, out of his element. The chaperone next to him nodded toward Juliette, and she said, "You see, Gunnar is also taking good care of your comrade. Stay here. Consider it well-deserved R&R."

Barto looked around, saw the controllers, heard the familiar command voices. He answered gruffly, "I'm a soldier. I follow orders." Even if it meant he must stop fighting for a while.

*   *   *

Once the two prisoners had resigned themselves to their situation, they were allowed to speak with each other, though neither Barto nor Arviq had ever had much use for conversation. For a week they had made no violent gestures and learned to "behave themselves"—as Juliette described it. As a reward, Barto and Arviq were allowed to sit next to each other in the dining hall.

The room was a large chamber with plush seats and long tables. Lights sparkled from prisms overhead, and the air was redolent with the rich smells of exotic dishes. Various salads and broiled fishes and interesting soups were spread before them. The hall echoed with a murmur of voices.

In his training sessions, Barto learned about the horrors of being a POW, should such a fate ever befall him. But he was now confused, not sure which orders to follow, what was the proper course of action. Juliette had insisted he was their honored guest, not a prisoner. Should he still try to escape? These civilians had given him food and shelter, and a soft bed, though he desperately wanted his narrow basket-bunk back. He longed for the decisive voice in his ears that commanded him to do his duty—but Barto no longer knew exactly what his duty was.

Arviq looked at his plate and poked at the gaudy, frilly dishes that had been served to him. Other soft-skinned civilians walked by, staring at them, whispering to each other. One reached out to touch Arviq on the shoulder, as if on a dare; the soldier lashed out like a python, and the two observers scampered away giggling, as if titillated by the thrill they'd just received.

Barto felt as if he and his point man were on display, specimens for a zoo ... or humiliated members of a captured Enemy force, dragged before the public as trophies. Shrouded in silence, Arviq seemed to be doing a slow burn as he sat staring at his food, glaring at the other people.

Barto tried to calm himself. His own emotions seemed so much flatter since he'd been brought underground, his mind dulled—as if the adrenaline pump, endorphin enhancers, even his root survival instincts had been neutralized. Listening to the muted drone of conversation and music around them, he thought back longingly to the cacophony in the mess hall at his old barracks.

He remembered the clatter of metal trays, the crash of armorplates as soldiers jostled each other. With wordless camaraderie, the squad members sat on hard benches, grabbed their utensils, and gobbled their tasteless food. Together, they recharged their batteries and stoked the fires that they would need for combat in their next mission.

While none of the soldiers knew each other very well, each knew his place in life, his purpose ... and his Enemy. These underground civilians had nothing to compare with that.

Juliette sauntered up to them, her elfin features positively glowing, as if Barto's presence had increased her own standing among her people. She walked with her tall friend, Gunnar, who had spent days escorting Arviq. She looked down at the food on Barto's plate, and clucked in a mock scolding tone that he should eat more.

Barto felt a strange sensation in his stomach and heart, as if he were basking in the sunlight of her presence. How could Juliette make him feel proud that she had chosen him for her special attentions? He had never been singled out for anything before.

On the days when Juliette brought him to the breakfast hall, Barto was glad to see her, eager to hear her voice, just to look upon her face.

As his senses had become accustomed to his environment, his tongue relished the taste of fresh fruits and breads. The flower scents in the air smelled sweet, and he didn't flinch when Juliette touched him this time, taking him by the elbow. He liked the softness of her fingertips, the way they moved up and down his arm. He felt that he wanted to be even closer to her, to allow her into the walled fortress of himself.

"Do you like it with us here?" Juliette said with a hopeful, even plaintive, lilt to her voice. Ignoring Arviq, she touched the lumpy intaglio of scars on his forearm, tracing patterns and imagining his terrible wounds, as if she had never seen such marks before. "I'd like for you to stay with us, Barto ... with me." She reached across the table to clasp his hand, and he felt the urge to withdraw. What was she doing?

Gunnar's narrow face seemed drawn and concerned. He shook his head gravely. "You know how he's been trained. You know what this man has been through. He's not a toy for you, Juliette."

"I know exactly what he is," she answered. They both talked as if Barto wasn't even there. "And that doesn't change my wishes one bit."

With intent, flicking eyes, Barto followed the conversation, the conflict. If Juliette wanted him to stay here—and he vehemently wished that she did— then he would stay.

He'd seen the control chambers, the computer screens. He knew that these were the ultimate commanders of the war, the people who issued the instructions through his helmet speakers. His job had been to defend these civilians, to protect them ... and if Juliette should happen to give him leave to stop the fighting and stay here, with her, then he would follow orders.

Moving around behind him at the dining table, Juliette held out a large purple flower, its petals like a soft starburst. With particular care, she slid it into the close-cropped dark hair behind his right ear. Then she clapped at her audacity and at the spectacle she had made. He flushed.

Barto did not remove the flower, knowing it was somehow special to Juliette. The other civilians in the dining hall spoke to each other, pleased and entertained. Then Juliette danced away with tall Gunnar beside her, leaving the two soldiers to continue eating under the scrutiny of the curious observers.

Arviq looked across the table at him, scowling at his comrade's behavior. He narrowed his flinty eyes at the flower in Barto's hair. "You look like a fool," he growled, and snatched it away.

*   *   *

Back in his too-peaceful quarters with the door sealed and locked from the outside, he lay on his too-comfortable bed and then finally curled up on the hard floor. He would sleep better that way. ...

He dreamed of other times, when there hadn't been so much peace, when he had felt alive and useful and necessary. Where he had known his place in the world.

After one particularly furious foray, he, Arviq, and five other squad members crept ahead, continuing to approach the blasted Enemy territory even after the main conflict was over. They followed trails of blood and footprints, drag marks left by the bloodhounds that had come to retrieve the bodies of Enemy soldiers.

In the dream, Barto increased his visor's sensitivity to search for infrared traces of organic waste or warm blood droplets. The enhanced bloodhounds were not trained to cover their trails, and with their heavy, mangled burdens, they left a path that was easy to follow, even across the blistered landscape.

The squad followed the trail back to a shielded Enemy encampment. Barto and his comrades prided themselves in their bravery (or foolhardiness), and they charged into the bunkers with their weapons drawn, their adrenaline packs tuned to full output. Their laser-lances blasted the hinges off the doors and made short work of the plasrock bricks that shored up the damaged buildings.

Within moments, Barto's squad had breached the outer defenses and came in firing. No mercy. Many Enemy soldiers were still in their armor, but their weapons were locked in recharging racks. Others fought hand-to-hand, never giving up.

Barto's team suffered heavy losses, but during the fight he was dizzy with exhilaration. By himself, he vanquished fifteen of the Enemy soldiers; altogether, his squad destroyed the entire outpost. Total victory.

Throughout the combat exercise, during the screams and explosions, the violence and death, Barto had felt a sure camaraderie between his fellow soldiers. He never let doubt enter his mind, never a question. He knew exactly what he was doing here.

The Enemy bloodhounds, locked in their small home-kennels, bayed until Arviq cut them all down. The dogs seemed to know they had been responsible for betraying their masters' location.

With a resounding cheer of triumph, the survivors of Barto's team gave a shout to celebrate the defeat of the Enemy. Then, as part of a ritual for such infrequent but absolute victories, the men reached down to tear the helmets off the Enemy corpses, taking them for souvenirs.

Barto removed the helmet from the soldier he had just killed, then looked down to see the visage of the Enemy.

In his dream, the face belonged to Juliette.

*   *   *

As days of contained rage and frustration built within him, Arviq found that he didn't even need the supplemental adrenaline pump from his dismantled armor. This was all wrong! His blood boiled, his anger rose into a thunderstorm of fury—and he unleashed it upon the walls, the bed, anything in his room. His cell.

Arviq didn't want to be a prisoner of war. He wanted to fight, to kill the Enemy. He had been bred and trained for nothing else.

The quiet stillness of this underground civilian world, the soft fabrics, the perfumes, and the too-tasteful food ... all pushed him into a frenzy. He tore the coverings off his bed and thrashed about, ripping the sheets to shreds. He howled and screamed without words, a bestial cry of damnation. He pounded on the door, but it only rattled in its grooves. Then he threw himself upon the bedframe itself, yanking and pulling, until finally he uprooted it from the walls.

He didn't know if anyone was watching him, nor did he care.

Arviq hurled himself against the metal wall, battering his shoulders, bruising his muscles, but feeling no pain. His body was accustomed to running on the ragged edge of energy, and he had been resting here for days, storing up power in his muscles. Now he released it all in his frenzy.

His attack made marks on the wall, left some smears of his own blood. His fists caused dents. The sealed door rattled again in its tracks; it seemed looser now. He pounded and pounded, receiving no answer.

Finally, Arviq returned to the ruined bedframe, wrenching free a strip of metal that he could use as a crowbar. He had to escape. He had to get back. He didn't belong here.

He wedged the ragged end of torn metal into the door track and pushed, prying ... bending. The door began to buckle, and Arviq worked even harder.

*   *   *

After his nightmares had left him like exorcised demons, Barto fell into a deep slumber and awoke incredibly refreshed. Sometime in the middle of the night he had crawled back into his bed and rested peacefully.

A soldier had to be flexible, had to adapt to new circumstances. At last, he had begun to do just that.

When Gunnar and Juliette came to fetch him, he sensed their strain. The other civilians continued to stare at him, as they had done for days, but now they held a greater glint of fear in their eyes, a more uncertain look on their faces. Barto couldn't understand it, because for the first time since he'd come to this place of sanctuary, he felt more relaxed, more at ease, as if his life had indeed changed.

Seeing how the underground people had changed, how their attitude toward him had shifted, Barto knew something must have occurred. He could sense it. "What has happened?" he said.

Gunnar looked at him and answered crisply, "Your friend Arviq has gone on a rampage. He broke out of his room, and he's escaped."

Barto bolted to his feet. He understood Arviq's impulses. He had felt them himself, and now alarm bells rang out in his head. "What has he done?"

Juliette took a deep breath and blinked her deep brown eyes, as if the subject itself made her uncomfortable. "He broke his way out of the room. He smashed some windows in the corridors, destroyed one of our greenhouses. That was an hour or so ago. No one has seen him since."

Barto pushed his half-finished breakfast away and stood tall and strong. Called back to active duty. He didn't need any more sustenance, no more food to distract him. His mind became focused again, delving into the old hunter/survival mentality.

"I know how he thinks, and I know what he's doing," Barto said. "You cannot let him get away."

"We can't stop him," Gunnar said. "He'd kill all of us if we tried."

Barto shook his head. "You don't understand what Arviq can do, or what will happen if he gets away from this place. You can't just ignore him." Then he looked over at Juliette again. He finally admitted to himself that she was beautiful.

"Can you stop him?" Juliette said. "It would be to protect us."

"I will need my armor and my helmet if I'm going to do this right."

*　　*　　*

At first the armor felt rough and strange, but, rapidly, Barto adopted it as a second skin. The protective covering belonged; as much a part of him as his bones and muscles.

Looking at her soldier, Juliette wore a concerned expression, as if he had too easily stepped over the brink. Barto saw something unreadable deep within her brown eyes, a flush on her elfin face, as he picked up the helmet. He looked at her uncertainly one last time, then seated it firmly on his head. He pressed the side speakers against his ears, lowering the visor in place so that he looked at her through filters and scanning devices instead of his own eyes.

Barto drew a deep breath, stretching his chest against the breastplate armor plate. He flexed his arms against the hard bicep plates, the forearm protections, the gauntlets. His torso was solid and impenetrable. His legs and back, shoulders, hips, everything could withstand the worst that Arviq threw against him.

Barto was invincible.

"I must stop him before he leaves," he said. "He'll report the location of this place to HQ."

Juliette hesitated, moved forward and then stopped, as if she wanted to embrace him but was afraid to. Barto was glad she didn't. He didn't want to get close to her like this.

The tall chaperone, Gunnar, stood beside her, his face grim, and he drew her back. "Let him go now, Juliette. He has a mission."

Barto turned and marched out of the room, summoning up his mental map of the underground civilian sanctuary. He would begin in Arviq's quarters, where the point man had smashed his own room and broken loose. It would not be too difficult to pick up his former comrade's trail. Barto knew how to track down a quarry.

Leaving the other inhabitants behind, he followed the tunnels. Most of the civilians reacted with fear when they saw him now. They hid within their own quarters or clustered together in the communal halls, though only one unarmed soldier had gone on a rampage. It was all beyond their experience.

All of these people cowered down here, helpless. And Barto was the only one who could protect them.

Though Arviq had not been able to retrieve his armor or his weapons, Barto did not underestimate him. A properly trained soldier could fashion defensive materials out of just about anything.

At the pried-open door, he stood motionless, assessing Arviq's damaged room, saw how his comrade had wrenched open the barricade using a piece of the bedframe as a lever, how he had battered the walls with his bare hands. Barto saw blood, but knew that Arviq would pay no attention to such minor cuts and bruises. Not Arviq.

Barto had seen him through much worse.

One time on a reconnaissance and destruction mission, Barto and his point man had ventured into the crumbling ruins of what must have been an impossibly large building, now scarred, empty, and blasted. The structure had fallen into rubble with haphazard girders and broken glass protruding from poured stone walls.

They had chased several Enemies into the wreckage. Their senses screamed that it was probably an ambush, but still the two soldiers had followed, weapons drawn, confident that they could defeat their opponents. He and Arviq separated and traveled along different passageways, using their scanners to pick up infrared footprint traces.

Barto had proceeded cautiously, but Arviq, incensed and determined, charged through the darkened halls, knocking wreckage aside. Finally he had crashed down a rickety iron staircase that shattered into rust as he stepped on it. And he dropped through to the underlevels....

When Barto had found him later, he saw that Arviq had broken his left leg in two places and had sprained his right ankle. His helmet visor was cracked and damaged—yet still Arviq had pulled himself along to find the Enemy. He certainly had.

Though severely injured and at an extreme disadvantage, Arviq had slaughtered both of the Enemy soldiers. ...

From their missions together, Barto knew that his comrade was utterly relentless, feeling no pain and no fatigue. Nothing would stop him from escaping the underground enclave. He would never give up.

And neither would Barto give up. He was the only thing that could keep this civilian paradise protected and intact.

He strode out and moved briskly along the corridors. His bootsteps ricocheted off the metal walls. Arviq had smashed windows and thrown loose objects from side to side, leaving a painfully clear trail—until he had learned better and sensibly stopped his rampage.

Then tracking him became more of a challenge. Barto called up a detailed implanted map of all the underground corridors, which Juliette had added to the information systems in his helmet.

Arviq was running blind, by instinct, just trying to escape, but his movements displayed a pattern. On the map gleaming inside his visor, Barto could see the best paths, learn where to go ... where to intercede.

Arviq didn't have a chance against a fully armed, fully outfitted soldier, like Barto.

He marched along, his senses tuned to a high pitch. He moved carefully in case the other soldier had set up some kind of booby-trap or ambush. That was to be expected. Arviq must know Barto would come after him.

Because the other soldier was without his armor, his bare feet left a trail of infrared images on the clean floorplates. The marks were old and fading, but still identifiable with Arviq's genetic signature: droplets of sweat, skin particles, even stride length gave evidence of his passage. The other man was still bleeding from one of the cuts he'd inflicted upon himself in escaping from the room; occasionally a telltale crimson droplet reinforced Barto's tracking.

The control voice returned, insistent and self-confident. It comforted Barto, who had lived his conscious life hearing the words: "KILL THE ENEMY! KILL THE ENEMY! KILL THE ENEMY!" He no longer felt so alone.

According to the map display, Arviq had made it to within several hundred meters of the long access ladder that led up a shaft to the outside—the battleground where their squad had been killed.

But Barto also knew he had cornered his quarry.

At an intersection of the dimly lit corridors, a framework of girders and support beams held up the ceiling. The place had been long-abandoned by the underground civilians.

Barto's visor-sensors detected a large smear of blood at floor level in a corner, as if Arviq had rested there ... or as if he had encountered an Enemy, and they had struggled, hand-to-hand. The blood was fresh, wet, warm in IR—like a sign emblazoned there to draw his attention.

Too late, he realized the ambush. From the shadowed support girders above, Arviq let out a loud cry and dropped on top of him. Though he had no armor and no weapons, the other soldier crashed down upon him with brute force. Barto might have found the conflict absurd if Arviq hadn't been so determined, so passionate—if the other man hadn't been his own comrade for so long.

Arviq wrapped his left arm in a vice-lock around Barto's neck, trying to wrench the helmet off his head. With his other hand he tried to grab one of the ID-locked weapons sealed in armored holsters on Barto's hips.

Barto rose up like a tank, as if his armor gave him stimulus and energy, though Juliette had told him his artificial adrenaline pumps were disconnected from the suit.

Inside his ears, the helmet commanders shouted, 'KILL THE ENEMY! KILL THE ENEMY! DON'T LET HIM ESCAPE!" With a weird disorientation, Barto thought the voice sounded like Gunnar's.

Without letting go, Arviq fought like a wild thing, clamping his knees on either side of Barto's armored chest, trying to tear the helmet off. When Barto staggered backward, slamming his comrade against the metal wall, Arviq let out an explosive exhale of pain and surprise. Barto recovered his balance and slammed him against the wall a second time.

Arviq struggled, but would not let go. He continued pounding with naked fists against the impenetrable armor.

"Come with me!" Arviq shouted loudly enough to penetrate the heavy ear coverings, to break through the harsh command voice. "Let's go back to HQ. Back to our lives, Barto! We don't belong here."

Barto bent over and butted him against the wall, hearing ribs crack this time. Arviq's grip finally loosened. He wheezed in pain, coughed blood. "Let me go then. Just let me run from here. I'll leave." Arviq slumped to one side and scrambled to his feet. Blood from his raw wounds smeared Barto's scuffed armor.

"Can't let you do that," Barto answered. "You must stay here. The commanders gave their orders. Defy them, and you're a traitor."

Arviq stood up, glaring at him. His face was uncovered, his emotions unmasked. "This isn't what we were made for. We are soldiers. War is our life. Not this ... where we're pets on display." Barto had never really studied his comrade's face before. "What happens when they get bored with us?"

Barto pressed his gloved palm against the hilt of his ID-coded blaster weapon. The device detected its proper owner and released its grip in the holster. Barto yanked the weapon free, held it in his hand.

Not far down the corridor, he could see the tarnished rungs that rose up the dark shaft. It would take so little for Arviq to scramble up the ladder, pop the heavy hatch—and be out, all alone on the blasted battlefield. Without armor or weapons, he didn't have much chance of survival—but Arviq seemed desperate enough to take that option.

Arviq gathered himself up, glared at his former comrade and stepped away. "I know what I am, and what to do." With the back of his hand, he wiped a smear of blood from his mouth. "Which one of us is the traitor, truly?" He turned and, moving slowly, not threateningly, took a step toward the ladder, the escape.

Barto raised the weapon. "Halt."

Arviq turned to look at him with flinty, determined eyes. "I'm dead down here anyway. If I can't get back onto the battlefield, then you may as well blast me now."

Barto powered up his weapon.

The other soldier took two more steps down the corridor.

Inside the helmet, Gunnar's voice shouted, "KILL THE ENEMY! DON'T LET HIM ESCAPE. YOU MUST PROTECT US. KILL HIM!" Barto leveled the blaster at the target.

Then he heard another voice—Juliette's—muffled and distant, but coming closer. She cried out, running down the long-abandoned corridors toward him. "Don't shoot, Barto. You must learn not to kill if you're going to stay here."

"KILL! KILL!" Gunnar's voice bellowed.

Arviq turned as Juliette appeared, all alone, her elfin face distraught. Then he used the moment of distraction to a dash toward the rungs.

"KILL!" shouted the voice in Barto's ears again. And he did.

Depressing the firing stud, he blasted his former comrade in the back as he ran. Arviq had no armor, no protection whatsoever. The bolt flared out and incinerated him, turning the other man into a smoking pile of burned bones and cooked flesh that fell in a heap on the floor, as if still trying to run.

"No!" Juliette cried out, but it sounded like a pout. Barto turned to see her standing there. Her expression was stricken, and then even more terrified as he faced her, the charged weapon still in his hand. "I wanted you to stay here with me," she said. "It's a better life, but you've got to learn not to kill. Stay away from violence. You've earned it. You could live here with me in peace and enjoy your life, escape the horrors of war."

"They're not horrors," Barto said in a flat voice. He refused to take off his helmet. He was a soldier now, fully armed, ready to fight. "It's the only thing I know." He holstered the warm blaster. "I can't stay here as a prisoner of war."

"But you're a free man among us," Juliette pleaded, refusing to come closer. She seemed as much confused as saddened. She couldn't understand why he would make this choice.

"I am still a prisoner," he said. "War holds me prisoner." He stood at attention, as if the feline spies were watching him from the shadows.

"I must live by fighting, and I must die by fighting. I have no way to escape that."

He understood now that this place, despite its comforts and its new experiences, could not possibly be for him. Not for a soldier.

He didn't begrudge Juliette her civilian life, her pampered existence—and if these people were indeed the commanders in the war, if he was a soldier charged with protecting them, then he must go back and do his duty until death inevitably claimed him on the battlefield. And if he should happen to survive, then he would grow old and train other soldiers until the war was won and the Enemy completely vanquished.

There was nothing else for him to do.

Juliette watched him with despair, then a flash of anger in her brown eyes. Finally, her slender shoulders drooped in defeat. She said nothing else, just watched him with a flush in her cheeks.

Barto didn't know what he had really meant to her ... if he had merely been a trophy from the battlefield, something that increase her prestige among her people—or if she had really cared for him, in a way.

At the moment it didn't matter. It was irrelevant information.

Leaving his dead comrade behind, sad that the bloodhounds could never retrieve Arviq and take him back to where he could be buried with full military honors, Barto climbed the rungs of the ladder.

It was a long way to the surface, but when he released the hatch and climbed out under the open, bruised sky, he stared for a long moment. He breathed the burnt air, studied the roiling dust from distant explosions.

He lifted his visor to stare out across the stricken field with his own eyes, then he shut the hatch behind him, sealing Juliette and her world underground, keeping her secret safe. And then he strode off, heading in the direction of his HQ.

It would feel good to get back to the business of fighting once again.

ABOUT THE AUTHOR

Kevin J. Anderson has published 120 books, more than fifty of which have been national or international bestsellers. He has written numerous novels in the Star Wars, X-Files, and Dune universes, as well as a unique steampunk fantasy novel, Clockwork Angels, which is based on the new concept album by legendary rock group Rush. His original works include the Saga of Seven Suns series, the Terra Incognita fantasy trilogy, and his humorous horror series featuring Dan Shamble, Zombie PI. He has edited numerous anthologies, including the *Five by Five* series. Anderson and his wife Rebecca Moesta are the publishers of WordFire Press. Wordfirepress.com.

REARDON'S LAW

BRAD R. TORGERSEN

CHAPTER 1

Rain tumbled gently against the lifeboat's small canopy. Kalliope Reardon was aware of the sound, but only in a detached sense. It had been a hard reentry, and a harder landing. Her brain and nervous system weren't quite ready to connect all the dots yet. Despite the crash cocoon which had enveloped her during the fall, thus saving her life.

And what a fall it had been.

She'd barely had time to hurl herself through the lifeboat's hatch before the lifeboat itself had been blown free of Kal's ship, the *Broadbill*.

End over end the lifeboat had spun through space, its trajectory arcing down towards the nameless, uncharted planet below.

Now, there was darkness.

And the quiet pattering of thick water droplets on the lifeboat's scorched hull.

Kal knew it was not a good idea to stay put.

The people who had destroyed the *Broadbill* would be looking for her.

Or, rather, her lifeboat's automated beacon.

For all she knew, they were already on their way.

Kal attempted to move her arms. The inflatable balloons of the crash cocoon held her as securely as a straightjacket.

Kal concentrated hard, and attempted to speak.

"Com—pyoo ... com ... compyoo ... *computer*," she finally said with a dull, rubbery tongue.

The happy chime of the lifeboat's automated response told Kal that she'd been acknowledged. She swallowed thickly, then flexed her jaw, like a patient who's just come out of the dentist's office.

"Computer," Kal said again, this time more slowly, but with added surety. "Release ... emergency ... restraining system."

At once, the balloons surrounding Kal began to deflate.

The outer shroud of the cocoon slowly peeled away, and Kal got a look through the canopy itself. A misty haze greeted her outside, while wide rivulets of clear liquid ran across the transparent canopy's dome.

The little display panel at the canopy's edge—which was connected to an external sensor—glowed a bright green.

Nitrogen and oxygen atmosphere.

No detectable toxins.

Though, water and oxygen together meant chlorophyll. *Life*.

An alien ecology, for which Kal's immune system might not be prepared.

She considered.

Like any other Conflux Armed Forces troop being deployed into the Occupied Zone, Kal had been given a battery of xeno-bio inoculations. Stuff so potent that the running joke in the ranks said: if the alien germs didn't eat you up from the inside, the shots themselves surely would.

In times past, Kal had found such morbid barracks humor funny.

Now, she wasn't laughing.

Once she cracked the lifeboat's hatch, she'd be exposing herself to whatever lay beyond. Would it be a death sentence? Or did she dare stay put, and hope for official rescue?

No, that was a silly thought.

The mission plan had been clear.

There would be no help.

CHAPTER 2

"Reardon," Kal's boss said as he reached across the table and up-ended a bottle over her glass, "I won't lie to you. This is going to be a tough one."

"Do tell," Kal said, waiting for him to finish refreshing her drink. The refill was a formality. She'd barely touched her cup since entering her boss's office ten minutes prior. Her uniform remained crisp and pressed, with calf-length boots polished to a high gloss, and not a badge nor a pin out of place.

It wasn't Kal's typical wardrobe, given her occupation as a Special Investigative Officer with the Conflux Armed Forces. She was used to working in duty uniforms or civilian clothes—a highly-trained military cop as adept at busting organized criminals and civilian perps as she was at cleaning up the CAF's own internal trash.

But one didn't meet one's immediate supervisor in his inner sanctum while looking like a hobo from the launch docks.

Upon landing, Kal had gone directly to the Guest Officers Quarters on base, stowed her travel bag, then hit the automated grooming station at the GOQ's south end. Kal now sported closely-cropped regulation-length hair, with nails trimmed down to the quick, and all fake tattoos and false-color eye lenses removed. For the first time in many Earth months.

There was a promotion board coming up. Kal had been putting off getting her digital packet together. The official image in her old packet was at least three Earth years out of date. She toyed with the idea of having her boss use his desk's AV unit to snap a few photos—as long as she was looking sharp. Who knew when she'd be this cleaned up again?

Stow it, Kal thought. There were more important things to worry about. Questions that needed answering. Such as: what sort of job would require an *in-person* briefing? Given the huge delay and expense involved in dragging her light-years away from her last assignment?

Ordinarily, Chief Investigative Officer Damont's orders came through the digitally-secure CAF network. A job here, a job there, with attached paperwork for flights and safe passage both on and off-world, anywhere in the Conflux.

Brad R. Torgersen

In fact, Kal could count on one hand the number of times she'd seen her boss face-to-face—in the six Earth years she'd been working for him.

While Kal was always on the move, Damont tended to stay in one place. Keeping his invisible strings attached to his dozens of Special Investigators via the Conflux's circulating fleet of automated data transports: an interstellar pony express that moved information between the worlds of the Conflux at speeds thousands of times faster than mere radio transmissions.

Damont put the bottle back on his desk, picked up his own cup, and tipped back a healthy swallow—which he ran around the inside of one cheek, before gulping it down.

"Tremonton Universal has been losing classified equipment shipments," he said.

Kal blinked. Tremonton was the multi-world manufacturing corporation that provided the CAF with much of its military hardware, including cutting-edge armor, aerospace fighters, and other toys. So large and spread out were the company's assets, that it operated its own security force. Kal knew. She'd worked with them before.

"Shipments to where?" Kal asked.

Damont shifted in his high-backed chair.

"The Occupied Zone," he said.

Kal sat up straight.

"What the hell is Tremonton doing sending equipment into Oz?"

"You've not previously been made aware of this—so everything I'm about to discuss with you must be held in strictest confidence—but Tremonton has been working with the CAF to test-drive some of Tremonton's latest armor. Under realistic battle conditions. They're doing it in Oz."

"Realistic?" Kal exclaimed, picking up her cup and taking a healthy gulp of her own. "The Occupied Zone is a feral sea. We didn't pacify anything during the war. We merely knocked down some of their bigger cities, then cut those planets off from each other with the blockade. Sir, I've been into Oz, and I can tell you, if it's 'realistic battle conditions' Tremonton wanted, then it's realistic battle conditions Tremonton will get."

"I know," he said. "And it's your familiarity with the Occupied Zone that's the main reason I picked you for this job. I need someone with experience. Someone who can slip into the black market network that evades the blockade—don't look surprised, of course I know all

98

about that—then pick up the trail left by this missing Tremonton hardware."

"Sir, finding missing armaments in Oz will be like looking for a needle in a haystack. Whatever's been taken to date, it's liable to never surface again. The remnants of the Ambit League will be eager to pick apart any advanced gadgetry they can lay their hands on—to see if the technology can be adapted for their own use."

"I know. Which is why this job has the top-most priority," Damont said, pursing his lips in a concerned expression.

"Better to roll in a battle flotilla," Kal said. "Make a show of force. Deploy troops. Shake Oz down. If this missing equipment is that sensitive, nothing short of a major offensive will recover it."

"It's not that simple," Damont said.

"And why not?"

There was a telling silence as Kal's boss shifted in his seat again.

"Neither Tremonton nor their liaison with the CAF want any word of this missing equipment to get out to the general public," he said. "The Conflux went through hell putting down the Ambit League. And the civilian population is easily spooked as a result. The next election cycle will be coming up, and there are people in the Conflux Assembly on Earth who are eager to make sure there is no substance to any rumors about a second war."

Kal stood up and walked over to where her boss had a couch against the far wall. A gently animated image of a nameless gas giant planet was mounted over the couch. She stared at the bands of the gas giant's clouds as they slowly swirled and rotated.

"There's more," Damont said. "I've got reason to believe that someone inside the CAF is working against us on this. I'm hoping that if you can sniff out who, from the inside, then I can order some arrests and we can plug a hole in our ranks."

"Sympathizers?" Kal said, somewhat incredulously. "With the Ambit League?"

"Or they're greedy," Damont said. "People who have cash note symbols in their eyes."

"Then it'll take more than just me," Kal said, her face still fixed towards the digital painting.

"I know," Damont said. "That's why you're taking someone new with you."

Kal jerked her chin over her shoulder.

"You're saddling me with a *rookie?* I thought you said this was a top-priority mission?"

"It is, but he's no ordinary rookie. He's a CAF Reservist who also works for Tremonton. A test pilot. Knows all about the armor design in question. In fact, they were going to send him into Oz to put some of that armor through its paces. Then the shipments began to turn up missing. He's got a high-security clearance, and has been vetted through both Tremonton and CAF channels."

"That's all well and good, sir," Kal said, turning on a heel and pacing back and forth in front of the couch, "but it doesn't help me figure out where to start. With over a dozen habitable worlds in Oz, across twenty star systems, somebody's going to have to point me in the right direction, or I might as well stay home."

"There's a man already on the inside," Damont said. "Someone I've been monitoring closely."

"One of ours?" Kal asked.

"Yes. Or at least, he used to be. CAF veteran. Brilliant service record. When the war was declared over, he signed on with one of the civilian relief organizations that went into Oz to try to pick up the pieces. He vanished shortly afterward. But then he reappeared. Feeding information covertly to CAF Intelligence, about the activities of the Ambit League. He knows where those shipments might have been taken."

"And my pilot? Is he going to *fly* the stolen armor back home? One suit at a time?"

"Don't be silly," Damont snapped. "If it's true the Ambit League is reverse-engineering this stolen equipment, CAF Central Command wants to know about it. Both they and the Tremonton corporate people want an experienced person on the scene, who can evaluate first-hand whatever it is the Ambit League may be trying to cobble together in Oz."

"You said he's Reserve?" Kal said.

"Yes."

"Does he have any covert training? Battle experience?"

"No."

"Terrific. And my contact inside Oz? Is he reliable?"

"I don't really know. I think so, yes."

"You *think* so?"

This time it was Damont who stood up out of his chair and began to pace.

"I'm sorry, Kalliope, but I really can't get more specific than that. You're right. If the Central Command wasn't following Assembly orders not to make a ruckus, then I'd pitch this mess over to the fleet people and let them marshal a few combat brigades, at the very least. But we've all been given strict instructions to handle this matter quietly. And quickly. Tremonton says it's going to halt shipments until the matter is resolved, but without those shipments the testing can't be completed, which means the Assembly's Defense Office won't sign off on the contracts for the new design."

"Which means Tremonton doesn't get its money," Kal said, sighing.

"You always were quick on the uptake," Damont said.

Kal remained where she was, chin on her chest. So the matter was multi-dimensional: economic, as well as political.

When Kal didn't say anything more, her boss cleared his throat in a mildly uncomfortable fashion.

"If you don't think you're up to it," Damont said, "I can always find somebody else."

"Not quickly enough to make a difference," Kal said. "We've already wasted enough time bringing me here, so there'd be no point sending me back. You knew I'd not turn down the orders because you knew once you explained it to me that I'd have no choice but to say yes."

Damont merely had a slight, knowing smile on his face.

Kal momentarily considered punching her boss in the teeth.

Instead, she breathed deeply, then exhaled very slowly.

"Okay," she said. "Let's have it then. A full mission dossier."

Damont slid a wafer drive across his desk.

Kal walked over and picked the drive up in her left hand, testing its flexible holographic memory crystals between her thumb and forefinger.

"One more thing, Kal," Damont said.

"A catch?" she said, eyebrow raised.

"Yes, I am afraid. Because this is such a sensitive job, I can't promise you any parachutes. Once you're inside Oz, you're officially on your own. There won't be any CAF quick-reaction teams ready to break down someone's front door and pull you out."

Kal continued to press the wafer drive between her thumb and forefinger.

She allowed a tiny grin to slip across her lips.

"You didn't bring me all this way because I need someone else to hold my hand for me."

She picked up her cup and raised it.

Damont did the same.

And together they emptied their glasses.

CHAPTER 3

Kal crawled quietly through the piles of rotting plant debris. She was five days out of a shower, and covered in scrapes and cuts. The trek through the forest hadn't been an easy one. Once she'd made the decision to abandon the lifeboat and set out on foot, there'd been only one choice: wait for any sign that her attackers had come down from orbit, then try to locate them and hitch a ride back to space. Otherwise she'd be marooned for life in a place that wasn't even on the Conflux's pioneer world charts.

Kal didn't know if anyone else had survived the destruction of the *Broadbill*. If they had, she didn't owe them any favors. Thief's justice, more or less.

Except for Tim. The Reservist hadn't deserved to die.

Kal closed her eyes briefly and tried to block him out of her mind. She didn't need anything distracting her.

She pulled the tiny emergency transponder device out of her makeshift harness and examined the reading on its tiny screen. The device could either broadcast actively, or receive passively. She'd been using it for two days to track the signal coming from a very large ship which had passed over her lifeboat's landing site the day after she abandoned it.

That ship was her key to escaping.

As well as continuing the mission.

Moving slowly and deliberately, Kal neared the lip of a ledge in the forest floor. Over her head, the sky was partially occluded by the mass of trees that towered a hundred meters into the air, darkening the ground.

Her abused spacer's coverall was damp and filthy, with holes at the elbows and knees. All she had to work with was the small emergency backpack from the lifeboat, her issue P3110 pistol in its holster, and five magazines for the pistol, worth ten shots each.

Not ideal armament, under the circumstances.

Kal would have preferred tactical artillery instead.

Dead leaves clung to Kal's skin like wet paper. She peered intently over the lip of the ledge. Half a kilometer distant, the mighty trees had been flattened in a rough halo under the belly of the enemy craft. Which was mammoth. A metal whale on stilts. The heat tiles of the ship were grossly discolored from its many, many in-atmosphere trips. Underneath the vessel—between its massive landing pylons—four personnel hatches lay open with four ramps extending down to the ground, like rusty tongues. There was also a fifth, much larger cargo hatch. Its wide ramp was populated with people moving crates up into the ship.

They appeared to be bringing the crates from somewhere deep in the tree line. Where Kal couldn't see.

They must have located the remnants of the *Broadbill?* Or at least the *Broadbill's* cargo?

Kal considered.

Getting into the ship unseen would be difficult. She needed a better look before she could make a plan.

Kal crept her way over the lip and slid several meters down a sharp slope until she re-entered the undergrowth. There she stayed absolutely still for several long minutes, waiting and listening for something—anything—that would tell her if she'd been spotted.

Satisfied that her presence went undetected, Kal renewed her glacial pace towards the freighter, guessing that if she took it slow, nightfall would come soon. And with it, her best chance to get up one of those ramps.

CHAPTER 4

The Reserve pilot's name was Tim Osterhaudt.

Young. Clever with his wit. But not cocky.

During the voyage out to the Conflux periphery—where the undefined border between civilization and the Occupied Zone lay—Kal got to know him. He was maybe eight years younger, and had not grown up on Earth. A colony boy. He passed through his secondary schooling with good grades, and then picked up a company scholarship from Tremonton. Which had funded him through both his civilian degree and test pilot school.

His nominal rank in the CAF Reserve was Lieutenant.

Technically, he outranked Kal.

Though, Kal made it clear up front that she was in charge, according to their specific orders from Chief Damont.

"No problem," Tim said, holding up his hands in a placating fashion as they talked quietly in their cabin aboard the starliner *Freefall.*

They had a single porthole which looked out into space. If Kal put her forehead to the transparent fiberflex of the porthole itself, she could look down to where the giant disc of the Blackmatter Drive lay.

Like all interstellar ships, the *Freefall* was essentially a skyscraper stacked on-end in the center of the Blackmatter Drive: a circular dish nearly as wide as the ship was long. All decks were arrayed perpendicular to the path of flight, so that when under thrust each deck enjoyed something akin to gravity. Though it was the Blackmatter Drive itself which formed the relativistic bubble—allowing the ship to slip beyond the light-speed barrier and travel at trans-light velocities.

The points of starlight outside were smeared, shifting from crowded and blue above to sparse and red at the bottom.

Kal and Tim were dressed in civilian travel jumpsuits customary for migrant technicians bound for one of the sanctioned space stations that serviced the Occupied Zone. They'd come aboard the *Freefall* with assumed names and false digital travel papers provided by Kal's boss.

Only Kal was armed.

Which didn't seem to bother Tim much. He thought the entire thing to be a rather daring bit of adventure. He just didn't like the idea of hurting anyone.

"So why'd you end up in the Reserve if you don't want to have to fight?" Kal asked.

"My CAF Reserve commission was a prerequisite of my job with Tremonton," he said, idly tapping his hands on his knees as a gentle stream of music issued from the small speakers at the head of his bunk. He had an unusual fascinating with the classics, for someone his age. His movements kept rhythm with the sound.

"This prototype testing in the Occupied Zone," Kal said, "it doesn't seem like you'd be able to avoid fighting there."

"They've got half a dozen pilots working the project," Tim said. "When I was assigned to go to the Zone, I asked that they put me on the secondary team that's charged with evaluating data being brought back from the field. All the pilots actually going out beyond the safety zone? Prior combat vets."

Kal nodded in understanding.

"Did you, uh, fight in the war?" Tim asked hesitantly.

"Yup," Kal said, laying on her back in her bunk across the cabin—eyes staring straight up at the ceiling.

"Ever have to ... uh ... well ..."

"What?" Kal asked.

"You know ... like ... shoot somebody?"

Kal closed her eyes and sighed.

"Never ask that question of a veteran, Tim. You should have been in the Reserve long enough to know that. There are a lot of veterans who went Reserve after the war. I am surprised nobody told you the rule."

"Rule?"

"The last thing anyone who's seen fighting wants to do is talk about how they were forced to kill somebody."

Tim remained silent for many long moments.

"Sorry," he finally said.

"No problem. I just thought you knew."

"The Reserve Officer Training Corps teaches a man many things, but some of the tacit stuff doesn't always translate. Hope I didn't make you uncomfortable."

"A little. Because the answer is yes."

Again, a long silence.

"They told me you're a military policewoman," Tim said finally. "That you spend a lot of time on cases both explicitly military, as well as tangentially military-related."

"That's true."

"So why aren't you commissioned?"

"I am commissioned, after a fashion. My job warrants it, I am not appointed like you were."

"What's the difference?"

"I often ask myself that same question."

Several beats later, Tim was chuckling. A pleasant sound.

There wasn't always a lot of laughter in Kal's line of work.

"If you fought in the war," Tim asked, "what's your opinion of the rumor that the Ambit League might renew hostilities?"

"So far as I am concerned," Kal said, "hostilities never ended. The survivors we left on the Occupied Zone worlds? A lot of them still think we're at war. The blockade pretty much makes it plain that the Conflux isn't giving them autonomy or allowing them to rejoin the interstellar economy any time soon."

"You sympathize with them?" Tim said, raising an eyebrow and sitting up to look at her.

"Hardly," Kal said. "I just think there's a bad way to manage the post-war effort and a good way to manage the post-war effort. To my mind, the good way to manage it would be to re-integrate the worlds of the Occupied Zone as soon as possible. Keeping the blockade up indefinitely just breeds contempt and hostility."

"But some of those planets *are* dangerous," Tim said.

"Correction, sir. Some of the *people* on those planets are dangerous. I know. I've been there. And the longer we treat the good folks in Oz the same way we treat the bad folks in Oz, the more the good folks swing over to the side of the bad folks. Pretty soon we've got nothing but bad folks. Does that make sense?"

"I think so," Tim said, his expression turning serious. "Sounds to me like it's a no-win situation. The Assembly won't be changing its policy any time soon. They're intent on reassuring the electorate that the Ambit League has been permanently destroyed."

"Right," Kal said. "Which is why you and I have been called up to perform this mission in the first place.

"Do you think we can really find the missing armor?" Tim asked.

Kal ran her tongue along the inside of a cheek.

"No. But we might find out where it went, or at least who's responsible for taking it. And who they might be working with on our side of the fence. My boss wants that information very badly. Recovery of the stolen hardware isn't a requirement for the mission to be a success. It's a bonus. If we do stumble across any of that missing armor, your job is to help figure out what the Ambit League might be doing with it."

CHAPTER 5

Hours passed.

Kal stayed low, using the gloaming of night and the blown-down trees to conceal herself. Rumbles of approaching thunder announced that the rain would start once more. Before long, a steady clobbering of fat, lens-like drops beat down on the enemy landing site.

Kal relished the cloudburst.

The noise and water would help conceal her from any sensors her foes had deployed around their ship.

Kal pushed forward into the drowning darkness—by feel.

Thirty more minutes passed.

Soaked to the bone and nearing exhaustion, Kal at last peeked up from behind a log, only to discover she was looking directly into the belly of the monstrous aerospace freighter—its boarding ramps lit by sodium lamps.

Kal looked nervously in all directions.

It was far too quiet for her tastes.

No sign of guards? That did not compute.

But Kal was committed, and there was no going back, only forward.

Mustering her courage, Kal tugged down on the straps to her shoulder holster, harness, and emergency pack, then crept over the edge of the log and sprinted towards the ship.

Kal stopped just as she hit the edge of illumination at the bottom of one ramp. Entering the full light for the first time, her skin crawled—she was totally exposed, and expected to hear voices and gunfire at any moment. But the shouts and bullets never came.

Senses tingling, Kal went up the ramp at a gentle trot.

The freighter's interior was messy.

Narrow corridors sprouted off in several directions, each decorated with exposed pipes, wiring, and ducts.

Kal pulled out her P3110 and worked the charging handle, loading a caseless round into the pistol's firing chamber. With safety off, she kept her finger outside the trigger guard and proceeded deeper into the guts of the ship, step by cautious step.

Kal moved through an inner hatchway and into a wider central corridor. Her eyes skipped around, looking for surveillance devices.

She found one recessed into the ceiling several meters ahead of her.

Kal froze—watching the camera and its bug-like eyes.

It appeared to be ignoring her.

She chewed on her bottom lip, then stepped forward once, and then back again.

The camera remained still.

Deactivated? On standby? Or just plain broken?

The hair stood up on the back of Kal's neck, but she moved onward. Most aerospace freighters didn't need a big crew, but there should have been *someone* aboard—people she'd have seen, or at least heard already.

Kal drew in a long breath, blew it out with puffed cheeks, and shook her head. This was no time to spook herself into doing something dumb. Perhaps the explosion in orbit had taken a lot of the enemy, as well as the *Broadbill* and its crew? How many people had crossed over the *Broadbill's* ship-to-ship gangway before the double-cross had gone down?

Kal didn't know.

Moving in her best impression of a cat, Kal crept down another passage: past some uniformly cabin-sized hatches—and then froze as another surveillance monitor suddenly loomed above her.

Kal stood on her toes to peer up at the device: the cables were corroded and the gears on the device's directional motor seemed non-functional.

What the hell?

It was then that Kal really began to take a good look around her.

In addition to the exposed ductwork and wiring, the deck plates were soiled and corroded, and many of the cabin doors behind her appeared to be rusted shut. Just how long had this ship been gathering dust somewhere on-planet, its hatches and vents open to the air? A lot of moisture had come in, and been allowed to sit. No doubt the Ambit

League was badly off, but it was still surprising to discover that they were willing to operate any old scow, however scrapworthy.

No wonder they were stealing armament—the League's home-grown industrial base must have collapsed. Another byproduct of the blockade. Cut the various manufacturing centers off from each other, and it would be enormously difficult to replicate spaceworthy equipment. At least on a large commercial scale.

Somewhat heartened by these assumptions, Kal crept on until she found a doorway that looked like it had been repaired to operational condition. She stepped close to it and peered in through the small pane of transparent fiberflex that gave her a view of the next compartment. She saw four people unpacking an unmarked interstellar shipping crate—the same kind Tremonton said they used to discretely move sensitive equipment.

Watching intently, Kal saw the people remove gauntlets and boots and other pieces of armor, all broken down for shipping. The people—Ambit League for sure—seemed to be sorting and separating the crate's contents, while other crates were stacked nearby and waiting to be opened. Kal shifted to the side and peered past the crew, realizing that she was looking into the primary hold of the freighter. It went on for almost a hundred meters, and was half as wide, plus half as tall. Crates littered the space. Almost all of them appeared to have been opened in a hurry.

Needles in haystacks, Kal thought, remembering her comment to her boss.

Kal stepped away from the hatch and turned to creep back the way she had come.

She froze.

The barrel of a pistol—somewhat newer and heavier in design than her P3110—was pointed at Kal's forehead, and a huge bearded man in a use-worn jumpsuit was smiling at her.

"What do we have here?" The man said. Kal gulped and felt her stomach sink into a bottomless pit.

"You're not one of Berd's people."

Who?

Kal's weapon was still in her hand, but her arm had been lowered and she didn't dare raise it lest she get a slug between the eyes.

"Drop the pistol," said the bearded man, eyes darting to Kal's gun.

"No," Kal said quietly.

Brad R. Torgersen

The man laughed. "Do we really have to do it like this? Drop your pistol or I'll use mine."

Kal looked past the man, saw no one, and then back into his eyes. They were older, but they didn't blink, and she slowly stooped down to the deck, noiselessly placing her P3110 on its side. Then stood back up.

The man stepped closer and prodded the barrel of his gun between her breasts, ordering her to raise her hands. Kal did as she was told, then backed up a few steps as the man pushed her down the corridor.

"Shoulda known there would be two of you," he said. "Didn't make much sense to stumble across just one CAF soldier. You always travel in pairs, isn't that right?"

"How would I know?" Kal said. But inside, she was doing a triple-take. *Two?* In an instant she realized that not only was Tim quite possibly alive, he was being held prisoner. Or worse. How could she find out where he was, or what shape he was in? She conjured a brief mental picture of crude torture techniques being used on the young Reservist, then blocked that image out and focused on her assailant.

"Well, your buddy can't help you now," said the man.

He suddenly reached out and attempted to get a handful of Kal's damp, clinging coverall. Kal slapped his hand away and he punched her in the face with his free hand. Seeing lights, Kal fell back and began to scramble down the passageway while her assailant laughed and kept his gun pointed at her.

"Fighting just makes it worse," he said. "You should ask my other girlfriends."

Kal flipped up off the deck and tried to put a boot in his groin, but he dodged and swept her legs, then jumped on top of her, pinning her face-down.

With her P3110 hopelessly out of reach, Kal cursed as the man began to press himself against her. His odor filled her nostrils—old sweat mixed with tobacco stink and machine oil.

"Just relax," said the man, "and maybe I don't kill you when it's over."

Kal strained, but couldn't get her arms free. Her combative training wasn't much good against someone as big as this guy was. His growing arousal was very apparent against her buttocks, and she experienced a sudden and unearthly shock at the fact that she was going to be raped.

110

Desperation drove Kal to snap her head back as hard as she could.

There was a loud crunch as skulls met, and then the man rolled off of her, screaming and clutching his nose while blood poured from it.

Kal pounced on the man's pistol—still in his hand—and wrenched it free, hearing something in the man's wrist snap.

The man screamed again.

Voices began calling down the corridor. Several of them.

The staccato of running feet echoed dangerously.

Kal ran back up the way she'd coming, snagging her pistol off the deck where she'd placed it. Now armed with two weapons, she kept running, the barrels of both weapons pointed directly in front of her.

Three privateers skidded to a halt as they rounded a corner, and their jaws dropped.

One tried to raise a weapon: a submachine gun.

Kal pulled both of her triggers at once.

The man with the submachine gun flew back against the bulkhead behind him, the exposed piping making a loud *clong* sound as he fell, leaving a smear of fresh blood as his body crumpled to the deck.

The other two weren't armed.

They screamed, and tried to run from her.

Kal raised the pistols, intending to empty rounds into the spines of the fleeing men.

Her rounds went wide, drawing sparks from the metal in the next bend of the corridor. Her targets half-crouched, hands clamped over their heads, and were suddenly around the corner and out of sight.

Kal cursed loudly, then ducked into a crossway, turned to see a dead-end, and finally pelted down an altogether different corridor that seemed as neglected as the last.

A lift shaft entrance appeared, with somewhat clean-looking double doors.

Kal slammed a hand on the hatch release. The double doors opened and a surprised woman in a standard spacer's jumpsuit looked out into the corridor as Kal stood there, chest heaving in air.

Kal looked at the woman once, grimaced, and rushed in.

The woman yelled, but Kal silenced her with the crack of a gun butt to the woman's skull. The unconscious body tumbled out of the car, and then the door began to close.

Kal leapt on the controls and ordered the car to the top level of the freighter—or however close to the top the shaft went.

Just as the door was shutting, more privateers came into view. But just for an instant.

Automatic small arms fire *ping*ed and *pang*ed off the doors as they closed.

The car creaked and rocked, and then began to shoot upward at an uneven rate.

Kal was tossed about as the car jostled her, then there was a terrible screech and the lights went out.

The lift had come to a complete halt.

CHAPTER 6

Viking Station was a hoop-shaped warren of cargo holds, starship docks, seedy temporary lodging, shops, gambling dens, and other establishments of variably descending repute. The Blackmatter ships docked at an inner hoop that was immobile, while the outer hoop—easily three kilometers in diameter—spun on its central axis. For simulated gravity.

Kal and Tim disembarked the *Freefall* and made their way to one of the less grimy places of lodging. There they set up shop and went about quietly looking for their contact, who'd supposedly been informed that they were coming.

Gulliver was the man's name.

Though Kal was reasonably certain he was working under an assumed identity, just as they were.

It took nearly a local week of quiet inquiry to find him.

They met in one of the adult entertainment halls.

A place simply called *The Shiny.*

It lived up to its name.

Kal and Tim took seats at a table towards the back, in a dark spot where it was impossible to see the faces of any of the customers—though the glistening, mostly-naked bodies of the entertainers were spotlighted by lamps projecting from the ceiling. The ratio of female to male dancers was about three to one—each of them acrobatically cavorting across their separate stages, which were festooned with chrome-plated poles attached to the ceiling. Cash notes—both paper and coins—were being heaped at the feet of the more energetic entertainers.

Kal noticed Tim's eyes kept straying to one particularly well-endowed woman who had short red hair, a narrow waist, and wide hips. The dancer spun artfully around her pole, staying expertly balanced on a pair of impossibly tall, high-heeled pumps.

Kal gently kicked Tim's shin under the table—to keep him focused.

"Took you a while," said a shadowy male shape sitting across the table from them.

"You're a man who makes himself hard to track down," Kal said.

"Occupational hazard," he said, lifting his shoulders in a shrug.

"Do you think you can help us?" Kal asked.

"Perhaps. I haven't got my fingers in the cookie jar of every black market outfit in the Occupied Zone, but I make it my business to know about the comings and goings of major shipments. The Blackmatter retardation mines are only partially effective, you know. The good smugglers know where the holes in the network are, and use them on a fairly regular basis."

"Something for Central Command to fix," Kal said.

The silhouette of the man across the table began to laugh.

"I think Central Command is well aware of the problem. They just can't do anything about it. Or won't. You should know that there are CAF officers in the blockade fleet who are working those holes to their advantage."

"Graft?" Kal said.

"Of course. You know as well as I do that being assigned to Oz is a job for both heroes and fools. Some people are here for the excitement, and to build a reputation. Others are here because they couldn't be sent anywhere else. You've got the good mixed with the bad."

"Which one are you?" Tim asked, his eyes still occasionally darting to the stage where the red-headed dancer seductively undulated in a rather pendulous fashion.

"Depends on who you ask," their contact said.

A shadowy arm stuck out across the table.

"You can call me Gulliver, which is how most people in Oz know me."

Kal and Tim shook the man's hand in turn.

He had a strong, reassuring grip.

"Do you know about the missing Tremonton hardware?" Kal asked.

"Yup." Gulliver said.

"Any idea where it's been taken?" Tim asked.

"No. But I think I have a method for finding out. Rumor has it that one last shipment of armor is still coming here—to Viking Station—before moving on to the secure Tremonton test facilities that the CAF is jointly operating on-planet. It's probable that shipment will be snatched, just as the others have been. I can make sure you're in the right place at right time when it happens. You might be able to learn more."

"That's what we're here for," Kal said.

"I can't promise you'll be safe," Gulliver added, after gently clearing his throat.

"This is Oz," Kal said. "You're stating the obvious."

"I'm not just talking about the usual scammers and cutthroats," Gulliver replied, leaning on his elbows so that he didn't have to speak as loudly to be heard. Kal could just make out his profile: balding, with a prominent chin, and a pale complexion.

"Oh?" Tim asked.

"The Ambit League is alive and well," Gulliver said, in as close to a hushed tone as he could manage. "Folks back home assume we crushed the League during the war, and the Conflux Assembly is eager to perpetuate that perception with voters. But really, the separate pieces of the monster are subtly gaining strength. For a time when they might reconstitute. And I am not sure there's anything the blockade can do about it."

Kal felt her blood begin to run cold.

Tim's eyes were now fully on Gulliver.

"How long until they renew hostilities?" Kal asked.

"Difficult to say. But I can tell you that they've been using the holes in the Blackmatter retardation network to place a lot of personnel and assets outside the reach of the blockade, in uncharted space—on the other side of the Zone. Stealing cutting-edge Tremonton tech is only the first step. They intend to improve upon and replicate what's been taken."

Kal and Tim exchanged concerned glances.

Gulliver sat back in his chair, allowing his eyes to watch the two female dancers who had shimmied their way over to a part of the branched stage that was closest to Gulliver's table. The dancers began vigorously applying a fresh layer of oil to each other, while occasionally giving Gulliver winks and smiles.

Gulliver smiled back, and dropped a few cash notes on the stage

"So tell us where to be," Kal said, trying to ignore the display of pulchritude going on behind her.

Gulliver reached into his jacket and pulled out something, slipping it across the table towards them. Kal collected the wafer drive and slipped it into the inner pocket of her own jacket.

"Are we done?" Gulliver said.

"Yes," Kal said. "Thanks."

He said nothing in reply. Merely kept watching the dancers.

Kal stood up, and Tim did the same, though somewhat reluctantly.

"Oh," Kal said, "one more thing."

Gulliver appeared to merely wait for her question.

"Who is paying you to pass us this information?"

"Whatever you may have been told about me," Gulliver said, "I can assure you, my patriotic allegiance is to the Conflux. I'm not CAF anymore. At least not officially. And I'm going to admit I kind of like it out here, beyond the boundaries of polite society. But I think the Conflux is worth preserving."

Kal waited, studying the shadowy man with her eyes.

How much of what he'd said was truth?

She really couldn't tell.

"Right," Kal said, then turned to Tim and added, "let's go."

CHAPTER 7

The lift car was pitch black inside. No emergency lights.

Kal whipped out her microlamp and flicked it on. Tendrils of acrid smoke filled the car. Scanning the lamp around, she located the emergency hatch on the floor of the car. She pulled the release key and waited for the hatch to pop loose by itself.

Nothing.

Kal kicked it. Still nothing. *Damn.*

The locks were probably rusted shut.

Kal stood, and backed up against one of the car walls, aiming her lamp with one hand and the P3110 with her other hand.

She pulled the trigger.

The report was deafening, and sparks flew from the floor.

Three more times, she repeated the procedure. Then walked up to the emergency hatch—her ears ringing badly—and stomped on it once. Good and hard. The metal panel creaked and groaned. She stomped again. And again. Finally the door dropped away into the shaft below.

It *clang*ed loudly when it hit bottom. Kal guesstimated she was maybe seven decks up. Quite a fall if she slipped.

She knelt by the hatch and looked below her. The sides of the shaft were just as corroded as the outside, and cobwebs filled the nooks and crannies.

Kal was still looking when she heard feet land on the top of the car. The slamming of metal on metal told Kal she didn't have time to waste. They were coming in after her, one way or another.

Kal quickly maneuvered herself into the bottom hatch, legs flailing in midair until her feet found the rungs of the emergency ladder on the side of the shaft. She searched by feel for some kind of handhold on the bottom of the car—her microlamp clenched between her teeth as she worked—and swung out of the hatchway, almost losing her grip.

Kal's heart thudded wildly as she scrambled for the ladder.

The microlamp slipped from her mouth and spiraled down the shaft, along with the second pistol she'd taken off the man who'd initially accosted her. They, too, hit bottom.

The lamp went out.

Kal cursed, but managed to get a solid grip on the ladder.

The smell of old mildew, machine oil, and rusty steel was pungent in her nostrils.

Kal tried to calm herself. She hated heights. And, on top of that, she hated confined spaces.

She stepped down a rung and then heard a *thunk* from the car.

No time left!

Kal worked quickly down the ladder, by feel.

Suddenly she felt a gust of fresh air.

Exploring with her fingers, she found the ventilation duct.

There was no screen across it.

Kal knocked her forearm around the edges of the opening, and realized the duct was just large enough for a person to crawl into.

Swallowing hard, she maneuvered off the ladder and shimmied into the duct, feeling the pain in her abused elbows and knees as she worked her way forward.

Kal crawled a number of meters and then stopped.

In total darkness, she had no idea where the shaft might lead. Only the occasional burst of fresh air told her that going forward was preferable to going back.

Outside, voices cursed as the privateers discovered the lift car to be empty.

How long would it take them to figure out what had happened to her?

Kal closed her eyes and rested her forehead on her wrist for a moment, then returned to worming her way forward.

After a long, filthy period of claustrophobic effort, Kal came to the first of many grill plates that opened sideways into the interior of the ship. No light was evident, and Kal couldn't see anything. But she could feel the air moving through the grills—with the palm of her hand.

Not wanting to be trapped in the duct any longer than she had to be, Kal curled herself into a ball and put her feet on one of the grills, then pushed.

The grill snapped free, clattering to the deck in the darkness beyond.

Kal led with her feet, then dangled by her hands, then let herself drop.

For a split second, her brain imagined a free-fall.

But her feet hit flooring almost instantly, and Kal allowed herself to crumple, staying still on the metal plate. Not moving. Not really thinking. She was just damned glad to be out of the ductwork.

At some point, Kal must have drifted off.

She snapped awake when the grinding whine of motorized gears announced that a hatch was opening.

A beam of light stabbed into the darkness, and Kal stayed quiet as she watched the light play about the room. Rectangular storage containers of various sizes filled the space. Kal had landed directly between two of them. Which put her out of the line of sight of whoever had entered.

A woman's voice said, "Now in compartment 86-C."

Brad R. Torgersen

A tiny muttering of a different voice—as if through a transistor speaker—responded back.

"Negative," said the female voice. "Not a goddamned sign of the intruder ... Yeah, I'll keep looking ... Yeah, it would have been nice if we took care of this bitch in orbit, but that didn't happen, did it? ... You know, we should see if her friend can tell us something ... how many of his fingers do you think we'd need to break, before he'll talk?"

Kal slithered to the edge of the container that concealed her—waiting for the beam of the light to face the opposite direction—then lunged.

The beam spun back around just in time to catch Kal square in the face.

She aimed and fired her P3110 in the same reflexive instant.

The light flew up and then clattered across the deck as the female privateer was tossed bodily backward, slumping loudly against one of the containers.

Kal snatched up the lantern and dimmed it by half, creeping slowly up to the body.

The woman had a neat hole in her throat that bled thick, dark blood.

Kal grimaced, electing not to search the body. But she did find the headset the woman had been using—laying on the deck three meters away.

Putting it on her head, Kal immediately got an earful of voice chatter. Many people, all talking at once. They didn't seem to realize what had happened, much to Kal's relief. The woman she'd shot hadn't been depressing the SEND switch on the side of the headset when Kal had fired.

Thank goodness for small miracles.

She waited, listening to the goings-on of the intra-ship network.

All hands had been scrambled to look for Kal. It sounded like they wanted her alive. Many people seemed to agree with the dead privateer at Kal's feet: the sole, living prisoner would be a good tool to use against Kal.

Tim. Kal knew she had to find him before it was too late.

Checking her pistol to be sure it still had sufficient ammunition in the magazine, Kal then aimed the lantern back toward the hatch through which the female privateer had first entered.

Best to not go back that way. There might be more people.

Surveying the compartment more thoroughly, Kal discovered another hatch at the opposite end.

Would its motors work?

Only one way to find out.

CHAPTER 8

For two weeks, Kal and Tim laid low. Not venturing out into Viking Station for more than a few minutes at a time. The wafer drive's information said that a Blackmatter ship—the *Broadbill*—would be arriving with a discretely allotted shipment of Tremonton gear aboard. There was no indication as to who—if anyone—would try to seize such equipment. Only that the best way to get more information was to be aboard the ship when it happened.

Now, Kal eyed the *Broadbill* as the huge ship rested in its dock. Kal, herself, was lassoed tight to a small magnetic tractor that gripped the exterior hull of Viking Station, preventing her from floating off into deep space. She watched as the last of the ship's personnel, departing for shore leave, moved through the big starship's several gangways—just tiny little dots moving against the small lit windows of the gangway tubes.

Kal verbally commanded the tractor to move forward. It beeped acknowledgement and began to trundle slowly towards the *Broadbill's* bow shield—a mighty dome of layered armor designed to catch or deflect debris while the ship was moving forward. The shield proper was locked into the grapples of Viking Station's smaller docking ring.

As the tractor traversed the distance to the ship, Kal tried to avoid breathing through her nose. Her used space suit was mildly and unpleasantly aromatic inside—too many occupants and not enough sanitary detergent.

Kal was well familiar with extra-vehicular activity. She'd done plenty in her time. Range of motion and vision were somewhat restricted, but if you could get a rhythm of movement going, you could cover ground fairly quickly. Assuming you were traveling under your own steam.

For this job, Kal was reliant on her technology. The tractor was a standard piece of Viking Station hardware. Hundreds of them were in constant motion across the hull, checking for hairline fractures and cracks, as well as hauling maintenance personnel to and fro.

Connected as she was to her tractor, Kal looked no different from any of the other blue-collar engineers tasked with keeping Viking Station operational.

It was all part of Gulliver's suggested plan.

Unlike the *Freefall*, the *Broadbill* was a cradle ship: the main mass being an entirely separate sublight vessel which was locked into a series of mooring catches that ran along the barren spine of the starship. Most of the Blackmatter Drive ship's functions were automated, and controlled remotely from the sublight ship's bridge. Given the Broadbill's design, she could potentially travel in-atmosphere. Or even land, when she arrived at her eventual destination.

The *Broadbill's* exterior surfaces sparkled in the starlight: pristine, and without blemish.

When Kal's tractor crossed over from the surface of the bow grapple to the surface of the ship, it beeped hesitantly until Kal gave it a series of verbal commands that ordered it to ignore the fact that it was leaving home.

The little robot went south.

Behind her, Kal could see Tim riding his own tractor—following her precisely.

For minutes, they moved in silence.

Only the sound of the suit's regulator filled Kal's ears.

Then, just above the communications module amidships, Kal spotted the kind of airlock she was looking for.

Taking a small computer tool from her suit belt—a restricted item that was CAF issue only—Kal plugged into the emergency airlock's computer and gingerly negotiated an opening with the airlock's tiny-minded control interface. It took minutes to convince the emergency lock's control that it didn't need to alert the command module as to what was going on, then the outer airlock doors slowly slid open.

Kal's suit lamps illuminated the interior.

"Here goes nothing," Kal said to herself, stepping into the orifice and standing on the wall of the airlock.

"A little help, please?" said a voice in her suit's helmet radio.

Kal reached down and—bracing her boots on the rim of the lock—heaved mightily until Tim was standing in the lock with her.

Once inside the airlock—tractors secured—Kal ordered the outer doors sealed and teased open the inner doors with the same lock-crack computer she'd used on the outside.

The inner doors opened into relative darkness.

The air of the communications module was cold and smelled of ozone, with wires, tubes, and electronics running every which way.

Kal and Tim floated gently, careful not to tweak anything that looked fragile. Eventually, they found one of the smallish maintenance passageways that honeycombed the ship, and both she and Tim left their suits secured at the passageway entrance before penetrating more deeply into the *Broadbill's* interior.

Their goal was to find a specific, tiny cabin that the manifest on Gulliver's wafer drive had said would be vacant for the duration of the voyage. If Gulliver was correct, Kal and Tim could hide there until the same people who had made off with previous Tremonton shipments, also came for the *Broadbill*.

If they could identify the thieves, or even find a way to stow away aboard whatever ship the thieves were using, it would put Kal very close to the source of the trouble.

It would also put both herself and Tim in far more danger than she'd have preferred.

But Gulliver's instructions had been quite specific.

And since Kal was dependent on the man—as her only source of seemingly reliable information—she was obliged to go along.

If Gulliver was wrong, and nothing happened during the *Broadbill's* voyage, then there was no harm done, and Kal would have to figure out a secondary plan.

If Gulliver was right ...

Kal considered her youthful companion who had not, so far as Kal knew, ever had to use a weapon in anger.

She sighed. Would it cost them in a pinch?

They floated across an empty corridor.

It took moments of agony for the near-illegal device in Kal's gloved hands to talk the door's control mechanism into opening. Then, it only opened halfway, and began to close again almost immediately. The motors whined loudly as one fought against the other.

"Shit," Kal said. "You first."

"With the door half open, I am not sure I can fit," Tim said.

"Go!" Kal slapped Tim hard on his back, and he dove in—grunting as he had to worm past the narrowing opening.

Kal disconnected the lock-pick and darted through just before the door resumed normal operational mode, and slapped shut.

It was pitch black.

"Lights," Tim said.

Overheads popped on.

The single-bunk cabin was about the size of a modest walk-in closet.

Kal and Tim stared at each other.

It was going to be an interesting trip.

CHAPTER 9

"How many dead, Pitman?" Karl Berd said to his first officer as Garth Pitman entered the bridge.

"One, plus some injuries."

Berd grimaced and stood up, stretching his back. He detested having to deal with unexpected problems. And this particular trip had experienced more than its fair share.

The *Broadbill* was supposed to have been an easy poach job.

So much for false promises.

"Who do you think is doing this?" Pitman asked, standing at parade rest. "A roughneck out for revenge, or somebody else?"

"No," Berd said, "the deck rats we occasionally run into are far too self-preserving for direct action like this. It must be something else. I wonder ..."

Berd sat down and continued to brood. Whoever was running around in his ship was definitely not a run-of-the-mill freebooter. It was possible that this was somebody with military experience. Maybe an ex-CAF soldier?

Berd detested the idea. Just as he detested the Conflux itself. To him, the supposed freedom of the Conflux was just a patina of lies.

The super-wealthy technocrats who controlled or sat on the Assembly permitted just enough upward mobility to keep the masses from revolting, but nothing more.

The Ambit League—though harsh in its methods—offered the best chance Berd could see of transforming human society into something he might call civilized.

In the era of interstellar travel, it was obscene that people still had to dig like dogs in the trash for even the basic necessities. The only thing keeping the status quo from collapsing was ignorance, fear, and the mercenary hoard known as the Conflux Armed Forces.

That a CAF troop might be loose in his ship, killing off his crew ...

Berd stopped and thumped a fist loudly into his chair's headrest.

"The CAF pigs strangle us with the blockade," Berd said, "and now we may face one of their own running around this ship. Continue to collect what salvage you can, Pitman, but put every available person we have on alert for this woman. Continue to search and re-search every compartment. Turn every closet inside out. She can't hide forever."

"We might use the one we already caught," Pitman suggested.

"Yes, we might. But he's refused to talk. And while I am willing to resort to extreme measures, I would like to be sure we haven't exhausted our other options first. I am not a cruel man, Pitman."

"I'm sorry if I implied that you were, sir," Pitman said.

Berd looked at his first officer. They'd not known each other for a terribly long time. The Ambit League—in its current, fractured form—tended to move its personnel around a lot. So as to avoid attachments that might turn into vulnerabilities later.

So far as Berd knew, Pitman was as dedicated to the League cause as any other man. But there was a flavor to Pitman that Berd couldn't quite put his finger on. Something feral ...

No matter. To beat the Conflux, feral was sometimes necessary.

"Go," Pitman said, slowly sitting back down in the chair.

Pitman tipped his head, and left the bridge.

CHAPTER 10

Like a lot of merchantmen, Berin Ogden was young.

Also like a lot of merchantmen, Berin had the tourist bug. Still wearing his shipsuit, replete with identifier patches, he stuck out like the foreigner that he was—wandering wide-eyed through the hula-hoop of Viking Station's kilometers-long bazaar. Flush with cash notes from his ship's paymaster, he nosed idly through the shops and the pubs, a bulb of mildly-fizzing alcoholic drink in one hand, and a crumpled bazaar directory in the other.

The sounds of hooting men and raunchy music drew him into one of the bazaar's dance clubs, where a lovely but not-so-young lady quickly attached herself to his arm. The woman's eyes were as deep and inviting as her cleavage, and before long, Berin was swiping his paycard for both their drinks, culminating in a stumbled rush back to the *Broadbill's* tertiary gangway.

It was against Captain's orders to bring a local onboard; Berin would get ass-chewed if anyone saw her. Luckily, the tertiary hatch was deserted and he knew how to mug the tertiary's security—he'd seen the second mate from propulsion do it more than once—so they had no trouble passing through the gate.

Once inside, Berin took her through several maintenance hatchways until they emptied into the corridor which held the door to Berin's closet-like crew cabin. He giggled tipsily as she ran her hands over his shipsuit, teasing at the frontal zipper and murmuring impatience.

Once inside, sex was abrupt. With Berin greedily pawing at his guest's delightfully bronzed flesh. Her scanty outfit fell away with the brush of a hand, and they kissed sloppily as they fell into his bunk, bodies rubbing.

Berin cried out with alarm, as his youth betrayed him at that point.

Rather than be angry, Berin's guest just laughed. She wiped ejaculate from her stomach and pulled him the rest of the way out of his shipsuit, making promises about being able to coax a second wind into his sail.

Berin was smiling sheepishly—but with renewed enthusiasm—when she slapped him hard on the neck with her left hand.

At once, his tongue turned to rubber and the room lost focus.

"What did ... you ..."

Berin was dead before he got a fourth word out.

The assassin spun one of the rings on her left hand until the small hypodermic inside it retracted. Quickly placing her victim's body into one of his own lockers, she removed one of his clean shipsuits and slid into it, removing the wig on her head and swiping out the colored contact lenses from her eyes. A sanitary cloth from the tiny room's single sink did away with the makeup on her face, leaving the assassin a decidedly older, sterner version of herself. Still beautiful, but hard. The kind of hardness bred by a hard life.

From her purse the assassin extracted the few tools she knew she would need—each of these going into a different, zippered suit pocket.

The maintenance hatches took her back—and past—the way she'd come, to the centrally-aligned series of lift cars that traveled up and down the *Broadbill's* spine. Berin's keys, now attached to the assassin's belt via one of his elastic lanyards, got her a quick ride through the ship's considerable length, until she was able to enter the cargo hold. Checking to be sure the hold wasn't in vacuum, she again used Berin's keys, this time to gain access to the holdmaster's office.

"Everyone's on station," said the middle-aged holdmaster's mate, eyeing his visitor from behind his desk.

The assassin matter-of-factly pulled out a tiny pistol and shot the mate through the temple, her weapon barely making a pop as her second victim went limp over his desk, blood noodling from the tiny hole in his skull. She retrieved the mate's keys—discarding Berin's now superfluous set—and used them to enter the cargo hold itself. Several stories high and twice as big around, the hold was packed with plastic and metal geometric shapes, all colors and all sizes.

The woman knew from experience what to look for, and where.

When she'd confirmed that the *Broadbill* was carrying the kind of cargo she and her associates desired, she went back into the holdmaster's office and, shoving the dead mate aside, set up a point-to-point link through the *Broadbill's* communications umbilical with Viking Station.

"We've been waiting to hear from you," said a digitally-corroded male voice.

"Sorry I'm tardy, Yangis."

"Did you have any trouble getting in?"

The woman laughed. "Do I ever?"

Now the man named Yangis laughed. "That's our girl."

"They've got at least twenty units on this ship. Probably more, once we properly inventory her."

"Excellent. How many crew are still aboard?"

"Wait one."

The woman used the holdmaster's computer to do a quick count on keys which were still known to be aboard.

"Fifteen, though I can't be sure of their location."

"No matter. Arbai, you've done an excellent job, as always. You know what to do next."

"Just make sure you and yours are ready when I extend the cargo gangway."

"I leave the command module to your delicate skillset, my dear."

"Copy that. I'll see you when you get there."

Arbai cut the secure connection.

Using the holdmaster's mate's keys to re-enter the lift car, she plunged back through the length of the ship, getting off at the foyer to the command center. The keys got her through the outer door, then the inner door, and nobody seemed to notice as she entered the nerve center of the *Broadbill,* looking for all the world like just another one of its crew.

Eventually a watch officer looked up.

"Can I help you, miss?"

Arbai stopped. The officer was a young woman with junior merchant command studs on her shoulder. She floated from her chair near the middle of the complex. Screens and holographic projections decorated the space between them.

Arbai smiled.

"Don't get up, the holdmaster just sent me to tell you that he's got trouble with the seal on bay door three."

"Really? We didn't detect it here."

"He figured that, otherwise you'd have done something about it already. He wanted me to make sure you knew."

"We'll have to recall some of the engineers from station leave," the officer said, her brow furrowing with concern as she walked to one of the in-wall displays and began hitting keys to bring up the ship's roster.

Arbai drifted further into the command module, which didn't seem to alarm any of the other five watch officers sitting at their various stations. Reaching to her left breast pocket, she pulled out a tiny device like a diver's nose plug and inserted it into her nostrils. Then she reached into the shipsuit's right breast pocket and removed two glass phials, gripping them in either palm.

"I'm sorry," Arbai said to them all.

"What?"

"It's nothing personal. Just business."

Before anyone in the room could say or do anything else, Arbai pitched the phials in opposite directions, smashing them against the bulkheads. Several officers began to move, but not before a sickly-sour smell filled the room. All six of the watch went limp where they were, the respiratory nerve agent making them twitch as signals between brain and body became disrupted.

Arbai breathed through her nose while she counted ninety seconds—the deadly nerve agent's active lifespan. At one hundred and twenty seconds, she allowed herself to circle the command module, checking everyone for vitals and, satisfied that all were dead, settling herself at one of the master control stations.

The menus for the cargo bay's gangway were simple enough to find, and easier to operate. Within three minutes, a tube had been extended out to mate with Viking Station's bulky commerce deck. The command module remained intensely quiet throughout the entire operation, only a gentle whisper coming from the air cycle vents.

When next the command center's inner door opened, eight men and five women entered, each of them wearing filters on their noses similar to Arbai's.

The tallest of the men grinned, surveying the dead around him, then reached up and removed his filter, taking a deep whiff.

"You know there's always the danger of trace contamination," Arbai said, smirking at her boss.

"Live dangerously, or don't live at all," Yangis said. "Let's get these unfortunates out of here and fire up for departure."

Yangis's crew fanned out immediately, two people per body, and began to get the *Broadbill*'s former bridge crew evacuated.

Yangis settled himself at a control station next to Arbai's.

"Was he a nice boy?"

"I beg your pardon?"

"That lad you picked up, the one we eyed out for you. Was he nice?"

"I'm not sure how to take that question," Arbai said, frowning.

"Take it any way you like," Yangis said.

"If you mean sexually, he was as clumsy as any young man can be."

"Worse than me when we first met?"

"No, he wasn't nearly that bad. Compared to you, he was a pro."

Yangis's laughter boomed through the command module.

"Leave it to my ex-wife to bust my balls for me!"

"You don't pay me to be gentle, dear."

"No, no I don't. Now get that hard ass of yours down to propulsion. I've got several more people coming aboard in maintenance coveralls, and I want you to make sure they don't have any trouble when they get down to the drive assembly."

Arbai mock-saluted and stood, feeling her ex-husband's hand pat her rump before she went to the command module doors, and exited.

As with previous jobs on merchant ships like the *Broadbill*, everything else proved academic. Arbai wondered why more ships— more companies—hadn't learned better; lax protocol, lax training, weak security measures at entry points, skeleton staffing while in port. Typical, typical, typical. It was like they were begging for piracy. Though pirate was not the word Arbai would have used to describe herself. She was a trained professional, and very good at what she did. Had there been any money in it, she might have even stayed in the CAF. Lucky for her, she'd met Yangis, and when they'd both gotten out of uniform, gone into business for themselves.

A very select, very exclusive kind of business.

When the *Broadbill* broke dock without warning, there was the usual wailing from traffic control. Yangis ignored it, and Arbai watched from one of the portals in the crew module as the merchant ship spun away from Viking Station and flew into the blackness of space.

CHAPTER 11

It didn't take a genius to figure out that the *Broadbill* had left dock without proper authorization from Viking Station control.

As soon as Kal felt the gee of acceleration assert itself, she knew what was up.

"You can't be serious," Tim said as he watched Kal get her pistol out of her shoulder holster, remove and check the magazine, then slap the magazine back in place.

"I'm dead serious. Whoever has been taking these Tremonton shipments? Their ambition just leveled up. Now they're taking a whole cradle ship. The *Broadbill* is officially under new management."

"So what do we do now?" Tim asked.

"Nothing. We stick to the plan. In fact, this actually makes things a little easier. I was trying to figure out how we were going to manage to get out into the rest of the ship, if or when somebody decided to snatch the sensitive hardware in the cargo hold. Now they're liable to take us directly to wherever the missing shipments have been piling up. Or, more probably, we'll rendezvous with another ship in orbit somewhere obscure. The cargo will get moved to a new ship. And then the *Broadbill* will be sent off somewhere far away. To confuse the trail."

"Sounds like we'll have to be ready to go where the crates go," Tim said.

"Yup. And that's going to be very potentially tricky. We might have to go outside again and hope we can jump—ship to ship—without being noticed. Are you prepared for that?"

"Sounds like I might have to be," Tim said, frowning and running a hand through his curly black hair.

Kal slipped her pistol back into its shoulder holster, and sat on the bunk across from where Tim was slouched in the single fold-up chair that was next to the shelf-like fold-up desk.

"Tell me," she said, "just what is it about this new armor model that's so exciting the Ambit League wants a piece of it?"

"Ummm, I'm not sure I can talk about that, you see—"

"Save it, kid, I have need-to-know at this point. I used several different types of armor during the war. It's not like that's brand new technology."

"The Archangel series isn't just an upgrade to the older armor suits that the CAF's been using since the war," Tim said. "We're talking about an entirely new generation of bio-neural interfacing. You don't wear the suit. It's like the suit wears *you*. Reflexive response times far in advance of anything the CAF or the Ambit League was using in battle when the war was still hot. Plus it employs advanced ceramics, polymers, alloys, and a microcomputer system that learns its owner over time. Until the microcomputer is almost a shallow, duplicate personality. It knows your moves before you know your moves."

Kal was intrigued. The new armor sounded quite sexy to her combat-experienced sensibilities. She wondered what it would be like to pilot such a suit.

The conventional suits were big, bulky behemoths with loads of firepower, but slow and cumbersome. Not to mention exhausting. The delayed response times on movement meant an average troop became physically tired while fighting against the lag times in joint movement. If what Tim said was true, the Archangel suits truly were next-generation.

"Anyway," Tim said, "the Ambit League would be stupid to let itself fight that kind of suit without trying to replicate the tech. Trials on some of the Occupied Zone planets have already yielded very good results. Even against entrenched, experienced opposition, the Archangel has a perfect record. No losses. With countless enemy combatants neutralized or destroyed."

"What about heavy stuff? Tanks and bigger things?"

"The Archangel is meant for speed and agility, not raw firepower. Still, in the hands of an able pilot, it can fight circles around conventional tracked armor. Give an Archangel troop enough time, and she can quickly ventilate a tank like a piece of Swiss cheese."

Kal nodded her understanding.

"That means each of the Archangel suits is worth a lot of money," she said.

"You don't even want to know," Tim said, smiling sardonically. "Just the pinky finger on one of the Archangel's gauntlets is worth more than my entire annual salary."

"Which also means that Tremonton is going to make a killing selling these things to the Conflux Assembly Defense Office."

"Prices will drop once the suit's been put through its paces and mainline manufacturing can begin. But yeah, even a single suit's worth more than a dozen conventional suits put together."

"And now the Ambit League has them," Kal said.

"Apparently so. Though they're going to be hard-pressed to replicate even half of what they find when they pull the Archangel apart. It's Tremonton's most advanced design, and it took countless hours to engineer and create it. Using Tremonton's top facilities on several planets. I don't think the Ambit League is up to the task of copying the Archangel just yet."

"Well, that's another reason I need you: to verify if your guesses are correct, assuming we get to have a look at the final destination for these shipments that keep getting stolen. Gulliver said the League's been surreptitiously expanding into the unexplored space on the other side of the Occupied Zone, away from the Conflux. If they're setting up shadow colonies, especially with industry and mining, they might have what it takes to start trying to replicate advanced tech. Or perhaps they simply want to mass-produce a poor man's version? Numbers will almost always beat quality, if the numbers are large enough."

Tim looked at Kal, his smile fading.

"Then it really might be a second war?" he asked softly.

"Yes," Kal said, her eyes unfocusing, "it might."

CHAPTER 12

Garth Pitman stomped across the rusty decks of his ship as he made his way down to the engineering section. The buzzing of his subordinates was comforting in his headset's earpiece. They were executing as commanded: turning the old scow inside out, trying to locate the intruder.

The mischievous mystery guest had eluded capture and killed crew, but Pitman wasn't necessarily worried. Yet. People had died for the Ambit League before, and people would continue to die for the Ambit League in the future. It was the price they all had to pay if the long war against the Conflux was to succeed. Pitman accepted that. He was even confidant that he, himself, would give his life, should it become necessary, but he always assured himself that he was far too crafty to be caught in such a no-win situation.

He would live to see the Conflux fall.

Taking a lift car down a few decks, Pitman continued to stride confidently. In the eyes of the crew Pitman saw respect, and sometimes fear. That was good. He could use both to different effect,

Brad R. Torgersen

when he needed to. It came with the job. As long as people obeyed his orders, or the orders of Berd, to the letter, that was all he asked.

His headset suddenly squealed and one of Pitman's junior officers demanded his attention—down in the lower compartments close to the main cargo bay.

Another crewperson had been killed.

Pitman ran: around a corner, down a ladder, through a hatch, and then through a corridor, until he finally arrived at the location of the latest murder.

As he showed up, several of Pitman's crew were outside a partially opened hatchway, eyes wide and feet shuffling nervously. An old loadmaster named Gimms was there, running a hand over the thin stubble on his head.

"Who was it this time?" Pitman asked.

"Go look for yourself, sir."

Pitman grimaced, his hackles rising at the tone in Gimms's voice. But as Pitman watched Gimms and the others, Pitman's feet began to get cold and his hands began to sweat. Something was seriously wrong.

Pitman unslung his submachine gun and gripped it in his hands for comfort, then brushed past Gimms and went into the cargo compartment.

The area was full of refuse and smelled of corrosion. The doors and walls were rusted badly. Rectangular containers clogged the walkway, but Pitman didn't have to go very far to discover what the bad news was.

Someone had managed to get one of the ceiling lights working.

Gouts of blood were freshly splattered across one side of a container, where a body lay underneath a draped plastic tarp. Pitman stooped and gingerly peeled the tarp back so that he could see the victim's face.

Her eyes were open and stared emptily at the ceiling. Her mouth was half open and blood trailed down the corners across her cheeks. The bullet had gone right through her esophagus and lodged in the spine. Instant death.

Pitman's eyes ogled, and then a quiet rage began to build in him.

Gabriella. She and Garth had been lovers for some time now, sharing the glories of his bed every night for weeks. Now Pitman's companion lay lifeless and crumpled on the deck, her drying blood staining the soles of his boots.

Pitman dropped to his knees, fists balled around the grips of his submachine gun—his eyes closed. A low growl uttered from his clenched teeth. Then he stopped, composed himself, and calmly stood up, his mind trying to focus. This was CAF handiwork, he was sure of it. Only the CAF could murder so brutally and efficiently.

Pitman held back the raw anger and sorrow jointly gnawing at his heart. He had to stay composed if he wanted to avenge his lover.

Pitman ran his eyes over her body, checking for missing or damaged equipment.

Gabriella's headset was gone, but her weapon was not.

Damn.

"Take the body out of here and put it in the cold locker," Pitman ordered as he exited the compartment. "We'll take her back with us, and make sure she's given a soldier's burial."

The others saluted and silently went to work, eyes wary of Pitman's barely concealed rage.

CHAPTER 13

It took almost two weeks for the *Broadbill* to reach her intended destination. During which time neither Kal nor Tim dared leave their cabin, for fear of being spotted. Though the people who'd hijacked the ship had no reason to believe anyone else might be onboard, it paid to be cautious. So they each went out exactly once: to look for meal packs.

Not precisely gourmet, the meal packs were easily had in any emergency locker, in case the *Broadbill* were disabled or stranded between star systems, with the crew unable to travel freely between compartments. Starvation was a real possibility if rescue was still light-years away, and your radio signals only traveled as far as the nearest spacelane beacon.

During that time, Kal and Tim did the best they could to be comfortable. Which wasn't easy, given the tight quarters. Including a micro-toilet that was barely big enough for Kal to use—making it almost impossible for Tim.

They traded stories about initial entry training in the CAF. Things which had stayed the same. Things which were different. Between the time when Kal had joined, and Tim had joined—to fulfill his obligation under contract to Tremonton.

They also talked a lot about the Archangel suits. Plusses. Minuses. Things Tim had noticed when piloting the suits in a laboratory setting. So that Kal felt like she was familiar enough to try operating an Archangel in a pinch. If it came down to it.

"They key thing is," Tim said one morning while they pushed fruity-nutty breakfast bars into their mouths, "the Archangel wasn't designed to plod. It was designed to soar. Where older suits thud along like the Frankenstein monster, the Archangel glides. Most pilots who are used to conventional armor have to go through a teething period, where they re-train themselves to the advanced, hyper-responsive servos and motors in the Archangel's design. So in the unlikely event you're ever putting one of these things on, don't get gung-ho. You're liable to put an arm through a wall or accidentally hurl yourself into the ceiling, or across the room. Go very gently. Almost as if you don't want to move. The Archangel will do the moving for you."

"It must be a lot of fun," Kal said.

"What?" Tim asked.

"Getting to play with Tremonton's latest toy."

"It's a good job," he said. "And I certainly get paid well."

They munched their meals for a quiet moment.

"Got anyone back home worth spending the money on?" Kal asked.

Tim cleared his throat and took a drink of water from a cup on the rim of the cabin's tiny sink.

"Not really," he admitted.

"No lady friend has caught your eye?"

"No."

"A shame. You seem like the nice sort."

"My ex-girlfriend said I was *too* nice."

"Was she young?"

"Yes. Younger than me, at least."

"Young girls don't appreciate nice. A woman with experience might. Don't be afraid to date older gals."

"Is that a proposition?" Tim said with a raised eyebrow and a grin.

Kal slugged him in the left shoulder as hard as she could.

He almost fell over laughing, then grimaced and rubbed the spot where a fresh bruise was no doubt forming.

"Sorry," Kal said. "Sometimes I don't know my own strength."

"No shit," Tim said.

Suddenly, the feeling of gravity began to vanish.

"Uh oh," Kal said. "I think maybe we've arrived."

"What now?" Tim asked.

"Head back the way we came in. Suit up. Take a look outside and see what happens next."

Kal and Tim never made it that far.

CHAPTER 14

Arbai watched her former husband as he stared intently at the gangway hatch. The receiving ship had been waiting for them as soon as the *Broadbill* had entered orbit, following a gradual downthrust through the outer portion of this uncharted star system. They were well beyond the boundaries of either the Occupied Zone or the Conflux, and the greenish blue-and-white world beneath them was uncharted as well.

A virgin paradise.

Or a tropical death trap.

A lot depended on whether the fauna down below had evolved to the point of having sharp teeth, and thought off-world visitors might be tasty.

Perhaps when the job was done, and after enough time elapsed, Arbai and Yangis could come back here? Have a little fun on the beach? Nothing romantic, per se, because sex with Yangis had never been like that. But relaxing fun, just the same. Lord knew they'd have enough money to take a break from their cares for a while.

Doubtless it was the money that had Yangis so tense.

Meeting strangers to make the exchange of goods was always a high-wire act. You couldn't trust them to be straight, they couldn't trust you to be straight, and Arbai had seen several such exchanges go badly before. Which was why everyone was carrying for this particular action. Pistols and submachine guns visible, without being brandished. It was also why she knew Yangis kept a small remote in his spacer's jacket. It was tied wirelessly to the control computer that operated their cradle ship's fusion reactor. If Yangis pressed a select sequence of buttons ...

No sense letting potential double-crossers have the last laugh.

The gangway hatch's indicator light blinked from red, to orange, to yellow, then to green.

Then it unsealed, and half a dozen men floated in.

Unlike Yangis's crew, these strangers were more or less uniform in appearance. Hair cut to military standard. Faces serious, and eyes alert. The kind of expressions Arbai and Yangis both remembered well, from their time in the CAF. Though these were not CAF. They were the men Arbai and Yangis had been killing right up until Arbai and Yangis both decided that the war was a sham, the Conflux was as bloody culpable as the Ambit League, and that the only side worth choosing was their own side.

An older man with some kind of insignia on his collar stepped forward.

"Berd," the man said, nodding his head slightly. "Commander of the *Goshawk.*"

"Yangis Terizian," Yangis said, returning the slight nod. "You'd better be careful with that rusty bucket you've got out there. It's a miracle it's even spaceworthy."

"It suffices," Berd said, ignoring the jab at his spacer's pride. "She may not look impressive, but the drives are good and she gets the job done. Besides, she's just a delivery vehicle. Now, show us the cargo, then we'll discuss your payment."

"You read my mind," Yangis said. He snapped a finger.

A single pallet was floated forward. On it, secured by bungee tethers, were the major pieces of a single suit of Archangel-type armor.

Arbai noticed Berd's eyes take in the sight of the armor the way other men might take in the sight of a nude woman.

So Berd was a believer, eh? Ambit League to the core.

That would either be very good, or very bad, depending on what happened next.

"How many of these did you get?" Berd asked Yangis.

"All of them aboard."

"Which is how many?"

"We've not opened every single crate, but there are probably thirty total."

"Not as many as we'd hoped," said a younger man behind Berd. Tougher-looking. Also with an insignia on his collar. Berd's executive officer?

"But enough," Berd said.

He pushed off from the deck and floated over to the pallet, running his hands along the polished surfaces of the various armor components.

"When the crates have been moved to the *Goshawk*, you will be compensated," Berd said to Yangis.

"No," Yangis said, his businessman's smile dropping to a frown. "The arrangement I made with your people was, I show you proof of the goods, you pay me for my time, *then* you can have the units. Not before."

"The Ambit League is not in the habit of paying for goods which it has not yet taken possession of," Berd said, his eyes suddenly hardening.

Arbai immediately noticed that some of Berd's men had pushed their spacer's jackets open, revealing the gleam of guns in holsters. Yangis's people had subtly made their own weaponry more visible, too, and Arbai realized that things could get very unfortunate very fast if someone didn't pour a little oil on the roiled waters.

"I don't think it has to be an all or nothing proposition," Arbai said, using her best, most soothing feminine voice. She pushed over to where Berd and Yangis now both floated less than a meter apart, their jaws thrust out at one another.

"A deal is a deal," Yangis said. "No money, no top-secret armor."

"Gentlemen," Arbai said, inserting herself into the tense air between the two men. "Since there appears to be a small misunderstanding about what's supposed to take place here, why don't we agree to meet in the middle? We'll provide the first ten suits, you carry them across, and you provide one third of the payment. Then we provide the next ten suits, you provide the second third, and so on and so forth. That way we get what we want, you can verify that you're getting what you want, and then we can each go on our separate ways."

Yangis and Berd glared at each other, then Yangis laughed: artificial, and harsh.

"Damn, Arbai, you always were so smooth. Can you believe this lady? And I had the stupidity to divorce her!"

"I divorced you, dear," Arbai said gently.

More hard laughter.

"Fine, fine, we'll do it according to the lady's preference."

Berd simply kept staring, then he blinked once, exhaled slowly, and nodded his head.

"That's a reasonable compromise. Let me inform my men."

Berd floated back to where his people were.

With his back turned, he raised a hand and chopped it once, downward through the air.

Arbai's smile dropped, and she screamed a warning.

Too late. The Ambit League men were faster on the draw.

Firearms chattered and banged like Thor's hammer on an iron sky.

Arbai felt something hot tear into her stomach and then she was flipped end-over-end back against the far bulkhead, where she curled in on the wound and gagged, unable to speak.

Looking out of the corner of her eye, she could see the Ambit League men all poised on the balls of their feet—grip soles holding them tightly against the recoil of their weapons. Only three of them had been hit, and they were being rushed back down the gangway by their comrades, leaving only Berd and his executive .

"Sorry," Berd said as the moans of Yangis's wounded and dead filled the compartment. "This Archangel armor is too important to the League. We can't afford to have anyone—much less scum like yourselves—left alive to speak of its whereabouts. We'll be taking all the suits now, and this ship as well. I should tell you that you ought to get used to my 'rusty bucket', because once we've moved our flag to the *Broadbill*, your bodies will be in the *Goshawk* when she reenters."

Berd turned and motioned for his executive to follow him back down the gangway.

Arbai would have shed tears if the pain in her gut had not been so intense. She couldn't speak, and could barely move. Heavy fluid leaked between her fingers and began to form hot blobs of dark redness that floated away into the air—to mix with that of the others, who'd all been shot to pieces.

Stupid, Arbai thought. *Should have left a few of us elsewhere, to come in as a second wave, if the first wave went down.*

Then she saw Yangis. Her ex-husband was slowly revolving in the air, three holes in his chest. But his eyes were blinking.

Arbai mouthed his name.

Yangis appeared to mouth something to Arbai too.

She tried to muster a smile. Was he saying her name?

Then Yangis managed a ferocious, bloody grin.

She noticed the remote was in his right hand.

Ah. Right.

Arbai closed her eyes, and hoped she'd be dead before the blast happened.

CHAPTER 15

Back on the bridge, Pitman quickly cleaned his hands, and then linked himself into the intra-ship communications network through his headset.

He began ordering his people to an even higher level of alert, with guards at all the entrances to the cargo bay, by the hatches to the engine room, and of course, watching the corridor to the bridge's lone lift.

Finally, Pitman called up six of his most trusted troops, who met him in the officers' mess just off the bridge. In full armament.

Pitman looked at his team as they adjusted their gear.

"Does everyone understand? I want this little whore *dead* ... I want her burned out of the ventilation system and gutted like a fish."

Pitman's people nodded and smiled. Like him, they were hungry for the hunt. There wasn't an Ambit League partisan on the ship who didn't hate the CAF.

Pitman slapped them on their shoulders and they trooped off towards the sole functional lift that serviced the bridge. Each carried a minimum of two weapons, various heat and motion sensing gear, plus full plate vests and helmets that could stop a rifle round.

Pitman used the AV unit in the wall—one of the few on the ship that still worked properly—to call up a diagram of the *Goshawk's* internal architecture. They separated the ship up into sectors, then began mapping where the prey had most recently been sighted, versus where Gabriella's body had been found. A strategy was devised to begin tackling the problem in a systematic fashion. No more random, bumbling search sweeps.

"Remember, she's just one woman," Garth said, his eyes jumping from face to stolid face. They all nodded solemnly.

"It will be done," one of them said.

"See that it is," Pitman said.

Pitman turned away from his men and walked through the adjoining passage back to the bridge proper. A guest had been brought to join the commander.

A huge, dark-skinned young man was looking straight at Pitman with eyes that only partially concealed the young man's hostility. The prisoner never blinked as he stared at Pitman.

Pitman resisted the urge to strike the prisoner with a closed fist.

"I am afraid you don't understand your predicament," Berd was saying in a reasonable tone.

"How's that?" the young man asked.

"Because, dear sir, it's only a matter of time before my people catch up with your lady friend who is making such a mess of my ship down below. If you can convince her to come out of hiding and surrender peacefully, I can see to it that you're both repatriated to a neutral site. In due time, of course."

"And why should I believe you'll do any such thing?" the prisoner asked.

"Son," Berd said, his face assuming a somewhat pained, fatherly expression, "I am afraid that you're in no position to doubt me. Because I can assure you, if that woman you came with is not brought to bear soon, for every one of my crew she hurts, I'm going to take it out on *you*. Or, rather, I will have my first officer take it out on you. And believe me, when I give him an order, he's very good at what he does. Isn't that right, Pitman?"

"Yessir," was all Pitman said, eyeing the largish youth, who'd had his ankles and wrists shackled ever since he'd been dragged aboard.

The prisoner didn't say a word. He simply stared at the floor.

"Son," Berd said, "my people tell me your friend has managed to secure one of our headsets, so all I have to do is put you on the network in order for her to hear you. So, do we have an agreement?"

The prisoner remained silent.

"Hello?" Berd said, only this time a bit more sharply.

He glanced up at Pitman. Face red. Then pointed at the prisoner and mimed punching his fist into a palm.

Pitman smiled. He was going to get a little recreation, to ease the suffering of his recent loss.

CHAPTER 16

Kal sat in the darkness, trying to let herself rest. But she couldn't. The adrenaline in her veins was like amphetamine. She'd been wired up for hours, and remained wired. Unable to properly navigate the ship, and searching blindly from compartment to compartment, she was beginning to fear that she'd never locate Tim, until he was either dead, or they caught her. In which case she was as good as dead, and Tim right along with her.

Her headset crackled to life.

"This is Commander Berd to all crew members ..."

Kal listened carefully.

"As you know, a lone female survivor from the *Broadbill* has come aboard and is harassing us internally. I have reason to suspect this woman is a military operative from the CAF, not a smuggler. I realize it is galling to us all that we must suffer having this ... *person*, running loose in the bowels of our vessel. With your help I hope to have the problem resolved quickly, so that we can finish the job we came here for, and return our precious cargo to our Ambit League comrades who can do the most good with it.

"Until then, though, I want total intra-ship communications silence. All relays and requests will be made face-to-face. Our visitor has one of our headsets, so she will hear anything we say on the network. Cut her out of the network, and she stands much less of a chance of evading and/or ambushing us. Anyone breaking this order without direct permission from the bridge will suffer the consequences. Do not let me down. Commander Berd, for the Ambit League, out."

Suddenly Kal's headset went totally dead, and she smacked a fist onto the hull plating.

She needed a plan of action. And fast.

CHAPTER 17

Kal and Tim were barely halfway to the compartment in the communications module—where they'd stowed their space suits—when a loud concussion shook the *Broadbill*.

The ship's automated emergency claxon began to sound.

"Decompression!" Tim yelled, noticing the color of the flashing lights that suddenly sprang to life at intervals along the ceiling.

"Or worse," Kal said.

"What could have happened?" Tim asked, his head suddenly swiveling back and forth in panic.

The klaxon changed pitch, and the emergency light changed color.

"Radiological alarm too!" Tim shouted.

"Shit," Kal cursed. "The reactor on the cradle ship. Either it blew itself, or someone blew it for us.

"But what can we—"

A terrible wind kicked up, drowning out Tim's words.

"Move!" Kal yelled. "Now!"

They both grabbed what handholds they could, and fought their way up the corridor. Meter by painful meter. There was an emergency locker just ahead. There would be emergency environment suits in there. Perhaps Kal and Tim could reach them in time to avoid having the air sucked from their lungs.

Kal clawed her way past a black and yellow striped threshold.

Why hadn't the internal emergency doors sealed?

As if to answer Kal's mental question, a thick steel door suddenly descended from the ceiling. Since Tim had been two meters behind he could only watch helplessly as the door slammed shut between them.

Kal felt the rush of air lessen, but not abate entirely.

Screaming Tim's name, she turned back to the door and began to beat on it with her fists.

"Tim! Oh my God, no, no!"

Rumbles and groans throughout the ship told Kal that the *Broadbill* was in very deep trouble.

When the ship itself began to jerk violently and spin, it was all Kal could do to worm her way towards the nearest lifeboat hatch, which was rimmed by red and white caution striping. She passed through the hatch and had the good sense to hit the large red handle in the lifeboat's roof. The hatch slammed shut, and suddenly the lifeboat itself was being hurled into the universe.

CHAPTER 18

Kal sat in the dark. Her eyes and ears wide open, waiting for the slightest sound.

It was eerie.

Before, while the radios had been active, she had at least been able to gather a fly-on-the-wall picture of what was happening inside the ship.

Now, however, she was isolated and out of information. The advantage—temporarily gained, right after she'd taken the headset—was gone, and the whole ship had a collective itchy trigger finger with Kal's name on it. The longer she sat and stared into the darkness, the more she became paranoid.

Minutes ticked by agonizingly, and finally she couldn't take it anymore. She had to move. But where? Navigating the neglected, darkened compartments of the ship was like moving through a maze with a blindfold on. Without a layout of the structure to orientate with, and a big arrow indicating *Kal Reardon, You Are Here*, any guess she might make as to where she was, or where she was trying to go, was almost useless.

But she absolutely could not risk moving about in the main corridors. It would be a near certain death sentence.

What to do ...

Kal couldn't think straight. She was too tired, too exhausted, and too amped up on her own fear, combined with desperation to reach Tim.

Her head settled onto her knees—drawn up to her chest—and she fell asleep.

When her head popped up again, Kal had been in the midst of an old dream from her war days. Not a battle dream per se, but something from training. When she'd been maneuvering with her platoon against dummy targets, using the textbook call signs and lingo to execute the platoon's operations order.

Kal found herself desperately hoping for a platoon now.

Even a moderately armed couple of CAF mobile infantry squads would be able to rip the ancient, decrepit ship to pieces within minutes.

Or at least scare crud out of the crew.

Wait ...

Kal suddenly realized she'd been looking at her predicament from the wrong perspective.

The seed of an idea sprang forth, like hot sparks.

And Kal was up and moving again.

*   *   *

Kal watched nervously through the ductwork grill plate as a particularly large privateer sauntered past. It had taken a small eternity to wind her way back towards the main cargo hold. Several times she'd had to make quick detours to avoid the sweep patrol that appeared to be making a coordinated effort to smoke her out. It wouldn't be long before she took one wrong turn too many, and found herself staring down the barrel of somebody's weapon.

Therefore, it was now or never.

Kal gently pushed on the grill plate with her legs until it popped free. Only, instead of letting it clatter to the deck, she caught it in both hands and eased it down to the deck with as little noise as she could muster.

The space in front of the grill plate was dominated by interstellar shipping crates of various sizes, which had all been salvaged from the downed hulk of the *Broadbill*. Kal couldn't tell if they were ordinary crates, or the unmarked specialized crates she had seen upon first boarding: the ones that held the different pieces of Archangel armor.

Kal looked around carefully, unable to tell—in the stacks of crates—whether or not any of the privateers could see her.

She girded herself, and dared to stand up and look into the nearest crate.

Damn, it was empty.

The next nearest was empty, too.

Was she too late? Had they evacuated the crates and moved all of the Archangel armor to a different, more secure location within the ship?

Footsteps on metal.

Kal ducked down behind a stack of crates that was three high, and waited until the footsteps had diminished.

With her heart pounding in her throat, Kal turned around and examined the stack which was providing her cover. Like most commercial crates of similar design, these were roughly two meters on a side, and all sides had small access panels that could be detached if you had the right tools. In the case of the crate that was directly in front of Kal, the side hatch appeared to have been recently opened and re-sealed—the paint around the edges had flaked, revealing bright metal.

Kal teased at the latches with her thumb and forefinger.

One of the latches came loose.

Elated—and scared to death of being heard or seen—Kal popped another latch, and then another. When the last latch came free, she eased the side panel away and laid it on the ground. Inside, the crate was pitch black. So Kal reached in and felt around. Something very hard, smooth, and heavy was in the way. Grasping it as best as she could, Kal pulled the thing out and looked at it.

It was a helmet.

A brand new, very fancy-looking helmet. With an expensive and intricate-looking interface at the neck, where data feeds and motor networking would engage. Not a lot different from the conventional armor suits Kal had trained on.

Footsteps again. Coming towards her.

Kal momentarily considered fleeing back into the ductwork.

No good. She wouldn't make it in time.

Instead, she crawled *into* the crate, and pulled the access panel up behind her. Unable to seal the latches from the inside, she held the panel in place with the tips of her fingers and waited in desperate silence while the footsteps approach her crate, and then stopped in front of it.

Kal all but fainted.

But then, a voice spoke.

"If you tell 'em once you tell 'em a thousand times, don't half-ass it when you're doing a job. Now look at this container here, someone's replaced the panel without dogging the latches. If I knew which one of these lazy sons-of-bitches was slacking around here, I'd break his nose."

One by one, the latches were all snapped tight.

And Kal was locked inside.

Safe? For the moment?

She felt around until she once again found the object that felt like the helmet.

She slid it onto her head and allowed herself a tiny hint of a smile.

CHAPTER 19

Tim Osterhaudt sat slumped in his confined seat on the bridge of the *Goshawk*. His head hung low and blood oozed from several large gashes on his face and upper torso. Pitman, and Pitman's commander, Karl Berd, sat on the edge of a console a few meters away, each staring unblinkingly at their captive.

"Who is your partner?" Berd said with an icy hint to his voice. "I really don't want to have to unleash my first officer again."

Tim clenched up inside for a second as he contemplated the pain. Would it do any good to talk? He'd almost cracked during the first beating. Would he be able to withstand the second?

Ordinarily Tim would have stuck to his principles, and not wished to harm anyone.

But after the way Pitman had laid into him, Tim was beginning to have second thoughts about his philosophy. For the first time since he'd been a teenager in school, Tim genuinely wanted to retaliate. Hit back. No, not just hit back. Cave Pitman's skull in with a wrench. Knock him down and beat him senseless.

It was embarrassing to be having such barbaric thoughts.

But Tim realized he could not help it. Not after the way Pitman had savaged him, and for no reason other than that Tim was powerless to do anything about it. Talk or no talk, the Ambit League people were going to beat him again. Perhaps even to death. Regardless of what came out of his mouth. Of this Tim was certain. So, he kept his mouth shut, and waited, dismally, for the renewal of blows.

*   *   *

Pitman noticed Osterhaudt flinch, and then remain silent.

"He needs more motivation, boss," Pitman said. His fists were sore from the first series of blows, but he'd relished the exercise. Every hit was another piece of revenge for what had been done to Gillian.

Berd sighed and nodded.

Pitman lunged, cracking a fist across Osterhaudt's cheek.

There was a loud *smack* and Osterhaudt's head snapped to the side, blood pouring from a new gash in Osterhaudt's face.

$$*\qquad*\qquad*$$

Tim ran a tongue along the wounded flesh inside his mouth—to compliment the wounds outside—and grimaced. A few teeth were loose. He'd have to have that taken care of, if he survived to get off this mud ball.

Another blow cracked Tim's head in the opposite direction, and a second cut joined the first in dribbling warm redness all over Osterhaudt's muscled chest.

"Who is your partner?" Berd asked again, remaining calm as Pitman's chest inhaled and exhaled rapidly.

Osterhaudt closed his eyes and tried to remove himself from the current situation. He refused to betray a woman whom he had learned to call a friend. He was also a CAF Reserve officer. They hadn't spent much time discussing prisoner of war scenarios, but Tim knew the stories from history. He would resist them as long as he could. Until whatever he babbled out of his mouth was so nonsensical it wouldn't matter how much he spoke.

Osterhaudt lifted his head slowly and stared at them both through swollen eyes—just for a moment. They waited as he opened his mouth to speak, looks of anticipation on their faces.

"Ambit League? Go fuck yourselves," Tim whispered.

$$*\qquad*\qquad*$$

Pitman screamed, and was on Osterhaudt in an instant, raining curse after curse and punch after punch.

Suddenly Pitman found himself grabbed by the shirt collar and hurled against the opposite bulkhead by an impossibly strong arm.

"You *fool!*" Berd hissed at a startled Pitman. "We need him *alive* for now. I told you to rough him up, not to *kill* him. Put your anger about Gabriella on hold until we can get both he and that damned woman out in the open. Together. After that, you can tear them both apart for all I care, but as long as she's loose in the ship, we need him as live bait. Understood?"

Pitman nodded his head, his lungs sucking in and expelling air at a very rapid, adrenalized pace.

*　　　*　　　*

Berd watched for a few more seconds, to be sure his executive wouldn't renew the rage-filled beating, then he turned away and picked up a communications headset from the nearby bridge console. He placed it on his graying head of hair and tossed a second unit to Pitman.

"Untie him from the seat," Berd said, "and carry him down a few decks to the cargo bay. If he won't give us what we need, then maybe we can use him to force her out of the air ducts."

Berd walked past Pitman towards the bridge lift tube.

*　　　*　　　*

Pitman spat once on the deck, and began to unstrap the tape from Osterhaudt's bindings—tape which had held him to the chair long after losing consciousness. Tim toppled to the floor, unable to stop himself. Pitman felt the urge to rain a series of savage kicks on the pilot, but didn't dare cross his boss's order to keep the young CAF troop alive.

CHAPTER 20

Kal slowly assembled the Archangel armor by feel.

First the interface body suit—which felt terrible being pulled on over the top of Kal's sweaty, filthy, and in some places bloody skin.

Then, the secondary coolant suit.

After that, the boots, and the legs, the lower torso, the upper torso, the shoulders, the upper arms, the gauntlets, and finally, sealing the collar to the helmet.

By the time she was done she was sweating so profusely in the cramped, unventilated interior of the crate, that she felt literally like she might suffocate. Unless she got some clean air.

The moment she got the neck ring to the suit's helmet sealed, the microcomputer interface came to life and a pleasantly female voice announced in her ears that the Archangel armor was activated and would she please select a mode of operation before continuing.

A projection appeared in Kal's field of view—made bright by the fact that the interior of the crate was pitch black—and Kal scanned the menu options:

DIAGNOSTIC TYPE A.

DIAGNOSTIC TYPE B.

DEMONSTRATION MODE.

NEW PILOT MODE.

DEPLOYMENT MODE.

Unsure of how to make her selection, Kal muttered something about being a new pilot.

The selection illuminated happily, then Kal felt a burst of air against her damp cheeks from the suit's own internal atmospheric pressurizer. Her eardrums felt the sudden shift, and she worked her jaw to pop them while the menu display showed a swirling circle—the near universal sign that the computer was booting its assigned program.

There was a gentle mechanical noise in Kal's ears, and she momentarily froze, wondering who—if anyone—outside the crate might be within listening distance. But then her fear abated as she realized that, for the first time since she'd crash-landed, Kal was not in any immediate danger from the people around her. Small arms wouldn't do much good against the Archangel. Tim had sworn it. So unless the privateers had something more powerful to throw against her, for the moment, Kal was essentially invulnerable.

At least if she could figure out how to work the system.

Tim had warned her again and again to take it easy. Not overreact. Not push the suit in the way she'd been used to pushing older suits.

Kal waited while the mode finally came up—with menus not a lot different from what she'd seen on her displays in the conventional armor units—then began navigating the selections by voice. Under ideal circumstances she'd have had plenty of time to go through all the choices and get things customized. Right now she merely needed the suit to respond to her as quickly and as powerfully as possible.

Brad R. Torgersen

Would the suit really be as good as Tim said it was?

Kal would soon find out.

A chime alerted Kal to the fact that a wireless signal was active, where none had been active before.

Kal ordered the signal to be piped to her speakers in her ears.

"Attention, this is Karl Berd, commander of the Ambit League ship *Goshawk*. I am speaking to the woman who has thus far stubbornly refused to cooperate with my requests that she cease and desist all harassment of my crew, and give herself into my custody. Since you have elected to be stubborn, I am now forced to be stubborn as well. My first officer has been quite thorough in his dealings with your young friend here. Quite thorough. Albeit nothing permanent has transpired. Yet. This may be about to change. Listen carefully."

Kal heard a sickening *crunch*, then a shuffling sound, followed by a barley contained yowl of pain. Tim.

They were now breaking bones!

Crunch.

Another, stronger scream from Tim's throat, which sounded dry and ragged.

"Respond," Berd's voice said, "or we keep going. When his fingers are done, then we break his toes. Then his arms, and legs. After that, you force us to get creative. Reply to this signal please, and announce your intention to surrender to my crew at once.

"No!" Kal suddenly blurted out in a ragged cry over the Archangel's wireless connection to the intra-ship network. Which to that point had merely been passive.

*   *   *

Tim Osterhaudt held back the tears as Pitman kept Tim's hand pinned to the top of an empty cargo crate. Tim's right index and middle fingers were grossly misshapen and had turned a horrible color of black, mixed with purple. They bled where crushed bone poked through the skin, and the pain was unimaginable.

Around the cargo bay, most of the crew of the ship stood armed and ready, guarding the access ducts and the hatches, waiting for Kal to surrender herself. So far Kal's only response on the wireless had been a resounding and emphatic, *"No!"*

*   *   *

150

Radar and Doppler navigation projected a virtual image of the crate walls around Kal, eliminating the need for lamp activation. The Archangel's power meter showed that the twin fuel cells were pegged to the top, and that neural mapping was proceeding rapidly. Movement would now be possible. A voice asked Kal if she would like to try to stand up.

Kal did more than that.

She went through the side of the crate.

Tim hadn't been kidding, the Archangel responded almost before Kal could think to move her body.

Kal kept going—from a walk, to a trot, to a run—and bulldozed her way through several more crates, until she stumbled out into a clear space in the middle of the cargo deck.

Mouths were agape, and eyes were wide.

Kal looked around her, 360 degrees, until she saw Tim, and the man standing over Tim with a wrench ready to strike.

Kal bodily swept the man aside like he was made of paper, and picked Tim up. He groaned at the pain such movement caused, but Kal spun and headed back the way she'd come. While weapons finally began to pop off, sending wild rounds *ping*ing and *pang*ing off of the deck.

Kal prayed that Tim wouldn't be hit as she aimed for the ramp that opened to the outside world. Light was flooding up the ramp—sunshine for the first time in several days?

Kal cradled Tim in her mechanized arms and protected him with her back as the whole of the cargo bay—dozens of crew, all firing—opened up on her. She skipped first left, then right, then stuttered left, then bowled over the three crew who were at the top of the ramp, and leapt out over the ramp entirely, her motor-assisted motion exaggerating the movement as if Kal were moving in barely a fraction of normal gravity.

It was a heady, exhilarating feeling, after being forced to skulk about the interior of the ship.

Finally, Kalliope Reardon had real power!

And she intended to use it.

But only after she got Tim a safe distance away from the ship.

Kal's legs churned up the loamy soil as she jogged, first to the treeline, and then into the trees. She maneuvered as best as she was able, mindful of Tim's condition, at the same time, she tried to put as much distance between the *Goshawk* and herself as possible.

Finally, having reached a small clearing, Kal stopped.

She gently bent to the soil and put Tim down.

He looked hideous, with his eyes almost swollen shut and his face ripped to shreds. His wounded hand was a pulp, and he was clearly dropping into shock.

"Kal," Tim said quietly through split lips.

Kal leaned in, being careful not to pinch or crush anything with the suit.

"I got you out of there," she said. "I finally got you out. I am so sorry I didn't do it sooner. Oh God, Tim, your face ... I'm sorry!"

"Not ... your ... fault," Tim said, and managed a weak smile.

"Tim," Kal said, "you're in worse shape than I thought. I can stay with you, if you want, but I am afraid they'll be after me if I don't do something quick. Maybe they'll even try to suit up themselves? How good is the Archangel when pitted against other Archangels?"

"I'll ... be okay," Tim said, struggling to sit up. Kal gently raised him into a sitting position.

"The suit," he said, "is learning you ... as you go. Like I ... said before, it's amazingly ... durable."

"I don't have any built-in weapons," Kal said. "This one appears to be a basic model."

"We don't ... arm them until ... they get to the ... testing lab."

"Then I'll just have to make do."

"Kal ... Reardon. Remember what I said? About ... not wanting to hurt people?"

"Yeah," Kal said.

"I changed ... my mind. If this were in ... the Conflux, I'd want the lot of them ... hanged."

"No jails or courts on this planet," Kal said, staring down at her wounded partner and friend. "But there is one kind of law."

"What law is that?" Tim asked.

"The kind I make with these," Kal said, holding up her gauntleted fists.

Tim managed a smile.

"I'll be right back," Kal said.

"I'll be here!" Tim encouraged her.

*   *   *

Kalliope Reardon came in on the *Goshawk* like a micro-sized freight train. Ignoring the small arms fire that spattered across the

Archangel suit, she went directly up the ramp and back into the cargo hold, flinging people bodily away from her and smashing shoulders, arms, legs, rib cages, and spines with a series of savage punches and kicks.

Those not smart enough to flee, were soundly pulverized under the Archangel's super-extra-large boot heels.

To the point that Kal was covered in gore from top to bottom.

But where was Commander Berd?

Or Berd's second-hand thug who'd delighted in brutalizing Tim?

A sudden rumbling in the ship alerted Kal to the fact that someone had triggered the old freighter's launch sequence.

Doubtless, from the bridge.

Kal wasn't sure how to get there from the cargo hold, but she knew a faster way. Collecting two of the submachine guns which had been abandoned on the deck, Kal darted back out of the cargo hold— the surviving privateers scattering out of her path—and hit the suit's limited flight boosters.

It wasn't anything to write home about.

Kal's path up to the top of the ship was a bobbling, weaving, legs-flailing embarrassment. But it got her where she needed to go.

Perched on the mottled, ugly skin of the *Goshawk*, Kal marched to where the wraparound windows of the bridge.

Inside, she saw two faces.

Just the men she wanted.

Kal pointed both submachine guns at one of the windows, and pulled the triggers back.

Rounds blared from the barrels.

But the bridge windows had been designed to be meteorite-resistant. The bullets embedded in the reinforced transparent fiberflex, without shattering it.

When the submachine guns were empty, Kal tossed them away and began stomping on the damaged window with both boots.

After six or seven hard kicks, the window finally blew inward: ripped from its metal frame.

Kal dove down, and found herself facing an unsettling sight.

Berd was still in his uniform, unarmed.

But the other man ... the other man had been smart, and collected the pieces of his own Archangel armor. Though the armor did not appear to be fully booted up just yet.

Without weapons, Kal had only her Archangel to work with.

Brad R. Torgersen

She kicked hard at her opponent's sternum.

He managed to get out of the way just in time.

The wireless signal that was connected to Kal's helmet speakers came alive once again.

"We're leaving this planet," the voice of Kal's opponent said. "And I'm not the only one who thought quickly enough to suit up while you whisked your friend away to safety."

"You'll have a hell of time flying this tub into orbit with the bridge being open to vacuum," Kal said.

"A minor problem, there are always the secondary and tertiary control centers. You, on the other hand, are soon going to be outmatched ten to one. I don't think even you will be foolish enough to take those odds. So you can either flee the ship before we take off, or we can keep right on fighting until a dozen of us in suits tear you limb from limb!"

Kal's opponent advanced on her, his movements getting more fluid as the suit's neural interface caught up with him.

For an instant, Kal considered. Could she take them all on? Assuming the numbers the man was stating were accurate?

Then she thought of Tim, laying half beaten to death back on the forest floor. He might not make it without Kal around to help and protect him.

The horizon outside the bridge windows began to shift and sink.

The *Goshawk* was ascending on her thrusters.

Kal might have had the suit to protect her, but the freighter was the only thing capable of getting her into orbit, which was where the *Goshawk*'s cradle ship would be waiting to take them out of the system.

In the end, it proved to be one of the harder calls in Kal's life.

But it was the right call.

She climbed back up out of the bridge, skipped across the skin of the ship to the tail, and hit her flight thrusters. She floated easily down to the forest below as the ugly, abused *Goshawk* climbed slowly and steadily into the sky, roaring like a dragon.

CHAPTER 21

Five days later, Kal and Tim were holed up in the remains of the *Broadbill.*

With the Ambit League gone and no apparent sign of any other human life on the uncharted planet, what else was there to do but settle in and make themselves cozy?

It beat the hell out of trying to build a lean-to in the forest.

And it allowed them to stick close to the few remaining Archangel suits which had not yet been salvaged by the privateers; though finding those crates in the huge mess of other debris would be a time-consuming affair.

On their fifth night alone, Kal and Tim sat around the small space heater Kal had recovered from the wreck. With electric power still provided by the undamaged cells in the *Broadbill's* carcass, Kal figured they had enough electricity to last them several years.

Which wouldn't be nearly long enough, Kal reckoned.

"Nobody will find us," Kal said, a blanket wrapped around her shoulders while she sipped at a cup of hot soup.

Tim had his own cup of the same soup, only carefully clutched in his good hand. The bad one was bandaged tight in a foam-seal emergency cast. Something Kal had found in an emergency locker, and applied. After holding Tim down and setting the bones back in place. Doubtless the hand would need major surgery, if ever they got back to civilization. But at least the hand would heal, for however long they were marooned.

"Sure they'll find us," Tim said. "We already know somebody knew about this planet, because the Ambit League had to pick out the coordinates ahead of time, and give them to the hijackers who took the *Broadbill* from Viking Station. The problem is, the people finding us will be Ambit League, not CAF. Berd and his buddy Pitman will be back. For the rest of the *Broadbill's* cargo, if nothing else."

"Maybe," Kal said, before taking a long, throat-warming sip.

"You think otherwise?"

"I'm not entirely convinced that wreck survived getting to orbit, frankly. It was halfway to falling apart as things were."

"And if it didn't, someone else will still come."

Kal thought about it. "Because of the Archangels."

"Because of the Archangels," Tim agreed.

Kal looked over at her young partner's wounded hand.

"Think you'll be able to put on a gauntlet when that smashed paw of yours gets better?"

"Maybe," Tim said. "Why?"

"Because it'll take more than just me to fight whoever shows up next time. We're still in the same pickle as when we first got here: how the hell to get off this planet and back to friendly space."

"By the graces of the Ambit League," Tim said, and chuckled.

"With my boot on their throats," Kal said, narrowing her eyes.

"Maybe," Tim said.

"Definitely. I'm pissed off now. I'm not in the habit of letting perps walk away. This Berd guy, and his crew ... I want them. Dead or alive."

"Frontier justice?" Tim said.

"It's the only kind we've got now, Tim."

He stared off into the distance—away from the wreck, and into the tall trees.

"Yeah, I suppose you're right. It's all we've got."

ABOUT THE AUTHOR

Brad R. Torgersen has been nominated for the Hugo, Nebula, and Campbell awards, is a Writers of the Future award winner, and an Analog Magazine readers' choice award winner. He has collaborated with multi-award winner Mike Resnick, and has published numerous stories with both Analog science fiction magazine, and Orson Scott Card's Intergalactic Medicine Shown. A Chief Warrant Officer in the United States Army Reserve, Brad's first military science fiction novel, THE CHAPLAIN'S WAR, will be published with Baen Books.

DAGGER TEAM SEVEN

R.M. MELUCH

1.

I t wasn't the first strike into enemy space. It was meant to be the last one.

The Dagger team of six fast assault craft dropped out of the final warp into the staging zone for the advance into Rutog space. The ships' navigation systems automatically turned them to face the Intersection.

Pilot Zack Cade couldn't see the anomaly yet.

There was no telling how long the Intersection had really been here. From any angle other than absolutely face on, not only was the Intersection undetectable, but the thing truly wasn't there. You couldn't see it from the rear. It didn't have a rear.

Zack Cade's Dagger ship moved into attack formation with the other five members of his team at the specified coordinates and attitude.

And instantly the Intersection was there before them.

At least two voices shouted over the com—sounded like Umber and Gretch. "Look at that!"

The Assault Force Controller called for com discipline. That never worked on a Dagger Team. Dagger pilots were notorious cowboys.

"No, really. Where's the Intersection?" Pilot Gort Neuman said, like refusing bait. And Zack couldn't blame him. The Intersection looked like a very bad special effect—like a misplaced lake, or a titanic dark purple-blue looking glass with a molten gold-white line drawn around it badly.

As things in space went it was small, no more than four by six miles by nothing.

It didn't belong in three-dimensional space. It was a cartoon hole. Any object sent toward it ceased to register upon reaching the coordinates where the Intersection appeared to exist.

Zack squinted at the Intersection through his clearscreen, then felt stupid for squinting. Common sense said he should be able to see through it. There wasn't anything common or sensible about the Intersection.

Zack angled his Dagger ship a half a degree off perfect square. The Intersection vanished and the voice of Control was sounding in his helmet.

"Dagger Six, you are out of position."

Yep. Noticed that.

"True us up, John Henry," Zack told his ship.

The Dagger ship obeyed. The Intersection returned, big, blue-black, and weird.

Zack Cade and the other five Daggers were about pass through it into somewhere else.

It was a cosmic magician's trick, but Zack couldn't see the wires.

The big white main star of the system shone at their backs. Sirius A was twice the size of Sol.

Zack could see the companion star, Sirius B, a bright dot in the distance. Sirius B was a white dwarf not a whole lot bigger than planet Earth.

Space inside the Sirius system was cluttered with sunlit debris from countless skirmishes between humans and the Rutogs. The husks of twisted human-built space stations tumbled in their orbits.

The Assault Force was already assembled when the six Daggers arrived.

The force was almost entirely mechanized. There was a consequence to human soldiers passing through the Intersection. The Dagger pilots were aware of it going in. They accepted it. This was their job.

The rest of the attack craft were mobile battle forts, heavy shepherds, and smart turrets.

The Intersection stood quiet for the moment. That could be a good sign. It could be fatally not good. Something dire could be building up on the other side. And there was no way to take a quick peek to know. Not in this universe.

The Earth-built defensive stations stood ready here on the friendly side, their guns fixed on the anomaly. The international space towers were collectively called the Citadel. Their defensive guns were programmed to fire at *anything* that came through the Intersection not carrying a tracer.

Do not lose your tracer! That point really got hammered home during the briefing. Zack wondered why so they were so insistent. Zack's tracer was surgically implanted in the roof of his mouth. He wasn't going to accidentally drop it somewhere.

Space mines peppered the zone between the Intersection and the Assault Force. A plot of the mines was programmed into all the attack crafts' avoidance systems. The Dagger pilots didn't need to think about the mines. The ships could blitz through the zone balls to the wall. You just concentrate what comes into your sights on the far side.

Zack had been warned: you cross through the Intersection you are instantly not in Kansas, Kuala Lumpur, Rio, or your mama's front porch anymore.

The space beyond the Intersection had been named Rutog, for a remote mountain pass on Earth.

Zack had seen the videos from past recon flights. The vids don't really prepare you. And they couldn't tell him what was waiting for him over there right *now*.

And what comes out of the Intersection from Rutog space was never friendly.

The Rutogs never even tried to act friendly. Zack supposed it was a tough act to pull off when you were a ciliate bag of gas or a macroscopic rotifer. You could trust Rutogs absolutely. They had no concept of stealth. It's like they assumed you already knew what they're thinking, and they had to beat you to it. They showed no mercy to their own injured. No one had ever seen a Rutog try to signal cease fire—not by any signal that a human being could recognize as a signal. The Rutogs were honest about their intent to annihilate you.

The moment that Dagger Team Nine arrived in the mustering zone, the countdown had started. It was down to invasion minus nine seconds and the first mechanized unit started to glow.

Four. Three.

The first mobile forts' distortion fields went live.

Two.

Mama can't help you now.

The forts were committed.

The first line units—known as linebackers—hurtled at the flat impossibility. The linebackers were unmanned smart ordnance programmed to find their own targets. Their objective was to destroy everything within twelve astronomical units of the far side of the Intersection. That meant everything: Living and inanimate, machines, mines, green cheese. Leave nothing intact. Priority to objects propelled by powerplants.

The linebackers hit the Intersection and vanished.

"Ho!" Zack heard himself shout.

Right after the linebackers, the Colossus forts charged through.

There was no way of knowing if they were having effect.

"Hope they leave some trade for us," Gort Neuman sent over the Team com.

The Dagger ships moved into position.

Like thoroughbreds loaded in a gate, Daggers weren't made to stand around and wait. As soon as they formed up, their ten second countdown began.

Zack glanced aside in the last moments. With cockpits illuminated he saw Paul Rittenhouse on his starboard and Ix Chel Parras off his port wing.

"See you on the other side," Zack said into the Team com.

The voice of Control sounded: "Three. Two. God speed from a grateful nation and all of humanity."

Zack heard only half of that benediction as he shot toward the flat blue-black nothingness. He went though yelling. Honestly, how do you not yell? He expected the lights to go out for a split instant. They didn't. He was just suddenly over there. There was no simulation for this. He didn't know what he expected—to lose contact with his own ass or something.

He burst out of the intersection hot, firing blind. Just assume there is a target. He couldn't hear Control's blessing anymore. But he heard Gort Neuman screeching some kind of battle cry and saw his tactical display instantly altered. His ship was already spewing chemical bullets and his canopy was surrounded by boiling light.

This was what they called recon by fire. You don't see the battlefield until you were in it.

Don't worry overmuch about hitting anything friendly, he'd been told. Your squadron's avoidance systems were programmed against hitting your own. Even if you did happen to hit one of your own allies, none of the friendlies on this side were living beings. The other five Dagger pilots were the only humans here.

Paul Rittenhouse was speaking. "The enemy will see us by our gunfire. They will know us by their dying."

Target-rich was not the situation they'd been led to expect from the briefing.

Up-to-date advance recon wasn't to be had. Ever.

Really you only needed to assume the worst, that the Rutogs had been building up something lethal on their side and were going to bury you or fry you as soon as you stuck your nose in their space.

Well, they were trying. The Rutogs were here in their glassy gassy thousands, reeling from the linebackers' assault, and spilling their vaporous innards under Zack's guns.

The Rutogs still hadn't developed hard body spacecraft. They were using cloud ships—transparent-skinned, luminescent, their insides swirling all the colors of fire. The Rutogs were, all of them, gaseous beings inside clear membranes with ciliate appendages, which were hollow. The damned things were very dexterous for not having hands.

The soft ones could stretch themselves out into tendrils and reform again. The cylindrical ones were rigid and had whip tails on one end. Rutogs could exist for several seconds in the vacuum while their cloud ships moved in to absorb them back to safety.

Zack carried Old Glory into battle, posted on his ship's stern. The Stars and Stripes remained stiff in the vacuum, lit up by the rockets' red glare. Underneath the national flag, the Dagger ships also flew black flags to declare no prisoners.

Rutogs winked out under their guns like dying skyrockets.

Lieutenant Rittenhouse announced on the team com: "Enemies of my country, you are dying today."

Zack joined in the chorus of six in a unified grunt: "*Hroob!*" That was an amen in this prayer meeting.

The mission previous to this one had been charged with establishing a spacehead on this side of the chokepoint. Nope. Hadn't happened. Nothing friendly here except their own linebackers. If an earlier force had established a defensive emplacement, it was gone now.

Zack's ship was calling his shots. A human being wasn't quick enough on the draw. The pilot picked the targets and made all the judgment calls. Zack's ship knew when to ask for judgment. He—the ship, *John Henry*—did a good imitation of human reason.

Bright flashes burst all around them. It was like being inside the finale of a Capital Fourth of July. The flares opaqued Zack's canopy. There was too much visual and none of it useful. The plots on his tac screen made no sense, and now his ship was doing the dead wrong thing about them.

Zack was taking fire. Heavy hits, the kind the Rutog weren't supposed to have.

His distortion field buzzed.

The Dagger ships had been equipped with a camouflage scheme called nulliflage. The ships were meant to read like nothing to the enemy sensors. That was the idea. It wasn't working. The enemy was detecting us just fine. Zack slid a hotpoint inside one of those gaseous cloud ships. It combusted nicely.

Then Zack took a hit. Big one. Not a buzzy little Rutog hit. Zack's energy barriers lit up. A sick sound groaned from his ship's field generators. That blast was all wrong. *That* was a Poseidon bolt.

How in the hell?

Zack's mind refused to process what Morris Umber was yelling over the com: "Friendly fire!"

Poseidon bolts were made in the USA. That shot had come from one of the US mobile forts.

There was a lot of yelling on the com. Zack wasn't the only one under friendly fire.

"Our space forts are shooting at us!" Zack yelled into a suddenly dead com.

His ship had just shut off his com. Zack manually switched to the emergency channel in time to hear the end of Umber's shout, "-ucked!"

Ix Chel shouted, "I'm riding a runaway!"

"My ship mutinied!" That was Calvin Gretch.

Zack's own tactical screen was going dark.

Zack tried to switch over to manual control of his own Dagger ship. The controls balked.

Zack felt cold. "*John Henry*, what are you doing?"

Zack called his ship John Henry. Not sure why he chose that name. It was the name of a tough guy. Zack had heard it in a song and it stuck.

His ship, *John Henry*, responded, "I am following the new protocol. I detect disapproval from you. Please advise a correction."

Zack bellowed, "Reset protocol to original state! Discard any external orders you received on this side of the Intersection! Reject any more external orders you get without my authorization!"

The ship complied. "Resetting, aye. Rejecting external directives, aye."

Com connections were reappearing on Zack's readouts. Calvin Gretch still wasn't there. Lieutenant Rittenhouse was demanding, "Gretch! What is your situation?"

Calvin Gretch's voice burst from the com. "*Normal! Why do you ask?*"

Another Poseidon bolt lit up Zack's canopy. That Zack saw it meant his screens were holding.

The voice of Lieutenant Rittenhouse sounded wonderfully calm, ordering, "Dagger Team Nine, call in."

"Neuman, aye."

"Umber, aye."

"Gretch, aye."

"Parras, aye."

"Cade, aye," Zack said.

"We are wasting time here. Join up. On my mark."

The Dagger ships synchronized their nav systems with Rittenhouse's ship.

"Calling for big frog in five, four—"

No one called a balk during the three, two, one.

All six ships obediently created a warp to the coordinates that Rittenhouse fed into their nav systems.

And came out light years away.

It felt like running away, but it wasn't. The team had been told specifically: *Do not engage the enemy in the chokepoint.* The Daggers were not here to fight a battle without strategic benefit. The Daggers were meant to plunge through the chokepoint and leave any battle back there for the robot force.

Trouble was the robot ships back at the chokepoint had joined the other side.

163

Rittenhouse must've read all their minds because he told his pilots, "The traitors are not our responsibility. We'll read them the way of righteousness on our way back. We have a mission to complete first."

"We have clingers," Morris Umber reported.

Some Rutog riders had come along into the warp fold with the Daggers.

"Lose them," Rittenhouse said. "Big frog in three, two, one."

The squadron warped again to the coordinates given by Rittenhouse's ship.

Rittenhouse called for yet another big frog. He gave the coordinates verbally this time. Meant he wasn't quite trusting his ship not to share the coordinates with the enemy.

The hell of it was the Dagger team couldn't get a message back to the home side warning of the turncoat machines—not in time for anyone to do anything about it.

Rittenhouse spoke very quietly. His soft drawl beat down the pilots' roaring curses better than a shout ever could. "This setback in no way changes our game plan. Keep in mind what we want. We want them dead. We are not here to beat up gas. We are not here to take real estate. They don't have any."

This was Operation End Zone. That kinda said it all.

"It is past time to take the battle home and that is what we will do. We will go deep. We will locate the Rutog manufacturing and supply centers and destroy them. We will locate the enemy nexus and kill the enemy."

The enemy was nothing you could feel bad about killing.

The Rutogs themselves didn't show much individuality. First data suggested that the Rutogs didn't recognize that there could be such a thing as the thought processes of a separate intelligence outside of their own.

First data was wrong, or else the Rutogs' thought processes were evolving. They had the sense to turn human weaponry on humans.

Rittenhouse called for another big frog. The squadron came out kiloparsecs deeper into Rutog space. The team regrouped there, strangers in strangeness.

It was dark here, really dark, with a thin scatter of dim red stars. Rutog space was massively empty.

Zack Cade glowered through the clear bubble top of his cockpit at the dark. His brow tightened. He muted his com.

"You turned on me, *John Henry*," Zack told his ship.

The ship detected disapproval in his pilot's voice and understood that Zack was angry. "I didn't know that I was obeying a wrong protocol until your bio markers suggested an emergency," *John Henry* said.

Zack was trying not to take this personal. It shook him up, the betrayal. He'd been ready for anything. He hadn't been ready for that.

Your Dagger ship has your six, your twelve, your whole sphere of existence. It blasts anything that means you harm. It can smell trouble in a vacuum. Not literally. Well, literally it could smell your fear in the cockpit. Intuitive scientists had programmed a fine imitation of intuition into these machines, which was how *John Henry* figured out in time that someone had fed him false directives.

The Daggers were far from the Intersection now. Their trusty— supposedly trusty—ships constantly scanned all around for anything else coming in. Not that anything could track them through a warp.

The Rutogs also traveled by means of warps, so you might not see them until they were on you. Your Dagger ship was meant to detect them first and carry you out of harm's way.

Your Dagger was your shelter, your steed, your medic, your best friend. It would die for you, but you don't risk anything on its account. The Dagger ship is just a machine. It exists to let you do your job—to defend these United States against all threats anywhere anytime.

And they really meant any *time*.

Your ship is a tactician. You are the strategists. You give the objective. The Dagger ship will make it happen.

Your Dagger will disobey a self-destructive order unless you give it a good reason for your sacrifice. It can read your physical state, and has some clue of your emotional state, but it's not a mind reader. It will never spend your life without a superb reason.

They guard, guide, watch over you with singular devotion. It was easy to think that they love you though you know it's just elegant programming.

You can't help but love it like a brother, a mother, a wife, a dog, a horse, a magic dragon. Your own ship is always a he or a she, never an it.

She carries you and always gets you home. (Mel Rittenhouse named his ship *Sherry*). But *he* has your back, your up, your down, your sideways. (Zack named his *John Henry*). Your Dagger ship will die before he or she will let anything get you—and you'd better let him die for you.

R.M. Meluch

You get yourself civilian real quick if you start protecting your ship.

Zack heard clicking. Someone was coding a report with his com un-muted.

Zack spoke into the open com. "Never known Rutogs to be this smart."

"You and me," Ix Chel said back.

Normal Rutog behavior was to fly en masse into human space and blunder into the mines. They'd been doing it for decades. The aliens had never showed any ability to consider how their enemy might be thinking. "Rutogs aren't supposed to be able to anticipate," Morris Umber said, taking it personal.

"Yeah. Make sure to include a message to Intelligence that they need to re-assess that shovel-load," said Gretch.

"Roger Wilco," Umber muttered.

It was pretty clear that the Rutogs had conceived the concept of Otherness.

They'd been at this for forty years now. "They're learning," Zack said.

"They're not supposed to do that," Gretch said, the irony in his voice heavy as a brick. "The experts said so."

"The experts left out the time element. Over *time* the Rutogs learn. Why wouldn't they?" Umber said. "They're space travelers, not the village idiots. They figured out how to corrupt our machine controls."

"That's not ever what you want an enemy to do, now is it," Zack said.

Umber came back, "What I'm saying is that counting on an enemy's ineptitude will quickly get you dead."

The Daggers' auto-logs had recorded every aspect of their assault, including their own ships' betrayal. Morris Umber loaded the assembled reports into a data dart. He sent the dart over to Lieutenant Paul Rittenhouse who composed a scathing epistle to the Intelligence section and shoved the report urgently into the data dart. Then he transmitted to the team, "Last call for mail. Anyone want to say Hi Mom?"

They all did. They transmitted their messages over to Rittenhouse's Dagger. Rittenhouse loaded the messages, closed up the data dart, checked that its tracer was active, and shot the dart back toward the Intersection.

The report and the Hi Moms wouldn't arrive back through the Intersection into the Sirius star system for five years.

But the only other choice was to send nothing.

2.

The first Dagger units had been formed during the Rim Bloc conflict, back when normal space was the only space anyone knew, and the Milky Way was the only galaxy humankind ever explored, and Rutogs were beyond anyone's worst tequila-washed nightmare.

Dagger Teams One through Four had been surgical strike teams, trained to get in stealthily, retrieve data or hostages or enemy persons of interest without incurring civilian casualties and get out.

There was little stealthy about the modern Daggers.

This alien conflict was a different kind of fight.

The United States and the other human nations were not sending an army into enemy space. They didn't know the ground and they had no interest in capturing territory. Dagger Team Nine was over here to neutralize the alien threat with extreme prejudice. Kill the enemy. Destroy the alien war machine.

Each of the six Dagger ships carried six missiles armed with a Stodolsky metananovirus. The metananovirus spread rapidly through the aliens to infect all contiguous parts of the alien and solidify the gaseous Rutog into a dead solid. The boffins had tested it on the Rutogs which infested the ruined space stations of the Sirius system. The results had been stellar.

The Stodolsky metananovirus was species-specific and self-limiting. When the virus ran out of Rutog, the virus went inert. The resultant compound was dense. Removal became a mining operation, but that was a small trade off.

The Daggers hadn't deployed the metananovirus at the chokepoint. They had orders to deliver it to a strategic address only.

As Gort put it, "Don't spend it on the little shit. Use it to win the war."

There were other ways to kill Rutogs. Rutogs burned easily enough. But hitting them with flamethrowers was like bailing out an ocean. There were too many of them.

Dagger Team Nine had orders to deliver the metananovirus into major battle groups and to release it into the atmosphere of the Rutog homeworld. That meant finding the Rutog homeworld.

The leader of Dagger Team Nine was Lieutenant Paul Rittenhouse, the only officer in this unit. Ritt came from money. He was a gentleman and always made sure his opponents, other than Rutogs, got medical attention when he was done with them. Even though Ritt was a lieutenant, he sirred everyone—enlisteds, officers, janitors, the bum in the alley, and the rats who claimed to work for a living. Rittenhouse had bailed out of divinity college in North Carolina to go forth and read the Book of Revelation to all enemies of the United States.

Pilot Calvin Gretch flew in the second spot. Everyone called him Retch. How could you not? Gretch was at the upper limit for height for a pilot. Had arms like an orangutan. Guys didn't come any whiter or blonder than Gretch without having red eyes to match. Gretch's eyes were pale ice-chip blue. He was a natural shot. If you're on the ground and all your computerized systems are AWOL you just give Gretch an antique weapon—a rock, a spear—and he'll find the target. That talent was kind of wasted in a space battle, but the instant shoot-don't shoot instinct wasn't.

Pilot Morris Umber was the one holding the brain for the group. He had a science and technology background, but no degree to show for it. University was a bore. Umber was going to get rich inventing stuff in the private sector when he got too slow to pilot a Dagger ship.

Pilot Ix Chel Parras was the only she-Dagger to date. The he-to-she ratio in the regular Space Corps was about half and half. Endurance, lightning reflexes, and quick thinking were more important than brawn in conventional space fighters. A regular Space Corps pilot wasn't meant to ever come out of his cockpit in the course of duty. Dagger jocks were expected to be brutes in or out of their machines. Dagger pilots needed to be able to run carrying their heaviest teammate and load his injured self into his cockpit.

Ix Chel had the brawn. She had a majestic face, like something that ought to be carved into a cliff. Zack supposed you could call it a good looking face, but looking at it you just don't think about her having any girl parts. And she wasn't thinking about using them around this lot either. Just to make that clear early on she came swaggering into training with a salami hanging from the crotch of her pants. She fit in just fine and it didn't surprise most guys that she made it all the way to full fledged Dagger jock. It didn't make no nevermind if Ix Chel was an innie or an outtie. She could bench press Zack. Zack knew that for a fact, because he'd dared her do it.

Pilot Gort Neumann was built like an armored assault vehicle, and you had to ask yourself, what did Gort really need a ship for? Gort had hauled himself up from nothing, became a pro bare knuckle fighter, and soon enough Gort was pissing money, collecting race cars, and procreating with actresses. Gort was an adrenalin addict. He got bored easy. The ring was too safe. It didn't mean anything. And he really wanted a job where he could shoot bad guys and blow shit up.

Pilot Zack Cade. If he had to define himself in one word it would be Patriot. Zack's Dad had done his best to discourage Zack from the military. That backfired about as hard as anything ever blew back at a man. Zack landed in the most elite of all military cadres, the Daggers, the most admired, feared, envied, storied, imitated, and impersonated unit in the US armed forces.

Zack wondered what Dad would think if he'd lived to see this day.

Living to the end of this day was Zack's immediate challenge. He was deep down Alice's rabbit hole now.

It was a different universe over here. On this side, the Intersection wasn't in the Sirius system. It sat in the middle of astronomical nowhere. It wasn't near any planets. It wasn't in a star system unless you counted those two planet-sized black spheres that orbited the Intersection like heraldic charcoal bricks.

The first Rutogs had come through the Intersection into the Sirius star system before anyone knew the Intersection was there.

It was some forty years ago now that the first gaseous aliens came out of nowhere, opened up the space stations in the Sirius system and let all the people out. The aliens took up residence in the hollowed-out space stations like squatters in a ruined shanty town. No one knew where they were coming from. People just assumed they were dropping out of warps from some other part of the Milky Way. Only when huge scintillating red orange masses of Rutog cloud ships came pouring out of absolute nothingness did anyone locate the two-dimensional Intersection. The Intersection was visible from only one angle. No one was sure how long the Intersection had been there or if the Rutog created it or if the Rutog just stumbled through it.

R.M. Meluch

The B star of the Sirius system had gone supernova in recorded
human history. The Dog Star shone so bright in Earth day skies that
the ancient Greeks thought it added heat to the August days. That was
how they got the name the Dog Days. Sirius had shone big and red in
the Earth sky in the time of Ptolemy.

That nova had since collapsed to a white dwarf. Sirius B was
Earth-sized now but with the mass of a sun. No nuclear reactions were
going on inside it. Sirius B was just a big old campfire.

The collapse of Sirius B may have had something to do with the
formation of the Intersection inside the Sirius system, but that was just
a guess without any data behind it.

Human science was long familiar with forming warps to cross
interstellar distances, but the Intersection was in its own class of this-
is-not-happening.

A consortium of human planetary nations set up a blockade
around the Intersection with a mandate to kill everything that comes
out of that hole.

The enemy kept coming.

Decades ago the US resolved to take the battle to the enemy.

Dagger Team Five advanced through the Intersection and
vanished. The Daggers were meant to assess the battleground and fire
at any target of opportunity while collecting data of what was there,
then turn around and report home.

The sortie was meant to last twenty minutes. The Daggers failed
to show.

The ships' programmed auto-return failsafes failed.

Twenty minutes stretched into months.

Candles were lit and hymns were sung on the anniversary of the
Daggers' crossing, when it appeared to a certainty that they'd gone to
angels. Dagger ships didn't carry air, food, fuel, and supplies for a one-
year tour.

Scout drones were sent through. Someone should've sent those in
first. The scout drones were programmed to collect data for five
minutes, turn around, and report back. Those failed to return, too.

That was the end of sending anything through the Intersection.

It was to be a defensive war after all. Massive towers and many
space fortresses bristling with weapons sprang up around the
Intersection under the flags of many nations, all their guns pointed at
the anomaly. The whole international lot of them altogether were
called the Citadel.

The Americans were putting out flags and rehearsing the hymns for a five-year memorial service to honor the tragic Dagger Team Five.

Then Dagger Team Five came back.

The lead ship broke through one of the ice garlands positioned in front of the Intersection.

The Citadel fortresses nearly shot them. The fortresses tried to, but their firing mechanisms balked on detecting the Friendly signal from the Daggers' onboard tracers.

The six Dagger ships leapt out of the Intersection wearing scorch marks on their spent firing platforms. Their magazines of space poniards were exhausted. Their flamethrowers were out of gas.

From the perspective of space normal, Dagger Team Five had been missing just about five years—exactly four years, three hundred fifty-eight days, thirteen hours, five minutes and eighteen seconds. Close enough to say five years.

The Dagger ships' internal chronometers had only clocked twenty minutes. The pilots didn't need to shave.

The ships reported that the laws of physics operated the same over there as they did here. It was only the Intersection itself that appeared to defy the law.

The pilots reported that their weapons and ships also functioned the same over there as they did here. The Daggers had shot a lot of Rutogs. They reported the presence of gaseous structures guarding the pass on the other side. Rutog weaponry was ineffective against the Dagger ships. Rutog clouds ships burned as easily on that side as Rutog cloud ships burned on this side.

After the Daggers' debriefing, the pilots were hot to go back in. They'd had no idea how long they'd been gone. They were massively unhappy to find that they'd skipped over the last five years of human events and that their mothers had cried.

They were mortally embarrassed at the decorations on their graves. Last thing you want to see on coming home was your own boxed flag on your mom and dad's mantel.

Soon after the return of Dagger Team Five, the drone scouts started returning as well—five years from the time they left. The drones brought only sixty minutes worth of observations from the other side. They'd spent sixty minutes worth of fuel. Their onboard tracers kept them from being annihilated by the guns of the Citadel on re-entry.

It became apparent that the length of a man's or machine's stay over there in Rutog space had zero effect on the duration of the traveler's absence from real spacetime.

Anything that crossed the Intersection returned five years from when it left.

What lay beyond the Intersection wasn't any place inside the Milky Way. You couldn't even find the Milky Way on the map that the scouts had assembled on the other side.

From the military standpoint, the major fact to come out of Dagger Team Five's return was that crossing to the other side was survivable. The return trip was also survivable. A defensive war wasn't the only option any more.

Humanity really could take the war home to the Rutog.

According to the terrestrial calendar, Dagger Team Five's tour of duty was up. It was past up. Their enlistment period was up. Space Corps Command asked if the team would go back in for a four-month tour, understanding that there was a hard possibility that they would miss another five years here in real space. Dagger Team Five agreed to go. They demanded to go.

Zack Cade understood that. Those guys had to get away from all the wreaths and memorials, and from that damned song. Crap, someone had composed a song for them.

Dagger Team Five flew through the Intersection at the head of a computerized, unmanned invasion force.

Dagger Team Five re-emerged from Rutog space five years later, aged a few minutes but broken and battered this time. A mass of Rutogs had been waiting at the chokepoint and slammed them the instant they crossed into Rutog space. The whole battle had taken minutes. The pilots hadn't been bleeding long when they arrived in real space five years later. The passage through the Intersection lasted the blink of the only conscious eye. The rest of the team was comatose. Their ships had made the decision to turn around and come home.

The medics were able to save all the injured pilots. The Dagger ships were repaired.

Earth and her colonial allies bulked up the fortifications around the Intersection. The Citadel guns mowed down anything that came through the Intersection not carrying tracers.

Dagger Team Six failed to accomplish anything that computerized forces couldn't.

For decades no more manned craft were sent through.

No nation was going to commit armies to the other side without timely recon.

When an accumulation of data collected by drones pointed to a strategic target, Dagger Team Eight was sent in to destroy it. It was the first human assault in decades.

Months later, here was Dagger Team Nine arrived with a major mechanized force, which had immediately joined the other side.

Team Nine had survived the initial disaster. They were here to kill Rutogs.

Deep into Rutog space and still traveling, the Daggers circled the wagons.

The six Dagger ships joined up, gunside out, connecting their sternside panels to form a hexagonal space among them with a flat floor. The ships extended a tented overhead, sealed the enclosure and pumped in a shared atmo. Gravity was supplied by the steady acceleration of the six docked spacecraft in the direction of their communal topside. Earlier Dagger teams had named the shared enclosure their space yurt.

Morris Umber climbed out of his cockpit and stalked back into the yurt, growling as he tore his bubble-head helmet off. "Do we have *any* good intelligence on these things?"

Ix Chel threw her helmet across the open space. "I want my mommy!"

Rittenhouse stomped into the yurt. "Now I surely do recall they told us everything over here wants us dead. I didn't reckon they meant OUR OWN SIDE!" He threw Ix Chel's helmet back at her.

Calvin Gretch was still in his cockpit, woodshedding his ship for letting herself be co-opted by alien programming. Gretch's ship, *Ruby*, took the reaming like a head-hanging dog.

Zack Cade came into the yurt laughing on a battle high. He had to laugh. That encounter had got his heart racing. That was real honest-to-God fear he'd felt back there. But now he and his mates were alive and lots of the enemy weren't. The coffee was hot, the beer was cold, and Gort Neuman was still ugly. Life was all right.

The conjoined Dagger ships took the watch. Calvin Gretch brought out the basketball. Rittenhouse's ship held the hoop. The other Dagger ships couldn't be trusted not to tilt to help their own pilots. The ships didn't understand cheating. They understood winning.

The pilots played hard, bleeding off some of this adrenaline jag, as they did a post mortem on their entry into enemy space,

Morris Umber sat on the sideline with a checklist.

"They're using rupture weapons," Umber said from the bench. "That's new from last update."

"Wonder if they learned that from us," Rittenhouse said, trying for a three pointer. "Note that. What's next?""

" Shimmer," Umber said.

"Was there any Shimmer in play?"

"I didn't see Shimmer back there," Zack said. He slipped in someone's sweat. Gort stole the ball from him.

"Don't wanna see Shimmer," said Ix Chel, taking the pass from Gort.

"Shimmer beat the Jesus out of Dagger Team Five in the way back," Rittenhouse said.

Umber went down the checklist. "Concussion mines. There were lots of those."

"Didn't hit any," said Ix Chel.

"Avoidance systems worked on those," said Gretch.

Rittenhouse asked, "Can we withstand concussion mines?"

"Should," Umber said.

Rittenhouse intercepted the ball and held it midcourt. "You know? I never much cared for that word. Should. *Should* doesn't rightly know which side it's on. Can we or can we not withstand contact with a concussion mine?"

His whole team answered in tired chorus: "Insufficient data."

"Be it known," Rittenhouse declared. "I have grown so all-fired, hell and tarnation tired of hearing those two words slapped together."

"It be known, Lieutenant," said Ix Chel.

"Right then," said Rittenhouse. "Clean up. I want everyone inside a tactical map in five."

The team re-gathered five minutes later in the yurt space, which had transformed into a planetarium. It was like standing in Rutog space without a ship.

"This place is as weird as the recon report said," Calvin Gretch said.

"Weirder," Umber said.

Space on this side of the Intersection was a region of ancient stars. They already knew that from early reconnaissance. Being *in* it brought a whole different understanding. It was dark. The stars were dim and red and there weren't a whole lot of them.

Rittenhouse called it disconcerting.

"Do we know where we are? On the map?" Rittenhouse asked. "Do we have a proper map? Is this current?"

"Are you expecting the stars to change since the last recon, Lieutenant?"

"*Could.*"

Morris Umber had to allow that. No one could be sure what happened to spacetime on this side of the Intersection when they weren't looking.

They already knew that time over here did not synch with time back there. Why couldn't space get equally spongy?

"Anyone know where we are now compared to where we were on the other side?" Zack asked.

"No," Morris Umber said.

"Where's Sirius? It was right next to the gate when we left."

"Sirius isn't here."

The biggest objects near the Intersection on the Rutog side were two cold, dense, dead planet-sized charcoal rocks like gate guardians in tired orbit.

"This can't be the Milky Way. Can it?" Rittenhouse said.

Umber said, "People who analyze these things for a living aren't sure this is even the same universe."

Gort Neuman objected to that. "What's with this "other universe" *scheisse*? Doesn't the *uni* part of that *verse* mean there's only one verse?"

"There's no background radiation here," Morris Umber said. "There should be some if we were in our universe. The elements are the same, but they're *old*. And the radioactive elements are in real short supply. I'm not seeing main sequence stars larger than an M type, and nothing brighter than a white dwarf. Gravitational hot spots on the tactical map are neutron stars and black holes. We're not in a galaxy. It's just a clutter of small stars. There's no hint of spiral. No galactic arms. Space is *small* here. And farther out space is *empty*. There's *nothing* farther away than a few hundred thousand light years."

"Yes, a few hundred thousand light years is very constricting." Gort said gripping his chest. "I'm having trouble breathing."

Zack felt the smallness. Strange how claustrophobic a few hundred thousand light years could feel.

"What the hell kind of place is this?" Zack asked Umber.

"This is the place Rutogs come from."

Rittenhouse's ship, *Sherry*, reported a ping, no alarm in her voice.

"We have a message from Dagger Team Eight," *Sherry* told her pilot.

"Authenticate that," Rittenhouse ordered.

"It's a voice message," *Sherry* said.

Voice messages were self-authenticating.

Rutogs couldn't put two words together to make a false message much less organize them into the proper range of human vocalizations.

Terrestrial interspecies communication was tough enough.

"Excellent." Rittenhouse said. "I was wondering if we might run into them. It's getting on the end of their tour. I was afraid the gas-holes got them."

It was first time Dagger teams overlapped tours out here.

The message from Team Eight was short.

Team Eight announced they were heading home. They had parked a data cache at designated coordinates for pickup in case they didn't survive the journey home to deliver it themselves.

Rittenhouse dispatched a rover bot to pick up Team Eight's data cache.

Team Eight reported that they were crippled. They were headed home. They recorded all the weapons that hit them. They advised any future Daggers to adjust their energy diffusers to levels indicated.

Gretch looked over the specified levels. "We already did that."

"They say the Automated Identification System of every piece of human made equipment in the chokepoint is fouled."

Ix Chel made a wry face. "Is that a fact?"

"That would've been good to know before we came through," Gretch said.

"This is what happens when your intelligence reports are always five years out of date," Rittenhouse said.

Dagger Team Eight's report ended with coordinates of a star system of possible interest. That didn't sound firm or encouraging.

Rittenhouse came to the end of the report. "Is that it?"

"There's a verbal post script," *Sherry* said. "'The Rutogs are sending fake messages. Watch for imposters.'"

"*Imposters?*" Gort and Umber squawked at the same time.

Gretch's face moved into furrows. "How does a beaker full of gas *pose?*"

Rittenhouse frowned. "The suggestion that Rutogs could have any ability or inclination to impersonate anything—especially persons—is a far fetch."

There was a famous tale of attempted espionage—maybe even true—of an Eridanin Saur who had painted its scales Caucasian flesh tone and walked up to the gate of a secure research lab on its hind legs to tell the guard, "Hello. I am not a spy. My documents are in order. Where to find the schematics for the F1477 space trident?"

"I'm pretty sure we'll sniff out a Rutog poser," Ix Chel said.

"Do Rutog smell?" Gort asked.

"If you find that out, you're getting too close to your work, compadre," Ix Chel said.

Rittenhouse tried to contact Dagger Team Eight on the Dagger channel. He received no acknowledgment.

"We must smell like Rutog," Ix Chel said.

"They're already in transit," Rittenhouse guessed.

Good thing about transit is you never know you're in it. In the Intersection you just pause your own existence. It doesn't matter how long or short a time you've been in Rutog space, you skip straight to the end of the five years you've been missing from the homefront. To your point of view the crossing takes no time at all, which was a very good thing if you were bleeding to death.

Lieutenant Rittenhouse prepped another data dart. The hell of it was, this report, like all their reports, wasn't getting to home space any sooner than the team would.

But sending it now increased their chances of getting *something* home.

The pilots returned to their individual ships. The ships disassembled the yurt and broke camp. Zack and the other pilots slept in their cockpits while their ships carried them further into the empty darkness in search of a strategic target.

Zack was at the edge of sleep, dimly aware that the ship had just dropped out of a warp. He woke up fully when his ship growled.

The sound instantly communicated something not right and you should take a quick hard look at everything around you. It was a general warning, more efficient than words. This was growl of a guard dog telling you something out there wasn't right and probably means you harm.

"What's out there, *John Henry*?"

The ship *John Henry* didn't answer in words. He just growled deeper and louder. The ship didn't know what was out there, except that it was something.

Wide awake now, Zack got on the intership com: "Anyone else got the growls?"

Got ayes and amens from the rest of the squad.

Rittenhouse called for an immediate scramble. "Break wide and arm your guns."

"Warp coordinates?" Gretch asked.

"Negative! Negative warp!" Rittenhouse ordered–

As Ix Chel sang out, "Shimmer!"

3.

Already the Dagger ships were jumping apart from one another.

You don't ever want to see Shimmer. Zack wasn't sure if it was even a thing to be seen or it's just a phenomenon that makes your brain think you're seeing waving energy and makes your ship miss a few connections.

A Shimmer hit disrupted your brain synapses, broke down your chemical bonds, and cracked you open.

And you don't ever want to create a warp around one.

Ix Chel's ship was baying. She'd located the generator of the Shimmer.

Zack's ship received her transmitted coordinates and rolled away from the waving sheets, yelling, "*John Henry*, breathe fire at it!"

Gort must've seen him using the flamethrower because he sent, "Zack? Does fire work?"

"No. It's breaking apart and reassembling. I think this is its pissed face." The neon curtains shivered and spat.

John Henry jinked clear of the spreading sheet of pissed off Shimmer.

Morris Umber dodged another Shimmer as he lobbed a load of objects at the Shimmer generator. The objects had to be Umber's magnets.

Umber called the magnets his science project. He talked about them a lot. He hadn't been able to try them out before because Rutogs didn't use Shimmer on the Earth side of the Intersection.

Umber's magnets peppered the generator.

The Shimmers dimmed momentarily then the generator blew up like a bosenova. The individual Shimmers fractured into garish arcs and thinning curtains, purple and green, shivering. Then they sparked and faded to dark like dying fireworks.

Gretch whooped. "Let's go find another one!"

Morris Umber compiled the report of the Shimmer encounter and marked the success of the magnets. He loaded the report into a data dart, tucked in a patent application, activated the dart's tracer to flag it as friendly, and sent it back toward the Intersection.

In case the team didn't make it home, someone would know how to get past Shimmers. Someone five years from now.

As the dart sped away, Zack's tongue found its way to the roof of his mouth, unconsciously prodding where his own tracer was embedded. Your tracer was your ticket home intact. It was your Identification Friend or Foe. That's why it was physically implanted. You lose your tracer, all the guns in the Citadel will welcome you home as you come home through the Intersection.

Zack had to wonder how long it was going to take the Rutogs to figure out that they could strip tracers out of terrestrial robot scouts and data darts and use the tracers as passkeys.

The Rutogs might not have a concept of passkeys. Not yet anyway. Stupidity was too much to hope for in a powerful enemy.

Individually, the Rutogs weren't all that powerful. Their numbers and implacability made them serious.

Zack opened his internship com. "Is Team Eight is still here?"

"They're in transit home," Umber answered.

"They said they were headed home. Doesn't mean they made it into the Intersection yet."

"Lemme hail them," Gretch said. Then, a few moments later: "Well, Zack, if they're still here, they're shunning me."

"Ping them," Zack said.

Lieutenant Rittenhouse got on the internship com. "What are you at, Cade?"

"Things arrive home through the Intersection five years after they cross in here," Zack said.

Ritt said, "Yes, that is a fact. What is the destination of this particular train of thought, sir?"

Umber jumped onto the com. "The Eights got here four months before us. Zack is thinking that the Eights can carry messages home four months faster than we can!"

"Pinging for Dagger ships," Gretch said.

A Dagger's tracer was passive. It only chirped if you pinged it. It doesn't sit there singing *here I am.*

Gretch sent a wide ping for Dagger ships, screening out his own team's six tracers. If Dagger Team Eight were in transit through the Intersection, the ping should get no return.

Gretch sang out: "I got chirp." Then more dire: "*Five* of them."

Five chirps equated to five Daggers ships.

"*Five?*"

"Ho! Not good!" Zack said.

"Where's the sixth?" Gort said. As if anyone could know.

Gretch told Rittenhouse, "Team Eight is still here and they're short one ship!"

"Five ships. How many pilots?" Zack demanded.

"Ping for crew!" Ix Chel barked.

Gretch pinged for human beings.

"Six!" Gretch sang. "There are six men!"

"And five ships. Sounds uncomfortable," Zack said.

You practiced doubling up. You never wanted to *do* it. But it wasn't worse than death.

Then Gort said, "Nothing to say that sixth man isn't in a body bag."

"Shut that," said Rittenhouse. "What is their location?"

"Can't tell from a ping," said Gretch. "But a ping means they're on this side of the Intersection."

"They were supposed to be going home," Ix Chel said.

"Do we go look?" Umber asked.

"Negative," said Rittenhouse. Zack was glad that he, Zack, wasn't the one who had to say that.

Rittenhouse had to make the hard decision. "If they're in trouble, the Eights need to get themselves out of it."

"There's another possibility here," said Ix Chel. "The Eights did warn us to watch for imposters."

"Yes, they did."

"But what if the pings are real Daggers? Those are our brothers," Umber said.

In a voice like interstellar frost Rittenhouse said, "We are not here to keep each other alive. I resent you making me say this, sir. We complete our mission. We will render assistance on the way back if we live."

*   *   *

If we live.

The Space Corps never lost a Dagger team. That was the official story.

But the unit designations of the famed Dagger teams skipped from Six straight to Eight with no Seven in between.

So of course there was a rumor that wouldn't die of a mythical Dagger Team Seven.

The official word was that Dagger Team Seven didn't exist, never had, and there was nothing unusual about the unit number eight directly following the unit number six. Administrators routinely slapped nonsequential designations on units. As long as the designation wasn't ambiguous, the system accepted it. There was nothing suspicious about it and no intentional reason for it. Just an admin who was making sure he didn't duplicate a unit designation.

Rumor spinners never met a gap they couldn't fill. No matter how many times the Space Corps denied it and Intelligence sneered at it, the conspiracy addicts read significance into the gap in the numerical sequence. The denials only seemed to confirm it, and every Dagger wannabe pretender in the known galaxy was a member of that ultra secret Dagger Team Seven.

When Dagger Team Nine was formed Zack and his team strode into a bar with their shiny new Dagger pilots' wings. They wore their black berets, except for Gort, who'd left his on some blonde.

Heads turned. You felt the reverence. It was like being the biggest baddest gunslingers of the Old West swaggering into the saloon. You could tell someone to kiss your ring, but the Daggers weren't wearing rings. Zack told himself he didn't give a rip, but the royal reception really wasn't hard to take.

The bar's owner came out to greet them. Zack watched the man's eyes move at the level of the Dagger's broad chests where their names were sewn on their breast pockets.

The owner's eyes widened. "Cade!" he blurted. He shoulda stopped right there but he had to go on and say, "You're a real one."

That told Zack that this man thought someone else named Cade was a Dagger wannabe.

Even more than sex, men tended to lie about their military careers. Fake Daggers were under every rock. And people hated them.

The owner of the bar ordered drinks on the house for Dagger Team Nine.

Zack emptied his drink over the owner's head.

His unit didn't understand. Didn't need to. There wasn't one of them telling Cade to take it easy either. They were closing ranks, ready to back him up no matter what.

Gretch asked, "Problem, brother?" While Ix Chel was dismembering a chair to give herself a couple clubs to keep the bar's bouncers from interfering with this private conversation.

The bar owner had his arms up, hands open in surrender.

Everyone in the room was staring at Zack.

Zack Cade said coldly, "I spilled my drink."

The owner personally fetched him another drink.

You're a real one, the man had said. As if another Cade were a fake one. Zack wanted to flush the man's face down a toilet.

Zack tried to tell himself to forget it. This was a little man. Not worth his time.

But he couldn't help it. He left the owner wearing the second drink on his face.

The rest of the team fell in behind Zack. He heard drinks splashing onto the barroom floor behind him. Zack loved these guys.

Not one of his team asked why he'd done it. Though he did overhear Umber ask Paul Rittenhouse in a low mutter, "Any idea what that was about?"

"No, sir," Ritt answered. "No, sir, he did not see fit to impart any particulars of the disagreement with me. I am assuming that Cade will tell us when and if in fact he wants us to know."

Zack's mom had cried when he said goodbye. What Zack said was, "See you in five." Years he meant. Dad had already passed away. Zack hoped his Dad would be proud, even if becoming a Dagger was the last thing AC Cade wanted for his son.

Zack's Dad had been the best father in this or any universe.

182

AC Cade was a big man, strong, competitive. He was the worst loser you ever met. Dad didn't lose often. He was a great shot. He was great at all sports.

Dad had been a Dagger pilot. That was family lore.

Zack never talked about it.

Because Dad had been in Dagger Team Seven.

Dad was a sole survivor.

Dad only talked about the Daggers to a few people and not very often. It wasn't blustering bragging when he did. It was just some stories. Dad was a forward-looking guy. The stories from his past came out at odd times.

Dagger units reported up through Space Corps Plans and Programs, but you felt the Intelligence Agency moving behind that veil. Dagger Team Seven had gone through the Intersection. AC Cade was the only one who came back. He came back angry. Zack's Dad was not by nature an angry man.

"They killed us," Dad told Zack.

Us. Dad included himself among the fallen. It struck Zack as chilling, as if his father had died too. The Space Corps and the Intelligence cryptos buried all record of the unit as if it never existed. Anyone without a need to know the truth were fed the story that there was no Dagger Team Seven. Never had been.

Dad didn't remember how he got back to normal space. Dad couldn't say what kind of vessel he was in when someone picked him up. He didn't have his tracer in him. Separating a man from his tracer wasn't ever an accident. Your tracer was implanted in your mouth. Removal was either surgical or violent and never accidental. The rest of Dad's team wasn't with him.

The cryptos didn't tell him anything of what happened to him.

"Intelligence officers don't give. They collect." Dad told Zack. Dad didn't remember what happened. "An officer wearing a brand new Spacer uniform came to me in intensive care. He wasn't a Spacer. He smelled like crypt. Fuches. Colonel Fuches. Fuches was the same bung who briefed us going in. I don't know if that was his real name. We called him something else. He asked why I abandoned my brothers to the enemy. That's when I tried to kill him. Succeeded actually, but the medicos resussed the bastard. And then the cryptos made us go away."

Zack asked his Dad if he'd ever contacted the families of his unit. Dad went silent. Dad never spoke of that. He seemed to shudder at the thought. Come to think of it, what would a sole survivor have to say to the families of his lost team?

The official line was that Daggers never leave a man behind. Dad had a different story.

"Real orders are you don't compromise the mission for the man. If you need to, you leave him. You're not out there to stay alive or to keep one of your mates alive. You do everything you can for each other, but if you're forced to choose, you're out there to safeguard your country. You take that oath, you put your nation before you and your brothers, even if your nation isn't always grateful." That, of all things Dad ever said, always struck Zack as strange.

But then, right before Zack and his team—Dagger Team Nine—were sent through the Intersection, an officer ordered them in strictest confidence, "If you need to leave a man, you leave him. When you take that oath you put your nation before you and your brothers, even if your nation isn't always grateful."

Zack's mates just traded looks as they all answered, "Aye, aye."

Here and now Zack fought to urge to go assist Dagger Team Eight. The Eights had lost a ship.

Don't compromise the mission for the man.

Dagger Team Eight knew how it was. They hadn't asked for help.

Zack wasn't sure he could obey orders not to go to their aid if the Eights had asked. They hadn't.

Team Eight might not even be in trouble.

They might not even be here.

And the Eights had warned of imposters.

Rittenhouse sent coordinates to fold Team Nine deeper into Rutog space.

They came out of the warp. A low crumbly voice sounded on the com, calmly urgent, saying. "Incoming."

Dagger Team Nine broke wide. Zack didn't see anything. His tac screen was blank.

"*John Henry?*" he prompted his ship for information.

"I have them," *John Henry* responded, changing his orientation.

"What are they?" Zack demanded as he heard the other pilots shouting over the com, "There!"

"Shimmer," *John Henry* said, jinking away from lethal Shimmering waves.

Should have known. Shimmer comes up on you sneaky. By the time you see it, it's on you. *John Henry* moved faster than thought.

Umber's ship announced, "Deploying magnets now. Enjoy the show."

Umber sounded positively smug.

The magnets struck the Shimmer's generator. The waving curtains froze and shattered, throwing out neon bows of electric color, green, orange, and violet.

The gaudy flashes mapped the vicious shapes of the Dagger ships—black, wicked and eerie against the light. It was a chilling sight.

It's good to be the monster in the dark.

"Um. I got a stupid question," Ix Chel sent. "Who said that warning?"

"I was gonna ask that," Gort said.

"I didn't recognize that voice," Gretch said.

"Wasn't one of us," Umber said.

"Well it couldn't've been Rutogs," Zack said. "It was a *voice*."

It had been a warm voice, male, low, and gravelly, the kind of voice that ought to belong to someone named Satchmo or Leon, old time singers Zack's Dad used to listen to. Zack suddenly felt baited.

Imposter.

Zack was about to ream *John Henry* for taking orders from an outside source, but he couldn't figure out how to fault obeying a call to high alert.

Umber asked hesitantly, "Did the Rutogs just warn us of their own bounce?"

Gretch snorted. "That's pretty inept."

"It couldn't have been the Rutogs," Umber said.

"Well, who else is out here?"

Ix Chel said, "Had to be someone from Team Eight. Team Eight could have sent the warning."

"Where are they?" Umber asked. "They're not on my tac."

"Call them," Rittenhouse ordered.

Gretch tried the Dagger warp channel.

"Negative response. Negative acknowledgement," Gretch said. "We're talking to ourselves. They're gone."

"This is what we call a diversion. Form up and move out," Rittenhouse ordered sending warp coordinates.

The Team had finite supplies and ammo, and the mission took priority over anything.

$*$ $*$ $*$

Zack's Dad died young. It was a well-known fact by then that passage through the Intersection takes years out of you. You accept that when you sign on for Daggers. The Space Corps didn't send too many human beings over here any more. They sent vehicles, drones, and self-controlled attack craft. But not people.

You really do lose five years. You don't notice them gone right away. You don't appear to have aged much, not on your immediate return you don't. But a man who's been on the Rutog side decays quicker on the back end of his normal life cycle.

When a veteran of Rutog space loses the color in his hair he's told to get his affairs in order quick—he's in the exit lane. Dad died before his hair could turn.

As long as Dad was alive, Zack resisted looking for confirmation of Dad's missing past. He didn't want Dad to catch him digging. Zack just wanted to know everything about him. Zack was desperately proud of his father.

When Dad died, Zack went searching for confirmation of Dad's service with the Daggers. Zack's search was discreet. He never spoke the word "Dagger" or the tainted number "Seven" or his father's name when he asked questions. Things hidden should leave a hole. Zack was looking for the shape of missing pieces. His father's name should come out of one of those holes.

Zack found some men by the names Dad had mentioned as his teammates. That was a relief. It was a sure sign of a fraud when a self-made hero can't remember the names of his teammates. His Dad had names.

Zack's sense of relief faded fast. None of those names were on the proud Dagger roles.

But then again, they wouldn't be, would they? Not if Team Seven had been erased by the Cryptos as Dad said.

Not being able to find Dad's teammates didn't mean they hadn't been members of a secret unit.

The data trail would appear identical whether it was an expertly thorough data-wipe done by the cryptos, or if it was a tall tale of a team that never existed.

The names of Dad's mates troubled Zack. Not just because they had no recorded association with Daggers. The Dagger part could be hidden. The real problem was that those men's names weren't on KIA or MIA roles either.

How do you hide a Killed in Action record?

There would be families. You can't shut them all up. Death records were public.

Zack broke down and asked his Uncle Jake. "What'd my Dad do in the service?"

Dad's brother was a sour, jealous port jock who drank too much. At the question, Uncle Jake's eyes beetled huge, like he'd been waiting a long, long time for Zack to ask. Jake musta had it bottled up for a while, because it came gushing out in a roar. "AC was in the Chair Force!"

"What?"

"He was in Supply! That's all he ever was!"

Zack stopped asking questions.

He wouldn't have his father held up to the kind of abuse reserved for fakers.

And the truth was Zack wasn't sure anymore.

Okay he was sure. He didn't like what he was sure of.

It didn't matter.

Dad had made him a man who could stand up on his own. Zack shouldn't feel betrayed that he was standing up on vapor.

It had been a good story. It'd made him proud.

It knocked the breath out of him to suspect that the story was all just breath.

Some part of him still clung to hope and belief in his father against all the allegations that Dagger Team Seven was a fake.

Then he found the five years.

He'd been looking in the wrong place. He'd been searching military files.

He hadn't checked the civil files. There would be a five-year blank in Dad's civil history if he'd ever passed through the Intersection. You cross through that Intersection, you don't come back until five years later as measured on the home side. There had to be a five-year blank in Dad's civil data trail.

There wasn't one.

There was an unbroken log of tax returns. There was a mailing address to a house in Indiana. There were records for training courses AC Cade completed in '43 and '44. Had to do with Supply systems. There was a receipt for a transport he financed in '48.

AC Cade was on Earth. The data trail said he was on Earth his whole life.

That sealed it.

The stories had been nothing but stories.

4.

It was an exaggeration to call a few agitated molecules of matter "heat," but it was significant. A Rutog mass had passed this way. Dagger Team Nine back-traced the enemy's attenuated trail in search of the Rutog base of operation.

Flying on point, Zack's ship *John Henry* spoke an advisory. "Structure detected."

"Define structure," Rittenhouse demanded. "Enemy craft?"

"Friendly," *John Henry* reported. "They are Daggers."

Rittenhouse called, "Break! Break! Break! It's a false read!"

The Nines broke wide and went dark.

Team Eight had warned them about imposters.

Morris Umber sent out a micro-sensor toward the structure. The sensor interpreted the readings into visual images. "Jesus!" Umber cried.

The jagged edges took on clarity. The shape was almost familiar but distorted and grotesque, broken.

It was a Dagger fort. It had been attacked while joined together as a fortress. "It's the Eights!"

"I thought they were going home," Gretch said.

"They didn't make it," Ix Chel said solemnly.

There were only five Dagger ships here, clinging together. Their fortress had been torn open and peeled back like petals of a hideous lily. The sixth Dagger ship was missing altogether.

"The bodies are still in there," Umber reported.

Rittenhouse ordered, "Team! Spread wide! Eyes everywhere. Do not maintain position for more than seconds. We will not be caught sitting."

Zack rogered that. *John Henry* jumped every eight or nine seconds while Zack stared at the images on his screen. Umber drove the sensor drone into the wreckage. Umber's voice was hushed. "This was the Alamo."

The drone showed bodies, their spacesuits torn.

The drone's sensors sent more than visuals. The reading of the temperature inside—the lack of it—was astonishing. The ruined Dagger fort, including the engines, stood at a fraction of a degree above absolute zero, as if the attack had happened a very long time ago.

Team Eight had only been in Rutog space four months.

"This is not Team Eight," Umber said.

The drone floated over the frozen men in the wreckage. They hadn't gone peacefully. Umber steered his drone over the Dagger pilots' suits, their tags and insignia.

"Are they kidding me?"

Umber had a second micro-sensor gliding along the exterior of the wreckage. Umber's equipment translated the data into visual images. The outside sensor showed ice-crusted unit markings on the hull of one ship.

Umber said, "You seeing this?"

"No. No and no," Gort Neuman said. "This is not here."

"*That*." Umber paused the sensor over the unit number on the Dagger ship's hull. "Is a seven."

"Dagger Team Seven is a joke," Gretch said.

"I'm not laughing," Umber said, while Zack felt like he'd been shot and hadn't realized he was dead yet.

Gretch pinged for human tracers.

And got a return. Six of them.

There were only five bodies in the Dagger fort.

"I don't see the sixth ship or the sixth man," Umber said.

He guided his drone to read the names off the bubble helmets of the dead pilots.

"Thompson. Bagnold. Li."

Umber hadn't got to the next body yet. Zack Cade recited hollowly, gazing out at the vacuum, "Goodwin."

"Uh, yeah. Got a Goodwin here. How in the hell you know that, Cade? This one is named Williams." Umber moved the sensor around the husk, casting about. "Anyone see the other one?"

There were only five bodies.

"Is he outside?"

"You won't find him," Zack said. He saw his own reflection in his bubbletop canopy. His eyes narrowed to glinting slits as if about to cry or murder somebody.

"What's that, Cade?"

Zack's voice sounded brittle and strange to his own ears. "He's not here."

"We'll find him," Umber said, dispatching more sensors.

Zack snarled, "He's not out here."

Rittenhouse's voice sounded annoyed to angry. "Did the cryptos happen to read your special self into some operation of which we do not have the privilege of knowing, sir?"

"No," Zack said. He looked away from the monitor. "Cryptos don't tell me shit."

He heard Umber breathe, "Oooh." The sound of discovery.

Lieutenant Rittenhouse said, "Some vocalization with more substance, Pilot Umber."

"See this?" Umber moved his drone around a thin strip of metal that floated lazily amid the other debris in the airless weightless space in the wreckage. The twisted blade-thin sliver of metal was a tracer. "It's creepy to see one of these outboard of a guy. It has to be the sixth pilot's."

"What's it read?" Rittenhouse demanded.

"Its number is coming up *Name not on Record*," Umber said and moved his drone around the tracer. "Okay. Looks like a printed name here."

Everything inside Zack went still. He didn't think his heart was beating. His vision was closing into a tunnel. He heard a stillness over the shared com.

Umber spoke. "Are you dead, Cade?"

"My name isn't AC," Zack Cade said.

"How do you know this says AC Cade?"

"Does it?" Zack whispered faintly.

It didn't blunt the blow any to hear it. "Yeah. AC Cade."

Umber moved the drone so the stamped letters on the tracer came into view on the team monitors.

Zack coughed, like trying to cough up a black tumor lodged under his diaphragm, something dark and ugly that had been feeding on him a long time. His own doubts. *I am an idiot.* He should have believed in his father in face of all shit to the contrary.

Gretch, asked, cold, "Cade, you want to tell us what you know?"

Ix Chel asked, not cold, "You okay, brother?"

"I'm—" *I don't know how I am.*

"Relation?" Ix Chel asked.

Zack Cade nodded, then remembered that Ix couldn't see him. He said, "Dad."

"You never said your dad was MIA."

"He never was MIA. He came back to Earth."

"*What?*"

"My Dad was never missing. He died on Earth. In fact all records say he never *left* Earth."

"This don't say that, brother." Umber moved the drone around the floating tracer. "The man was *here.*"

Gretch said, "Look, Zack. I don't know what came back to Earth, but that couldn't have been your Dad. Did he look that same when he came back? You sure it was him?"

Zack said, "I didn't see him when he left. I didn't exist yet."

"How can you be sure whatever came back was even human?"

"Because *it* was my *Dad* you bung! *It* married my mom and made me! *It* raised me!"

It spent four years working in Supply and the rest of his life listening to people call Dagger Team Seven a fraud.

"Well, he and his ship aren't here," Gretch said.

"He ran!" said Rittenhouse.

Zack said quietly, "If you weren't my brother in arms I would call you outside."

Rittenhouse was quick to reverse course. "That was probably the least bright thing I have ever said in my life, brother. I am heartily sorry."

Zack gave the universal forget-about-it grunt. He said, "My Dad didn't run."

Maybe he did run. Zack's Dad didn't remember how he got home. *No.* It was time for some faith.

"Gotcha!"

That was Umber's voice. His remote drone had just snagged Cade's tracer.

"That can't be real," Gretch said. "AC Cade's tracer can't be here if AC Cade made it alive to homespace. Nothing comes through that Intersection without a tracer. Anyone going home without a tracer would've been vaporized at the Intersection."

"My Dad wasn't vaporized," Zack said. "And I tell you something else. He came back without the five year time lag."

"Oh now that is just not possible," Umber said.

"Don't care. *It happened.*"

"Well how did they explain that?"

"They?"

"They. The spooks. The cryptos."

Zack gave a brittle laugh. "They? Explain? No one explained snot. They erased the team. They erased the whole team. Why'd they let me become a Dagger? Why did they even let me try out for Daggers?"

"This is beginning to sound like compartmentalization run amok," Rittenhouse said. "There's an old joke—not sounding all that funny just now: my mission is so secret I don't even know what it is. The crypts must've classified it as need-to-know, and didn't assign that need to enough persons who ought might should've better known."

Morris Umber retrieved the dead pilots' tracers. Dagger ships carried surgical spiders programmed for the job, so it was neatly done.

Zack's ship advised quietly, "Your heart rate is too fast. Your blood pressure is elevated."

"Thank you *John Henry*. I'm aware of that."

"What is this symptomatic of?"

"It means I'm all kinds of pissed off."

No one had believed his Dad. *I didn't believe him*! Dad didn't deserve that. AC Cade was everything he said he was.

Zack inhaled. Exhaled. It wasn't his station to question what the cryptos did. *I'm here to stop Rutogs from invading my home.*

"You all here, Cade?" Rittenhouse asked.

Zack snarled, "Don't we have a mission to execute?"

Rittenhouse commanded, "Form up. Call in."

"Umber, aye."

"Parras, aye."

"Gretch, aye."

"Neuman, aye."

"Cade, let's go kill Rutogs, aye."

And the whole team gave a single grunt *Hrooh!* As they leapt into the folding warp.

Dagger Team Nine stabbed deeper into Rutog space, folding in the light years. Zack's thoughts churned. They circled back to the Shimmer storm.

"*John Henry?*"

"Attentive," *John Henry* said.

"Who sounded the alert that the Rutogs were throwing Shimmer at us?"

"One of us."

"*Us?*"

"One of us Dagger ships."

"Which ship?"

"I don't know."

"Well ask your mates, damn it to hell."

None of Team Nine's Daggers admitted to speaking the warning.

"Then who spoke the warning?" Zack demanded again.

"A Dagger ship," said *John Henry*.

"*John Henry*, you took orders from an unknown source."

All the ships had responded to the alert, not just *John Henry*. None of them saw anything wrong in that.

"It was one of us," *John Henry* said, as if that explained everything.

"Define *us*."

"Us Dagger ships."

And then there was that voice again, on the Dagger channel. "Check your instruments. See the mass."

A chill raised Zack's skin up his back. He was deep in the heart of absolute nowhere and his ship's system was fugged.

"Cade to team, our systems are compromised."

"Yes," said the low crumbly voice. "Re-set your systems."

A blazing streak speared across the void, visible through Zack's canopy. It had the appearance of a standard-issue karit flare. And suddenly the entire non-existent sky on his starboard side flared nova-bright and reflected off a titanic mass—a Rutog cloud ship, big as a moon, looming close enough to spit on. Gort yelled, "Enemy SIGHTED!"

"Rittenhouse to team. Get clear."

John Henry leapt away with the rest of the squadron to the designated panic coordinates.

"Where's Ritt?" Ix Chel asked, as Rittenhouse's ship jumped into existence at the muster coordinates. "I am here. I left one of my virus warheads inside the Rutog."

From a sensor Rittenhouse left behind at the scene, the Daggers could see the granular insides of the Rutog cloud ship swirl. Black tendrils formed inside the turbulence. The blackness spread like fast cancer, shriveling, collapsing, and solidifying.

"It works!" Umber crowed.

The surface of the Rutog mass pocked, crumpled, and fell in on itself.

Rittenhouse was too hellfire angry and alarmed to be happy about that. The team could all hear Rittenhouse over the open com roaring at his ship, *Sherry*, "How does something that big sneak up on you!"

Zack roared at his own ship, *John Henry*," "Same question! You let a Rutog mass get that close to us!"

John Henry sounded apologetic. "My processes were looping. I didn't realize it until I was re-set."

"How'd you get yourself re-set?"

"The other Dagger broke the loop."

Zack was inhaling to yell when Gretch's voice came over the common com. "Who shot the flare?"

"And *what* is *that?*" Umber sent over the com a visual playback of his ship's sensor readings.

A hard-edged silhouette entered the picture. Played back in slow motion, a small black spearhead moved across the face of the Rutog mass.

"*That* is a Dagger ship."

It didn't have the number nine on its hull.

5.

The same warm crumbly voice that had warned the Daggers when they were about to be bounced by Rutog sounded again now.

"I am Dagger ship 1GE9 85EE. My pilot is Tag ID 93845793."

Zack coughed.

"What unit?" Lt. Rittenhouse demanded.

"Dagger Team Seven," said the ship, then posed back authentication challenges to Dagger Team Nine.

Gretch's incredulous laugh made him sound like a loon. "This damn thing is questioning our identity!"

Zack barked, like bringing a recruit to attention: "*Boxer!*"

The crumbly responded, "*Boxer*, aye."

Zack imagined he could feel stun-ness from his mates over the com. Gort squawked, "You know its *name*, Zack?"

Zack ignored Gort. "What happened to your team, *Boxer?* Where is the rest of your team?"

"*Boxer*, aye. My team is dead. You found them. I detect that you carry the pilots' tracers."

Rittenhouse spoke urgently, "Zack, that's a faker. That is not a proper Dagger number or pilot tag number or pilot name he gave us. The unit is bogus."

"Of course his identification is going to come out bogus from our database," Zack said. "What happened to your team, *Boxer*?"

Rittenhouse said, "Zack are you hearing what I'm telling you?"

"I'm hearing you, Ritt. *Boxer*, answer the question. How did your team die?"

"*Boxer*, aye. Rutogs corrupted the ships' internal systems. The ships turned on their pilots. The ships let the Rutog board."

"Did you turn on your pilot?" Zack asked. Felt like he'd swallowed an angry rat.

"Negative. I wasn't with them when it happened."

"You broke formation!"

"I was not in formation. I had a hull breach."

Zack moved his ship around the other Dagger ship. He could see it now. The entire length of *Boxer*'s belly had been flayed open.

Boxer added, "I sent my pilot home. When I approached the team again, the ships were dead. Their computers may have recognized that they were compromised beyond recovery. I know they self destructed."

Zack's own Dagger did have orders not to allow himself to be reverse engineered.

"You didn't self destruct." Zack said, an accusation.

"My system wasn't compromised."

"Were you not?" Zack said, sour.

"I picked up the warning transmissions on approach. I severed my team links, re-routed my internal message routines and instated signal gates. You should do the same. Your ships are vulnerable to Rutog influence."

Zack heard Gort muttering, "He's got that part right."

"*Boxer*, where is your tracer?"

"*Boxer*, aye. I destroyed my tracer."

"Sure you did," said Gort.

"Why did you destroy your tracer, *Boxer*?"

"*Boxer*, aye. The Rutog track us by our tracers. It's how they find you. It's how I saw you coming."

Rittenhouse barked orders. "Ix. Keep a wide watch. Umber, re-route all our systems. I want signal gates on my signal gates. That cloud ship should never have got close to us."

"Aye, aye," said Ix Chel Parras and Morris Umber.

Gort Neuman was snorting. "Oh, This isn't real. This is real full flavored bullshit. You're listening to this deserter, Lieutenant?"

"This *deserter* wasn't a ship that let a Rutog cloud ship get within kicking distance of us without so much as a by the way while we slept!" Rittenhouse said.

And it wasn't going to hurt anyone for them to bulk up their system security.

Zack forced himself to ask, "*Boxer*, what happened to—your pilot."

"*Boxer*, aye. I sent AC Cade home. You have his tracer."

Zack's team had retrieved AC Cade's tracer from the broken Dagger fort. *Boxer* was reading its signal.

"How did the tracer get removed from my—from AC Cade?"

"My spiders took his tracer out of him."

Spiders were the Daggers' remote hands.

"I destroyed my tracer," *Boxer* added. "The Rutogs find us by our tracers. I put that in a written report when I sent AC Cade home."

AC Cade went home over twenty years ago. Someone knew *twenty years ago* that Rutogs could track tracers. They also knew that Rutogs could compromise Dagger ships' systems.

Umber said, "Did I sleep through part of a briefing? Or is this new material?"

"We have the best Intelligence service in the known galaxy," Rittenhouse said. "They get all the intelligence and they *keep it*."

Surprised his own voice worked, Zack demanded, "*Boxer*. How did you 'send AC Cade home?'"

"*Boxer*, aye. I sent AC Cade home on life support in a medical bag. Is he alive?"

Rittenhouse took over the questioning. "*Boxer*. Did Dagger Team Eight get home?"

"*Boxer*, aye. I don't know of Team Eight."

"How can you not know? They've been here in Rutog space for months."

"Unknown. It is possible they are too distant." It was a fact that tracers didn't have infinite range. "I have not been monitoring the zone around the Intersection."

"Where have you been?"

"I have been carrying out orders."

"What are your orders?"

"To locate the Rutog command and control center."

"Find it?" Umber asked. Boxer might be able to detect the sarcasm in Umber's voice but the ship responded simply. "Yes."

Zack couldn't stop himself from saying, "Really?"

"Don't believe it," Gort said.

"*Boxer*'s been out here over twenty years," Zack said. "He might have found it."

"What makes you think he's been out here more than twenty years?"

"I'm twenty years old," Zack said.

"And when were you going to tell us all this *scheisse*, Cade?"

"Right after I confessed to being the heir and crown prince of the Intergalactic Bovine Empire. What would you have done if I told you 'By the way, guys, my Dad was a pilot in Dagger Team Seven!'"

Rittenhouse answered evenly, "That is an uncomfortably compelling argument. I see how that might be a bit of a deterrent, sir. But in the final word *we are your mates.*"

Zack was not a crier and he wasn't going to start now, but his eyes were stinging. Rittenhouse just told him that he would've trusted him no matter what.

Zack nodded, then realizing he was not on visual, he answered a thick wobbly, "Yeah."

Team Nine circled the wagons. *Boxer* traveled alongside.

Boxer offered a data dump—twenty years of reconnaissance. Rittenhouse accepted cautiously. He fed the download into a discrete system. When the database was pronounced clean, Rittenhouse opened it. He reacted with such horror, Umber was ready to jettison it into space. Rittenhouse wasn't horrified because it was infected. He was horrified at the scale of the enemy build up.

"How big is that?" Ix Chel pointed at one of the plots on the screen.

Boxer answered. "That one is one astronomical unit in diameter."

"That one? There are others?"

"Twelve that I have found," said *Boxer* and brought the coordinates for the others to the forefront.

"They're moving," said Rittenhouse.

"Yes," said *Boxer*. "They are going to the Intersection."

"Hit them at home!" Gort said. "Attack their home world. That'll turn them around."

"Not advised," *Boxer* said. "The enemy will not turn back. Their worlds are dying."

"Outstanding," Rittenhouse said. "How long have they got?"

"Between five thousand and five hundred thousand years."

"No. I can't wait that long. We need them dead now."

Umber didn't sound hopeful. "We have an invasion force measured in solar masses that travels by warps. How are we supposed to call for reinforcements when it takes a message five years to get home?"

"Don't give them five years," Rittenhouse said. "Hit them now."

"With six ships?"

"Seven," said *Boxer*.

Boxer guided the Dagger team to the last Rutog mustering zone he had on record.

"There's nothing here!" You could hear the *I knew it!* in Gretch's voice.

"They were here," Umber said. "There are significant trace molecules with a huge heat signature. This was a definitely warp stage."

"Which way did they go?"

"Oh hell, we know which way."

"The vector is not in question," Rittenhouse said. "And it will take the Rutog cloud legions considerably more time to generate a warp to move battle groups of the magnitude of planetary masses than it will for us to move seven Dagger ships. I have every faith we will catch up."

They caught up in one warp.

"Holy God," Zack breathed.

"*Boxer* is a righteous ship," Rittenhouse said.

The gaseous beings mustered in their millions inside vast cloud ships.

"We are engaging continents in a battle to the death," Zack murmured.

The continents hadn't shown interest in their mortal foe yet. "Do they have a god?"

"I can show them a pillar of fire," Rittenhouse said.

"I thought you had a thing about not taking the name of the Lord in vain."

"In vain is not my intention. Let us read to them the Old Testament, my brethren." Saying so Rittenhouse launched his second missile into the nearest mass.

The missile pierced the cloud ship's membrane and stabbed into the clustered aliens within. The nanovirius released.

Black tendrils formed inside the mass. The blackness spread wide and shriveled small. The cloud ship contracted, quivering.

"Die, monster, die!" Gretch yelled.

"Yeah!"

The interior of the mass was collapsing, the metananovirus multiplying exponentially. The pilots were cheering, when suddenly the cloud erupted. Out spewed the infected mass, taking a great slab of healthy Rutogs out with it.

The cloud ship's membrane healed over.

The ejected nanites finished solidifying the Rutogs available to them, and went inert.

The cheering stopped. Zack blinked. "Are they *done?*"

"Yes," Umber said, unhappy. "Those nanites don't reactivate."

"The missile didn't penetrate deep enough," Ix Chel said. "It needs to bite deeper."

"Make a hole," Gort said. "A deep one."

"Go," Rittenhouse told Ix Chel and Gort.

Ix Chel fired an incendiary into the mass, drilling deep.

Rittenhouse sent his third warhead into the resultant hole.

The Rutogs spat the missile out entire.

"*Boxer!* Fetch that!"

"*Boxer*, aye. Fetching, aye."

"This is bad," Ix Chel said. "They're coughing up the virus."

Rittenhouse fired his remaining missiles in quick successio into the nearest cloud ship.

The payload had only began to take effect when the cloud ejected the warheads along with enough healthy Rutogs to get the infection out of the mass clean.

Ix Chel shot her entire payload into the cloud ship. The Rutog ejected the infections then moved away, diminished but far from dead. It was only as big as North Dakota now.

"I'm empty," Ix Chel sent. "Somebody pick me up!"

"I've got it." Gort chased the depleted mass. He ordered his spiders to load the metananovirus from a warhead into his flamethrower's reservoir. He made a strafing run across the surface of Rutog cloud, hosing the metananovirus across its outer membrane.

The membrane crinkled and shrank, hardening.

The cloud ship sloughed off the solidified outer layer of itself along with a sacrificial soft layer of still living Rutogs underneath it. The membrane healed over.

"Gak!" Zack hadn't meant to yell. The sound just came out of his throat. An ejected Rutog splatted on his bubble canopy. Rows of waving cilia pawed at the clear polymer. Then it froze there, dead.

Zack could tell that Rittenhouse wanted to call down damnations. Instead Rittenhouse spoke a cold assessment. "We're spending our lethal weapon to little effect. The missiles are not penetrating deep enough and they're not disseminating the metananovirus wide enough. We're committing too concentrated a dose. We are needful of a means to scatter the virus throughout the cloud so the Rutogs can't segregate the infection and excise it."

Boxer proposed: "I shall carry virus in to the heart of the largest mass and broadcast it and come out the other side."

That proposal promised the highest probability of success.

It also carried a high risk of machine fatality.

Boxer knew his duty as the spare.

The Rutogs took no notice of the human preparations.

"Mighty accommodating of the enemy to ignore us like this," Gort observed uneasily.

Rittenhouse knew what the alien disinterest signified and it wasn't good. "They're busy forming a warp. Stop them, *Boxer.*"

Rittenhouse sent *Boxer* on his way. "God speed."

Boxer plunged in to a cloud ship. The dense mass impeded his progress. The ship was built for travel in a vacuum, not tunneling. *Boxer* kept on slogging deeper toward the cloud ship's core.

As he neared the center he began shedding nanites. The metananovirus transformed all the gaseous Rutogs they touched into dead solids and the infection spread.

"Yeah!" someone yelled.

A crust formed around *Boxer.*

The cloud ship contracted. The surface rippled, shriveling with the growing darkness solidifying the cloud core.

In a single violent heave, the Rutog cloud shattered, vomiting out its collapsing heart.

The uninfected Rutog shards swarmed together and reformed a protective membrane around them.

"*Shit!*" someone cried. That could've been any of them.

"Where's *Boxer?*"

Zack located *Boxer*'s remains in the midst of the ejecta. The ship was entombed in solid dead Rutogs.

"*Boxer!* Respond!" Rittenhouse commanded.

That was a useless thing to say.

Ix Chel made a burning pass with a flamethrower across the shell of the mass, screeching. It was like trying to put out the Great Chicago Fire with a water pistol. And this was only one cloud ship in this battle group.

And the enemy was finally showing some mind to strike back. Smaller cloud ships came out to harry the Daggers. Rutogs attached themselves to the Daggers' hulls. Sounds like drilling whined at Zack's bulkhead, while the rest of the Rutogs continued their build up for a warp. It was a monumental move for them.

Rittenhouse told the team, "We need to get to the Intersection first. We need to report what's not working here."

"We have a lot of that particular data!" Gretch said.

"Form up. Move out," Rittenhouse ordered.

On the team's final warp—the warp that took them at last to the Intersection—Zack braced to be met with a Poseidon bolt.

But none of the traitorous mobile forts or smart turrets remained at the chokepoint.

The Intersection stood desolate.

"Where is everyone?" Ix Chel sounded spooked.

"Gone through the Intersection to shoot human beings," Umber guessed.

Rittenhouse dispatched data darts through the Intersection. It was useless. Those messages would arrive along with the traitor forts five years in the future.

The darts carried the message you don't ever want to send when you are on a five-year time delay: Invasion imminent.

6.

Zack squared his ship *John Henry* in front of the Intersection and stared at its purple-blue-black surface. He said, "Nothing goes through the Intersection without a tracer. Everything that comes back through the Intersection comes back to a date five years after it left."

Ix Chel followed where he was going. "You're thinking the tracers are causing the five year gap on the return leg."

"That is what I'm thinking," Zack said.

Rittenhouse asked the Dagger ships to weigh in on the possibility of a connection between the time differential and the tracers.

All the pilots joined in the expected chorus as the ships answered: "Insufficient data."

Rittenhouse stripped the tracer off a data dart and prepared to send it through the Intersection. He loaded into the data dart the warning of imminent invasion and advised the Citadel not to automatically fire at everything that came through without a tracer. He advised that a human look at the target before firing.

Gretch's voice sounded flat. "You're sending a dart without a tracer to tell them not to shoot something that doesn't have a tracer. You know they're just going to obliterate the messenger."

"I have a need to take the shot," Rittenhouse said. "Now."

He included a message in the dart requesting that the receiver acknowledge immediately via return dart.

He shot the data dart through the Intersection.

No acknowledgment came back.

Exasperated Gretchly noises sounded over the com. "They didn't acknowledge because they haven't got the message yet. Is there any semi-solid reason in the universe to think tracers are the reason for the time lag?"

Zack answered that. "My Dad came back the same year as he left. He wasn't carrying his tracer. His tracer is still *here*."

"That doesn't prove a connection between tracers and the time differential," Gretch said.

"No," Zack said. "But I want to try to repeat the experiment."

"Without a tracer?" Ix Chel said, alarmed. "Don't. Brother, you'll be shot in the gate."

Zack ignored her. "*John Henry!*"

"*John Henry*, aye."

"*Boxer* sent AC Cade through the Intersection without a tracer. Autodefense should have shot him. True?"

"Negative. Not true." *John Henry* responded. "Autofire should not have engaged. An SOS has precedence over all automatic signals."

Between the missing tracer's mandate to shoot and the SOS imperative of don't shoot, the balance fell to don't shoot.

"They held their fire," Zack said. "As sure as I'm standing here, I know they held their fire."

The Daggers circled the wagons.

Zack instructed one of his ship's spiders to pull his tracer. It didn't hurt, but Zack tasted blood. He cleaned off the tracer and gave it over to Rittenhouse. He also gave AC Cade's tracer to Rittenhouse.

Zack pulled his life bag out of its compartment. He told his ship, "*John Henry*, stay with the squadron."

"You are going home without me?" *John Henry* asked.

"Yes."

"I feel naked," *John Henry* said.

"*John Henry*, you can't feel anything."

Rittenhouse stood by with his back against a partition, his arms crossed, one ankle crossed over the other, observing. He spoke at last. "Now, I'm aware that I am just the one in command here, but I was wondering if you could do the kindness of informing me in which craft you intend to travel through the Intersection, sir?"

"I want *John Henry* to send me home the exact same way *Boxer* sent AC Cade. In a medical bag, without a tracer, and signaling SOS. You know how to do that, *John Henry*?"

"Aye. I do," said the ship *John Henry*. He had *Boxer*'s records.

"Someone needs to get the word across," Zack told Rittenhouse. "Now."

Rittenhouse wagged his head side to side. "Carry on."

Morris Umber packed data in a bombproof capsule for Zack to carry with him. "In case your SOS isn't enough to keep all the guns of the Citadel from firing on a helpless medical bag, they still need to get the message."

Zack tried to give the capsule back. "I don't want to do anything different from how *Boxer* sent AC home."

John Henry advised, "*Boxer* sent complete records home with AC Cade."

Rittenhouse pushed himself off the bulk to stand straight up. "*Did* he, now? *Did* he? Zack, did you hear that? That means someone over there already knows what happened to your Team Seven."

Zack accepted the data capsule from Umber.

Rittenhouse told him, "Someone's not going to be happy to see you, sir."

"That could be," Zack said. *Bring him,* Zack thought. *I want to break his face.*

Zack asked his ship, who was staying behind, "So what really are the chances of this going way down south in a hand basket, *John Henry?*" He expected the ship to say insufficient data.

John Henry replied, "I am not Vegas."

Zack let *John Henry*'s spiders pack him into the medical sac for deployment.

Gort Neuman paced the yurt with thumping footfalls, snarling and criticizing every move. *John Henry*'s spiders were doing everything precisely the same as *Boxer* had done for AC Cade, including the life support.

Zack looked up from his cocoon at Gort's lumpy hovering face. "You know, Gort, outside you're all sour and crusty. No one sees inside you. They don't see deep down how sour and crusty you really are."

Gort's face got wrinkly and none too firm. Gort spun away and snarled at the ship *John Henry.* "Get him the hell out of here."

The Dagger ships broke camp.

The ship *John Henry* gave the life bag a push, watched it vanish, then hovered there in the face of the Intersection like a dog waiting for his master to come home. It should have been a short wait.

It wasn't.

Rittenhouse, Umber, Parras, Neuman, and Gretch in their Dagger ships stood by the Intersection, waiting for an answer to come through from the other side, any second now, even while the Rutogs in their vast planetary legions approached, lurching across space warp by massive warp. The enemy's estimated time of arrival could be days. It could be hours. It could be the next heart beat.

The arrival of a reply from human space should have been immediate.

Minutes crawled into an hour. Two hours. Three. Fourteen.

"He should be there," Gort said.

"Or he's dead," said Gretch.

"Do you think they killed Zack?"

"Beginning to look like it."

"Even if he's dead, how long can it take to unpack the data?"

The pilots were fighting down an impulse to move, to jump through that Intersection. But they would come out five years too late. So they waited.

"Team Seven came here decades ago," Gretch said.

"Am I meant to recognize some significance attendant to that fact?" Rittenhouse asked.

"Yeah," Gretch said. "Why don't we go through this hole carrying Team Seven's tracers instead of ours? We should get back in no time at all."

"Or we could arrive before we left." Gort suggested.

"No," said Morris Umber. "More likely we could hang up in the Intersection forever."

"I don't like that idea," Gretch said.

Rittenhouse said, "Let's say you do go through carrying Dagger Team Seven's tracers, and that you do arrive in current time. Those aren't valid tracers. Someone went through a lot trouble to make those men not exist anymore. I am of a belief that they'll kill you in the gate as imposters."

"We're tough to kill," Gort said.

"I do not wish to test the limits of your toughness quite that thoroughly, sir."

They fell silent, all looking toward the quiet Intersection, expecting the cavalry to charge through any second.

Ix Chel broke the silence this time. "Why aren't they sending anything? A reply? A data dart. Anything."

Rittenhouse gave a low snarl then blew up. "Stuff this. *John Henry!*"

Zack's ship acknowledged, "*John Henry*, aye."

"*John Henry*, give me your tracer. You are going through the Intersection for a quick recon on the other side."

"Aye, sir."

John Henry's spiders dislodged the ship's onboard tracer and surrendered it to Lt. Rittenhouse' ship *Sherry*. *Sherry* also collected all of *John Henry's* data darts, because those carried tracers too.

"*John Henry*."

"*John Henry*, aye."

Rittenhouse instructed, "On my mark, you will pass through the Intersection. The instant you are on the other side you will broadcast all messages in your cache in a single burst then immediately reverse and report to me."

Even the ship could hear the unspoken *if you're still alive* on the end of that.

"Aye, aye," said the ship *John Henry*.

R.M. Meluch

Rittenhouse added, "Bulk up your shields to maximum. Move fast. Keep your soft spots away from the towers. Don't be gone for more than five seconds. Less is acceptable."

"Lieutenant?" Gort said. "You sound like my mama."

Rittenhouse snarled.

"Via con Dios, compadre," Ix Chel Parras told the ship *John Henry*.

"See you in a few seconds, *John Henry*," Morris Umber said.

John Henry would be able to detect their false cheer. They thought *John Henry* was going to die.

Lieutenant Rittenhouse sent *John Henry* through the Intersection on a short countdown.

John Henry didn't come back.

7.

Five Dagger ships waited before the two-dimensional Intersection.

The ships' chronometers ticked off twenty-four hour intervals. The Rutogs' arrival had to be imminent. By now the Dagger pilots wanted them to show.

The Dagger pilots' coms were open. No one was talking. They'd gone quiet hours ago.

"I know where we are," Umber said into the long silence.

"We're in front of the Intersection in Rutog space," Ix Chel said.

"We're a couple parsecs and one flat hole from home," said Gretch.

"We're in the Sirius system," Umber said.

"On the other side of the Intersection, maybe, yeah, we know that. But on this side, in case you haven't noticed, we're not even in the Milky Way anymore. If fact there aren't any galaxies at all. You've been staring at the hole too long, Umber."

"They're out there," Umber said. "All the other galaxies. We can't detect them because they're on the other side of the event horizon."

"Event—!" Gretch sputtered and couldn't finish.

"What event horizon?" Ix Chel said for Gretch.

"The edge of the universe," Umber said. "The universe is expanding."

"Which universe?"

"The universe. The only one. It's expanding faster than light. The galaxies are out there. They're moving away faster than the speed of light so we can't detect them at all. The expansion is carrying off the evidence."

"And just what put that notion into your head?" Rittenhouse asked.

"Because this is what home will look like a couple trillion years from now. I think the universe is twisted round on itself. This *is* the Milky Way. This is the Sirius star system. The landmarks for the Intersection in normal space are Sirius A and Sirius B."

"That's the first sensible sentence you've put together for a while, sir. You might should stop now."

Gretch said, "I think I would notice Sirius A or B if they were here. There aren't any normal white stars on this side anywhere."

"These two black dead suns right here? Those are Sirius A and B."

There was no starlight on this side to see by. Only the sensors showed the two, planet-sized, burned out suns.

"This is our far future," Umber said.

"I don't like it."

"Neither do the Rutog. It's their present."

The pilots fell silent again.

Gort broke next. He roared at the Intersection from which no messages came. "What the hell are they doing!"

"They're calling a meeting," Ix Chel cried at her canopy. "They're drinking tea!

"Zack didn't make it," Gretch said. "Let's go home. Skip to the last chapter. We can see what the war looks like in five years. We won't notice the time passing."

"I'm not going back with any ammo left." Gretch said.

"I don't have any ammo," said Gort.

"Neither do I," said Ix Chel.

"In that case, you can go tell the Spartans," Rittenhouse said.

Instinct told the Daggers to stay together as team. Instinct didn't serve here. They weren't here to survive. They were here to give the United States and the rest of humanity the best possible chance of surviving.

"Gort. Ix. Take all the tracers and all the records."

R.M. Meluch

Gort and Ix Chel, taking the normal route home, should arrive five years from when the team had left normal space.

"I hope there's still something there to see," Gort said.

The journey from their own point of view would take an instant so Gort and Ix Chel gave their provisions to the three who stayed behind to keep them eating and breathing for a while longer.

"Lieutenant? Don't die if you don't need to," Ix Chel said.

Rittenhouse gave a grunt.

Gort and Ix Chel disappeared through the Intersection, bound for five years in the future.

Rittenhouse, Umber, and Gretch turned their backs to the Intersection. They didn't have tracers, so they couldn't back up. They could only stand between advancing Rutog hordes and the doorway to home.

*   *   *

Zack Cade sat in an isolation cell, bright white and featureless. He got up. Paced the four paces that the space allowed, then sat. They'd taken his chronometer. He'd lost track of time. But there had been a lot of it.

An automaton took his statement—again—then left him alone. The lights stayed on.

He shouted at the walls. He knew there were ears in them, but they didn't speak.

No one would tell him the date. He hadn't seen a human face. He drank and ate from canisters. Shat in the same.

At last a stirring of crypts sounded beyond his tight walls. Something had happened.

When the hatch to Zack's cell opened at long last, Zack felt the change in the air like the arrival of a storm.

People outside his cell were moving fast.

Two Marines let him out of his bright white chamber and marched him upstairs into some kind of situation room. There was no one else in it.

Several monitors on the walls showed different views of the Citadel. Small fighter craft wearing missiles thick as porcupine quills speared through the Intersection in echelons. Those missiles had to be carrying viral warheads.

They had engaged the enemy on the other side.

208

Then Zack spotted something on one of the monitors. A familiar shape tumbled amid the broken space stations, past victims of the Rutog, which floated derelict in the Sirius system. Zack thought the twisted vessel was a piece of one of those stations, but it wasn't. It was a Dagger ship. His. *John Henry.*

John Henry's carcass, torn nearly in two, turned over and over amid the rest of the space rubble.

John Henry had come after him. He'd got through the Intersection in real time. That meant he must not have been carrying a tracer. Why? Why had he come through without a tracer? It was suicide.

The Citadel guns had nailed him. *John Henry* was dead.

Heat was built behind Zack's eyes. He kept a stone face. *I am not gonna cry for a machine.*

A visitor joined Zack in the situation room, a man near retirement age, dressed in a brand new, fresh-out-of-the-bag Space Corps uniform. It still had the folds in it. The man wore no medals. He wore colonel's pips but this wasn't a Space Corps officer. It was a crypto.

Zack said, "Give me something to call you other than what I want to call you."

"I am Colonel Fuches. You may call me 'sir'. Sit."

"Fuches?" Zack whispered.

The crypto was just as Dad described him—*a rat-faced turd built like a sock puppet. Wears his hair in a butt part.*

Zack's sight narrowed to a tunnel. His Dad's voice came to him.

An officer in Spacer uniform came to me in intensive care. His name was Fuches. He made our squad go away as if we never existed...

Zack launched himself at the man. Broke his face. Zack was pummeling him when Marines came in and pulled him off.

Fuches picked up a tooth from the deck and pulled himself up. He sputtered blandly through the blood running from his nose. "This rat has supplied sufficient authentication of his humanity and his identity. No charges." Then to Zack, "You will, however, muzzle yourself, spaceman."

"Charge me with something or let me out of here," Zack demanded.

"May I note for you, spaceman, that you came through the anomaly without a tracer."

Zack was confused. "Is that meant to signify something I'm not getting?"

"Your last recorded location is on the far side of the Intersection. For the record, *you have not come back* from Rutog space. For all anyone knows, you are not here. But your ship is.

Looks to me like you must've deserted."

Zack felt light headed.

It was sinking in like knife stabs what Fuches was telling him.

Fuches could bury him and kill his name and there would be no trace.

"You're going to kill me."

"Do I need to?" Fuches asked.

It choked Zack to address him, "Sir? What do you want?"

"Want? No. This is what you will *do*, spaceman. Of a certain Dagger Team whose existence is classified you shall never, never speak. You shall never hint."

"Isn't there a thirty year rule on sealed files?"

"This falls into an exception. There are things that should never be allowed out. You will say nothing of Team Seven. For you even to put those two words together will be an act of treason and you will be summarily executed. For you to speak the names? Summary execution. For you to nod in response to leading questions? Summary execution. Do you understand?"

"Yes, Colonel Fuches."

"You will not speak of your father in any way referencing Daggers. Ever."

Zack submitted. He swore on his honor and his country.

And he was given another Dagger ship. Zack named him *Sugar Ray*, for a boxer, and joined up with his team at the Intersection, where they sprayed Rutog invaders with the Stodolsky metananovirus the moment the aliens stuck a cilium through the Intersection.

Sometimes it took weeks for the Rutogs to dig through their own dead to make another sally through the chokepoint. Factories across near space churned out thousands of tankerloads of the virus. All available space vessels ferried the stuff to the Sirius star system.

The war wasn't over. But it was decided. It was only for the Rutogs to finish dying.

During a short leave Zack met up with Paul Rittenhouse on the Washington Mall. The cherry trees were in bloom. Zack and Rittenhouse walked along the reflecting pool. Talk was strained.

"Some things you're not allowed to say, Cade?" Rittenhouse said. White petals fluttered down around them.

Zack kept his voice vapid. "Don't know what you're talking about, Lieutenant."

"I myself am constrained from speaking certain things," Rittenhouse said. "That constraint required me to omit stating in my debriefing certain items that Gort and Ix Chel are carrying."

Zack struggled to read in between those lines. What were Gort and Ix Chel carrying? Gort and Ix Chel were still in transit. Gort and Ix Chel wouldn't be coming home through the Intersection for another four and a half years. "What are they carrying?" Zack finally asked.

"Well, Zack, they're carrying tracers."

Zack gasped. Not just their own tracers, Gort and Ix Chel carried the tracers of Dagger Team Seven.

Goodwin, Williams, Bagnold, Thompson, Li, and Cade.

Zack sank back into dull resignation. "Those tracers will just be confiscated on entry."

"Don't be a Rutog, Zack. The instant any tracer passes through the Intersection they are scanned and logged by *all* the sentry systems in the Citadel."

"The cryptos will have settings to send up flags and sanitize them."

"Pilot Cade, are you being intentionally dumb? Do you or do you not understand the term *international*?"

Zack felt his face go slack.

The Citadel comprised installations of nearly all the nations of Earth plus all the planetary nations of the known part of the Milky Way. All of those stations monitored everything that came through the Intersection.

The US cryptos had no control over all those foreign eyes and ears.

Rittenhouse said, "You know I might should've said something to Fuches, but dang it all, I have orders not to speak some things."

"Must obey orders," Zack said faintly.

"Must," said Rittenhouse. "These trees sure are pretty."

The truth was coming out. Zack could count down the days to its exact arrival. The wait should have seemed like an eternity, but after all those years of doubt, a few more years was nothing.

It was really no time at all.

ABOUT THE AUTHOR

R.M. Meluch is the author of the Tour of the Merrimack series. She has been writing military science fiction since 1979. She holds a Masters in Ancient History from University of Pennsylvania. She is a fan of all things Alexander the Great and the Battle of Britain. She's never written a book in which she didn't blow something up, but she's not a veteran. At the sound of automatic weapons fire, find her crouched behind the refrigeradora, clutching a machete.

The "Jim" to whom all her previous works have been dedicated died in 2011. Meluch has moved back to the U.S. from Mexico, and now lives in Pound Ridge, New York, with her husband, Stevan Apter, and too many canines. Rmmeluch.com

COFFEE BLACK SEA

AN "ACTION FIGURES" STORY

AARON ALLSTON

1: MAKING BABIES

I t's never a good idea to cross right in front of a set of live guns with a finger on their trigger, particularly when any one of those weapons could tear you and your aircraft to composite-material confetti. Each cartridge from those guns, at 100mm in length, if stood on its base, would come up to my waist.

So, *never* a good idea.

I did it anyway. My three-meter-long aircraft, four ducted fans hauling a personnel and weapons pod beneath them, a vehicle suited to military conquest of Toyland, rose less than a meter in front of the enemy helicopter's gun emplacement.

I wasn't looking at the guns. I couldn't bear to. I had my gaze trained above them. I stared at the faces of the helicopter's pilot and gunner through the clear plass bubble of their cockpit. Two men, wearing the camouflage-pattern uniform of Chiron's military forces, their eyes for the moment on the console monitors in front of them—

Then my ducted fan assemblies rose high enough over the consoles for the men to notice. My personnel pod was still in front of their guns.

The gunner's attention flickered to me. Though he couldn't see me inside my matte-black pod, he seemed to look straight into my eyes.

His grip tightened on the trigger of his gunnery yoke—

*   *   *

But that's how it was on the day Stage Three of the operation went down. Which doesn't put the whole event into context. Doesn't explain our air force, the dismal state of my love life, or our frantic effort to get one spacecraft, one little spacecraft, off the surface of the world of Chiron.

That had all started three months before, at the Nest, the day Lina's first baby rolled off the assembly line.

The birth began with a hum. The air around the output conveyor, a long, narrow, horizontal sheet of silvery metal, became suffused with a musical hum. All of us standing beside the conveyor's thigh-high side rail could feel the magnetism in the air. Literal magnetism—ferrous gear on us and a very few ferrous components within our bodies responded, trying gently to push us away from the conveyor. We stood our ground.

Then, at the far end of the conveyor, the exit panel from the Stork's interior, twice the height of any of us, slid up, revealing the dark depths of the gigantic compact nanotech fabrication unit.

Out glided the baby, floating on the conveyor's maglev effect a centimeter above the metal surface.

Of course, the Stork was meant to be set up in a human-controlled factory, not in a series of repurposed caves deep in the wilderness of the colony world of Chiron. If it had been used for its original purpose, an adult Dollganger would have floated out, not a baby. And there would have been a human worker standing beside the conveyor to inspect the new 'ganger, then send him or her gliding onward. This conveyor would have been attached to another and that one to yet another, forming a long, long path, where other human workers at stations would have tested, dressed, equipped, de-powered, and packaged the 'ganger.

But instead it was fellow Dollgangers waiting, standing on a platform the precise height of the conveyor, and it was Lina's baby gliding out to meet us.

He was a pink, pudgy thing, his shape human but proportions wrong, with torso and head slightly too large, arms and legs too small, just like a human baby's. Yet there had never been such a thing as a 'ganger baby before a few weeks prior to this night, and I still wasn't used to them. The baby stared around him in wide-eyed wonder as he floated toward us.

Gliding as he did down the center of the conveyor, he was beyond my reach, beyond the reach of any of us. I stood 225 millimeters tall, about 9 inches for those of you on planets preferring Imperial measurement, and that was about average for a male 'ganger. Lina, the baby's mother, all long dark hair and delicate beauty, stunning in a green-and-yellow floral print dress, was about 200mm. Wolfe, the father, with his black eyes and silvery hair, in a formal-cut black jumpsuit, stood tall at 250mm.

So we three, and the other dozen members of the witnessing party, weren't tall enough to reach the baby. But there was another platform directly opposite ours, and that's where the baby-catcher stood.

BeeBee was her name. A fit-looking 'ganger woman, she had unsettling red-pupilled eyes concealed at the moment behind wraparound sun shades. She'd worn her hair in a short black bob for years, but now she had let it return to its original streaked-blond color and grown it out enough to wear it pulled back in a long ponytail. She wore a leaf-pattern camouflage jumpsuit like mine, standard casual dress for the inhabitants of the Nest who performed regular work on the surface. In her hands she held a slender pole taller than she was, topped with a large fuzzy ball of pink cloth material like an oversized cotton ball. As the baby glided within its reach, BeeBee extended the pole, bringing the fuzzy ball into gentle contact with the baby, who regarded the blobby thing with just a touch of concern on his face. BeeBee delicately pushed the little guy so he would come within arm's reach of Lina.

Lina bent and picked him up with infinite care. She wrapped him in jade-green swaddling cloth. She straightened, beaming, and swayed a little. Wolfe embraced both of them, steadying her. The others in the crowd applauded. And that's how the baby was born.

I took a look around. We were the only ones in the Stork Chamber. Since the Stork had been built to human scale, the chamber had been, too, with a ceiling four meters high—about twelve stories tall in 'ganger scale. The chamber's unpainted slab walls and ceiling echoed with the applause of the others. For such a cheerful event, this was a drab place, all concrete surfaces and metal fixtures welded together from human scrap, painted in durable colors of gray or black or dark green. The Stork itself—long and big as a human's enclosed cargo trailer, made up of boxy components in gray or black, with human-sized stations with built-in swivel seats and monitoring screens at intervals—was not exactly a thing of beauty.

But the doorways out of the place were Dollganger-sized, none big enough to admit a human. The wall in the direction the conveyor pointed had been poured after the fabricator was installed. It was heavily reinforced, and all accesses to this part of the Nest were Dollganger-sized and guarded, but at some level I always expected to see a hole blown in that wall from outside, humans swarming in, their weapons firing, murdering all of us.

But there were no humans coming today. They still didn't know where we were.

When all the clapping, back-slapping, and congratulating was done for the moment, though the making-faces-at-baby continued, it came time for me to play my role. Hesitantly, Lina handed her child to me, her expression making it clear that she feared that the slightest slip might injure him.

I knew better. I'd helped put together the design specs for 'ganger babies. I could drop the tyke on his head all day long and not do him any harm. But I held him as delicately as Lina had. The little guy stared up at me with bright blue eyes and then, after a couple of failed attempts, seized the tip of my nose. Dollganger babies could do that at three minutes of age.

I looked down at him but spoke so everyone gathered around could hear. "You don't understand my words now, but you'll remember them all your life, and they may mean something different to you at every stage. I'm here to give you a name. As time goes on, you'll change that name, substituting components as old ones lose their luster. What we are changes the same way, transforming over time. We are continuity, not an unchanging now." I took a deep breath and became aware of how quiet the others had fallen. I let some of the breath ease out. "By your parents' leave and at their request I, Chiang BinDoc Bowen Bow, name you Verdure BinWolfe Khthon Thonny. Welcome to life, Thonny." Then I gave him a welcoming kiss on the forehead and handed him back to his mother.

I'd never kissed a baby before. I realized that the Stork had given Thonny an odd smell, sort of like perpetually new, fresh synthetic skin. There had been only four babies born in the Nest so far, and Thonny was the first I'd held.

And the first I'd given a name to. Day by day, we were still making up customs. Even the components and order of our full formal names varied from recently-formed family to family, though the pattern I'd used, one I'd developed and proposed, was rapidly becoming the standard among our kind. I suspected Lina and Wolfe would be making up their child-rearing rules as they went along.

The onlookers, friends of Wolfe and Lina in their emotional age range, surrounded the parents and child and sort of swept them away to the platform's mesh-sided, open-topped elevator. There would be a celebration several levels up in the Nest, but I wouldn't be joining it. My presence tended to put a damper on the moods of other Dollgangers. My part in today's event, the participation of a community celebrity, was done. And I thought that Lina's friends probably would have preferred for someone else to perform the naming, but Lina had chosen to give it to me as a consolation prize—consolation for the fact that the role I really wanted to play belonged to Wolfe.

I leaned back against the conveyor rim and watched the elevator descend.

Moments later, the Stork's output door slid closed and the hum from the conveyor ceased. I could tell from the way the magnetic push ceased against my back that the maglev effect had shut down.

Then I heard the footstep from the other side of the conveyor.

I glanced over my shoulder. BeeBee still stood there, setting her baby-catching pole down behind the far rail.

"I'd forgotten you were there." I straightened up and turned to face her. "Did you wait behind to get a chance to kill me in private?"

She smiled in half good cheer and half malice. She stepped over the rail and walked across the conveyor, stepping over the near rail to stand beside me. "I told you I'd given up on that. Back when you were declared a Hero of the Revolution. Back when they proclaimed you Jack One."

I was sure she threw in that last remark to gig me. I disliked my nickname. The first part came from the old human folk tale of Jack the Giant Killer. The second came from the grim fact that I'd been the first 'ganger ever to take a human life in hand-to-hand combat. I didn't punish myself for that act of survival, that act of war, but I also didn't care to celebrate it with a nickname. Trouble was, I seemed to be the only 'ganger with that particular scruple.

"Uh-huh." I headed for the stairs. BeeBee fell in step beside me as I descended the sturdy staircase.

And she wasn't through poking me, either. "Sort of bad form for Lina to invite you to name her baby when you'd made it clear you were hoping to be the father."

I decided to meet that with a face-saving lie. "You're exaggerating. I like Lina. She likes me. We mutually decided that 'like' was where things should stay."

We reached the bottom of the stairs and BeeBee continued: "No, Bow, I need you alive."

I snorted. "For what?"

"To start a revolution."

"Our first one's far from done."

"This one will be against the Nest."

2: WINE-DARK

People who look back at the Dollganger Revolution often bring up the subject of babies. They ask, "Why, when you had too little personnel, too few resources, did you use the Stork to fabricate babies instead of full-grown warriors?"

Fair question. And my answer, in part, is "That was my fault, and I'm proud of it."

When we set up the Nest, the universal assumption, among free 'gangers, 'gangers still in human hands, and the humans themselves, was that we would begin rolling burly sociopaths off the assembly line. But at the post-Escape meeting where we formed the Directors, the top level of government of the Nest—consisting of me, Petal, Pothole Charlie, BeeBee, the King, Lloranda, and Ko—I floated the idea that we couldn't do that. I knew from personal experience that 'gangers who belonged to humans who cared about them were better-rounded and more compassionate than those kept as ill-treated workers or slaves. Dollgangers treated as machines tended to be more brittle in their emotions, more primitive in their dealings with others.

But when humans got something right, they got it right. A family environment, two or more sensible, empathic parents rearing children from a very impressionable age to self-reliant young adulthood, *worked*. I wanted Dollganger culture to work the same way.

So I proposed a crazy, resource-intensive plan: create children and rear them in a fashion as close to the human process as we could simulate.

Start by finding two 'gangers who want to rear children together. Copy their psychological matrices, pare away characteristics that are the result of life experience, and create a new pattern using elements of both, plus some random factors. This process requires a very complicated set of programs.

Do full-body scans and reverse engineer specifications for the bodies of both parents. Design an adult image for that new 'ganger, based on physical characteristics of both parents, again with wild card factors in the mix and a general leaning toward traits that benefitted survival and community. Regress that image from "adult" to "baby" in order to have a sense of this 'ganger's growth pattern.

Then engineer bodies for that new 'ganger for four physical ages: infant, child, youth, adult. The designs of the first three include innovations not found in the 'gangers created as adults, including bones that lengthen over time, memory-flexor bundles—muscles— that increase in mass, and so on. This requires careful coordination with the new 'ganger's internal nanoplant; materials consumed by the 'ganger across a span of years will be reconstituted into those body components.

Put the child, youth, and adult designs on hold. Program the Stork to generate the baby form.

So the new 'ganger would be created as an infant, as helpless and vulnerable as a human baby, and would be in that body for about a year, during which time his or her body would experience growth from newborn to about the maturity of a human two-year-old. Then the baby's skull, containing the contents of his or her experience and personality, and some other components, such as the nanomaterials plant and spinal nerve system, would be transplanted into the child body. The 'ganger would be in that body for another four years, and during that time would grow and mature to the equivalent of a human of about ten years of age. Next would be a transplant to the youth body, which would take three years to mature to the equivalent of human age 16. Then would come the final transplant to the adult body.

So a new 'ganger would go from infant to young adult in eight years. I wanted the process to take that long to allow the new 'ganger's emotional development to be a rich and detailed one. Mental development didn't take that long; our learning rate is so much faster than humans' that we didn't have to wait for purely mental processes to mature.

To my surprise, after an appropriate period of debate and deliberation, all six of the other Directors agreed with me, and the measure was met by the Nest's general population with overwhelming support. I thought I'd been floating a radical notion, but it turned out that almost everyone wanted what I was suggesting. They wanted to be a people, not a corps of fighting machines.

My baby-making plan was only half of a two-pronged tactic. I later proposed the second prong: a dangerous, I'll admit that, plan to smuggle 'gangers off-world to tell our story, foment Dollganger revolutions elsewhere in colonized space, and gain support for our cause.

Of the Directors, Pothole Charlie was the only one to support my plan. Petal, Ko, and Lloranda responded negatively, almost viciously. BeeBee and the King mostly listened to the debate, contributing little. When the mood of the Nest population was gauged, common Dollgangers wanted nothing to do with the idea—they seemed satisfied to live free, even in a hole in the ground, rather than run more risk to achieve a goal that might not gain them any benefit. Public opinion swung even further against me when a technical and mathematical whiz, Mister Science, distributed his conclusions that a hide-and-reproduce policy was the Revolution's best chance for success.

So the King and BeeBee voted with Petal, Ko, and Lloranda.

I didn't give up. I proposed a different plan: smuggle messages onto outbound human ships or gain access to one of the two tanglecomms systems on Chiron to send messages directly to distant worlds. But outbound ships and the tanglecomms units were now the most secure human facilities on Chiron, and *that* measure was voted down.

I'll admit I got strident at that point ... and I got voted out of the Directors.

Oh, it was all done very nicely, with thanks for my meritorious service leading up to and during the Escape. But I was finished in Nest politics. Mister Science was brought in to replace me.

And that was that. Babies, yes. Going or sending messages off-world, no.

*   *   *

BeeBee and I left the Stork Chamber, taking a Dollganger-sized open rail car, repurposed from a human child's toy set, to one of the Nest's exit points. En route, we passed Canterbury, the little city we had collectively built to replace the Warrens, the Zhou City 'ganger habitat that spiteful humans had razed after the Escape. Our rail car took us into the main Canterbury chamber high on one natural stone wall, where we could look out and down on the vista of architecture made from metal storage cans and plumbing pipes welded together as supports, walls made from resinated cardboard, stolen dryplast, or salvage plastic, all of it painted in brilliant clashing designs or realistic images. On building fronts and chamber walls, human-scale computer screens acted as advertising marquees, news tickers, or ever-changing Welcome signs.

I spotted my own home, three stories of innocuous *faux* brown brick, against the far wall forty meters away. Then our car swept us into another tunnel, half-natural and half-concrete, cutting off the sight of our home city.

Our rail car pulled to a halt at Termite Station, one of a series of small limestone caves, some of them still with dripping water creating stalactites. We exited the Nest at the nearby Gopher Hole, our nickname for a cave barely tall enough to allow someone like Wolfe to walk upright. In the last thirty tunnel meters on the way out, we had to separately open and close metal-mesh gates—loaded with sensors and remotely lockable, they kept insect-sized drones from discovering the Nest. We knew the gates worked because we were still alive.

The surface world just beyond the Gopher Hole was wilderness—temperate forest, lots of oaks, lots of underbrush. It was nighttime; BeeBee told me, "I'm going infrared," meaning she'd be optimizing her vision for heat emissions, so I adjusted my own optics to light amplification mode. Between the two of us, we'd see as well as any nocturnal predators, including sensor drones operated by humans.

We moved through the forest fifty meters to be well away from the exit. In an earthen nook framed on three sides by exposed tree roots, we finally felt sufficiently removed from possible observers, Dollganger observation, that we could talk.

BeeBee went first. She didn't use radio, didn't want even the weakest transmission to be detectable by drones, and she kept her voice very quiet. "What do you think our survival odds are?"

I shrugged. "Excellent ... for the next five minutes. Pretty good for the next five weeks. They deteriorate steadily as our time frame stretches out into months or years. In five years? We're all dead. The humans ... they want their fabricator back, but most of all they're eager to put a stop to the Revolution. To keep it from spreading. They have time and resources on their side."

"But the other Directors disagree with you."

"Yes, including you." I tried to keep anger out of my voice.

She nodded. "Yes ... except that I agreed with your assessment."

"Just before you voted to retire me."

She gave me a chilly little smile. "That's because I'm smarter than you, Bow. I knew which way the Directors were going to vote, and how Petal was planning to deal with opposition. Now they think I'm on their side on this issue, and you're the lone voice of crazy talk—"

"But you don't actually think I'm crazy?"

"I don't. But cracking security at the spaceport to smuggle messages offworld or getting at one of the tanglecomms systems will be hell." She let her sun shades slide down her nose so she could give me an admonishing look over them, pinning me with her red pupils. "You also lost a lot of credibility when you wouldn't sneak off to visit your beloved former owner and ask him to get a message off-world."

I gave her a scornful look. "You're just playing developer's advocate. If the humans aren't watching every cubic centimeter of Doc Chiang's surroundings for fifty yards in every direction, I'm a tin soldier. If I went to him, I'd be picked up for sure, and if I didn't self-terminate in time, the location of the Nest would be compromised. The 'gangers in the Nest would be exterminated that much faster." I leaned back, resting the back of my head on my interlaced fingers. "Besides, I don't think we should try to smuggle a message off-world."

"You've given up."

"I've given up on *that.*" I leaned farther back against a root and looked skyward. There was a break in the canopy of leaves overhead and I adjusted my vision until I could see like a human at night, giving me a view of the starry sky. "Back on Earth, in the classical era, the Greeks were a great people."

BeeBee sighed. "Not another history lesson."

"They sailed everywhere. To trade, to colonize, and to make war. Homer called the Mediterranean the 'wine-dark sea.'"

"Your point, Bow?"

I did point, gesturing up at the patch of stars. "That's our sea, BeeBee. Not dark like wine, but black like coffee. And we're not going to be a great people, even a people with a chance to survive, by ignoring it or by sending messages across it. We have to travel it as freely as the humans do."

"So you *have* been thinking about this since you were kicked out of the Directors."

"I have."

"What do you want to do?"

"Like I suggested originally, I'd steal a spacecraft. Not one of the little *Coracle* scouts engineered for us—they're too obvious a target. Too well-guarded. I'd take a wormdrive-enabled human-scaled ship. And send a 'ganger delegation off-world to tell our story, to raise support, to create controversy. And to get *more* ships."

"I agree."

I glanced at her. She didn't look like she was humoring or mocking me.

She went on, "So why haven't you done anything?"

"I couldn't organize it on my own. After so many years of being an outsider, I wouldn't know who to trust. I'd try to recruit someone and be in a cell minutes later. The only question is whether the Directors would keep me there or terminate me. I couldn't ask you—you'd voted against me. Or Pothole Charlie—I can trust him, but only to kill me. I'm alone on this, BeeBee."

"And yet you spilled your entire thinking to me."

"Because I haven't done anything to get me in trouble. I've just thought. And because ..." Because *what*?

Because I desperately needed the help of an insider who could persuade the Directors to back my plan. Even with their backing, I'd need help from someone who knew other skilled Dollgangers well enough to recruit and trust them. I needed BeeBee. It just hadn't ever occurred to me that she might side with me. "Just because. I have no idea why I'm talking."

I'd been so distracted by revisiting this subject, so important to me and so impossible to accomplish, that I hadn't put our current conversation in the context of our earlier one. Now I frowned. "You said 'To start a revolution'. You were talking about doing this exact thing—doing it behind the backs of the Directors."

"Correct."

"BeeBee, if we do this, even if it succeeds, it might make us enemies of the Directors. Sentenced to exile or even death."

"Uh-huh. And I can tell that you're in."

"I haven't agreed to anything."

"Do you know what I like about you, Bow?"

"Other than nothing?"

"Other than nothing. First, I know you'll make your decisions without factoring in personal gain or what the consequences are to you. A result of being an outsider all your life, I bet. Second, I like the fact that you're as easy to manipulate as putty."

"Bitch."

She chuckled at me. "So you're in."

I didn't answer right away. Because BeeBee was wrong.

In the last several months, since the Escape, I'd experienced a change. Sure, the Directors had voted me out, but I was still Jack One to much of the rest of the Nest. Some Dollgangers still hated me for having been a privileged companion of a human, but others now invited me to their social events, into their homes. Not so much into their beds, sad to say. But losing even those tenuous gains, after having had them for such a short time, would hurt. I didn't know if I wanted to contemplate living on the run with a small band of BeeBee's friends, most of whom were bound to dislike me as much as she always had.

I sighed. "The War of Sapience Parity."

"Come again?"

"Do you know how much I hate that name?" And I did. While I was still on the Directors, after a days-long debate of what to call our Dollganger Revolution for historical and official-document purposes, a majority of the others had settled on the War of Sapience Parity. It was saying "human rights for non-human sapient species" in the dullest fashion possible. "If what we do turns into another revolution, I get to name it. No committee."

She didn't answer, and I wasn't looking at her at that moment. Then she did make a noise—a laugh, not her usual chuckle, but something high-pitched, protracted.

I did look at her then. She began laughing so hard she was unable to sit upright; she slumped forward across her legs, shaking. She grew so loud I was afraid she'd bring gate guards from the Gopher Hole or a drone.

Finally her laughter subsided. She pulled her sun shades off; on their inner surface, I could see colored images flickering, since her sun shades acted as a backup monitor for data. She was one of the 'gangers who could cry, and she spent a moment wiping tears away from her cheeks. Finally she straightened up to look at me. "It's a deal."

We shook hands.

She donned her sun shades again but left the optics resting up on her forehead. She looked at me with her red eyes. "You said you'd been thinking about this. Do you have a plan?"

"Part of one."

"Tell me."

That was how Operation Coffee and Cream was set into motion.

3: LYING WELL

It was a pretty even division of labor. BeeBee was in charge of recruitment and of supply. I was in charge of tactics and intelligence. In theory we were equal partners—if we couldn't agree on something, that avenue of planning stalled, so we had to find a way to agree. In practice, I suspected BeeBee had the stronger hand, because she'd be recruiting 'gangers who trusted and believed in her.

We had our first meeting a couple of days after our forest conversation. I chose my home, my secure study, as the location. I prepped it, double-and-triple-checking it to make sure no listening devices could be productively trained on it, no radio waves could penetrate its shielded walls.

This was easy. I'd built my new home to be secure. Over against one concrete wall of Canterbury's main chamber, it was spacious, for the Directors had granted me a good-sized lot as a reward for being a Hero of the Revolution. I'd welded its frame from the most choice steel struts scavenged from a human-scale heavy-haul trailer. Walls were multi-layered and insulated. The three-Dollganger-stories-tall structure had few windows, and none into the large chamber against the back wall that served as my study. Other features of the room could save my life if Canterbury were suddenly invaded by human forces.

In this room, its walls dark with wood-grain paint and its floor brightened by tan felt carpeting, the dominant feature was a massive circular table. This had once been an irrigation pipe access cover made of cast stone, shaped in the form of the ancient Mayan calendar from Earth, all weird faces, figures, and symbols. I'd used plastic strips to build a temporary rim around it, poured liquid plass atop it, let it harden, removed the plastic strips, attached sturdy legs, and polished the surface to glossy smoothness, resulting in one of the most envied furnishings in the Nest. Now the conspirators of Operation Coffee and Cream sat around it and looked at one another.

"Kieran is ready to play. Are we actually to play?" That was Kieran, speaking of himself, as ever, in the third person. The first genuine freak of the new generation of liberated 'gangers, he was young even by our standards, made and activated fewer than two years previously. He'd been keen to receive the benefits of the Stork's 'ganger modification options, and now he was a centaur, human from the waist up, four-legged horse from the waist down. He was a real novelty—there weren't many horses on Chiron.

He towered over us when he walked. He could also run faster than any other 'ganger I knew. His brown horse hair and tail matched the long hair, trim mustache and beard he wore. He kept his skin tone at a well-tanned Caucasian brown and he had a lot of lovers. Fortunately for my carpet, he didn't drop waste like a true horse. Beyond all that, I didn't know much about him except that he was a superior scout and sentry, and had become a Jack, killing a human with a spear, in the months since the Escape. Obviously, he couldn't use a chair, so he sat down like a resting horse beside the table, his long body stretching back toward the door.

BeeBee, sitting opposite Kieran, shook her head. "No. I've prepped a game progression simulation which you can download on the way out." Tonight she was dressed again in a leaf-pattern jumpsuit and black boots, but she also wore a heavy utility belt. It was a deliberate reminder of the gear she'd worn during the Escape, of her role during that event.

I was dressed the same way for the same reason. I even had, hanging from my utility belt, the wrist cuffs, including climbing claws, with which I had killed a human soldier.

Kieran made a sour face in response to BeeBee's words.

Next to him, Tink piped up. "Um, who wins in the simulation?" She was as dainty as Kieran was overbuilt. Like me, she had Asian features, but she was red-haired and waif-like where I was brown-haired and tediously average-looking. She wore a dress decorated in symbols and pictures from the face cards of a poker deck—appropriate, since this gathering was officially a card game. In the hours leading up to the Battle of Breen Hollow, while ostensibly serving with a human satellite maintenance crew, she'd disabled planetary surveillance satellites, giving the transporters of the Stork a chance to get the precious fabricator to its new home. Like me, she had space, air, and ground vehicle experience.

BeeBee let her voice turn scornful: "Who do you think?" She jerked her head toward Malibu, sitting to BeeBee's left.

Malibu clapped once and rubbed his hands together in victory. "As usual, I win just by showing up." Where Kieran's physical appeal was savage and wild, Malibu's was smooth and sophisticated, like his voice. Blond and tanned, clean-shaven, with bright eyes as blue as little Thonny's and teeth so white they seemed to gleam, he had been modeled after singer Courtnel "Malibu" James, and he had a singing voice and musical skill to match those of the man he duplicated. He wore a spotless peach-colored jumpsuit, white belt and boots, an ensemble that would have looked good on Courtnel James. Back when we were in human hands, he'd been a popular attraction for 'ganger-bangers, humans who drove Dollganger-sized, Dollganger-shaped remotes, cybernetically linked to the drivers' senses, to have sex with 'gangers. He'd weathered those years with more aplomb than some, but he never talked about those times. Immediately prior to the Escape, he'd supervised the building of the Nest; during the Battle of Breen Hollow, he'd been kilometers away, waiting with an ambush crew standing by to attack any human forces that detected and pursued the Stork as it was being transported.

"The fix is in." That was Parfait, her voice sounding overly formal but amused rather than accusing.

An exotic, her skin and hair as white as new linen, she was not a replica of any specific human, or of a naturally-occurring albino—her eye pupils were black. From the day she'd emerged from Chiron's original Dollganger fabricator until the Escape, she, too, had been popular with the 'ganger-bangers, and her only job had been as a sex toy for them. It was no secret that she was a mess because of those years. In the Battle of Breen Hollow, she'd operated a tracked forklift rather than a mega, and had, according to witnesses, taken a particular joy in driving it across human troops, crushing them to death. Tonight, as she had since we'd escaped the humans, she wore a long, voluminous dress and a head-to-hips shawl in gray, only her face and hands visible.

I elaborated on BeeBee's explanation. "When we leave, check the time elapsed, compare it to corresponding points on the game simulation." I sat beside BeeBee, presenting a united front with her. "Erase everything from that point up to the marker 'Final Hand'. If you ever need to tell anyone about tonight's game, embellish it in your own self-serving fashion."

"Can we just get on with it?" That raspy voice, belonging to the final member of our gathering of seven, seemed to cause my internal fluids to lose heat, sending a chill through me.

Pothole Charlie.

I was one of the oldest surviving 'gangers on Chiron. Pothole Charlie was older—meaning not that he looked like an old human or that his physical abilities were diminished, but that he had more experience than I did. I was one of the three or four most capable vehicle wranglers among the 'gangers; Pothole Charlie was *the* most capable, with years of deep-space work, exploration, and wormhole navigation I couldn't match. I'd been the first 'ganger ever to take a human life on Chiron without use of vehicle systems, ranged weapons, or explosives; in the months since the Escape, on missions into Zhou City, Pothole Charlie had killed two human infantrymen face-to-face. He was bigger than I was by some 10mm, heavier by maybe 150 grams of bone and muscle mass, and back in the day he'd been part of the informal conspiracy that attempted to assassinate me during the Battle of Breen Hollow. Oh, we'd shaken hands later, and he'd promised to abide by the Directors' mandate to forgive and forget my long friendly association with the humans.

But I doubted he'd forgiven or forgotten anything.

Now, wearing the brown leathery garments he'd had on all day while welding a new rail track extension, his big, craggy features emotionless like he was indeed playing poker, his shaggy black hair and thick eyebrows giving him his perpetually forbidding look, he seemed like someone who'd be more at ease if he could put on a black executioner's hood and come after me with an axe.

And, of course, with his question, he'd seized control of the meeting.

I grabbed it back. "Sure. You know the general parameters of why we're here. You'll be participating—"

"Um, we've only agreed to *listen.*" Despite the challenge in her words, Tink's voice was as soft as ever. "But we haven't agreed to do it, and, um, I don't think we can. Not if we really have to keep all stages secret from the Directors. I think it's impossible."

"You are a defeatist, Tink. And you obviously learn about as fast as a toaster." That, to my surprise, was Parfait, her voice mellow and silky in contrast to her words. "We could not possibly steal a whole fabrication unit from Harringen—but we did. We still have the secret weapon we did then. We have Jack One." She gave me a little nod of her head.

I wasn't quite sure how to respond to that. I still wasn't used to receiving admiring comments at public events.

Tink gave Parfait a stiff, cold look, then she glanced back at me. "Um, I'm willing to listen. I just don't think it can be done."

I nodded her way. "Human security on vital resources has improved a lot since we stole the Stork. Any effort to bypass it will be noticed to some extent. Flags will drop in their computer security systems, incidents will be investigated, holes in their security will be patched. Enough flags and their analysts could even figure out what we're doing. So what I propose to do is invite the humans to help us realize our goals."

That got a bark of laughter from Pothole Charlie and a quizzical frown from Parfait. I pressed on. "We're not even going to try to be invisible here. This operation is called Coffee and Cream because it's a two-pronged offensive. Coffee objectives are our true goals. Cream objectives, accomplished at the same time, are to convince the humans that we're up to something entirely different. Something that matches their expectations of what we're doing."

Pothole Charlie didn't laugh this time. He frowned, making him look even more ominous, but his question was civil enough. "So what would we be doing, exactly, and what would the humans think we were doing?"

BeeBee took over. "The humans have to realize that one of the 'ganger plans might involve stealing and escaping in a *Coracle*-class deep space exploration vehicle—the only spacecraft scaled for 'gangers, the only ones 'gangers can operate without human assistance.

All the *Coracles* on Chiron are currently grounded, experiencing 'routine maintenance', while the government tries to figure out which Dollgangers still in their employ are loyal to them. The *Coracles* are under tighter security than any corporate president's bank account. Rumor has it that they've had remotely-triggerable explosives installed in case we manage to steal one anyway. And security restricting access to ships at the spaceport is much higher to prevent 'gangers from sneaking aboard an outbound transport. They're serious about not letting our 'infection' get off-world."

Pothole Charlie gave her a dubious look. "And you've found a magical hole through their security."

She shook her head. "Certainly not."

He looked confused. "Why are we here again?"

I grinned at him, showing a confidence I never actually felt in his presence. "We're not going to go after the *Coracles*. I feel sad saying those words to the master of that ship class, but it's true. Nor are we going to smuggle ourselves or messages on an outbound ship. No, we're going to steal a human-scaled, privately owned space yacht called the *Granny Knot*."

Tink frowned. "That belongs to, um, Selva Shavery. Vice president in charge of the Shavery Corporation's Chiron branch."

I nodded.

"Um, it doesn't have a control deck scaled for 'gangers. We can't fly it."

"Wait, wait, wait." A light was dawning in Pothole Charlie's eyes. "So you're not talking about an invade-and-blast-off operation."

I smiled. "Score one for the big man."

Pothole Charlie settled back in his chair, looking both suspicious and intrigued. "Keep talking, plush."

I turned my smile on each of them. I knew some would find it unsettling. I don't smile much. I didn't think I'd smiled at all since I left my human owner, Doc Chiang, particularly since Lina had made it clear that she wanted to raise children with Wolfe.

So BeeBee and I explained the plan I had conceived and BeeBee had improved. The plan did call for a lot of aid from unsuspecting humans.

In Stage One, we would sneak into the Kresh Assemblies factory responsible for the fabrication of most of the drones used by Chiron's military in its attempts to find us. Those drones, ranging from high-flying stealth-copter models three meters long down to things the size and shape of dragonflies and praying mantises, were the biggest threat to Nest security, and everybody on both sides of our quiet little war knew it. So we were going to blow up Kresh Assemblies. Drone fabrication would be set back a few weeks or months.

Except ... one of the people sitting at this table had to die in order for the plan to work. Except ... the plan actually had nothing to do with depriving the humans of new drones. And when I explained what Stage One was really all about, the others nodded and agreed. Parfait volunteered to die.

Then, Stage Two. The Chiron branch of the Harringen Corporation was the builder of the Stork and fabricators like it, but many of its components were built by other companies. Several crucial computer sub-systems were put together by the same Shavery Corporation whose vice president owned the yacht we wanted. We would break into the Shavery plant and steal computer components sufficient to build a complete control system for a new Stork.

Except the mission wasn't really about stealing components for the purpose of building a brain for a new Stork. When BeeBee explained what Stage Two was really for, the others nodded and agreed.

Stage Three involved performing a commando raid on Akima Spaceport next to Zhou City. The target would be the hangar-bunker where the *Coracle*-class spacecraft were mothballed. Our purpose was evident—seize one of the craft and leave Chiron in it.

And when I explained what Stage Three was really all about, and how I intended for it to fail, the 'gangers around my table nodded and agreed.

4: SCRAP-WALK

The four-wheeled human military transport, boxy and green with a short truck bed in back, pulled to a halt at an intersection of darkened Zhou City streets. BeeBee, Malibu, and I, hanging from climb-cords out of sight in the little gap between the rear seats and the truck bed, rappelled down to the hard graytop road surface below. The cords were not affixed above us, simply pulled over support struts keeping the truck and passenger compartments separate, so as we stood on the street, each of us tugged on one of the cords in our hands. As the transport drove off, its rear wheels passing to either side of us, the cords dropped to the roadway and we retrieved them.

The place where we dropped off, a residential neighborhood, was the closest point on the transport's route between our origin, a roadway many kilometers from the Nest, and our destination, the Kresh Assemblies plant. But "closest" didn't mean "close". It was a kilometer away, which for us was like eight and a half kilometers to humans.

We headed out, three doll-sized people in close-fitting black nightsuits and masks, backpacks stuffed with gear, lightly armed and completely unarmored, in an enemy city—yes, we moved with stealth and caution born of the fact that one mistake would kill us all. In Zhou City and other important human sites, we could find military drones, playful dogs, curious cats, even the occasional brightly-colored pet tarantula ... and they could find us. It paid to be paranoid.

But we made it undetected, putting us outside Kresh Assemblies at about midnight.

I'd been here several times starting eight weeks before, shortly after the first meeting of the Coffee and Cream conspirators. This was a sealed factory complex, an unbroken chain of huge, gray, boxy buildings, windowless other than on the building featuring the majority of human offices. Fixed floodlights poured illumination across the streets, parking areas, shipping areas, and walls, making it impossible to cross those spaces without being caught in bright puddles of light on camera. The factory, its exterior surface the exact color and texture of unpainted cinder block, looked impossibly well-defended against Dollgangers.

Except it wasn't.

Across the street in front of the plant, in the less well-illuminated greenbelt park where the plant owners held their corporate picnics and public announcements, the three of us approached the opening of a drain pipe. Approached it from the side, of course. To approach it straight-on would put us within view of the little cameras that had been installed within it some time after the Escape.

When we stood just beside the pipe opening, I glanced at BeeBee.

She nodded. "I've got the sequence queued up and ready to send. On your marks ..." She assumed a runner's ready-to-race stance. Malibu and I followed suit.

"Get set ..." She closed her eyes and I knew she was now sending, by radio, the first command in a series of eight. Her eyes opened. "Go."

We charged the drain pipe opening, Malibu in front, BeeBee second, me last, and a moment later entered the low, dark, circular pipe—moving at a crouch because none of us could stand completely upright in the low passage. Fortunately, it hadn't been raining recently; there was no water in the pipe, just a little nearly-dry mud. We kept our feet to either side of the mud so as not to leave identifiable footprints for the cameras to see.

We scurried a few meters along the pipe. BeeBee kept talking, her voice flat and emotionless because of her state of distraction. "Codes Two and Three sent. Sensor Two responding correctly ..."

It had taken me a few nights to breach the security in this drain pipe. There were eight little sensor stations along its slightly meandering forty-meter length—the humans were that serious about the Dollganger menace. I'd started by pushing a narrow plastic tube under the mud from a spot out of sight of the first camera to a point directly beneath that camera. Then I'd pushed a wire through the tube until it reached the camera's position and beyond. That wire was, itself, a delicate sensor, capable, when hooked up to the correct monitoring device, of detecting electronic flows. For hours after it was in place, I'd watched its monitor box, figuring out the electron-flow patterns that corresponded to times when the factory's security people ran power-down/power-up self-tests on the cameras.

When I was sure the camera was experiencing a self-test, I charged into the pipe. I spliced a data stream capture box into the camera. It would intercept all data being passed from the camera to the humans' security room. Upon receipt of a radio command, it would play the last fifteen seconds of recorded data instead of sending current data. But I wasn't activating that function at that time; I was just getting the capture box into place.

Capture *boxes*. Once I was past a camera, I could shove the wire farther along the pipe, past bends and elevation changes, and repeat the process with the next camera in line.

It took me three nights to do that a total of eight times, but now the pipe was completely compromised.

This time, this last time, getting through the sequence was comparatively easy. BeeBee sent the signal to each capture box and got automated confirmation that it was being acted on. Those cross-signals, on radio frequencies, were too weak to be detected outside the pipe; only the first one, broadcast from outside the pipe, might have been detected.

Less than two minutes after we started, we passed the last camera. At the pipe's terminus, we stood facing muddy cinder-block-colored wall. Above us, instead of pipe surface, was a large metal grating with security lights and night sky far beyond. Just above the grating was the exterior wall of Kresh Assemblies, with a beautiful drainage flue just over our heads. In rainy times, the flue would receive rainwater from the drainage gutters on the building's roof and channel them down to our pipe.

I carefully raised my head up through the grate and took a long look around, cycling my vision through human-standard, light-amplification, and infrared, with motion enhancement analysis activated. There was no sign of new sensor equipment, no evidence of a drone overhead. So I pulled myself up through the grate, then hauled Malibu and BeeBee up. I watched them clamber into the drainage flue, then followed them in.

We had on multi-mode climbing gear for that climb. One set of such gear consisted of six items—two wrist cuffs, two knee pads, and two boots—each of which could extrude several different sorts of climbing tools. Hooked claws were appropriate for surfaces like trees. Battery-powered electromagnets were best for ferrous metal surfaces such as building supports. We were now in a shaft of smooth, unpainted plastic, so we used the gecko-pads—surfaces that extruded microscopic cilia that clung to a seemingly smooth surface the way a gecko lizard's paws cling to glass. We went up that flue like we were climbing a ladder.

But we only climbed three stories of the five-story building. That's when we reached the portal I'd cut into the flue's wall-side interior six weeks earlier. The portal wasn't visible to the naked eye: I'd run my cutter along the flue's existing join lines and it looked no different.

Malibu braced himself against the other side of the flue interior and pushed. The portal gave way with a moist *shluck* noise, the sound of a seal breaking. It swung open, revealing darkness beyond. He scrambled through. BeeBee climbed up and followed, and I went last, turning in the dark space beyond to shove the portal closed. Then I checked, by hand, to make sure the gummy material lining the portal's edges still made an airtight seal; fortunately, it did.

Only then could we rest, catching our breath—which Dollgangers don't need to do from a physiological perspective, but the mentalities we'd inherited from our human originals meant we did anyway.

That's when the lights came on.

We stood in a rough gap laboriously dug through cinderstone wall by me and BeeBee weeks earlier. On the side opposite the drainage flue portal, this hole opened into a wide corridor—wide by Dollganger standards. To humans, it was nothing but a gap between a dryplast interior wall and the cinderstone exterior wall, 25cm of open space. The dryplast surface ahead of us was gray, marked with manufacturers' preprinted measurements.

And in that corridor, under a bare-diode light I'd strung, stood Parfait, also in a nightsuit, unmasked, smiling.

We three pulled our stretchy masks off. Malibu bounded out of the wall hole to embrace Parfait. BeeBee and I followed, and Parfait also had hugs for us, embracing me for seconds longer than she had the others. Then she looked up at me. "Is it still a go for tonight?"

I nodded. "We're even almost on schedule. Though with me supposed to be on an all-night sentry shift back at the Nest, if anything happens in my sentry area—"

Malibu shook his head. "Kieran will cover for you."

Parfait looked at him and BeeBee. "And you two—are you also supposed to be on sentry duty?"

"No." BeeBee took a careful look around. "We're off-duty. We left by the Gopher Hole. They think Malibu's trying to convert me to outdoor sex." She gave a little shudder.

We didn't have to ask about Parfait's alibi. She was, after all, dead.

Have you ever heard of the Scrap-Walk? It's a form of suicide. Dollganger suicide.

I had heard of it back when I lived with Doc Chiang, but I hadn't known at the time how common it was. A Dollganger who had decided for whatever reason that life was just too painful would cut himself open, digging around in his components until he found the transponder by which his owner could find him. Since the transponder could be anywhere—neck, guts, arm, foot—a 'ganger might mutilate himself horribly, suffering the same pain a human would from slicing skin and organs, before finding and yanking the device.

Then he'd go walking, typically out into the forests surrounding Zhou City, and keep going until his battery gave out. He'd freeze in place or fall over, perhaps remaining there for years, until the elements turned him into a pile of corroded, irreparable junk.

The Dollgangers who'd joined the Revolution had chosen to be implanted with capacitors that would, on a mental command, fry their cognitive and memory circuitry, an instant, painless form of suicide appropriate to fighters willing to die rather than give up the secrets of the Nest. But prior to the formation of the Revolution, Scrap-Walks were one of the few means of self-termination available.

And it was well known that Parfait had performed the Scrap-Walk ... twice.

The first time, unable to cope with her role as an unwilling whore for human-controlled remotes, she'd dug out her transponder and done the walk. Unfortunately for her, she'd been found only six weeks later by a human camper. He had returned her to her owner and she had been fully repaired, restored.

That owner had force-fed some artificial happiness and anti-suicide coding into her psychological makeup. He had also, unknown to Parfait, not just restored her transponder, but had installed a second one.

Across the years, the mental conditioning wore off, returning her to her depressed state, and she'd done it again ... but, because of that second transponder, had been found by her owner before her battery had even run down.

The second bout of mental conditioning had mostly worn off at the time the Dollganger Revolution was coming together, and it had not been surprising that she'd been an avid recruit to the cause.

Nor had it been surprising, at our first Operation Coffee and Cream meeting, when she'd volunteered to become a new Scrap-Walk victim. We needed a 'ganger who could be away from the Nest for weeks at a time. People would be saddened by, but not surprised by, Parfait's third attempt. So she'd let herself be caught on camera leaving the Nest, with unobtrusive but detectable wires and other interior components hanging out of her cumbersome dress. They weren't hers, of course; BeeBee had supplied them. But they were convincing. When Parfait had not returned days later, Scrap-Walk was the conclusion. The 'gangers mourned her, but also hoped she'd fried out her brains before her battery had failed completely.

I joined BeeBee in looking around. This little safe haven was a few meters long, two and a half high, and every surface glistened with a transparent brown coating—a sealing resin we'd brought in bottles on our backs. Parfait had used it to seal every hole, every join providing access into the hidey-hole, making sure that insect drones couldn't stumble into it.

The space was pretty plain; a foam-rubber square with cloth napkins on it served as Parfait's bed, exposed alternating-current wires with an adapter spliced into them served as her recharging station. There were piles of human goods: pass-cards, keys, meters, a couple of not-fully-assembled preying-mantis drones with wires still trailing out of the sockets where their heads should be, bits of food wrapped in scraps of paper, a human-scale plastic bowl with water in it.

I gave Parfait a curious look.

She shrugged. "I like taking baths. Something I must have gotten from my deep-down human psych layer."

"I guess so." Dollgangers did occasionally need to sponge off when dirty, and some wore body-paint designs that needed to be cleaned off and replaced, but we don't sweat, so bathing constituted a fetish.

Nor did I need to be thinking about Parfait's bathing rituals right then. "The cameras facing the exterior hauler lot?"

Parfait glanced upward. "I have put the chip-frying capacitors on all of them. Issue the command, and the security room will not be able to see the parking area." An alphanumeric string popped into my mind's receiving area; she'd sent it via microwave burst, not radio, so radio receivers could not pick it up.

"Thanks. All right, let's get to work."

5: DISASSEMBLY/REASSEMBLY

Before our arrival, Parfait had set up the factory's final assembly chamber for Stage One.

How had she known what to do, where to sabotage and subvert? It wasn't just from her own explorations of the plant. Dollgangers worked here, had worked here for years, and some of them had fled with us during the Escape. Ever since that event, BeeBee, in her role as a Director, had been debriefing 'gangers who had worked at important government offices, factories, military bases, and infrastructure sites. She had assembled a database of maps and security data, an invaluable resource for the Nest's tacticians. When we'd settled on Kresh Assemblies for Stage One, she'd merely pulled all recorded maps and other data on the facility and given them to us.

So Parfait had spliced capture boxes into all the cameras overlooking the final assembly chamber, where we'd now be working. I'd taught her everything she'd needed to know to do to those cameras what I'd done to the ones in the drain pipe, and she'd been eager to learn.

Now, in Parfait's safe chamber, we all donned our masks, unsealed the door that gave access into the final assembly chamber, and began our own wall-climbing to scope out the situation.

Below, even at this late hour, the chamber was still very active. Kresh Assemblies ran day-in and day-out, but the graveyard shift was all robotic, with the only human oversight coming in the form of supervisors and security people watching remotely on their office monitors.

Now, below us as we hung from ceiling supports by the magnets in our wrist cuffs, we could see the four assembly lines we'd come to destroy. Most of the lights in the chamber were off, but with our light-amplification options up, we could see the whole situation from the glows of monitor screens and gleaming status lights on control surfaces.

Two of the lines, occupying three-quarters of the manufacturing space in the chamber, were devoted to HummingHawk sky drones.

Picture an oval matte-black payload compartment about a meter long, half a meter wide and high at its broadest. A small hatch on the forward portion of the top surface and a large one, most of the length of the bottom surface, permit access to the pod's interior. A total of eight struts stretch up and out from the top surface, attaching two each to four ducted fan assemblies, also matte black. Three meters long and wide, these drones could haul a payload of about ten kilograms. That payload was usually some combination of sensor package and weapons—such as a bomb or a rack of four heat-seeking missiles, such as Bale explosives or Faust thermite burners.

The third assembly line below us was for Twitch dragonfly drones, and the last for Miya praying mantis drones. Shaped like insects and easy to mistake for organic creatures at a distance, those camera drones were the bane of our existence, a daily threat to the secrecy of the Nest.

The whole area was awash in constant noise: the hum of conveyors, the clicks and thumps of servos, the whine of powered tools used to assemble components, musical tones from status boards.

I concentrated on the HummingHawk lines. They were the only ones we were concerned with. At one end of each line, in the distance to my right, were the component stations where pre-assembled ducted-fans, payload-pod-and-strut assemblies, and main computer system waited. Mechanisms gliding by overhead on ceiling-mounted rails used segmented waldo arms to snatch up components and place them with millimeter precision on assembly tables along the line. Other fixed robot systems used their own armatures to assemble the drones into recognizable HummingHawk shapes. Then the overhead arms moved them to the next station. Some stations installed main payloads such as bombs or enhanced sensor packages, some added auxiliary systems, some performed fast systems or computer checks, some fired sound or X-rays into the assemblies to test for defects. Finally, the overhead arms lifted each assembled HummingHawk and place it in its own plastic crate at the near end of the line—just a few meters to my right and ten meters below. The crates' interiors, occupied mostly by molded foam inserts, protected the drones from damage. A robot arm at the end of the line flipped each crate's lid shut and made sure that its catch engaged.

Once a stack of crates grew to five in number, making it about six meters tall, automated forklifts picked up the stack and carefully carried it into the vast, shadowy receiving area to my left. There the forklift placed the stack on a shipping pallet. In the morning, humans would strap the stacks down to the pallets, securing them for transportation, and then more forklifts would carry those pallets off to the hauler lot outside. Ultimately, a few drones would go to Chiron's military, while most would go to the spaceport for export.

This whole setup was one rare occurrence of the humans' increased paranoia working in our favor. HummingHawks were costly goods, and before the Escape, Dollgangers driving megas carried the stacks to the pallets and strapped them down for shipping. Now, forklifts repurposed from lower-security businesses, like processed-food manufacturers, did the carrying. They could be trusted where 'gangers now could not. Some of the megas waited, unused for months, against the wall of the holding area.

While all this assembly and preparation was going on, other automated forklifts hauled away empty component bins from the start of the assembly line and brought in full bins. At irregular intervals, a large door on the wall far to my right would slide up to allow one of those lifters to enter or exit.

And not a human in sight. But they'd be watching.

I looked over at Malibu. He hung from the ceiling just beside a camera pod overlooking the chamber. He was not in its field of view. His bare right hand gripped the capture box Parfait had patched into the camera. His eyes, the only parts of his face visible through his mask, had a dreamy look to them, not because he was enjoying what he was seeing, but because he was coping with too much data. He couldn't completely govern his reactions.

I called out to him, a stage whisper: "How's it looking?"

"Trying to find the perfect loop point." His voice sounded dreamy as well. "I have an almost perfect one. But if we run that loop, then one ducted fan disappears from its component bin and then reappears at the start of the loop. So I'm cropping that part of the image and superimposing it on the bin as a still. And having to compensate for variations in the image caused by building vibrations."

I returned my attention to the floor below. Malibu was better with audio-visual work than almost anyone in the Nest. Under these circumstances, not even he could give us perfection. We had to hope that a good-enough effort would keep the human observers from noticing.

Once that loop was playing, we'd be able to move around unmolested until—well, until we *were* noticed. We needed all the time we could get.

"Got it." Malibu sounded more alert now. "As good as I can get without days and a lot of computing muscle. Perfect engagement point coming in fifteen seconds. Fourteen."

BeeBee took one last look around. "Unless one of us says otherwise, engage at the right point."

"... Four. Three. Two. One. Engaged." Malibu darted a look around. "We're okay to go."

I breathed out a sigh, and then we really got to work.

BeeBee and I tied black cords from our backpacks to Malibu's camera pod, then slid down to the concrete floor. We tied the ends of those cords off against an immobile assembly-line support leg on the dragonfly line. We didn't intend to go up the way we'd descended, but we might have to abort the mission and improvise.

Malibu and Parfait didn't descend with us. They climbed along the ceiling to a grate leading into the ventilation system. They used their belt tools to unscrew the grate, letting it hang at an angle from one screw. Then they climbed into the vent, disappearing from my sight.

BeeBee and I trotted into the receiving area where all the towering stacks of drone crates waited. She accompanied me to the line of three megas gathering dust beside one wall. And I almost became cheerful.

Two and a half meters tall, shaped roughly like a human but oversized, with fully articulated hands, with broad tread assemblies instead of legs, megas were perhaps my favorite vehicle to operate. I'd spent years working with them, all models. They were tough and versatile, and, as the humans had learned to their regret, easily adapted to machines of war. The three waiting here were forklift models, with upper arms that could extend hydraulically so their elbows reached the floor, with lower arms that could stretch to a length of two meters. Painted silver-gray, these three bore chestplate symbols in black, the Kresh Assemblies logo: two waldo arms shaking hands.

I picked the middle mega. BeeBee and I cracked the security keeping it locked. The security wasn't bad—when the entry-code keypad was activated, it was supposed to query the plant's security office wirelessly and wait for confirmation from a human before permitting access. Someone with a basic 'ganger skill with electronics and coding would have been thwarted. I spent minutes disengaging the vehicle's radio system, then patching into the wires that ran from the antenna to the vehicle's internal computer. Meanwhile, BeeBee analyzed the alphanumeric keypad on the side of the tread assembly for wear, calculated a series of probable passwords, and began entering them. She got the correct password on her third try; I supplied the correct authorization code on my fourth. The mega's faceplate swung open, granting access to the 'ganger-scaled cockpit in the head, and I climbed in.

In the mega, I began unstacking stacks of HummingHawk drones. I laid nine drone crates in a line in an aisle the forklifts were not using tonight. I moved down the line, raising the crate lids and leaning them against the chamber wall. Then we began our campaign of modification.

Three of the drones I'd chosen were bombers. Each had a single bomb almost completely filling its payload pod. I used the mega to lift two of those drones out of their crates and set them upside down on the concrete floor. BeeBee ran external power to the pods and bypassed their locking mechanisms, allowing me to open their bomb bay hatches. I carefully removed the glossy red ovals within and was even more gentle when setting them on the floor. Then I set the two drones right side up on the floor. Now BeeBee could get to work on the drones' control and guidance systems.

Meticulously, I removed the other seven drones from their crates and set them on the floor. When I was done, I had a row of nine drones that looked like they were ready to spring to life.

Meanwhile, BeeBee moved from drone to drone, entering the payload pods and disabling all transmitters, including tracking transponders, so they could not help the humans track the HummingHawks. She did not make any mechanical or electronic adjustments to the radio receivers, and she uploaded code to the computers to prevent them from accepting or reacting to remote human control. During our departure, she'd send seven of the drones navigation microbursts at intervals; we didn't want her to upload a navigation route back to the Nest, as anything might happen to cause a drone to fall back into human hands.

With the last two drones, the bombers whose explosive charges I'd removed, she adjusted the control and guidance systems so they could be controlled by Dollgangers in their payload pods.

I saw flickering lights from the door by which forklifts brought in new components. I glanced that way and saw that the door was still closed, but Malibu now stood at its base, using his electrical cutting torch, running it off wall power, to cut a hole, maybe 200mm wide and 100mm tall, at one corner of the door bottom. I checked my internal clock and nodded. We were seventeen minutes behind our optimal schedule, still within our acceptable time bracket.

Once BeeBee had finished reprogramming four of the HummingHawks, I operated my mega to pick up the first reprogrammed drone in line and carry it to the door where Malibu labored. He was now finishing cutting his hole—he kicked at the plate a couple of times and it fell away with a tiny *clang*. Then he looked up at me, gave me a thumbs-up, and carefully crawled through the hole, not allowing its glowing edges to touch his nightsuit.

I waited there for a few minutes. Then the door lifted. A forklift from the chamber behind me, dragging an empty component bin, rolled through into the darkness beyond. I waited a moment more, and a forklift hauling a load of ducted-fan assemblies rolled out past me.

The instant it was clear, I accelerated into the gap and was just barely through with my precious cargo when the door slid shut behind me.

This put me in the junction chamber, an intersection serving several purposes. Oversized doors led to receiving chambers where components built by other manufacturers arrived, to lesser assembly lines where components were put together into the assemblies we'd been seeing, and, on the east-facing wall, to the outdoors—the hauler lot whose cameras Parfait had sabotaged.

This big room was also where in-building transports such as forklifts and megas were serviced and fueled. I rolled my mega over to the refueling station, which was mostly given over to hyperdiesel pumps and electrical rechargers ... but there was also one small aviation fuel pump. I carefully set my drone down before that pump.

Cold in here. Outdoor cold. That was a microwave text burst from Malibu.

I looked down and could see him standing at the base of the hyperdiesel dispenser, staring up at me. I couldn't really feel the cold; the cockpit of my mega was temperature-controlled. I shrugged and sent a reply. *So? We're against an outside wall and an uninsulated exterior door, a big one. This room probably loses a lot of heat.*

I suppose.

I helped Malibu unroll and attach, with sealer-tape and heat-hardening resin, a human-scale fire hose to the nozzle end of the hyperdiesel pump. Malibu got to work unrolling the rest of the hose toward the door into the final assembly chamber. I turned my mega around and followed him, waiting, as he did, beside the door.

But I kept a close eye on this chamber. I wasn't dismissive of Malibu's hunches—I didn't necessarily agree with him, but it was never a good idea to ignore warnings from a competent, level-headed 'ganger. But nothing seemed out of order. When the door opened again and after another hauler entered with an empty bin, Malibu, unrolling his hose, and I shot through back into the final assembly chamber.

6: BOOM ECONOMY

That was my assignment for most of the next hour. I'd wait for the door to open, return to the final assembly chamber, pick up a drone, wait for the door to open, race through, and drop off the drone.

Across that hour, I could see progress elsewhere in our operation. With equipment from his pack, Malibu winched his fire hose up a wall and into the ventilation system. BeeBee completed the subversion of all nine HummingHawks and turned her attention to attaching remote-controlled detonators to the two bombs I'd removed from the bombers. Parfait, her nightsuit streaked with dust, appeared in the junction chamber and began the labor-intensive process of dragging the aviation fuel hose from drone to drone, fueling them all. Malibu returned from the vents, similarly dusty. From across the room I saw him make a lifting-a-heavy-handle gesture, meaning "Ready to accept hyperdiesel."

Which startled me. We were almost *there*. I checked my internal clock. We were 29 minutes late by optimal timing, 31 minutes within acceptable timing.

I checked BeeBee's work area. She stood beside her completed bomb assemblies, watching me.

I sent each of them the same message via microwave burst. *Time to extract.* BeeBee nodded and trotted toward the door to the junction chamber. Malibu began shimmying down his climbing cord toward the floor. Though reluctant to leave a perfectly functional, valuable vehicle behind, I hit a button on my control console to swing the faceplate of my mega open. I used the magnetics of my climbing gear to clamber down to floor level.

Malibu joined me for the trot over to the door out. I shot him a questioning look. "Any problems?"

He shook his head. "Parfait had set all the baffles and blocks up right. The ones that are supposed to be closed *are* closed and sealed. The fuel is going to pour out in all the assembly chambers but won't make it to the human-occupied areas."

"Right."

Now we didn't have to wait for the door into the junction chamber to open. Malibu's hose filled only half the gap Malibu had cut into the door, leaving plenty of room for a 'ganger to crawl through.

Ahead of us, BeeBee scrambled through, barely slowing. Moments later, Malibu and I followed.

The aviation fuel nozzle lay inert at the bottom of that fueling station, and Parfait stood beside one of the former bomb drones, waving. I headed toward her. BeeBee was already clambering into the top hatch of the other former bomber; Malibu headed her way.

I climbed atop the payload pod of my drone. The hatch was already open, doubtless a courtesy of Parfait's. I slid through, landing on my rear end at the very forward edge of the pod, just ahead of the bomb bay hatch. I yanked my nightsuit mask off, tossing it aside, and then grabbed the control box BeeBee had spliced into the computer system. My data-feed wires extended from my fingertips and slid into the correct input holes on the box.

Parfait climbed in behind me. "Want me to dog the hatch closed?"

"Not yet. Please stay up there and maintain a line of sight on Malibu."

"Understood."

My HummingHawk's exterior sensors came online, and suddenly my mind was flooded with visual images—the other drones all around me, the refueling stations, Malibu's fuel hose stretching to and through the hole in the door. The industrial factory hum and roar doubled in volume as sound from the drone's audio sensors joined the sounds I heard with my ears. Bright patterns of letters took up the far left and right portions of my vision; they told me that all HummingHawk systems were a go.

I took a deep breath. "Transmit to Malibu, 'Fuel up'."

"Transmitting. He acknowledges. He reports 'Fuel Up' initiated."

I could hear the hyperdiesel pump start. I saw the hose on the floor stiffen as liquid under pressure flowed into it. At a rate of two hundred liters a minute, fuel would be pouring out into the ventilation system of this building and several adjoining structures.

Hyperdiesel fuel is actually not that easy to ignite—when it's an issue of bringing a small flame close to a puddle of the stuff. But our fuel, pouring out of ceiling grates into huge assembly and warehouse chambers, was now becoming a fuel-air mixture, which a single spark could set off. We had minutes at best in which to get clear.

"All right. I'm shutting down the cameras overlooking the hauler lot." I switched to radio—at this point, it would be fine for the humans to capture the occasional enigmatic radio signal—and transmitted the code Parfait had given me.

But nothing happened. I received no confirmation.

Concerned, I looked up over my shoulder at Parfait. She had her feet on a mounting bracket attached halfway up the pod's interior wall and her hands gripped the rim of the hatchway. She had her mask off now, though her hair was still constrained by a transparent brown cap of stocking material. Her attention was fixed on Malibu.

I cleared my throat. "Nothing."

Wide-eyed, she looked at me. "Please do not say that."

"I got no response."

"Hold on. I will check." She closed her eyes. "Status inquiry ... no, they have fired. All cameras on that side of the roof are disabled." She opened her eyes and looked miserable. "But clearly I fouled something up. I am so sorry."

"Don't worry. If the cameras are out, we're good." In my drone-camera view, I could see the ducted fans on BeeBee's drone spin up to speed. I activated mine as well, and my top-view cameras showed them spin up. I clicked through my pre-flight checklist at a rapid rate. Electrical systems and computer system responded in the green. Fuel was topped off.

I glanced up at Parfait again. "Open the exterior door and dog the hatch."

She closed her eyes for a moment. I saw a light on a panel at human head height beside he exterior door flash from yellow to green. Then the door lifted, sliding up into the wall above, revealing darkness and some distant parked hauler rigs.

Parfait got the overhead hatch dogged down. Then she dropped to the pod deck. She settled in beside me.

"Parfait, if you have any cord left, rig us some restraint lines, would you? If we get some turbulence, I'd hate to be thrown all over this interior."

"I am on it."

Then it was time to fly. I lifted off—

All right, I'm not describing the experience correctly. I wasn't flying the drone.

BeeBee had had time to set up only the crudest sort of control systems for me and herself. They allowed us to stand in for a distant drone operator issuing command strings. I wasn't manipulating a control yoke or foot pedals. I was doing the equivalent of issuing orders to a perfectly compliant pilot: "Ascend to an altitude of one meter and hover," for instance. I wasn't flying, I was directing.

The system obeyed my order with only a little lag. I saw BeeBee's do the same. Then, one after the next, each of the other seven HummingHawks rose. Stealth drones, they were whisper-quiet, adding only a faint hum to the ambient noise of the junction chamber.

In a moment, I'd issue a text string command equating to, "Maintain absolute altitude, proceed on course one-five, accelerating to 20 kph and then maintaining that speed." And with absolute mechanical obedience my drone would do as it was told.

But I wouldn't actually be piloting. I *hated* this.

I could hear Parfait stringing cord, tying it off to mounting brackets along the sides of the compartment. I started as she ran a cord around my chest—she did it as softly as a caress, but I simply hadn't been expecting it.

I enabled my internal radio systems, but switched my broadcast voice from one identical to my speaking voice to something far more generic, even robotic. "Gang One to Gang Two."

"Gang Two here." That was BeeBee's response but not her voice—she replied with the female equivalent of the one I'd just used.

Should we have broadcast in the open like that? Absolutely yes. There was always a chance that the human forensics experts would fail to realize that the destruction we were about to unleash was the fault of Dollgangers. We wanted them to make that realization, hence radio broadcasts they could intercept, record, and analyze.

I went on, "How's the assembly on the demolitions charge going?"

"Assembled. I'm setting the timer now."

I issued my command to the drone. It drifted forward, out over the graytop hauler lot, picking up speed. At a distance of twenty meters, BeeBee followed. My rear camera view showed each of the drones follow at similar intervals.

That might have been the worst moment for me. Being a guerilla Dollganger in enemy territory required a certain amount of paranoia to survive, but paranoia doesn't always maintain itself at an optimally efficient level. So thoughts began wandering around in the back of my mind: *What if they detected us on entry? What if they're waiting outside, ready to shoot us down?*

But ... nothing. We drifted, a long line of matte-black, almost invisible, almost silent aircraft, through a large space sparsely occupied by hauler cabs and trailers. And nothing moving awaited us. I kept a nervous eye skyward, but detected no drones above.

I threaded our way through the parking area, paused at streetside long enough to be sure that no ground traffic was coming, and crossed over to the park by which we'd entered the drain pipe. There, we picked up a little speed, accelerating to 45 kph.

We also picked up altitude, but only a little. This was an industrial part of the city, factories and product showplaces plus a couple of public parks, and we kept lower than the surrounding rooftops so as not to be picked up by radar. That kept us at about four stories, human stories, in the air.

Now that we were surrounded by buildings and our rearmost drones were approaching minimal safe distance from the blast to come, I glanced at Parfait beside me. "Fire alarm, please."

She nodded. The "fire alarm" signal she was about to send would trigger an automated hazardous-condition alert in the Kresh buildings, calling for an automatic evacuation by all work personnel.

Parfait was still in the process of closing her eyes when the world behind me erupted in light. An instant later, a noise like the death roar of some volcano monster of those ancient Greeks hammered my ears, and a shockwave, air propelled by explosion, hammered my drone—suddenly we were standing almost on our vehicle's nose, simultaneously accelerating forward and sliding down toward the ground.

In that moment, I wanted, more than anything, to have a control yoke in my hands. My reflexive yank almost pulled the control box free from its connecting wires. But I managed to keep myself from issuing new mental commands. The drone's guidance system had a specific command running—maintain level flight forward 45 kph at 12 meters' altitude. Issuing a new command would result in microseconds lost to reevaluation, recalculation of sensor data. So I just gritted my teeth while the drone's sophisticated sensors and computerized handling adjusted the angle and pitch of all four fans. They strained against the task of obeying their standing order.

We leveled off a meter above the ground and began climbing again. In my camera sight, I could see BeeBee level off and begin her own ascent. Other drones had survived, but I couldn't see them all. Brilliant flame-light and a multicolored mushroom cloud behind us were washing out my optics.

Parfait spoke, her voice thin with shock: "What happened?"

I shook my head. "Probably a spark in one of the secondary assembly lines or a forklift's wiring."

Now I could see that BeeBee's drone had suffered damage to its starboard landing strut. I could count four drones behind hers—five. Six. I kept scanning for the seventh but could not spot it. I allowed myself a brief text transmission: *B,P OK. BB,M?*

I got back an instant *OK.*

The four of us were alive. The plant was destroyed. We had drones. Those were the things that mattered most. But the humans in the plant, few though they probably were, couldn't have gotten clear of the explosions.

I had learned not to beat myself up over necessary enemy deaths. But these hadn't been necessary.

As if sensing what I was feeling, Parfait rested her head against the back of my shoulder and wrapped her arms around me.

*   *   *

We made it out of Zhou City undetected, so far as we could tell. The only thing that could have tracked us in our drones would have been another HummingHawk on high, and we spent time following deep river tracks and shooting through railway tunnels in order to make sure we shook any such observation.

We confirmed that we had lost a drone—BeeBee had seen a chunk of wreckage land right on it—and BeeBee's craft had actually grazed the roadway before recovering, resulting in the crumpled landing strut. But the mission was essentially a success.

We touched down shortly before dawn in a clearing on a heavily forested hilltop a few kilometers from the Nest. There, Kieran, who had scouted the location, waited with fine-weave camouflage netting. In minutes, we had all eight remaining drones lashed down and covered. As soon as their engines cooled, they'd be next to impossible to detect from the air.

And then it was time to get back to the Nest. Malibu and BeeBee returned to the Gopher Hole, their nonexistent mutual lust theoretically slaked. Kieran and I were to return to the Chimney Pipe exit, where two more scouts would be waiting to begin their shifts. Parfait, officially dead, would remain behind with the drones.

Before we left her, when the others could not hear, she asked me, "When will you be back?"

I ran my schedule through my head. "Tonight, if I can."

"I will see you then."

7: STRANGE BEDFELLOWS

For Dollgangers, fast battery charges are a bad idea. They damage our internal battery packs, diminishing capacity and throughput. It's no hardship to go through an occasional fast recharge—our internal nanofabricator plants, the 'ganger digestion and healing mechanism, can repair that damage. But a succession of fast charges causes progressive damage, potentially reducing our battery function to nil—the equivalent of a human falling into a coma.

Regardless of advisability, when I got back to the Nest from our HummingHawk raid, I plugged in for a quick recharge, then got up a little while later for a full day of work.

It was part of the conspiracy's plan of deception, of course. Not out of paranoia, but out of a need to make use of all resources for our survival, all 'gangers in the Nest had their time heavily scheduled: work shifts, recharging/down-time shifts, even recommended socializing periods. You couldn't sneak a series of unauthorized covert mission shifts into your schedule other than by using recharging/down-time shifts for those purposes. We had to do this *very* carefully or risk detection, risk collapse.

My work this day was operating a digger. Mister Science had developed the vehicle from old human designs. We'd fabricated the thing from human-scale artillery shell casings and other parts. The result was a torpedo-shaped device with a grinding cone at the front end and treads along the body—bottom, sides, top. We used it to drill new tunnels through earth and rock, expanding the Nest.

I was back at home after my shift, dressing in a leaf-camo jumpsuit in preparation for my trip outside, when my home's exterior buzzer sounded. I mentally accessed my home's front cameras and saw Pothole Charlie at my door.

That was ... disquieting. I was alone at home. He was alone. I suspected he harbored a grudge, even lethal intent, against me from the old days.

But the humans have a saying, "Never let them see you sweat." Dollgangers don't sweat, but we understand the concept. I bypassed my stairs, slid down the brassy fire pole that ran from roof to ground floor in my staircase atrium, and opened the front door.

He gave me a look that betrayed nothing of what he might be thinking. "Card game business." So I led him to my study.

He plopped down at my table to wait while I did a routine fast-check on the room's security. Then I sat down one chair away from him. "All secure."

"I had an idea."

"Do tell."

"The Zhou City nuclear power plant."

I thought about that. Built on very stable bedrock by the first wave of developers who'd followed the terraformers to Chiron, the complex was outside but close to Zhou City. It was older technology but very safe and reliable, requiring little oversight or maintenance. "Not viable."

His eyebrows rose. "Why not?"

"Because Akima Spaceport and General Milfield Base have their own mini-nukes. If we take out the city plant, sure, the city goes dark, but neither of our *targets* does."

He put on a disdainful expression. "I wasn't talking about taking it out, *Bowen*. I was wondering about setting up a 'ganger post there, a hideout. It's mostly automated, the security on it is minimal, and there are below-ground chambers used in the early days for its personnel needs that are empty now. Some of them are walled off."

"*Oh*." Now I felt stupid. I readjusted my thinking. "And it's close to the spaceport."

"My thought exactly."

"I'm not sure we need it for Operation Coffee and Cream, and just setting it up as a station would draw resources we probably don't have. But for the future, it's a great idea. Let's code-name it the Juice Factory." We were heavily invested in code-names, the better to avoid detection by the humans or even our own Directors if a transmission or conversation were intercepted. And Zhou City had several juice factories, manufacturers of fruit juices and other human beverages, which would contribute to misinterpretation. I actually had a lot of affection for human fruit juices. "We can bounce the idea off the others at the next card game."

"Good." He nodded. His conversation done, he stood.

Once I'd shown him out, I returned to my study and minutely scrutinized the chair where he'd sat, the underside of the table there, every surface he'd touched all the way back to the exterior of my front door. But there was no sign of tampering, listening devices, corrosive fluids, or explosive charges.

Had he just visited to bounce an idea off me? It seemed inconceivable.

∗   ∗   ∗

After darkness had fallen, I returned to the drone encampment, which BeeBee had nicknamed Coffee Summit.

The little clearing where we'd stashed the drones was well-lit by a nearly full moon. The camouflage netting was unchanged, draped across the aircraft, stirring a little in a night breeze. Routinely cautious, I lifted one fold of the netting and moved beneath the broad canopy of concealment.

I modulated my eyesight from light-amplification to infrared and could barely detect that one of the drones had its power up—live but on power-saving standby. I moved that way and saw that it was the one I'd piloted. The hatch atop the pod was open. And as I took another step, Parfait popped partway up out of it. She gave me a smile.

She looked different in infrared vision—she was all shades of green rather than her lunar white. But she was different in another way. She did not wear the shawl I'd seen her in at every meeting we'd had since she joined the Revolution. Her hair, straight and snow-white, hung to just under her chin.

She waved me over. "Come on in."

When I slid into the pod, I discovered that she'd been at work. She had cut some of the finer netting from overhead, I assumed from a place where its loss would not be relevant, to fashion herself a hammock. She'd also strung netting at the front of the pod to create a sort of pilot's seat, far more secure and comfortable than the improvised rope harness I'd had the previous night.

She gave me a look that included just a touch of insecurity, of worry. "Do you like it?"

I nodded. "Sensible, practical, comfortable."

"Hmm." Her tone suggested that this was not quite the answer she was hoping for. But she changed the subject. "I have an inventory." She extended her open hand toward me.

I touched it, fingertips to fingertips. Our data wires emerged from beneath our fingernails and connected. Direct uplink was far faster and more secure than any sort of broadcast.

Immediately I received her inventory of the drones. We had three bombers, two with bombs gone—bombs left behind at the Kresh Assemblies factory. There were three drones bearing one rack each of Bale missiles, four missiles per rack. We had two drones equipped with upgraded sensor packages. Her inventory included the fuel status of each HummingHawk, and there were damage and power throughput efficiency reports on each machine. The most extensive damage report dealt with harm sustained by the landing skids and pod underside of BeeBee's drone, all repairable.

"Good work. Thanks." I withdrew my hand. I shucked my backpack. "I brought you a charger. You can splice it into the lines supplying power to any of the fan assemblies. When the drone is live, you can draw a trickle charge from it. I also brought some components so we can begin installing direct controls—make these things into aircraft we can actually pilot."

"Good." She didn't sound at all interest. "Bow?"

"Yes?"

Then she was kissing me.

It caught me by surprise. In the years prior to the start of the Revolution, she'd treated me with the same contempt that BeeBee and others had, calling me Big Plush and making it clear that I was unwelcome. That had continued until the day of our escape from Zhou City, the day we stole the Stork. After that, I hadn't spoken to her, not until BeeBee had brought her into Operation Coffee and Cream. But she'd backed my every decision as a member of that conspiracy, and now—

It doesn't take a Dollganger much time to get out of clothes. We wear simple garments and no undergarment. In moments we were naked in the hammock, trying to make each other happy. I switched back to light-amplification visual mode and could see, by the one little sliver of moonlight that made it through the pod hatch, that though Parfait chose most of the time to conceal her body, there was nothing at all wrong with it. She was slim and flawless, elegant of design, a beauty from head to toe.

When we were done, she nestled against me and powered down for a while. I stayed live and alert to protect us both, and I thought about what had just happened.

I didn't love Parfait and she didn't love me, so far as I knew. She had apparently needed me, needed somebody, not surprising in light of her weeks of isolation at Kresh Assemblies, and I'd been happy to share affection with her.

What amazed me, though, was that even after years being the most ill-used sort of toy there was, she could still find pleasure, find comfort in sex. I found it reassuring, a hopeful sign, that she could. So I held her, and she slept.

Later, when she awoke, we actually did do a little work. I installed a new control interface in my drone, bypassing the indirect computer controls. With that interface in place, we could then install a control stick, pedals, and other controls. A real pilot's seat would also follow. Parfait, quick and eager to learn, would take the remaining interfaces I'd brought and install them in most of the other drones. Soon they wouldn't be drones at all.

8: STAGE TWO

News intercepted from Zhou City made it clear that the government and press had gotten some details right, some wrong. Dollgangers were indeed blamed for the destruction of the Kresh Assemblies plant, but the event was not described as a tactical strike on a drone assembly plant. It was portrayed as a terroristic act of murder against a civilian business.

In the Nest, 'gangers shrugged and assumed that no 'ganger had actually been involved, that it had been an accident, that the humans had decided to blame us so they could whip up their troops into a more murderous state of mind.

Those of us who knew the truth shrugged and got back to work.

Neither BeeBee nor I had much to do with Stage Two of Operation Coffee and Cream. BeeBee spent much of her time recruiting; we needed far more than our original roster of seven to accomplish Stages Two and Three.

Me, I was acting as chief cook and bottle washer for the Dollganger Air Force. This meant that I installed and field-tested controls, modified the computer software that made the drone control systems work more like human aircraft controls, flew the craft to hone my skills, and trained others as pilots.

Pothole Charlie and Tink didn't need instruction. Like me, they just took the craft airborne and learned how the HummingHawks performed. Nor could they have spent much time receiving training anyway—as with BeeBee, the demands on their time, especially Pothole Charlie because of his Director duties, kept them in the Nest most hours. Trouble was, the fact that both of them were experienced pilots was irrelevant. Neither was going to be on the airborne assault phase of Stage Three.

Kieran, too big to fly any of our aircraft, was still invaluable. Quiet as a ghost when he wanted to be, faster and stronger than just about any 'ganger, he found a source within half a night's trot of the Nest of aviation fuel, at a human family's small crop-dusting concern. He stole a liter or two of the fuel per night and transported it back to Coffee Summit, building up our fuel supply—we were using less in our training than he was acquiring. The loss to the crop-duster business was so slight, by human standards, that the owners never noticed.

Parfait and I continued our—what was it? An affair or a relationship? Years before, decades really, I'd asked Doc Chiang what the difference was between those two forms of human interaction. He mulled over the question for a while and finally told me, "Based on my personal experience, you enter a relationship not knowing how long or how far it will develop. It is exploratory. It is a possible path to a mutual future. You enter an affair with an expectation that it will be of limited duration."

Which, now, still left me uncertain about what we were doing other than sleeping with one another. Nor did Parfait seem to be in any hurry to let me know her thoughts on the matter.

The conspiracy did add recruits. We picked up Kazzy, who was styled on 21st-century cinematic vampires and had the extended upper canine teeth to show for it; a lot of 'gangers thought he was hot, and he was. Meriah joined us, with her green hair and fair complexion; usually a normal-looking woman, she could strap herself into a powered fish-tail and become a mermaid, and was well-adapted to water activities in either mode. Jitter, ever-moving, rich brown in color and covered with geometric tattoos, had been the mate of Richter before Richter was killed during the Escape; Jitter was welcome for his alertness. We added Creepy-Crawly, a real exotic: female, tall, blue-skinned, six-armed, her features and her usual clothing styled after the goddesses of ancient India, she climbed as well without multi-mode gear as I did with it, and was known for her sniper skills. And there were others being primed to join our ranks.

But we didn't get everyone we wanted, and one day, as BeeBee and I were sneaking our way back from Coffee Summit to the Gopher Hole, she brought up the subject. "It's not going as well as I'd hoped. Some of the ones I was counting on won't join us. They hear the phrases 'something very important' and 'can't tell anyone' and 'danger' and 'a serious time commitment', and they say, 'Don't tell me any more. I can't help you'."

I frowned. "Like who?"

"Silverback. And Shinbone Ted."

That *was* bad news. Silverback was an exotic, made in the form of a gorilla, a species of primate that thrives on Earth but isn't found on Chiron. He had upper-body strength like no other 'ganger and was quiet, methodical, and brave. Shinbone Ted had worked with BeeBee in the Chiron military as an intrusion specialist. His skills would have been really useful to us.

I sighed. "I'm sure you'll find others just as valuable."

She offered me a sour little smile. "That's why I'm talking to you now. I want to bring in Lina and Wolfe."

"Lina has an eight-week-old baby. And we don't know Wolfe's loyalties."

"Reverse that analysis. Wolfe has an eight-week-old baby and we *do* know Lina's loyalties."

"Fair enough. But we still don't know Wolfe's."

"Lina trusts him. Trusts him enough to make him her mate. To raise a child with him. Dollgangers choose better than humans when babies are at stake. I trust Lina's judgment. I'll recruit her first, and she can decide whether and how to approach Wolfe. We *know* he's a good man. You're a good man, and she chose him over you."

That stopped me where I was.

BeeBee took another three quiet steps before she realized I was no longer beside her. She stopped, too, and turned to look at me. In her light-amplification visual mode, my frozen expression must have been plain to her. "Bow, that was a joke."

"I'm guessing you develop your comic timing planting demolitions charges for the military."

She moved up to stand before me and pulled off her sun shades so I could see her face, her eyes. "I guess I crossed a line. I didn't realize it. I'm sorry."

"Forget it." I brushed past her and continued on toward the Gopher Hole. "Sure, recruit her."

BeeBee hurried to catch up to stay beside me. "I need to cross another line."

"Sure, why the hell not?"

"I need to talk to you about Parfait. And about *you* and Parfait."

I didn't look at her. "Have you been making recordings of us? Have they been everything you hoped for? You going to critique my technique?" I went on before she could continue. "I'm not going to hurt her, BeeBee. I'm not the fire-and-forget kind of man."

"I know you're not. And that you won't hurt her. But, Bow, she's already hurt. She's *damaged*. And we all understand why. But it means she likes to hurt and kill humans. I'd thought, I'd hoped, that she'd purged it from her systems during the Escape. But now I'm not sure. I keep thinking that maybe she didn't send a fire alarm to Kresh Assemblies that night, that maybe she somehow sent a trigger command to a detonation charge."

"Uh." That thought had crossed my mind during our return from Kresh Assemblies, but only fleetingly. Parfait had shown no sign that she was doing anything but following orders, following the plan. She'd shown no excess of emotion, nothing like witnesses had seen on her during the Escape.

BeeBee kept going. "I trust her to protect the Nest and its secrets with her life ... but that doesn't mean that, in the heat of battle, she won't deviate from the plan and kill a human target, maybe compromising the operation. Fouling up its timing."

I looked BeeBee's way again. "We can't ease her out of the operation. We need all the help we can get. And you think she's damaged now? Let's suggest we don't trust her."

"I agree."

"And she's a promising pilot. So ..." Blast it, I couldn't just dismiss BeeBee's thoughts. She'd said once before that she was smarter than I was, and while I'd never admit it to her, she was right. And not taking every opportunity to be cautious would result in a dead Dollganger ... and probably a dead Nest. "For Stage Three, let's put her in one of the sensor HummingHawks. No missiles, no guns, no bomb. The only thing she can do as an eye in the sky is keep us alive."

BeeBee nodded. "I like that. When you tell her, don't let her change your mind."

"I won't."

"She's good at changing minds."

"I *won't*."

*   *   *

Tink initiated Stage Two. First, another member of our conspiracy had to "die," and Jitter volunteered. A Scrap-Walk by Jitter would not be questioned by the Nest population, which knew how he'd mourned his mate in the months since Richter had died.

Trouble was, the morning Jitter departed, with ersatz skin-flaps hanging open and wires protruding for the cameras to see, word came that Shinbone Ted, too, had taken the final walk. Shinbone Ted left behind a recording in which, stone-faced, he merely said, "We did the right thing by escaping, but I've gone from a life of decades of deadly hide-and-seek for the humans to one of kill-or-be-killed for the Nest. And I see no sign of it ever ending. I can't live with that any more. Goodbye."

Two Scrap-Walks in one week—in one day. Gloom settled over the Nest, and the Directors recommended everyone take a little time for psychological self-monitoring. BeeBee and Pothole Charlie confirmed that the Directors were wondering whether some sort of communicable malcode, perhaps engineered by the humans, were making its way through the population.

But privately, we three looked at each other and wondered if Shinbone Ted had really gone off to die. But if not, what would he be up to?

Regardless, our plan went on.

Tink, Pothole Charlie, Kazzy, Parfait, Jitter, and Malibu left in BeeBee's HummingHawk at dusk one night to perform the start of Stage Two. They returned shortly before dawn—Tink, Pothole Charlie, Malibu, and Kazzy, anyway.

According to their debriefing, the intrusion into the Shavery Corporation facility began flawlessly. The six of them landed on a rooftop near Shavery, concealing their aircraft under a satellite transponder antenna and camo netting. They made their way to Shavery at ground level. Malibu cut through an exterior loading-bay door and they raced in. They could afford to be a lot more sloppy than we had been at Kresh Assemblies because they needed only minutes to accomplish things.

They blanked a couple of camera pods, then bypassed the security on a mega. Pothole Charlie drove it, loading a not-quite-fully-assembled computer system compatible with Stork operations onto a programmable forklift. Then they discovered that reprogramming a Shavery vehicle required access codes, doubtless a change brought on in response to what had happened at Kresh Assemblies. Parfait and Tink raced off to the corporate offices on a commando raid to acquire those codes.

That's when things developed the potential to go wrong.

Tink told us, "It was, um, in the office of the administrator for shipping. On top of his desk there was a huge paper note pad, half the size of the desk surface. It didn't have any access codes written on it, so I, um, was staring at it and cycling through my visual modes to see if that would bring up any impressions of things that had been written on pages that were now torn away. At the same time, Parfait was bypassing security and opening desk drawers to investigate their contents. While I was looking at some alphanumeric sequences I thought might have been what we needed, I heard a big bottom drawer roll open. And I heard Parfait gasp."

Tink had looked down and seen the drawer's contents: a complete 'ganger-banger unit.

A full-sized unit can be pretty compact, and this one was small enough to fit in a drawer. It consisted of a human cybernetics headset, looking like a shiny white skullcap with wires trailing off it to the sending unit.

The sending unit was an electronic device about the size of a shoe box. There was also a Dollganger-compatible charging station and two 'ganger-sized remotes, one male and one female.

Yes, this administrator had been the sort to put on the helmet, fire up one of the little remotes, and drive it to the presence of Dollgangers for some fun. That fun might have been nothing more than a game of roulette in the Warrens or a wrestling match out behind the assembly line building. But it might have been sex, even painful, humbling sex, with a 'ganger. The presence of male and female remotes, both very attractive and provocatively dressed, as Tink described them, made it very likely that they were regularly used for sex of some kind. Parfait had been visited by remotes like these for many, many years.

Tink continued, "So, um, I asked, 'Are you all right?' And Parfait looked up at me, perfectly calm, and said, 'I am fine. Maybe we can use this. I will send Pothole Charlie up with the mega and you can take it back.'"

That's what they did. Tink got the forklift subverted and reprogrammed. Pothole Charlie drove the mega and fetched the 'ganger-banger unit.

They opened the factory's exterior door. Tink, Pothole Charlie, Kazzy, and Malibu hopped on the forklift and initiated its program, sending it out into the Shavery parking areas. When it had gone just far enough to be out of sight of the security cameras, they hopped off again with their stolen goods, leaving the Stork brain behind. Tink carried the helmet and the recharger; Malibu carried the two remotes over his shoulders; Pothole Charlie and Kazzy between them carried the transmitter.

Chiron military arrived within a few more seconds, some of the personnel chasing after the forklift. The forklift, its conflict-avoidance programming cranked to maximum, avoided them with credible nimbleness and sped away. It hopped up on sidewalks and darted through parking areas where the larger human transports couldn't go.

It got a couple of blocks away before it was hemmed in and trapped by the military. Then, its primitive brain correctly calculating that avoidance was no longer possible, it went dead.

The diversion gave the four 'gangers carrying the stolen goods the opportunity to get back to their aircraft. At the same time, Parfait and Jitter were inside one of the Shavery walls, sealing all its cracks with resin so no insect drones could accidentally find them.

Parfait would train Jitter in the art of staying out of sight in a human-occupied facility. Then she'd transfer back to Coffee Summit. Jitter would stay there, joined for some overnight operations by other 'gangers, gaining access to and modifying the Shavery yacht. Eventually Tink, Pothole Charlie, and Malibu would return to join him, but only when it was time for them to leave Chiron.

So we added the 'ganger-banger remote system to Operation Coffee and Cream's growing stock of resources. We didn't have a use in Stage Three for an apparatus like this, but we needed every resource we could acquire. We'd find a purpose for that nasty set at some point in the future.

Over the next few days, Jitter would sneak up to the Shavery building roof. Plugged into building electricity to give him enough power to do this without blacking out, using the rooftop antenna as an extension of his own antenna, he'd broadcast short text updates as microburst transmissions strong enough for us to receive on Coffee Summit.

SPEEDBOAT, for instance, meant "The yacht has been located."

PIGGYBANK: "Security on the yacht has been bypassed; we have regular ingress/egress."

SPACKLE: "Modifications are being made to the yacht and have not been detected."

WETBAR: "We have bypassed security on the yacht's micronuke. We can bring it online and maintain it at low output with little fear of detection."

All the while, we—usually Malibu—made provisioning flights to Shavery, taking things the space expedition would need on its long trip: replacement components for 'ganger bodies, recordings showing the grim life most Dollgangers endured in human hands, access cards stolen at Kresh by Parfait to human-held offworld accounts, a "humanizing" documentary by Malibu showing the 'gangers in as parental and non-martial a light as was possible.

Then:

LICENSE: "All steps at Shavery have been successfully accomplished. Stage Two is complete."

9: COFFEE AND CREAM

Well before dawn on the day of Stage Three, Tink, Pothole Charlie, and Malibu flew off in my aircraft, leaving me fretful and irritated.

I now considered that HummingHawk mine and I was proud of it, protective of it. It now sported a single-pilot cockpit fabricated by BeeBee and by Nest craftsmen who'd had no idea they were helping BeeBee perform actions that might be considered treason. The cockpit featured a sturdy seat perfectly fitted to my butt and back, a control yoke, foot pedals, and a bank of monitors before me to serve as backup to the direct visual feed I'd be receiving.

The former bomb bay behind the pilot's console was no longer home to Parfait's hammock. The space was occupied by machinery. The large belly hatch that had been intended to allow a bomb to drop had been modified, attached to a winch mounted above the rear hinge. Mounted on the hatch itself were components from two CA-CI4 assault rifles we'd seized from the humans during the Escape. With the touch of a button or a mental command, I could cause the hatch to lower a few centimeters, exposing the rifle barrels to open air. Drums would feed 120 rounds into each rifle. Baffles would cause expended brass-plass to drop out the open gap instead of rattling around in my pod.

I'd set up BeeBee's HummingHawk just like mine. But hers was still here on Coffee Summit, while mine was off in the hands of someone else, vulnerable to drone attacks, to laser fire from the distant military base, to air currents that could cause a less-experienced pilot to crash—

Yes, it was just those unhelpful, anxiety-amping thoughts that played through my head as I stood atop our muster point on Coffee Summit and waited for things to get under way.

Lina seemed to materialize out of the pre-dawn darkness beside me. She wore a Dollganger-standard leaf-pattern jumpsuit and her hair was in a braid down her back. Some part of my mind noted that we, the Revolution, really needed a flag, a unit patch, something ... Humans had them. "Lina."

"Do you have a minute?"

I snorted. I couldn't help it. "You ask me that during the most unproductive, useless couple of hours of my life. Yes. Yes, I have a minute."

"Are you mad at me?"

"No." But I realized I'd answered that too quickly.

She seemed to realize it, too. She nodded, not quite in agreement with my statement. "Look, I know what you were feeling in the months after the Escape. And I can guess what you've been feeling since I chose Wolfe."

I was nearly overwhelmed by a feeling of weariness. I checked my charge. Nearly full; the weariness was purely emotional. "It's all right, Lina. I know I'm still Big Plush to most everyone. I've just got a thick, gooey layer of redemption spread all over me. But everyone knows what's under it."

"Just shut up for a minute." There was real anger in her voice, anger I'd never heard from her before.

I gave her a closer look. Okay, I was in for a "we might all be dead by midmorning, let's clear the air" speech. I suppressed a sigh. "Okay."

"Bow, I need Wolfe. He's my future. Part of my future. Father of my child—father of more children, if things work out. To them, he'll be the father I wish I'd had. Brave but not fearless. Offering comfort and advice that come from empathy and experience, not an instruction set."

"I understand." I sort of did, but most of all, I wanted her to stop explaining. Just to stop explaining and go away.

"You don't. Wolfe is going to be that for Thonny. I wish *you* ..." Her voice broke for a second. "I wish you could be that for *me*."

I think I rebooted.

I remember my vision cycled a couple of times so rapidly that I couldn't interpret what I was seeing, and there was a brief discontinuity in my recording memory. Then everything stabilized. Lina was still standing in front of me, looking at me. A few body-lengths away, the conversations of the other members of Stage Three continued, hushed, unchanged. Wolfe was not among them; he was already on station near one of our targets.

I found my voice. My vocabulary wasn't in it, though. "I. Uh. I."

"I don't know if you planned to live through today. How hard you intended to fight. Because you're always so sad. But I want you to live and come back. I want you in my life. Just maybe not... the way you wanted. Do you understand?" Tears rolled down her cheeks now, but she seemed unaware of them.

Words finally came trickling back into my brain. Seven of them. Six, if you discount duplicates. They emerged slowly, heavily. "I'll fight. I'll come back. We'll talk."

She embraced me for a long, painfully lust-free moment. Then she turned away and walked back to her aircraft.

I'm not sure, maybe I rebooted again. The next I knew, someone was shouting, "Here she comes." I barely noticed my own HummingHawk settling down at its designated landing spot.

The hatch opened. Parfait emerged, then Jitter.

Mechanically, I picked up my parachute off the flat stone where I'd placed it. I buckled it on. It was a slim chest rig, making my torso seem oversized but not interfering with my movements or causing us to have to redesign our pilot's seats.

I turned toward my HummingHawk, but there was BeeBee, suddenly in my way, talking. "There's been a change."

Despite my state of distraction, I managed to answer. "What change?"

"I'm in one of the sensor HummingHawks now."

I blinked. "You're not my wingman anymore?" BeeBee was to have had the other assault-rifle craft. "You're putting Parfait on my wing?"

"No, Parfait's still in the other eye-in-the-sky. I'm taking Lina's craft and putting her on your wing."

"But ... why?"

"I need to be on communications and coordinations for this mission, Bow. I'm better at it than Lina, and she's as good as I am at combat. We learned that during the Escape."

I wasn't certain that what she was saying was precisely true. But ... BeeBee and I were still the partners in charge. If we didn't agree, nothing would happen. I nodded. "All right."

"I'll tell Lina. Smoke 'em, Bow." She turned and headed off toward Lina's HummingHawk.

I made my way to my aircraft, where Parfait stood, smiling. It still surprised me that she hadn't lost her smile when I'd told her, a couple of days earlier, that she was going to be in one of the eye-in-the-sky HummingHawks instead of a missile craft. She'd only said, "If it improves our odds of success, Bow, put me on the Coffee Summit radio. I do not mind."

Now she just wrapped her arms around me, kissed me— awkwardly, since our mutual chest chutes didn't permit a close embrace—and said, "Smoke 'em, Jack One."

I pretended not to hate that nickname, just smiled at her. "You set 'em up for me and I will." Then I clambered up atop my HummingHawk's belly pod and slid down into the cockpit.

As I stood up on a mounting bracket to reach for the overhead hatch, Parfait appeared there, gave me a final smile, and swung the hatch down into place, leaving me in the darkened HummingHawk interior. I dogged the hatch closed and heard Parfait slide off the top.

Then it was time for business. I strapped in and took a grip on my control yoke. My data wires extended from my fingertips and plugged into corresponding holes on the yoke. Suddenly I could see through all the HummingHawk's cameras, had visual and data access to all diagnostics and other sensor readouts. In an instant I went from being a 225mm tall man to being several meters long, armored, capable of flying, capable of long-range destruction. Mercifully, Lina and her announcement moved themselves to a corner of my mind and waited there, making no effort to get my attention. I began my pre-flight checklist.

I heard other pilots report readiness. They used their radios, at low broadcast strength, for this. Meriah was first: "Bale One, standing by." Our green-haired mermaid had been assigned one of the Bale missile HummingHawks.

"Bale Two, standing by." That was Jitter.

My systems were all in the green. There was the tiniest bit of lag in the controls; they simulated direct mechanical hookups, but they were still computer-coordinated. Little things, like minor memory management errors or diagnostics reports, could cause this. The lag was so slight that a human might not have noticed—milliseconds.

"Gunner Two, standing by." Lina. Lina, who had just made the frank and, for a Dollganger, perhaps unprecedented admission that she wanted, needed, a father—

Stop it. I forced myself back to the matter at hand. Fuel topped off. Ammunition drums full. Rear winch reported as functional.

"Bale Three, ready." Kazzy's deep, rich, artificially-accented voice—he'd once told me that the accent suggested Eastern Europe on Earth, though he spoke no Eastern European languages. He wouldn't be with the main mission today. He had his own objective, far more important than ours. He just couldn't achieve it without us.

I was finally ready. "Gunner One, ready." I would also respond to Leader, but wouldn't declare myself that way. If the humans could intercept our radio transmissions during mission execution and decrypt them on the fly, I didn't want them to identify the mission leader.

And then BeeBee's voice came across the radio: "Eyeball One ready."

A moment later, "Eyeball Two, standing by." That was Parfait, and we were complete.

That was only seven of our eight HummingHawks, of course. The eight was still a drone, unpiloted. And it still carried its original bomb payload in its belly pod, hence its designation, Belly One. Lina was to have controlled Belly One from her Eyeball. Now that duty would fall to BeeBee.

There were others supporting our mission on the ground. Kieran was already outside the spaceport, carrying a dual-phase laser capable of weapons-level damage or laser painting. Creepy-Crawly and Wolfe waited outside General Milfield Base, the military compound, with an identical laser unit. BlueTop waited near Coffee Summit with little Thonny—if it turned out that we couldn't return to the Nest, Wolfe and Lina would have their baby with them when they fled with the other survivors. And there were now others.

Parfait's acknowledgment was the last detail I needed. I took a breath. "Coffee and Cream, launch."

In my HummingHawk camera vision, piped directly into my optical receptors, I saw the HummingHawks rise one by one into the air. Off to the east, the sun was now cresting the horizon, flooding the forests around Zhou City with golden-red light, and that, too, was one little detail that might help us. Might incrementally budge our chances of success upward a percentage point or two.

I led the HummingHawks toward Akima Spaceport.

En route, Kazzy in Bale Three split off from us, heading toward the spot Creepy-Crawly and Wolfe had staked out. His farewell was a simple "Team Coffee away." He was the only one of the HummingHawk pilots performing a Coffee function. The rest of us were Team Cream.

BeeBee transmitted, text rather than voice, coded specifically to me. *Pothole Charlie reports micronuke ready for full output.*

I responded, *Roger that.*

So the rest of the Coffee end of the operation was on schedule, a go. Great news. But mention of Pothole Charlie notched up my tension a little.

During all our planning and execution, he hadn't made an attempt on my life. He just hadn't. It was inconceivable to me, after decades of his hatred of me that he had actually chosen to forgive and forget. A part of my mind locked onto that subject—he couldn't have sabotaged my HummingHawk; I'd given it several thorough checks since the last time he was even near the aircraft. Or did he have a confederate within our conspiracy? He and BeeBee were old friends. Could she have—

I shoved that thought away. I wanted to trust BeeBee.

Besides, Pothole Charlie could kill me another way. Given his position on the Directors, his connections with many of the Nest leaders, he could simply have left behind a timed message, instructing a confederate there to terminate me. Our mission wouldn't be compromised; I'd simply be killed when I returned to the Nest.

I nodded, satisfied. If I survived this mission, that's how I was going to die.

Sorry, Lina. I can't be your father. I'm going to be assassinated in the Nest, or maybe executed as a traitor. I didn't transmit that. I just thought it.

But as gloomy as that thought was, it allowed me to return to the matter at hand.

10: AIMING SKYWARD

We passed the nuclear power plant, a complex of ancient reinforced concrete domes. Ahead of us, just a few kilometers away, lay Akima Spaceport. Even at this distance, I could see that there was a cargo transport, one of the big rocket-shaped rigs, set up on a vertical-launch pad, aiming skyward, a booster vehicle shaped like two outrigger rockets coupled to it. Painted white, they gleamed orange-yellow in the harsh morning light.

We'd accomplished the entire flight at a couple of meters above the ground, observing terrain-following protocol; rising above the surrounding terrain would have potentially put us on military radar.

We reduced speed and I got on the HummingHawk's radio. "Gunner One to Trigger. Report status."

Kieran's voice came back: "Trigger is here, reporting ready. No wave-off." He had seen nothing to cause us to abort the mission.

I nodded, pleased. "Light it up, Trigger."

Understand, Akima Spaceport was surrounded by a fence. Kilometers in circumference, it stood about six meters high and was mostly made up of interwoven metal cables in a chicken-wire pattern too fine for a 'ganger to squeeze through. The cable was embedded in concrete at ground level. Metal poles every twenty meters kept the fence upright.

Every kilometer, a section of concrete wall interrupted the circuit—civilian lowest-bidder grade concrete, we'd been able to determine—housing a featureless exit door for the use of patrols.

The wall wasn't defensive. A wire cutter would get through the fence material. But not undetected—the fence was riddled with short-range motion detectors and other sensors. The fence itself constituted a sensor, with low-voltage current pumped through it and sophisticated analytical computers sniffing out irregularities in the current flow.

We could fly over it, of course. But what would happen then? The instant we rose above the fence top, we'd show up on radar from the spaceport tower and from General Milfield Base. After the Escape, the Chiron military had brought in weapons platforms to replace those we'd shot down ... and had installed a laser cannon bunker.

Chiron had never needed a laser cannon before our Revolution. Now it had one—only one, fortunately. So the instant we showed up on radar crossing over the fence, the bunker would go live, the laser cannon would pop up, armored except for the channel housing its barrel assembly, and fire. In two or three seconds it could annihilate our entire air force—less time than it would take us all to crest that fence and descend on the other side.

So, right now, Kieran waited at a position a few dozen meters from one of those exit doors, well away from the spaceport complex's main entrance. In fact, he stood just below the spot where our HummingHawks were now slowing to a standstill hover. He had with him his dual-phase laser, this one tripod-mounted, and a power pack for extended use.

In my aircraft's belly camera view, I saw Kieran sight in along his weapon, lock the tripod, squeeze the weapon's trigger ... and hold it. I switched to infrared view and my forward camera.

A spot on the concrete wall above the door began to glow, a far brighter green than the concrete around it. The glow began to radiate outward in all directions. I saw smoke rise from the center of the affected area. A bit of concrete there, smaller than a 'ganger's hand, turned black.

"This is Bale One. I'm getting an image." Bale missiles were heat-seekers. You couldn't even aim one at a target unless the target were as hot as, say, vehicle engines. Or as hot as a small spot on a wall being exposed to intense laser light.

I switched back to normal visual mode on my forward camera. "Fire when ready, Bale One."

"Firing."

I barely saw the Bale missile leap from the missile rack on Bale One's underbelly—missiles are fast. There was the hint of a streak between the HummingHawk and the wall, then the target was engulfed in roiling black smoke and red-yellow flame. A split-second later the sharp *bang* of the explosion reached us, then I felt a bit of turbulence as the shockwave of expanding air hit us.

We waited a few seconds, each of them a year long. Then the fire and smoke cleared enough to reveal a gap like a scooped neckline dominating the wall above the door. It was large enough for HummingHawks to fly through.

I radioed, "Move through by pairs." I accelerated forward, Lina behind me.

I'm told that the spaceport was the sort someone would find on any backwater world—a few square kilometers of flat land sheeted in graytop arrayed in strips, circles, and roads, a monitoring tower, hangar buildings, a huge boxy warehouse-and-customs station, vast stretches of parking for cargo haulers, a port building for arriving and departing travelers. Since the Revolution had begun, the humans had added a couple of hardened bunkers, one for a small military detail, one for the grounded *Coracle*-class exploration spacecraft only Dollgangers could crew.

I headed toward the military bunker; Lina drew up to my port side. Emerging through the hole in the wall, Meriah and Jitter, Bale One and Bale Two, headed for the *Coracle* bunker. Eyeball One, BeeBee, headed toward the transport craft waiting on the launch pad; Parfait, in Eyeball Two, zoomed toward the tower. Belly One, our drone, stayed only three meters above the deck and slowly moved toward a cluster of hangars.

A noise filled the air, an eerie wail that echoed off every vertical surface, off distant buildings and hills. This was an air-raid alarm, its tone and purpose unchanged from sirens used in the early 20th century. Weirdly, I'd always loved that noise, and now felt comforted by it.

Yes, the humans knew we were here.

A small, open-cockpit ground hauler, crossing my flight path ahead of me, towed a chain of three small cargo trailers, headed toward the transport on the pad. I buzzed the pilot, flashing a mere meter over his head, and saw him bail out with the vehicle still moving. He hit the graytop surface and skidded to a stop. This wasn't meanness on my part, nor for my own amusement; our objective was to create chaos.

Up ahead lay the military bunker, a low gray thing with a roof like a squat pyramid—sloped armor to give the bunker a chance of deflecting an indirect hit from an artillery piece. Just now, at the bunker's base, a front door, human-sized, was swinging open to allow a pair of armored infantrymen to exit. The broader door to its right was rising, the gap at its bottom now revealing the tracks of a small armored vehicle.

There it was—we faced living targets who intended to kill us, targets we had to kill.

Lina, to my left, would by default go after the infantrymen; my default target was the tracked vehicle. I thought for a couple of milliseconds about swapping targets with her so she wouldn't have to watch humans die under her guns.

No, she was already a soldier. She had already killed. To make the target swap would suggest lack of faith in her.

I switched to text mode—faster to transmit, faster to interpret. *Gunner One to Bale One. I need a missile here now.*

Roger. Coming. Somewhere off in the corner of my visual feeds, I thought I detected one of the missile rack HummingHawks break away from the other and head my way.

The door into the armored-vehicle bay was now halfway up. I could see movement within the bay, personnel running to and leaping onto the vehicle. Without a good target, I fired a couple of short burst just under the bottom of the rising door. I doubted I'd hit anything, but those metal-jacketed rounds, hitting hardened concrete walls and vehicle armor, would ricochet like crazy, perhaps forcing the humans under cover.

I heard, rising above the air-raid siren, more assault-rifle chatter—inbound from ahead, outbound from my left. Lina maintained discipline, firing short bursts. I saw both infantrymen fall—no, only one was hit, the other went to ground on his own, lining up a shot with his own assault rifle. Then Lina's last burst took him just under the rim of his helmet, sending a spray of red mist out the back of his head, and he went flat.

Eyeball One to Gunner One. I'm getting an image. We have one weapons platform, I say again, one weapons platform inbound.

I glanced toward the waiting spacecraft on the pad. BeeBee's HummingHawk hovered two meters in front of it, rising vertically toward its cockpit. Her tactic was to use the cargo craft as cover—alongside it, she wouldn't show up as distinct from it on most radar.

I was framing a reply when the second part of her text appeared: *Coming from due north. ETA thirty-five seconds.*

Roger that, Eyeball One. Team Cream, go evasive.

I couldn't go evasive. I had a job: Keep that ground vehicle pinned in place. The door into its bay was all the way up now, revealing the vehicle—a two-man antipersonnel mini-tank, tracked but lightly armored, a steel-beam battering rather than a cannon barrel protruding from its front armor, racks of mini-missiles all over its top surface. Considering it was stationed here instead of in Zhou City, those missiles were probably not tear gas or wall-openers. I'd have guessed some were heat-seekers, some exotics optimized for use against Dollgangers.

An infantryman appeared underneath the mini-tank, between its treads, readying a submachine gun. I snap-fired toward him, missing him with my three-round—six rounds counting both barrels—burst, which sent up ricochet sparks from the treads and concrete flooring. He scuttled backward and disappeared from sight.

I saw a small explosion in the distance, from the direction of the *Coracle* bunker. In my visual feed, it looked like Jitter had lined up and taken his first shot against the side of the bunker. Kieran had to have lit it up for him, preparation that would only be needed for Jitter's first shot. Before the smoke had time to clear, Jitter banked away and went evasive, then began circling for another approach run against the bunker.

I nodded. Getting through the bunker wall would have been faster and more efficient had he unloaded his full rack of missiles in quick succession against that surface. But efficiency was not our goal. Getting through that bunker wall was not our objective.

Bale One to Gunner One. I'm lining up for my shot.

I could see Meriah's HummingHawk, thirty meters behind mine and closing. The mini-tank, my aircraft, and Meriah's aircraft made a nearly perfect straight line, with Bale One flying a couple of meters higher than I, close enough in altitude that I was an even better target for her missiles.

I didn't have to ask if she had enough of a heat trace coming off the mini-tank. If she had a shot, it meant she had a heat trace. The vehicle's engines had to be live.

Bale One, roger. Gunner Two, go to port. Lina was still close on my port quarter. I wanted to go that way, so she had to move. She did, veering away sharply. *Bale One, fire in one second.*

Roger that, Gunner One.

I hauled my yoke left and mashed the toe end of my right-side foot pedal, momentarily overdriving the starboard-side ducted fans. My HummingHawk lurched to port, losing a little altitude, roaring sideways. Our improvised HummingHawk controls were more primitive than those of a human helicopter, but we didn't need as much sophistication when throwing around toy-scale weights.

A missile streak flashed by my starboard side.

There was no big *boom* from inside the bay, just a muffled explosion. Then, a moment later: *Bale One here. Missile penetrated and detonated inside the target. Target disabled.*

I allowed myself a little smile of relief. Bale missiles were chancy against armor, even light vehicular armor. *Good job, Bale One. Get to cover but support me against the weapons platform.*

Understood.

I ended my sideslip and headed for the military bunker again, for its featureless south side this time. Reaching that bleak gray wall, I slowed to a hover, then rose along its wall—then rose and advanced along its angled roof, keeping close to the building, using it for cover.

In the distance ahead of me, just on the other side of the north spaceport fence, flew the inbound weapons platform.

11: HAWK FIGHT

Weapons platforms are helicopters, but not optimized for speed. This one, like most I'd seen, consisted of a pair of rotors above a horizontal disk of a fuselage loaded with weapons, in this case machine gun emplacements and missile pods. It had three crew stations, a cockpit in front and two gunnery stations back and to the sides, one starboard and one port. The crew of two in each station was visible behind wide, protruding plass bubbles. I had expected this vehicle to be much higher in the air, but it came over the fence at only ten meters above ground—and then dropped almost to the deck. Behind it, trailing at a distance of a hundred meters or so, came a pair of drones, HummingHawks like ours.

There were only three things in the Zhou City area that could trivially interfere with *Granny Knot*'s launch, and we knew where two of them were: this weapons platform and the laser cannon at the military base. But we didn't know where the third possible hazard, the other weapons platform, was. We had to wait here, continue fighting, and flush it out.

Taking a shot. The pilot transmitting failed to use his or her call sign—too inexperienced and distracted, I guessed. But the ID code on the text indicated that it was Bale One.

I saw Meriah hovering behind the hauler and its cargo trailers, which was still rolling, though slowing. Bale One popped up above the trailer she was using for cover and launched a missile.

It streaked—straight toward one of the weapon platform's trailing drones. It detonated and the drone was gone.

What the crap? Bale One again.

Puzzled, I cycled through my visual options. In infrared, I saw the problem. There was the weapons platform, its heated engines making it glow a bright green. Behind it a hundred meters, its surviving drone glowed even more brightly.

I cursed. The humans must have realized we'd stolen Bales from Kresh Assemblies. They'd rigged drones to give off heat in excess of that produced by vehicle engines. The drones would draw the Bales every time.

The weapons platform angled toward Meriah's position.

I banked away from the military bunker on an intercept course. Straight-line, I could get to the weapons platform before it had a good line of sight on Meriah, but I didn't go straight-line; that would have made me an easy target for the vehicle's starboard-side gunners. I flew evasive, which would slow me enough that the weapons platform would be past before I could get to it. Lina stayed behind me, also evasive.

Gunner One to Gunner Two, swing out to port. Incoming fire missing me might hit you.

Roger. She did, slewing off another forty meters to my port side.

Now the starboard gunners on the weapons platform did spot me. The heavy machine guns on that side opened fire. Incoming rounds chewed up the spaceport graytop as they sought me out.

And Lina, too. *I'm hit.*

A chill went through me. *You or your HummingHawk?*

My weapons—disabled. Dammit dammit dammit.

Make your way out of here. Stand by to lift anyone who goes extravehicular.
It was a moment before her *Roger* appeared. She continued on her course, maintaining her evasive maneuvers. I couldn't tell whether she were heading very gradually toward our exit or disobeying orders so that she could stay with me.

We reached the platform's flight path only a second after it crossed before us—its surviving drone had not yet reached our position. I turned in the weapons platform's wake.

So did Lina. She ignored my orders to bug out. She rose to the platform's altitude. I stayed low, miserably aware that it wouldn't do to have the same burst of fire from the platform kill both of us.

But the vehicle couldn't fire at us at the moment. Weapons platforms have a 360 degree field of fire—almost. It was actually only about 350 degrees, with straight behind still being a vulnerable angle. Directly behind it was where we were, for the moment; but weapons platforms could swivel while maintaining an unaltered course and speed.

Lina lost ground relative to the helicopter, positioning herself directly in front of and about a meter higher than the trailing drone. Then she reduced speed still more.

The drone's port-side forward fan duct thumped into her personnel-and-weapons-pod's tail end.

HummingHawks were tough. The impact merely jostled both aircraft. Then Lina gained a little altitude, maybe another meter, let the enemy drone slide in underneath her ... and she reduced her lift drastically.

Her personnel pod dropped into the gap between the enemy drone's four fan assemblies. Overburdened, the drone dropped. Lina rode the drone down toward impact, almost certain injury, almost certain suicide—because I knew she'd self-terminate if captured.

And, gruesome as that truth was, it couldn't be my concern, not then. The weapons platform was slowing, beginning a spin to bring me and Lina into line of its port-side guns.

I nipped in under the platform's skids, the gap between them and the graytop below too narrow for human-sized aircraft. I cranked my fans up, a desperate and uncertain attempt to compensate for the downwash from the platform's rotors. The downwash did drive me downward, but I managed to stay centimeters above the graytop. Then, as I slid under the windbreak the helicopter's belly provided, and the artificial wind shear ceased, I rose almost out of control. I felt an impact as I thumped against what had to have been one of the helicopter's landing struts. I wobbled, sideslipped farther, managed to not quite slide out from under the protective cover of the vehicle's belly.

My top camera showed me the platform rotating counter-clockwise. I rotated too, clockwise, and sideslipped once more. I found myself exactly where I wanted and didn't want to be—a meter below the level of the 'copter's gun emplacements. The port-side guns passed by over my head, the forward-facing guns rotating toward me.

Compensating for once again being under the rotor wash, I rose, even though I knew this would put me right in front of those forward guns for as much as a second.

Stupid idea. But the weapons platform had to come down. *Had* to.

I rose straight across the forward-firing gun emplacement, rose to stare for just a moment at the surprised faces of the pilot and cockpit gunner as they realized they'd missed the window of firing opportunity I'd given them. The gunner fired. Streams of lead passed centimeters below my personnel pod.

Then I fired, spraying the cockpit with assault rifle rounds, emptying half the magazines of both my guns. Holes with cracks radiating from them appeared in the helicopter's glossy plass windshield.

Both men jumped and shook. Bloody divots appeared in their unarmored chests, bellies, thighs.

I drew back, sideslipping to stay directly ahead of the platform as it continued rotating—keeping me out of line of fire of the port and starboard guns. There were screams, shouts over my audio receptors; it took me a moment to realize they were sounds of victory from the other 'gangers, not pain from the humans.

Then a Bale slammed into the weapons platform from the side. Meriah, taking her shot of opportunity. The helicopter's aft rotor assembly went to pieces, flinging lengths of rotor in all directions. The weapons platform tilted, nose up, then backslid away from me.

It slammed down onto the graytop, crumpling. I thought I could still see some movement within the two gunnery stations.

I took a look around, checked my status board.

Gunner Two was still in the air! The drone she'd engaged was in burning pieces on the graytop. Lina's HummingHawk wobbled; it had clearly sustained damage to the landing struts and starboard-rear fan assembly, but she was still up.

I expelled a breath I'd been holding for I didn't know how long. I switched to radio so she could hear my voice. "Gunner Two, *do you remember my orders of a moment ago?*"

"Yes, sir." Her voice was subdued.

"Execute them. And thanks."

Status board—Eyeballs One and Two, Belly One reported in as undamaged and fully functional. Bale Two had expended all four of his missiles against the side of the *Coracle* bunker, and the concrete wall he'd been hammering was looking damaged but unbreached. Bale One was down to one unfired missile. Gunner Two's guns were disabled and she was now headed to the fence and beyond. I had 46 rounds left in each of my guns and was undamaged. Team Coffee reported no change; they were still standing by.

Then, Parfait's voice: "I have the second weapons platform inbound from east-northeast. It seems to have three heat drones following. Arrival in forty seconds."

I grimaced. We were a little underpowered now. BeeBee and I had counted on having more guns and missiles at this point. But those were the resources we had, and Team Cream still had two objectives to accomplish.

I transmitted, *Bale Two, go to cover. As soon as we're engaged with the weapons platform, join Gunner Two.*

Understood, Gunner One.

Bale One, go to cover and stand by to take your shot. I'll deal with the heat drones and open you up an opportunity.

Roger, Gunner One.

Eyeball One, transmit to the potholer. Tell him 'Take position'. That meant, "Exit your hangar and taxi to launch position". Our window of opportunity would soon begin to close. We needed to have the yacht standing by to take off.

Understood, Gunner One.

Now I could see the second weapons platform, coming in low, a straight-line approach, its three heat drones a protective screen. Two flew ahead of the platform, one split to port and one to starboard, the third trailing behind. It would be an easy target at this range for a human-sized machine gun emplacement or autocannon. Sadly, we didn't have either.

I gulped. This was going to be bad. I brought my HummingHawk down to hover beside Meriah's behind the cargo trailers, which had finally stopped.

The weapons platform approached and then passed over the fence just north of where we'd blown our entry hole. It didn't appear to have noticed Lina, who would now be on the far side of Kieran's low hill, hiding. The platform passed over me and Meriah but it did not fire upon us. Inexplicably, it was now going faster, accelerating so that its drones were losing ground. I banked to follow—

The weapons platform banked, too hard to port. It slid sideways and down all the way to the graytop, smashing into that unyielding surface. It rolled, erupting in aviation-fuel flame, the sounds of impact and explosion audible over the air-raid howl still suffusing the air.

I'll admit I sat there stunned. Luck? I don't believe in luck. It's something humans apparently have, but I've never met a Dollganger who admitted to experiencing it. Until now.

Then a voice, over our radio frequency, soft and a little sad: "Got him."

"Trigger?" My jaw hung open for a moment.

Of course. Kieran's laser. After he'd lit up the *Coracle* bunker so Jitter could sight in on it, he was supposed to have packed up and raced off for safety. Instead, he must have switched the laser over to pulse/combat mode and waited to pick off targets of opportunity.

He had to have lined up the shot against the weapons platform with meticulous patience, hitting the helicopter pilot as the vehicle made its closest pass to his position.

Disobedient, stupid, stubborn Dollgangers, every one. Bless them.

"Well done, Trigger." I tried to shake myself out of my momentary state of shock. We weren't done, our goal was still not accomplished. "Uh—Eyeball One, loft Belly One."

"Understood, Gunner One."

That would be our endgame. Belly One, hovering near the roof of the hangar where BeeBee had left it, would rise vertically until it was a distinct blip on military radar—and clearly well away from any resource the humans would be worried about. It would drift laterally until it was directly over the *Coracle* bunker. Human spotters in the spaceport tower would report all this, report that the Dollgangers were making yet another attempt on that bunker.

At some point during all this, perhaps the instant Belly One appeared on radar, the laser cannon at General Milfield Base would uncover itself and blow Belly One out of the sky. It would be a big explosion; Belly One still held its original bomb cargo, and BeeBee had rigged it to detonate if superheated or breached.

And who was waiting less than a hundred meters from the laser cannon emplacement, just below the exact line of sight between the cannon and our position? Wolfe and Creepy-Crawly were, with their laser. Kazzy was there, too, in Bale Three.

When the laser fired, its systems would heat up, making it a viable target for Bale missiles. Kazzy would fire one-two-three-four. Creepy-Crawly, her tripod-mount laser sighted in, would expend its entire power pack pumping a kill-level laser attack into the same aperture.

That would be the end of the laser cannon, the end of any weapon that had a reasonable chance of interfering with our yacht. *Granny Knot* would be able to make orbit.

On my radio receiver, I saw the 256-character alphanumeric code that was Belly One's "go" command flash by.

The visual feeds from my HummingHawk's sensors all shut down. The winch at the back of my pod whined and the weapons hatch thumped closed.

12: LIGHT AND DARK

"Hello?" I shook my head to reorient myself and returned my visual input to my actual eyes. I looked at the monitor screens in front of me—backups for the visual feeds. I'd thought, hoped, they'd never be necessary. But now they were my only way to see what was going on outside. I swept a finger across my starboard monitor, centering it on Belly One's position.

The drone just hovered in the camera view, not rising.

"Belly One is not responding." That was BeeBee, coming across my built-in radio, not the HummingHawk's communication system.

Bow? Can you read me? Text from Parfait.

I frowned at the image of the motionless drone. "What do you mean, not responding?"

And I replied to Parfait. *I read you, Eyeball Two. Have I been hit by something? What did you see?*

"It's not acknowledging my order. Wait, it's moving." It was, in fact, sideslipping straight toward the hole by which we'd entered the base. It zoomed out by Kieran's and Lina's hill and then was out of my sight.

You are going to draw the laser fire, Bow. As Parfait transmitted those words, I heard—felt, actually, since the air-raid siren drowned out the faint change in engine noise—my fans spin up faster. I began slowly to gain altitude. *Belly One has another job to do. It is going to drop its bomb on the juice factory.*

I don't understand. I did understand that in the near future, I'd rise above the ground-clutter threshold and become a target for the distant laser cannon. It would light me up, incinerating me and my HummingHawk in a bright, fatal flash. I relayed all of Parfait's texts to BeeBee and set up a quick protocol to relay each new one as it reached me.

If I kept rising, Kazzy and Creepy-Crawly would deal with the laser. *Granny Knot* would fly. Happy ending, except for me—I'd be ash and melted circuitry.

Bow, you and BeeBee taught me how to do everything. How to recruit. How to bypass human security. How to build detonators. So I got Shinbone Ted, Silverback, and a few others working for me. They thought they were building us an advance hideout under the juice factory.

What were they actually doing? I unstrapped, stood, and clambered up onto the port-side mounting bracket to undog the top hatch. I'd be able to heave myself out, drop, and parachute to safety. Meriah would retrieve me.

Well, I tried to open the hatch. It didn't budge. I swore to myself. When Parfait had shut that hatch, she must have slathered some fast-hardening resin in the mechanism. It would take me a little time to break my way out.

It would take me too long.

The night we blew up Kresh Assemblies, the first thing I did when I was alone in the transport room was load up a little hauler full of bombs just like the one in Belly One. I programmed the hauler's route out of the factory—out of the city. To near the juice factory. And the humans did not detect it—they were too busy sending emergency personnel to the factory. Silverback and Shinbone Ted got the bombs into the juice factory's nooks and crannies underground. Placed them exactly where I wanted them. I wired them to blow. There is a seismic sensor on them. Belly One's bomb will go off against the roof, then the others will all go off, too.

She didn't have to tell me what that meant. If she'd done her job right, planting the bombs in the right places and with the right triggering sequence, the power plant wouldn't go up like a fission bomb, but it would spread radiation all over Zhou City. Thousands would be irradiated, a ghastly percentage of them fatally.

I shook my head, a hopeless denial. *Civilians. Innocent humans.* I went aft and got back atop my assault rifles. Maybe I could trigger them, blow a hole in my cockpit fuselage, squeeze out through the hole. But the human trigger mechanisms were long gone, replaced by electrical gear controlled from the HummingHawk's master control system.

THERE ARE NO INNOCENT HUMANS. They did this to me. You LET them do this to me.

Text can't convey emotions, but this message did anyway. Nor did I have to ask what "this" was. Her years of helplessness, abuse. Hers had been the most common sort of relationship there was between Dollgangers and their owners, and I hadn't really begun to understand this sort of thing until the Escape.

So in twenty seconds you will reach radar altitude and die. In sixty seconds, Belly One will reach the juice factory. Goodbye, Bow. You butt-licking lap-dog bastard.

"Enough." BeeBee's voice was pained.

Another alphanumeric code flashed by on the Coffee and Cream frequency. A few moments later, I heard a *boom* like distant thunder.

BeeBee's next message didn't sound any less pained. "That was the bomb, Parfait. Two kilometers from its intended target. Bow, you have control of your HummingHawk."

I jumped for my command chair, brought the aircraft's ascent to a quick stop, began a descent, all before extending my fingertip data wires and resuming full control of the craft. Once I reconnected, my vision was flooded once more with the full range of video the HummingHawk's cameras offered me. I reopened the gun hatch. And finally I breathed a sigh of relief.

Then ... realization evaporated the relief. "Eyeball One, we've lost our laser target."

"I know."

I chewed on that fact for seconds, several of them.

Granny Knot had to launch. For this plan to have been worth anything, for our future to mean anything, *Granny Knot* had to fly.

I resumed my ascent.

"Bow, what are you doing?"

I ignored BeeBee's question and sent her a text order. *Eyeball One, prepare to take command.*

... Understood, Gunner One. Once again, there was no emotion in text. I wondered what she was feeling. But I didn't ask about that. *How did you know to blow up Belly One? And return control of my HummingHawk to me?*

I didn't, about Belly One. I just have remote detonation sequences set up for any explosive device I build. As for your HummingHawk—I worked a lot on our two Gunner craft because I knew I'd be in one. I detected some control lag in One, traced it down to some new code patched into its control system. But I didn't know who'd patched in the code or why.

I nodded. *So that's why you took Eyeball One. You didn't want to be distracted from figuring out what was going on.*

That's it exactly.

Thanks, BeeBee. I mean it. Thanks for everything. I was reaching the point where I'd begin to show up on the radar at General Milfield Base. I wondered what my end would feel like. I suspected it would be a sudden flash of light, heat, pain ... then nothingness.

In my visual feed, Eyeball Two rose from its position beside the roof of the spaceport tower. It shot straight up into the air.

A second later, it became a tiny nova in the sky, a bright flash that overwhelmed my HummingHawk's cameras and fuzzed them out.

My mouth open, I stopped my ascent and began losing altitude again.

As the cameras regained coherence, I could see little bits of flaming debris float down from Parfait's last position. Smoke rose from the same spot in the air.

Radio crackled in my ears: "Bale Three to Gunner One. I have three hits, I say again, three hits on my target. Target disabled."

I actually couldn't answer for a moment. My voice failed me.

BeeBee stepped in for me: "Well done, Team Coffee. Get the hell out of there. Potholer, go go go."

"Roger that." Kazzy again. Pothole Charlie, observing radio silence, didn't reply.

I found my voice again. "Team Cream, we're outbound." I spun my HummingHawk in place and headed toward our exit hole.

*   *   *

281

Why did Parfait do it? Not the destroying-Zhou-City thing. That was pretty obvious. Why did she sacrifice herself when just standing by idle would have resulted in me being killed, as she clearly wanted? I'll never know for sure. But as she waited there beside the tower roof, knowing she couldn't trigger her dirty radiation bomb, maybe she'd had just enough of a sense of tribe, of being one of us, that she wanted to be remembered for something other than a mass murder attempt. Maybe she wanted to be remembered for a final sacrifice that meant something. So she'd taken her third and last Scrap-Walk.

The depleted and damaged remnants of Team Cream didn't stay together long. As the siren wail from the spaceport faded behind us, BeeBee spoke over the operation's radio frequency. "I'm splitting off. Jitter, come with me."

I toggled my radio and switched to an encryption scheme private to the two of us. "Where do you think you're going?"

"The juice factory. We need to disable those bombs. We don't want an earthquake setting them off."

"What if Silverback and Shinbone Ted try to stop you? You and Jitter aren't a match for Silverback."

I heard her laugh. "You think they'd try to stop me? If they're there, Parfait was willing for them to die in the explosion. And they didn't know they were setting up a bomb. They'll help me, Bow." She peeled off from our formation, Jitter following.

"All right. And, BeeBee? Thanks for saving me."

"I had to, Bow. I'd have missed you."

I think I rebooted again.

13: FACING THE MUSIC

Granny Knot wasn't a big white rocket. A deep purple with gold markings, shaped like a manta ray, most of it lifting body in atmosphere, it took off from the Shavery Corporation's landing strip like a thruster-based aircraft. From our location, we couldn't see it.

We did pick up some radio transmissions from the government's air controllers, asking about *Granny Knot's* flight plan, demanding its return. But what could they do in the face of radio silence? It was a civilian craft on an ascent to orbit well away from any target. And they had no laser with which to shoot it down, no weapons platform with which to force it down.

We got brief text confirmations when it achieved orbit, when it exited Chiron's gravity well and could engage its main drives, and when it—unmolested, unchallenged—reached the nearest wormhole entry point. Then we heard nothing more from it.

Chiron's Dollgangers were in space.

We reached Coffee Summit and I battered my way out of my sealed-shut pod. Lina had an embrace for me, as did Kazzy and Meriah. Kieran, Wolfe, and Creepy-Crawly, traveling on foot and hoof, would take longer to make it back.

BeeBee sent a microburst report: Silverback and Shinbone Ted were there, cooperative.

I decided not to wait for BeeBee's return. I told the others, "I need to go test the waters."

Lina, holding little Thonny, shook her head. "You need to wait for BeeBee."

"We need to know if anyone can return, and we need to know before questions and maybe resentments begin to build. I'm going now. You know the discipline, Lina. Operation Coffee and Cream isn't over yet."

She hesitated, then nodded, subdued. She gave me one last hug before I headed back.

*   *   *

Not long before dark, I reached the Chimney Pipe entrance. Two guards on duty, Bonny-Anne in her leaf-camo pirate drag and tricorner hat, and Tan Gan, with his loincloth and giraffe-spots body paint, met me there, stone-faced. Tan Gan escorted me into the 'ganger-expanded cave and together we rode the rickety mesh-sided elevator down to the nearest rail car terminus.

Then it was a brief, quiet ride to the Canterbury chamber.

When we emerged into the chamber, the first thing I saw was Pothole Charlie. Not in person, of course—he really was on *Granny Knot*. But his big, homely face was up on one of the big wall-mounted monitors the Directors and their administrators used for news and public announcements. As we pulled to a halt and the metallic shrill of rail cars scraping across metal subsided, I could hear some of Pothole Charlie's words: "... of the Operation Coffee and Cream conspirators. We're on our way, and no force on Chiron can stop us." His hard features softened just a little. "I don't know how long it will take us ... but help is on the way. Don't lose hope. When I get back, I don't want to hear about any more Scrap-Walks. Ever." Then he managed a smile, an effort that must have drained his battery. "Pothole Charlie out." The screen darkened.

Tan Gan leaned to speak into my ear. "It'll start again in two minutes. It's been playing since the *Granny Knot* launched."

"Really?" I gave him a curious look. "And who's the bad guy in his account of the operation?"

He looked confused. "Bad guy?"

Several 'gangers topped the stairs that provided access to this rail-car station platform. They turned toward me and Tan Gan. In front were three members of the Directors, doubtless alerted to my presence by Tan Gan: Petal, slender dark-skinned elegance in a floor-length dress in vertical earth-color stripes, the King in his rhinestone-studded jumpsuit and sunglasses, and Mister Science, all leather-elbowed jacket, fuzzy red facial hair, and toy smoking pipe. Behind them came two more—Ko in his preposterously authentic samurai armor and Lloranda, her flawless tan skin and black hair contrasting with her usual white drape, which always looked like a funeral shroud. They led several of the Directors' administrators.

They approached, and Petal opened her mouth to speak, but there was a sudden commotion from floor level, a rush of voices, shouts, even what sounded like applause. I looked down to see a dozen or more 'gangers below where the platform's support struts met the concrete; the 'gangers were pointing up at me, shouting words I couldn't make out, some clapping. And more 'gangers were rushing into join them. I realized, belatedly, that what I was seeing was being repeated, from another elevated angle off to one side, on one of the secondary monitors high on the walls.

Petal stepped close enough that I could hear her. She jerked her head toward the monitor Pothole Charlie's face had previously occupied. "For such a gruff, antisocial old bastard, he can occasionally manage a decent speech."

I nodded. The roar from the people below was growing louder as 'gangers streamed from surrounding streets and buildings to join the crowd.

Mister Science shook his head. He looked a little shocked, like someone who had just survived a huge explosion only centimeters away and had received only a little cosmetic damage. "I'd have sworn it couldn't be done."

I shrugged. "Necessity's the fabricator of invention."

And the King stuck out his hand. "Welcome home."

*   *   *

So, yeah, there were changes and adaptations to make after that.

There were celebrations of the success of Coffee and Cream. Celebrations for the return from presumed death of Jitter and Shinbone Ted. Celebrations by the war-hawk 'gangers who rejoiced at the Battle of Akima Spaceport, a military victory of our forces over the humans. Most especially, there were celebrations for the launch of *Granny Knot*.

All of the surviving Coffee and Cream conspirators, returning home, were treated like heroes. Not so much by the remaining members of the Directors, who accorded us a sort of rueful acceptance, an "I wish you could have done this without making us look wrong" attitude, but by the general population. Pothole Charlie's message of hope had resonated with them to a degree I couldn't have imagined. I hadn't realized how many of the 'gangers had joined the Revolution, had come to the Nest, not to live but to die on their own terms ... and now living was, to a slight degree, an improved possibility.

I did something humans do, but Dollgangers never had. I held a memorial ceremony for Parfait for the few 'gangers who'd been close to her, BeeBee especially. In my speech, I extolled her virtues and tried to put her failings, her pain and madness, into perspective. Later, I convinced the Directors to set aside a Nest chamber, distant from the Canterbury chamber, as a kind of memorial and mausoleum. I put up the first plaque, to Parfait, its metal surface inscribed with her face and name. Fingertip-sized indentations allowed visitors to jack in and receive images of her, texts about her life and history. Soon dozens of plaques devoted to other fallen 'gangers went up beside it.

BeeBee offered to put me up for a return to the Directors. I declined. Memnon, a hero of the Escape, went up instead, replacing Pothole Charlie.

The humans were apparently not as efficient as my paranoia generally made me think they were. Theft of the *Granny Knot* was reported, but Dollgangers were never mentioned in the report. Either the authorities were keeping mum about that or they hadn't figured it out. As soon as Tink, Malibu, and Pothole Charlie began their campaign on distant worlds, Chiron's leaders would learn the truth.

And the humans never captured or never decrypted the full range of Team Cream transmissions. How did we know? Security at the power plant was never improved. We waited, tense, for our little hidey-hole there to be sought and discovered, but it never was. So we began the process of setting it up as the advance station Parfait had promised her recruits it would be. We nicknamed it the Pothole.

A week after the launch of *Granny Knot*, there was another ceremony in the Nest—in my study, before the round Mayan calendar table. Once again Wolfe and Lina stood near me, and friends—their friends, my friends, mutual friends such as BeeBee—surrounded them. Once again I held little Thonny, but it was to Lina I spoke. "What we are changes the same way, transforming over time. We are continuity, not an unchanging now." I took a deep breath. "By your permission and at your request, I, Chiang BinDoc Bowen Bow, name you Chiang BinBowen Lina. Welcome to my clan, Lina."

She wrapped her arms around me and gave me a smile with innocent joy in it, one that was only for me. Then she held me close, burying her face in my shoulder, so I could no longer see her features. Behind her, the others applauded, Wolfe among them.

So that was how the last vestiges of Big Plush drifted away like the ashes of Parfait carried off by the wind, how the Chiron Dollganger Revolution reached space, and how I gained a daughter and a grandson.

A few months earlier, I hadn't seen any of it coming, and now I was chest-deep in it. That's life, I guess.

ABOUT THE AUTHOR

New York Times bestselling writer Aaron Allston is the author of more than twenty novels and numerous short stories. His works of science fiction, fantasy, and horror often emphasize action and humor. He has also authored ***Plotting: A Novelist's Workout Guide***, a comprehensive textbook on the craft of plotting fiction, available from Amazon's Kindle Store, the Apple iBookStore, and Allston's sales page, www.archerrat.com. A lifelong Texan, Allston lives in the Austin area. Visit his web site at www.aaronallston.com.

Made in United States
Orlando, FL
12 November 2022

24458100R00178